D0191350

The
Care and
Feeding of
Stray Vampires

MOLLY HARPER

Pocket Books

New York   London   Toronto   Sydney   New Delhi

Pocket Books
A Division of Simon & Schuster, Inc.
1230 Avenue of the Americas
New York, NY 10020

This book is a work of fiction. Names, characters, places, and incidents either are products of the author's imagination or are used fictitiously. Any resemblance to actual events or locales or persons, living or dead, is entirely coincidental.

First Pocket Books paperback edition August 2012

POCKET and colophon are registered trademarks of Simon & Schuster, Inc.

For information about special discounts for bulk purchases, please contact Simon & Schuster Special Sales at 1-866-506-1949 or business@simonandschuster.com.

The Simon & Schuster Speakers Bureau can bring authors to your live event. For more information or to book an event, contact the Simon & Schuster Speakers Bureau at 1-866-248-3049 or visit our website at www.simonspeakers.com.

Manufactured in the United States of America

10   9   8   7   6   5   4   3   2   1

ISBN 978-1-4516-4183-7
ISBN 978-1-4516-4187-5 (ebook)

For Manda Zeb

Acknowledgments

Completing this book was my first opportunity to write about sisters who get along. It was a refreshing change of pace, since this reflects my own relationship with my sister, Manda. No one makes me laugh like Manda. No one else will ever understand why my brain works the way it does. And I would imagine there are times when she sincerely wishes she was not privy to that information. Thank you, Manda, for putting up with me, and for not smothering me in my sleep during the sixteen years we roomed together. (Despite the fact that I snore.)

Thanks again to my family, to my parents, and to my husband, David, who keep me going. Thanks to my agent, Stephany Evans, for her patience and humor during the many, many drafts of this book. Thanks to Abby Zidle, my fabulous new editor, who has managed not to laugh at my many quirks, including the four-stage title-picking system. And of course, thank you to Ayelet Gruenspecht and the lovely people at Pocket for all of their hard work and support.

The
Care and
Feeding of
Stray Vampires

1

The thing to remember about a "stray" vampire is that there is probably a good reason he is friendless, alone, and wounded. Approach with caution.

—*The Care and Feeding of Stray Vampires*

How did an internal debate regarding flavored sexual aids become part of my workday?

I was a good person. I went to church on the "big days." I was a college graduate. Nice, God-fearing people with bachelor's degrees in botany should not end up standing in the pharmacy aisle at Walmart debating which variety of flavored lube is best.

"Ugh, forget it, I'm going with Sensual Strawberry." I sighed, throwing the obscenely pink box into the basket.

Diandra Starr—a poorly thought-out pole name if I'd ever heard one—had managed to snag the world's only codependent vampire. My client, Mr. Rychek. When she made her quarterly visits to Half-Moon Hollow, I was turned into some bizarre hybrid of Cinderella and the Fairy Godmother, waking up at dawn to find voicemails and e-mails detailing the numerous needs that must be attended to *at once*. Mr. Rychek seemed convinced that

Diandra would flounce away on her designer platform heels unless her every whim was anticipated. No demand for custom-blended bath salts was considered too extravagant. No organic, free-trade food requirement was too extreme. And the lady liked her sexual aids to taste of summer fruits.

I surveyed the contents of the cart against the list. Iron supplements? Check. Organic almond milk? Check. Flavored lube? Check.

I did not pretend to understand the dynamics of human-vampire relationships.

Shopping in the "special dietary needs" aisle was always an adventure. An unexpected side effect of the Great Coming Out in 1999 was the emergence of all-night industries, special products, and cottage businesses, like mine, that catered to the needs of "undead Americans." Companies were tripping over one another to come up with products for a spanking-new marketing demographic: synthetic blood, protein additives, dental-care accessories, lifelike bronzers. The problem was that those companies still hadn't figured out packaging for the undead and tended to jump on bizarre trending bandwagons, the most recent being a brand of plasma concentrate that came pouring out of what looked like a Kewpie doll. You had to flip back the head to open it.

It's even more creepy than it sounds.

Between that and the sporty, aggressively neon tubes of Razor Wire Floss, the clear bubble-shaped pots of Solar Shield SPF-500 sunblock, and the black Gothic boxes of Forever Smooth moisturizing serum, the vampire aisle was ground zero for visual overstimulation.

I stopped in my tracks, pulling the cart to an abrupt halt in the middle of the pharmacy section as I recalled that Rychek's girlfriend was a vegan. I started to review the label to determine whether the flavored lube was an animal by-product. But I found that I honestly didn't care. It was 4:20, which meant that I had an hour to drop this stuff by Mr. Rychek's house, drop the service contracts by a new client's house in Deer Haven, and then get to Half-Moon Hollow High for the volleyball booster meeting. Such was the exotic and glamorous life of the Hollow's only daytime vampire concierge.

My company, Beeline, was part special-event coordinator, part concierge service, part personal organizer. In addition to wedding planning, I took care of all the little details vampires didn't have time for or just didn't want to deal with themselves. Although it was appropriate, I tried to avoid the term "daywalker" unless I was dealing with established clients. It turns out that if you put an ad for a daywalker service in the Yellow Pages, you get a lot of calls from people who expect you to scoop Fluffy's sidewalk leavings. And I was allergic to dogs—and their leavings.

On my sprint to the checkout, I cast a longing glance at the candy aisle and its many forbidden sugary pleasures. With my compulsive sweet tooth, I did not discriminate against chocolate, gummies, taffy, lollipops, or even those weird so-sour-the-citric-acid-burns-off-your-tastebuds torture candies. But between my sister

Gigi's worries about the potential for adult-onset diabetes in our gene pool and my tendency toward what I prefer to call "curviness," I only broke into the various candy caches I had stashed around the house under great personal stress. Or if it was a weekday.

Placating myself with a piece of sugarless gum, I whizzed through the express lane and loaded Mr. Rychek's weekend supplies into what Gigi, in all her seventeen-year-old sarcastic glory, called the Dorkmobile. I agreed that an enormous yellow minivan was not exactly a sexy car. But until she could suggest another way to haul cases of synthetic blood, Gothic-themed wedding cakes, and, once, a pet crate large enough for a Bengal tiger, I'd told Gigi she had to suck it up and ride shotgun in the Dorkmobile. The next fall, she'd used her earnings from the Half-Moon Hollow Country Club and Catfish Farm snack bar to buy a secondhand VW Bug. Never underestimate a teenager's work ethic if the end result is averted embarrassment.

I used my security pass to get past the gate into Deer Haven, a private, secure subdivision inhabited entirely by vampires and their human pets. It was always a little spooky driving through this perfectly maintained, cookie-cutter ghost suburb during the day. The streets and driveways were empty. The windows were shuttered tight against the sunlight. Sometimes I expected tumbleweeds to come bouncing past my car. Then again, I'd never seen the neighborhood awake and hopping after dark. I made it a policy to be well out of my clients' homes before the sun set. With the exception of the clients whose newly legal weddings I helped plan, I rarely saw any of them face-to-face. (I allowed my wedding clients a little more leeway, because they were generally too distracted by their own issues to bother nibbling on me. And still, I only met with them in public places with a lot of witnesses present.)

Although it had been more than ten years since the Great Coming Out and vampire-human relations were vastly improved since the early pitchfork-and-torch days, some vampires were still a bit touchy about humans' efforts to wipe out their species. They refused to let any human they hadn't met in person near their homes while they were sleeping and vulnerable.

After years of working with them, I had no remaining romantic notions about vampires. They had the same capacity for good and evil that humans do. And despite what most TV evangelists preached, I believed they had souls. The problem was that the cruelest tendencies can emerge when a person is no longer restricted to the "no biting, no using people as food" rules that humans insist on. If you were a jerk in your original life, you're probably going to be a bigger undead jerk. If you were a decent person, you're probably not going to change much beyond your diet and skin-care regimen.

With vampires, you had to be able to operate from a distance, whether that distance was physical or emotional. My business was built on guarded, but optimistic, trust. And a can of vampire pepper spray that I kept in my purse.

I opened the back of my van and hitched the crate of supplies against my hip. I had pretty impressive upper-body strength for a petite gal, but it was at times like these, struggling to schlep the crate up Mr. Rychek's front walk, that I wondered why I'd never hired an assistant.

Oh, right, because I couldn't afford one.

Until my little business, Beeline, started showing a profit margin just above "lemonade stand," I would have to continue toting my own barge and lifting my own bale. I looked forward to the day when heavy lifting wouldn't determine my wardrobe or hairstyle. On days like this, I tended toward sensible flats, twin sets, and pencil skirts in dark, smudge-proof colors. I liked to throw in a pretty blouse every once in a while, but it depended on whether I could wash synthetic blood out of it. (No matter how careful you are, sometimes there are mishaps.)

And the hair. It was difficult for human companions, blood-bank staff, and storekeepers to take me seriously when I walked around with a crazy cloud of dark curls framing my head. Having Diana Ross's 'do didn't exactly inspire confidence, so I twisted my hair into a thick coil at the nape of my neck. Gigi called it my "sexy schoolmarm" look, having little sympathy for me and my frizz. But since we shared the same unpredictable follicles, I was biding my time until she got her first serious job and realized how difficult it was to be considered a professional when your hair was practically sentient.

I used another keyless-entry code to let myself into Mr. Rychek's tidy little town house. Some American vampires lived in groups of threes and fours in what vampire behaviorists called "nesting," but most of my clients, like Mr. Rychek, were loners. They had little habits and quirks that would annoy anyone, human or immortal, after a few centuries. So they lived alone and relied on people like me to bring the outside world to them.

I put the almond milk in the fridge and discreetly tucked the other items into a kitchen cabinet. I checked the memo board for further requests and was relieved to find none. I only hoped I could get through Diandra's visit without being called and ordered to find a twenty-four-hour emergency vet service for her hypoallergenic cat, Ginger. That stupid furball had some sort of weird fascination with prying open remote controls and swallowing the batteries. And somehow Diandra was always shocked when it happened.

As an afterthought, I moved Mr. Rychek's remote from the coffee table to the top of the TV.

One more stop before I could put in my time at the booster meeting, go home, and bury myself in the romance novel I'd squirreled away inside the dust jacket for *The Adventures of Sherlock Holmes*. If Gigi saw the bare-chested gladiator on the cover, the mockery would be inventive and, most likely, public.

My new client's house was conveniently located in the newer section of Deer Haven, at the end of a long row of matching beige condos. As usual, I had to count the house numbers three times before I was sure I was at the right door, and I wondered how wrong it would be to mark my clients' doors with big fluorescent-yellow bumblebees. And yes, I knew it seemed inconsistent to name a company that dealt with vampires after a sunny, summer-loving insect. But bees were so efficient, zipping from one place to another, never forgetting the task at hand. That was the image I wanted to convey. Besides, way too many vampire-oriented businesses went with a Goth theme. My cheerful yellow logo stood out in the "undead services" section of the phone book.

Entering the security code provided on his new-client application, I popped the door open, carrying my usual "Thank you for supporting Beeline" floral arrangement inside. Most vampires enjoyed waking up to fresh flowers. The sight and smell reminded them of their human days, when they could wander around in the daylight unscathed. And they didn't have to know that I'd harvested the artfully arranged roses, irises, and freesias from my own garden. The appearance of an expensive gift was more important than the actual cost of said gift.

Mr. C. Calix certainly hadn't wasted any money on redecorating, I mused as I walked into the bare beige foyer and set the vase on the generic maple end table. The place was dark, which was to be expected, given the sunproof metal shades clamped over the windows. But there was little furniture in the living room, no dining-room table, no art or pictures on the clean taupe walls. The place looked barely lived in, even for a dead guy's house.

Scraping past a few cardboard packing boxes, I walked into the kitchen, where I'd agreed to leave the contracts. My foot caught on a soft weight on the floor. "Mother of fudge!" I yelped, then fell flat on my face.

Have I mentioned that I haven't cursed properly in

about five years? With an impressionable kid around the house, I'd taken to using the "safe for network TV" versions of curse words. Although that impressionable kid was now seventeen, I couldn't seem to break the habit. Even with my face smashed against cold tile.

"Frak-frakity-frak." I moaned, rubbing my bruised mouth as I righted myself from the floor. I ran my tongue over my teeth to make sure I hadn't broken any of them. Because, honestly, I wasn't sure I could afford dental intervention at this point. My skinned knees—and my pride—stung viciously as I counted my teeth again for good measure.

What had I tripped over? I pushed myself to my feet, stumbled over to the fridge, and yanked the door open. The interior light clicked on, illuminating the body stretched across the floor.

Shrieking, I scrambled back against the fridge, my dress shoes skittering uselessly against the tile. I couldn't seem to swallow the lump of panic hardening in my throat, keeping me from drawing a breath.

His shirtless torso was well built, long limbs strung with thick cords of muscle. Dark waves of hair sprang over his forehead in inky profusion. The face would have been beautiful if it hadn't been covered in dried blood. A straight nose, high cheekbones, and full, generous lips that bowed slightly. He had that whole Michelangelo's *David* thing going—if David had been an upsetting religious figurine that wept blood.

A half-empty donor packet of O positive lay splattered against the floor, which explained the rusty-looking dried splotches on his face. Had he been drinking it when he . . . passed out?

Vampires didn't pass out. And most of them could sense when to get somewhere safe well before the sun rose. They didn't get caught off guard and collapse wherever they were at dawn. What the hell was going on here?

I eyed my shoulder bag, flung across the room when I'd fallen on my face. Breathing steadily, I resolved that I'd call Ophelia at the local World Council for the Equal Treatment of the Undead office and leave her a message. She would know what to do. And I could get the hell out of there before the hungry, ill vampire rose for the night and made me his breakfast.

I reached over him, aiming my arm away from his mouth. A strong hand clamped around my wrist. I am ashamed to say that I screamed like a little girl. I heard the telltale snick of fangs descending and panicked, yanking and struggling against a relentless vise grip. A tug-of-war ensued for control of the arm that he was pulling toward his chapped, bloodied lips. He tried to lunge for me, but the effort cost him, and his head thunked back to the floor with a heavy thud.

With my hand hovering precariously over his gaping, hungry mouth, I did the only thing I could think of—I poked him in the eye.

"Ow," he said, dully registering pain as I jabbed my index finger against his eyelid. The other eye popped open, the long, sooty lashes fluttering. It was a deep, rich coffee color, the iris ringed in black.

"Ow!" he repeated indignantly, as if the sensation of the eye-poke was just breaking through his stupor.

With him distracted, I gave one final yank and broke free, holding my hand to my chest as I retreated against the fridge. I took another donor packet from the shelf. I popped it open and held it carefully to his lips, figuring that he wouldn't care that it wasn't heated to body temperature. He shook his head faintly, wheezing. "Bad blood."

I checked the expiration date and offered it to him again. "No, it's fine."

His dry lips nearly cracked as they formed the words, "Poisoned . . . stupid."

"OK . . . jerk," I shot back.

The faintest flicker of amusement passed over his even features. "Need clean supply," he whispered.

"Well, I'm not giving you mine," I said, shrinking away from him. "I don't do that."

"Just wait to die, then," he muttered.

I had to bite my lips to keep from snickering or giggling hysterically. I was sure that crouching over him, laughing, while he was vulnerable and agitated wouldn't improve the situation.

Shouting for him to hold on, I scurried out to my car, carefully shutting the door behind me so that sunlight didn't spill into the kitchen. I had a case of Faux Type O in the back, destined for Ms. Wexler's house the next day. I grabbed three bottles from the package and ran back into the house. Sadly, it only occurred to me *after* I'd run back into the house that I should have just grabbed my purse, jumped into my van, and gunned it all the way home.

But no, I had to take care of vampires with figurative broken wings, because of my stupid Good Samaritan complex.

Kneeling beside the fallen vampire, I twisted the top off the first bottle and offered it to him. "I'm sure this is clean. I just bought it. The tamper-proof seal's intact."

He gave the bottle a doubtful, guarded look but took it from my hand. He greedily gulped his way through the first bottle, grimacing at the cold offering. Meanwhile, I popped the other two bottles into the microwave. I even dropped a penny into each one after heating them to give them a more authentic coppery taste.

"Thank you," he murmured, forcing himself into a sitting position, although the effort clearly exhausted him. He slumped against the pine cabinets. Like all of the Deer Haven homes, the kitchen was done in pastel earth tones—buffs, beiges, and creams. Mr. Calix looked like a wax figure sagging against the pale wood. "Who are you, and what are you doing in my house?"

"I'm Iris Scanlon, from Beeline. The concierge service? Ophelia Lambert arranged your service contract before you arrived in the Hollow. I came by to drop off the paperwork."

He nodded his magnificent dark head slowly. "She mentioned something about a daywalker, said I could trust you."

I snorted. Ophelia only said that because I hadn't asked

questions that time she put heavy-duty trash bags, lime, and a shovel on her shopping list. The teenage leader of the local World Council for the Equal Treatment of the Undead office might have looked sweet sixteen, but at more than four hundred years old, Ophelia, I'm pretty sure, had committed felonies in every hemisphere.

Scary felonies.

"Well, you seem to be feeling a bit better. I'll leave these papers here and be on my way," I said, inching around him.

"Stop," he commanded me, his voice losing its raspy quality as he pushed himself to his feet. I froze, looking up at him through lowered lashes. His face was fuller somehow, less haggard. He seemed to be growing a little stronger with every sip of blood. "I need your help."

"How could *I* help you?"

"You already have helped." As he spoke, I picked up the faint trace of an accent, a sort of caress of the tongue against each finishing syllable. It sounded . . . old, which was a decidedly unhelpful concept when dealing with a vampire. And since most vamps didn't like talking about their backstories, I ignored the sexy lilt and its effects on my pulse rate. "And now I need you to take me home with you."

"Why would I take an unstable, hungry vampire home with me? Do I look particularly stupid to you?"

He snorted. "No, which is *why* you should take me home with you. I already know where you live. While you were running to your car, I looked in your purse and memorized your driver's license. Imagine how irritated

I would be, how motivated I would be to find you and repay your *kindness,* after I am well again."

I gasped, clutching my bag closer to my chest. "Don't you threaten me! There seem to be a lot of handy, breakable wooden objects in this room. I'm not above living out my fonder Buffy fantasies."

His expression was annoyed but contrite. Mostly annoyed. He cleared his throat. "I'm sorry. That was out of line. But I need to find a safe shelter before dark falls. I have a feeling someone may be coming by to finish me off. No sane person would attack me while I was at full strength."

I believed it, but it didn't stop me from thinking that Mr. Calix was a bit full of himself. "How do I know that you won't drain me as soon as you stabilize?"

"I don't do that," he said, echoing my earlier pronouncement while he swept my bag from my hands. I tried snatching it back, but he held it just out of my grasp, like some elementary-school bully with a My Little Pony backpack.

Scowling at him, I crossed my arms over my chest. "Considering you just vaguely threatened me, I have a hard time believing that."

"Check my wallet, on the counter."

I flipped open the expensive-looking leather folio and found what looked like a shiny gold policeman's badge. "You're a 'consultant' for the Council? In terms of credibility, that means nothing to me. I've met Ophelia."

His lips twitched at my reference to the cunning but unpredictable teen vampire.

"Why can't you just call her?" I asked. "She's your Council rep. This should be reported to her anyway."

"I can't call her. The Council supplied me with that blood. Left here in a gift basket before I arrived," he said, giving a significant look to the discarded packet on the floor. "Therefore, I can't trust the Council. I can't check into a hotel or seek help from friends without being tracked."

"I have a little sister who lives with me. I don't care how you ended up on the floor. We don't need to be a part of it." I grunted, making a grab for my bag as his tired arms drooped. "I am not running a stop on the vampire underground railroad."

"I can pay you an obscene amount of money."

I'm ashamed to say that this stilled my hand. If anything would make me consider this bizarre scheme, it was money. My parents had died nearly five years ago, leaving me to raise my little sister without much in the way of life insurance or savings. I needed money for Gigi's ever-looming college tuition. I needed money to keep up the house, to pay off the home-equity loan I'd taken out for Beeline's start-up capital. I needed money to keep us in the food that Gigi insisted on eating. And despite the fact that the business was finally becoming somewhat successful, I always seemed to just cover our expenses, with a tiny bit left over to throw at my own rabid student-loan officers. Something always seemed to pop up and eat away at our extra cash—car repair, school trip, explosive air-conditioning failure.

An obscene amount of money would provide enough

of a cushion that I might be able to sleep for more than a handful of hours per night. Mr. Calix slid to the floor, apparently drained by the effort of playing purse keep-away.

"How obscene?" I asked, coughing suddenly to chase the meek note from my voice.

"Ten thousand dollars for a week."

I quickly calculated the estimate to replace the aging pipes in my house, plus Gigi's first-semester tuition and the loan payment due next month, against what the Council paid even the lowliest of its underlings. I shook my head and made a counteroffer. "Twenty-five thousand."

"Fifteen thousand."

I pursed my lips. "I'm still saying twenty-five thousand."

"Which means you never quite learned how negotiating works."

It was a struggle, tensing my lips enough to avoid smirking. "How badly do you want to get off that floor, Mr. Calix?"

He grumbled. "Done."

"One week," I said as I knelt in front of him, my voice firmer than I would have thought possible under the circumstances. "That means seven nights. Not seven days and eight nights. Not seven and a half nights. *Seven nights.*"

"Done."

"Excellent." I gave him my sunniest "professional" smile and offered my hand for a shake.

"Don't push it," he muttered, closing his eyes.

I sighed, pulling my cell phone out of my bag to call Gigi. I wasn't going to make that booster meeting, after all.

2

The first rule of caring for a stray vampire: Don't tell anyone you're taking care of a stray vampire.
—*The Care and Feeding of Stray Vampires*

The moment I started dialing the phone, his hand snaked out and smacked it away. My precious Black-Berry shattered against the kitchen wall into splinters of black plastic. I shrieked indignantly, my mouth agape as I watched the shards tinkle to the ground.

He killed my phone. He ruthlessly *murdered* my phone! Mother . . . fudger.

My phone was my lifeline, my tether to my clients. It was what kept me available for their needs, their wants, each and every whim. I never ignored a call. Ever. If I wasn't able to answer, hair-trigger frustration and un-dead diva temperaments could lead to lost business. Lost business meant lost income, and lost income meant . . . I fought the rising panic clawing at my throat.

"What the hell is the matter with you?" I seethed.

"I said you couldn't call anyone." He wheezed, as the effort to bat my phone into shrapnel had apparently cost him some energy.

"I was calling my sister to let her know not to come home tonight," I said. "There's no way in hell I'm letting her walk through the door unless I know you're . . . house-trained." He snarled at that, pulling his lip back from sharp white teeth, but he remained quiet. I supposed that expecting an apology for the pulverized phone was futile, so I continued. "You're replacing that phone, by the way. And if I didn't have backup assistance to replace all of my contacts, I would leave your butt here on the kitchen floor, to hell with you and the Council."

"You're that attached to your phone?"

"It's the most dependable relationship I have."

If he'd made a joke about the vibrate feature, I would have walked out the door with a clean conscience. Unfortunately, he drew his own phone out of his pocket and handed it to me without comment, which took that option off the table.

Shunted to Gigi's voicemail, I told her to ask if she could stay at her friend Sammi Jo's house for the night and to call me before she came home. Behind me, Mr. Calix sat leaning against the cupboards, drinking the last bottle of clean synthetic blood.

I turned, crouching in front of him so we were at eye level. He didn't seem to like that, his big, honeyed-chocolate eyes pinning me as I hovered outside of striking distance. I squared my shoulders and tried to force as much authority into my voice as I could muster. "Here are my rules. I will set up a comfortable, light-tight place for you in my root cellar. I will stock bottled blood and whatever you need at my home. You will not be welcome in any of the living spaces above the first floor. I will not be feeding you any of my blood. Ever. And neither will my sister. In fact, if my sister is in the house, you are not allowed to be in the same room with her alone. The *minute* your week is up, you are out."

"You're making an awful lot of rules, human."

I smiled sweetly. "I'm not the one stranded half-naked on a cold tile floor, vampire."

"Get me up and out of here before the sun sets," he grumbled.

"Like I want to be here after dark," I retorted, standing so that I could pull him to his feet.

He shook his head when I held out my hands. "First, you need to clean up the blood."

I cocked my fists on my hips. "I think you'll find, if you look at your contract on the counter, that I am not a maid service."

Mr. Calix closed his eyes, as if he was praying to some fanged deity for patience. "If someone comes to my house, I don't want them to think they've gotten to me. I don't want them to know I'm weakened, unprotected. So, we make it look like I got a sudden whim to go out of town. People who do that generally don't leave large puddles of blood on the floor."

"Fine." I huffed, grabbing a new sponge from the drawer beside the sink. I wiped down the floor while Mr. Calix struggled into a faded black Rolling Stones T-shirt. After watching him unsuccessfully attempt to pull the right sleeve over his arm three times, I helped him settle it over his shoulders. It left us in an awkward position, him partially leaning against me, his face inches from mine as I supported his weight with palms pressed against his chest. I found myself staring at his mouth. His top lip was just the tiniest bit heavier and rounder than the bottom, given his mouth a bit of a bee-stung appearance. His lips looked soft, although I could see the barely concealed razor-sharp fangs lurking behind them. My hands curved around his pectorals, cradling rather than pushing him away. I bit my own lips to prevent a strange little sigh from escaping.

This was not a good beginning.

Five minutes in his employ, and I was already struggling with the very valid, sensible reasons for keeping my client at a professional, fully clothed distance. My eyes flicked up to his and saw wary calculation reflected back at me. I pushed up, helping him settle more firmly on his feet, and the spell was broken. The moment I moved away, I was able to breathe a little easier and remember all of those very valid, sensible reasons, which included:

1. Humans who slept with vampires sometimes ended up missing or worse.
2. Three months of carefully considered celibacy was not something to be thrown away on pretty lips that happened to be attached to a client.
3. After working with the vampire community for years without incident, I didn't want to develop the reputation of being an easy mark for horny male vampires.

4. The phrase "sex with the guy who sleeps in our basement" is not used by most responsible parental figures.

"Look under the sink," he said, nodding toward the cabinet in question. Where most people stored their garbage bags and empty grocery sacks, Mr. Calix had stored a canvas duffel bag and a carrying case for the laptop in the living room. I unzipped the duffel to find an emergency stash of clothes and toiletries. Oddly, this level of preparation warmed my heart. I did not want to top this strange day off by searching around in a vampire's underwear drawer. Nothing good could come of that.

By the time I turned around, Mr. Calix was standing on his own two feet, albeit leaning against a counter. Even weakened, at his full height he cut an imposing figure. He loomed a good foot taller than me, his frame solidly built. And I didn't think he got those muscles from painting or baking during his human years. Mr. Calix was someone who charged and fought until his last remaining enemy was destroyed . . . like my poor phone.

I had a sudden sense of foreboding. How smart was it to take an unstable, phone-crushing vampire home with me? I didn't know anything about this guy beyond his last name, address, and credit history. Sure, he was referred to me by Ophelia, but she was the type who would probably find trapping a human in an enclosed space with a vampiric sex offender rather droll.

I should just call Ophelia, I told myself. I should tell her about her poisoned consultant, go the hell home, and pillage the bag of York Peppermint Patties hidden in my freezer.

Just as I was flipping through Mr. Calix's contacts to do exactly that, he pulled open what most people would have used as their utensil drawer and began carefully counting out cash into small, banded stacks. I could see a wealth of green still in the drawer as he snapped it shut.

"Ten thousand dollars," he said, nudging the neatly stacked bills toward me. "Consider it a good-faith down payment. If I survive the week, you'll get the full amount."

My hands shook a little as my fingertips brushed the precious green paper. I had never seen so much cash in one place before. This couldn't be real. This amount of cash shouldn't just fall into my hands so easily. This couldn't be a good idea. But the money ended up in my hand somehow and was safely zipped into my purse. And that seemed like the point of no return, in terms of negotiating.

"You keep that kind of cash in your knife drawer?" I asked. "I think I know why someone poisoned you."

"The person who poisoned me didn't have use for my money," he said dryly. "Just so you know, I'll be changing the security code on the way out. I would hate for you to be tempted to come back and clean me out while I'm sleeping."

"I ask you, where's the trust?"

"Tucked safely into your purse," he retorted.

I took a moving blanket from a heap in the living room and tossed it over his head. He slipped into some shoes, and we carefully exited the house. He used his vampire speed to reset the code so that even if I'd been tempted, I couldn't follow it, and we moved swiftly toward my car. Just dusk, there was no one outside in the neighborhood yet, so I was able to load him calmly into the back of the van without so much as a wisp of smoke rising off his skin.

With my client snugly situated under a blanket, I stopped on the way home to pop into a local blood bank where the staff knew me and told them that I was filling an order from Mr. Rychek. Knowing the way he stress-fed when Diandra came into town, they didn't question the extra units of O positive and fresh plasma that I withdrew.

The sun was just setting as I turned into my own driveway. I was relieved to see my house, even if I was technically bringing a monster into it. My place was nothing special, a rambling old farmhouse that my parents had purchased just after they married. The original owners had added rooms here and there over the generations. The effect was like several cracker boxes stacked against one another and then covered with cream-colored aluminum siding. But the trim was covered with a fresh coat of robin's-egg blue, and the gutters were new.

I didn't have as much time to maintain my flower beds as I'd like, so I tried to give them a low-maintenance, wild fairy-cottage look, with fluffy white spikes of crepe myrtle and low-lying purple and golden clouds of shrub verbena. Creeping carpets of periwinkle phlox spilled over the stone circles that contained the beds. I liked the way their color contrasted against the lush basketball-sized purple-blue clusters of the hydrangea bushes.

I knew every plant, every bloom, because I tended them with my own hands. I could mentally catalogue them by genus and phylum, but I chose not to. This was one area where my botany professors and I didn't agree. I didn't like calling plants by their Latin names. Yes, it was more appropriate in an academic setting, but it was so impersonal. Plants had personalities. Referring to happy, open sunflowers as "helianthus" was like calling them by the ugly middle names they only listed on their tax forms. If plants paid taxes, that is.

Despite the use of a wide-brimmed straw hat, my skin was brown and slightly freckled from the hours I spent weeding, watering, and warding off pests. My hands were callused, and my nails were nonexistent. Some days, all I wanted to do was collapse on the couch after work rather than break out the aphid spray, but I could no more neglect my plants than I could leave Gigi "Appliance Killer" Scanlon to cook for herself. Like Gigi, they'd been left to me, and I took care of them.

I caught Mr. Calix looking at the house over my shoulder as I helped him out of the van. The expression on his handsome face screamed "not impressed." He cleared his throat and managed, "It's . . ."

I gave him an arch look. "Yes?"

"Quaint. Very homey."

"Because it *is* a home, my family's home," I reminded him. "Which I am bringing you into."

"I understand," he said, gritting his teeth a bit as we

negotiated the front steps. I wasn't sure why he seemed so pained. I was pretty sure that I was bearing more of his weight than he was. And negotiating a locked front door while attempting to prop up a slumping vampire is quite the feat of concentration.

Contrary to those talented storytellers' theories, vampires can, in fact, enter your home without an invitation. In general, they don't, because they consider it rude. There were a lot of little myths that the humans had to let go of once vampires came out of the coffin—crosses, holy water, guys with cute English accents who wandered around in long black coats being all adorably evil.

Sigh. Oh, Spike.

Believe it or not, this whole public vampirism thing was started by an out-of-control undead accountant. In 1999, a newly turned Milwaukee tax consultant named Arnie Frink requested evening hours so he could continue his job at the firm of Jacobi, Meyers, and Leptz. But the human-resources rep, as ignorant as the rest of the world about the existence of the undead at the time, insisted that Arnie keep banker's hours because of security concerns. Because God forbid anyone should be able to use unsupervised night hours to make unlimited copies.

Arnie countered with a diagnosis of porphyria, a painful allergy to sunlight, but the evil HR rep could not be moved. So Arnie responded just like any typical wronged American.

He sued the absolute hell out of them.

When the allergy-discrimination argument failed to impress a judge, a sunblock-slathered Arnie lost his composure in court and declared that he was a vampire, with a medical condition that rendered him unable to work during the day, thereby making him subject to the Americans with Disabilities Act.

After several lengthy appeals, Arnie won his lawsuit and got a settlement, evening hours, and an interview with Barbara Walters. While initially furious that some schmuck accountant from Milwaukee had destroyed millenniums' worth of undead mystique, the international vampire community eventually agreed that it was more convenient to live out in the open, anyway. Blood was easier to get when you could just ask someone for it.

An elected contingent of ancient vampires officially notified the United Nations of their presence and asked the world's governments to recognize them as legitimate beings. They also asked for special leniency in certain medical, legal, and tax issues that were sure to come up. Apparently, organized financial records are beneath vampires' notice.

The first year or so was a pretty dark chapter in human history. When the media did anniversary reports on the Great Coming Out, they tended to leave out the part about mobs of people dragging vampires out into the sunlight or setting them on fire for no reason other than that they existed. The federal government issued mandatory after-dark curfews out of fear that the vampires would retaliate en masse. So the humans found ways to fit all of their raids in before sunset.

The same international contingent of vampires, who called themselves the World Council for the Equal Treatment of the Undead, appealed to the human governments for help. In exchange for providing certain census information, the Council was allowed to establish smaller, local bodies within regions of each state in every country. The Council was charged with keeping watch over newer vampires to make sure that they were safely acclimated to unlife, settling squabbles within the community, and investigating "accidents" that befell vampires.

I wasn't sure if working for the Council made Mr. Calix an authority figure or less trustworthy. While I generally stayed on Ophelia's good side, I'd been witness to some significantly shady dealings on the Council's part. The vampire authority believed in "any means necessary" to maintain order, including intimidation, cover-ups, and the occasional disappearance. I tried not to witness anything, because that sometimes led to disappearances. It was a vicious cycle.

I helped Mr. Calix settle onto the couch with a warmed packet of donor blood, then went downstairs to organize his living space. The basement was pretty tidy, thanks to my postfuneral outburst of boxing and labeling. My parents' camping equipment was stored neatly in the southwest corner, farthest away from the set of small windows at ground level. Clearing a space among the boxes, I set up the little two-man tent that my dad said was "idiot-proof." Inside, I covered the low camping bed with fresh sheets and blankets. An upturned orange plastic dairy crate served as a little nightstand.

Because vampires are highly sensitive to heat and sunlight, I covered the windows in two layers of heavy-duty aluminum foil and then taped cardboard panels over them. A sunburned vampire was not a pretty sight. Every vamp had a different level of reaction. There was a rumor floating around that it was like a personality test. If a vampire's skin engulfed quickly, he or she had a passionate nature. A slow, smoldering burn indicated a more controlled character. Personally, I thought it was mean to sit around and look for signals in the smoke while someone was on fire.

As long as Mr. Calix stayed inside the tent and didn't mickey around with the window coverings, he would be able to avoid direct sunlight and smoky, fiery death. That was my main selling point, should he gripe about having to sleep between boxes of old yearbooks and an inflatable Santa Claus.

I made my way up the stairs to find a slightly less gray vampire dozing on my comfy blue sofa. It was utterly bizarre to see a corpse in the room where my family had once held Monopoly tournaments. This was clearly a family room, with its careworn furnishings and cheerful mint-green paint. My dad's wooden duck decoys "swam" on the mantel. I'd taken down Mom's framed cross-stitched floral samplers, featuring platitudes about hearth and home, and replaced them with black-and-white photos of our family in better days. There was a shot of preteen Gigi finishing her first 5K with Dad. Mom kneeling among her rosebushes. The four of us playing a particularly violent game of Spoons that nearly derailed Thanksgiving. To usher in a little life, I'd set little arrangements of roses and hydrangeas around the room in square glass vases. This was not your typical crash pad for the undead.

I sat in the chair opposite the couch, a delicate, brocade-covered wingback my mother had favored when she needed to have serious discussions with us. We called it the Report Card Chair. I tilted my head to the side and studied my charge. Although his feet dangled over the end of the sofa and his head was bent at a weird angle, his face was relaxed. He looked sort of sweet and untroubled . . . when his mouth was closed.

The nearly drained blood packet rested precariously against his chest. At that angle, it was in danger of dripping onto my upholstery, so I reached over him to take it away. His eyes snapped open, and he hissed at me, fangs in full play, as his fingers circled my left wrist and squeezed. Even in his weakened state, the crushing force of his grip dropped me to my knees. I braced my feet against the chair legs and tugged frantically as he pulled my arm toward his mouth. I threw all of my weight back, hoping to knock him off balance, but he didn't budge. Finally, I bopped him on the end of the nose with my other hand, shouting, "No!" in my sternest voice.

His grip loosened as he stared up at me, dark eyes boring into mine as if there were secret codes scribbled on my corneas. He blinked rapidly as my face came into focus.

"Did you just slap me on my nose like a mischievous dog?" he asked incredulously as I tried to rub the circulation back into my wrist.

I nodded, cringing away from him. "I think I did."

His tone was at once menacing and amused. "And am I mistaken, or did you poke me in the eye earlier?"

"I saw it on Shark Week," I murmured.

"What was that?" he asked, although I knew good and well that he could hear me.

"I saw it on Shark Week," I repeated in a louder, irritated tone. "The narrator said that if you're attacked by a shark, you should jab it in the eye, and it might distract the shark long enough to let you go. I figured as another apex predator, it might apply to you, too."

He chuckled, a hoarse noise that rattled in his chest like a cough. "So I went from shark to dog in a matter of hours? That's a considerable demotion. Do you always apply animal-behavior techniques to interactions with clients?"

"I try to avoid direct interaction with clients whenever possible, particularly when I'm alone," I griped, yanking my arm out of his grip. "And I've never interacted with a client who shows fang as much as you do."

"You have this way of sneaking up on me. My reflexes are generally better."

"Well, it would appear that you're not at your best right now," I conceded. "I think we've gotten off to a bad start, what with the violence and the destroyed cellphone hardware. Can we start over?"

His face slipped into a shrewd expression. "Does that mean a renegotiation of our financial arrangement?"

"No."

"Well, I'm willing to try it anyway," he drawled.

"Iris Scanlon, pleased to make your acquaintance," I

said, reaching out to shake his hand. A pulse of warmth buzzed along my palm. He squeezed my fingertips in a way that had the nerves along my skin singing and sizzling. It felt like part tickling sexual energy, part organic emergency flare; like my sensible superego was screaming at the dumber, hornier regions of my brain that whatever the id was planning could lead to no good. I pulled my hand away abruptly. His lips twitched, and his eyes narrowed, like a hawk circling a clueless little mouse.

"Cletus Calix, pleased not to be sprawled out on the floor."

I laughed at an indecent decibel level and clapped my hand over my mouth. "Cletus? As in the slack-jawed yokel?"

"In my language, it meant 'illustrious,'" he said grumpily.

I snickered. "Or that you shared a drinkin' gourd with your eleven brothers, also named Cletus."

He arched one sable eyebrow. "I'm going to assume I would have to originate from this lovely hamlet before I'd find the humor in that."

"Hey, I live in Half-Moon Hollow," I protested. "And no one in my family is named Cletus. No wonder you insisted on having only your initials on the contracts."

"As opposed to Scanlon, which means 'scandal' in the old Irish tongue? There's a proud lineage."

"Regardless of etymology, I'm calling you Cal. I can't call you Cletus with a straight face," I told him, pushing dark, errant hair out of my face. "OK. Now that my panic high seems to be fading, can you explain how we've found ourselves in this situation? I had quite a few things on my to-do list this morning. 'Take in stray, cranky vampire boarder' was not on that list."

"Cranky? Is my manner not suited to your delicate human sensibilities?"

"Oh, no, I've always wanted an abrasive, sullen creature of the night to call my very own. My self-esteem was getting too high." He scowled at me. I gave him the shallow, sugary smile I gave Diandra on the rare occasion our paths crossed. "I have enough of my own sarcasm, Cal. I don't need yours."

He eyed me for one long, speculative moment. I felt weighed and measured by those deep, dark eyes. And I got the distinct impression that he didn't like what he saw. Well, screw him and his "illustrious" lineage. I was a Scanlon, damn it. And my lineage was just as noble. I came from a long line of people . . . who were probably household servants to some very important people.

I opened my mouth to tell him that he was welcome to leave anytime he could drag his undead butt out the door, but he finally said, "Someone interfered with my blood supply. There was some substance in the blood that made me weak and sick. I knew something was wrong after consuming a relatively small amount. But by that time, I couldn't stay on my feet. I lay there on the kitchen floor, drifting in and out of consciousness, for most of the day. I didn't even feel it when you fell on top of me."

"I didn't fall on top of you, I fell *over* you."

His lips twitched. And I had this bizarre urge to slap

the smirk right off of his face, which wasn't exactly the best way to establish an amicable business relationship. What was it about this vampire that had me swinging on the mood pendulum so violently? I'd never had trouble behaving professionally around the undead. But something about my new charge made me want to kiss his mouth one minute and punch it the next. Neither of which was a good idea, because either would end up in my being bitten and/or maimed.

Drawing me out of the internal smacking/kissing debate, Cal said, "You're very concerned about semantics. Fine, when you *fell over* me, I didn't feel it. I only sensed you after you so foolishly stretched your arm over my face. I could feel your pulse beating that delicious tattoo right over my nose. You have a very nice natural aroma. Are you aware of that? Lavender with a hint of iron-rich earth."

"Am I going to have to get a rolled-up newspaper?" I demanded.

A little dimple appeared at the corner of his mouth. I was amusing him, like a petulant little pet. Fantastic. I rolled my eyes. "Are you sure it was the blood that made you weak? Did you do anything else last night that could have made you sick? Blood eventually expires, right? Do vampires have allergies beyond silver and sunlight? Could you have had a reaction to something in your new house, like a cleaning product or new carpet?"

Cal seemed mildly annoyed with all the questions. He yawned, something I'd never seen vampires do, and blinked as if he was having trouble keeping his eyes open. "I am sure it was the blood, perhaps something injected into the plastic packet. I wouldn't have noticed the tampering. And as for allergies, I'm not sure I should reveal my weaknesses to you."

"You think I'm going to attack you with Windex?"

He blinked again. "At the moment, I trust you more than the average human. But you might question your decision to let me into your home at some point tomorrow while I'm resting."

"You make a relevant but frustrating point. I'm actually questioning my decision as we speak." When he tensed, I added, "I figure if I tell you the truth now, you'll have no reason to drain me over a minor misunderstanding later. I have to ask: Why would someone interfere with *your* blood, in particular? Why would someone want to hurt you? I mean, some other reason beyond your lack of personal charm or regard for communicative technology."

His cheek barely twitched with the effort to frown at me. "That's classified information, Council business," he said, slurring the *S*'s slightly. "I can't discuss it with you."

"Oh, well, I'll just go right ahead risking my neck without the full picture, then," I muttered, crossing my arms.

"Full disclosure wasn't part of our agreement."

"The agreement is being amended," I shot back.

"And why am *I* not allowed to amend the agreement?" he demanded.

"I suppose 'Because I said so' isn't a sufficient answer?" I asked. When this failed to bring about a response, I rubbed my hand over my eyes. "I brought you into my home. The least you can do is tell me why I made such a stupid decision. And before you insult my trustworthiness again, I might remind you that I have access codes to the homes of nearly every member of the Council. I know who and what they eat. I know when they're fighting with their spouses, and when they're having sex with people they're not supposed to, and when they're fighting with their spouses *because* they're having sex with people they're not supposed to. And I never breathe a word to a single soul, living or otherwise. It's safe to say I can be trusted to use discretion."

Cal stared at me. I shot my best stern, irritated expression right back, which didn't seem to faze him in the least. I really needed to work on my stern expressions. Apparently, they only work on teenage girls . . . or Gigi was just humoring me.

"There has been a series of vampire attacks on humans," he finally said, his tongue thick and slow. "Sporadic, across the country. Horrific, bloody attacks with no apparent motive, vampires who have shown no previous signs of aggression lashing out at human companions and tearing them apart. The Council is doing its best to keep it quiet, because we don't want to cause a panic in the human community. As best we can tell, the vampires in question all suffered a form of poisoning. The compound is like steroids for vampires, on an exponential level. It brings out the worst of our aggressive, territorial behaviors while enhancing our strength and lowering our inhibitions."

"Why would someone do that?"

"How old are you?" he asked. "Twenty-two, twenty-four?"

"I'm twenty-nine," I grumbled.

"So you're old enough to remember what it was like following the Great Coming Out. The burnings, the 'accidents.' The all-out lynchings of vampires. While that's died down over the years, there are still conservative religious groups out there that would like nothing more than to prove to the world what vicious, dangerous animals we are."

"How many attacks have there been?"

Cal began to protest. I jabbed a finger toward his face, which he did not seem to appreciate. "If you tell me that's classified information, I will shove my size-seven shoe up your rear."

"Charming," he muttered. But my off-putting foot-to-rear threats might have been some sort of stimulant, because he seemed to focus more clearly on what I was saying. I would analyze that disturbing development later.

"There have been a dozen attacks over the course of the last two weeks. The first few were written off as random acts of violence by vampires who were too young to control themselves. But then the violence began affecting older vampires. Vampires with no history of harming humans. We went through the trash left at their homes. They all consumed Faux Type O, which in itself wasn't unusual. It's the most popular brand of synthetic blood on the market. But in each attack, the affected vampire had consumed Faux Type O that was part of an experimental batch made by Nocturne Beverages. The newer version was supposed to appeal to younger vampire palates, using a new botanical flavoring agent. The flavoring agent was mixed into a batch of product for test marketing, but rather than being set aside, as was intended, the modified batch was distributed along with the original product."

"I guess they didn't learn anything from New Coke." I snorted.

Cal's lips twitched, but he continued, all business. "I traced the supplier that produced the flavoring agent, Blue Moon Additives. Blue Moon submitted preview samples to Nocturne for testing, and they received positive responses from company taste-testers. I reviewed the manufacturer's safety-testing records. Everything seemed to be in order, until I tried to contact Blue Moon after the attacks. The company simply doesn't exist outside of paperwork. The address listed in Louisville is a vacant office park."

"What was the flavoring agent supposed to taste like?" I asked, curious about what vampires could find appetizing. Cal opened his mouth to answer. I held up a hand like a shield against the potentially icky information. "Never mind. Some things can never be unheard."

"Blue Moon is a front, registered by a cleverly constructed dummy corporation. The whole mess has been infuriatingly difficult to sort out."

Releasing that torrent of information seemed to exhaust him. He slumped back against the couch and closed his eyes. The slight ruddiness of cheek that the donor blood had given him was fading, leaving a waxy, nearly gray pallor.

"So why come to the Hollow?" I asked.

One brown eye popped open, staring balefully at me. "Because the first attack was here. It was written off as newborn blooklust. The Council managed to cover it up quickly and quietly. I suspect it was an initial test case, so to speak. It seemed a reasonable place to start."

"Why wouldn't you let the Council staff know you'd been poisoned?"

"Because of the circumstances of my own poisoning, I believe it's possible someone within the Council hierarchy is assisting in this effort. Only someone within the Council office would know why I am here. And only someone within the Council office would have access to the donor blood that was included in my welcome basket. It would be easy to tempt a younger vampire with money. As you know, the lower-level Council bureaucrats are pitifully underpaid."

"Shouldn't people know about this?" I demanded. "Shouldn't you warn the human authorities, at least?" He opened both eyes, just so he could roll them. I nodded, blushing a little. "Right, discretion, sorry."

"We don't know if the person responsible has plans for poisonings on a broader scale. Since we would like to get through this crisis without the human government instituting an extermination program for my kind, we're trying to handle this quietly," he said in a wry tone.

"All but a few of the affected bottles of blood have been tracked and recalled."

"Which plants were used in the flavoring agent?" I asked, thinking of the botany textbooks I had upstairs. If Cal had access to them, he might be able to—

He chuckled derisively. "Why would I share that information with you?"

Arching my eyebrow, I mentally nixed my impulse to offer to let him go through my bookshelves. Act like a jerk, get cut off from my treasure trove of information on plant life. I had to have some standards. Cletus the slack-jawed vampire could just deal with the consequences.

"Who among the local Council members knows why you're here?" I asked.

"All of them."

"Which doesn't help us narrow the pool of potential suspects for poisoning your blood," I conceded. "Is it unusual that the Council left blood in your fridge in the first place? I mean, wasn't that why you were hiring me?"

"No, I was hiring you to be polite. Ophelia was quite insistent that your services were essential. I was afraid I would offend her if I sent you away. To be honest, I thought your contract was a cover for her monitoring my activities."

"By that logic, wouldn't it make sense that I might be the person who tampered with your blood?" I asked. His eyes narrowed at me. "I really have to learn to shut up."

"I know it wasn't you," he said grimly. "The blood was delivered as part of a welcome gift basket from the

Council yesterday. You haven't used the access code for my door before today."

"My friend Jane says you shouldn't trust gift baskets around here," I told him.

"That would have been helpful to know a few days ago," he mumbled.

"So you're sort of a vampire PI?" I asked. "Without the office in a semidisreputable part of town or the cheesy mustache?"

The aforementioned unmustachioed lips quirked in response. "In a manner of speaking. You might say my gift is problem solving. If I stay fixed on a problem or a question long enough, I will eventually find a solution. It started in my early days as a human. I'd always been clever with puzzles, games of strategy, battle plans. And now I'm used in investigations into financial indiscretions between vampires and the human business world, finding vampires who have disappeared or died under mysterious circumstances, tracking the human descendants of vampires interested in getting reacquainted with their human families since the Great Coming Out, that sort of thing."

He was sprawled back on the couch now, exhausted and drained by my questions. I helped him to his feet and walked him to the cellar door. "So if you're the problem solver, why can't you figure out who's poisoning the vampires?"

He frowned at me, as if I was touching a tender subject. "It's not an instant-gratification sort of talent. It's more of an instinct that leads me in the right direction.

This time, the problem has a few more twists and turns than I'm used to," he said, his voice worn and as thin as paper as I helped him downstairs and into the tent. He barely glanced at his "room." If he was less than thrilled with my less-than-four-star accommodations, he didn't say anything. I suspected that he found conversation with me to be circuitous and pointless.

Mainly because he told me that he found conversation with me to be circuitous and pointless. To my face.

3

Your family will not understand your decision to take in a vampire. To avoid awkward conversations, think of excuses to avoid their visiting beforehand. Solid suggestions include: Your house is being fumigated. You have a contagious rash. You are trying to read the *North and South* trilogy from beginning to end.

—*The Care and Feeding of Stray Vampires*

I stayed up a good portion of the night, sitting on the couch, clutching my mother's heirloom silver pie server. Much like with sunlight, vampires are allergic to silver. For them, it's like touching every caustic, irritating substance in the world all at once, combined with the annoyance of listening to actress-slash-models talk about their "craft." It can actually burn the flesh from their bones if they're exposed to enough of it, which is why the vampire pepper spray I carried was mostly very pure colloidal silver.

For all I knew, Cal's impotent-kitten routine could have been an act. And I wasn't exactly pinning my hopes for personal safety on my houseguest's inability to climb the cellar stairs unassisted.

I used my insomnia time wisely. I finished a historical romance I'd started-and-stopped so many times I'd forgotten the names of the main characters. I reported the loss of my darling BlackBerry to my cell provider's online insurance site and was slightly mollified by the promise that a replacement phone would be shipped to my house overnight. My business landline rang several times. There were calls from clients asking for various deliveries, pickups, and errands . . . And asking why I wasn't picking up my cell phone, which had me grumbling and cursing Cal's very existence. Ophelia called at around two A.M. and was surprised that I'd answered the phone instead of letting it go to voicemail. It was interesting to hear any emotion in her voice beyond smug boredom.

"Aren't you normally asleep at this hour, Iris?"

Pressing the phone to my ear, I blew a cooling breath over a cup of valerian root tea. I needed my special "It's two A.M., and the infomercials are starting to make sense" blend to counteract the bag of espresso jelly beans I'd found in my desk drawer.

I am a constant contradiction.

I yawned for effect. "Yes, Gigi has a school project due. Nothing like last-minute extra credit in hopes of saving a biology grade."

"What an exciting life you lead," she said dryly.

"What can I do for you, Ophelia?"

"I was curious. The Council arranged for a new contract with a Mr. Calix, one of our freelance employees. Did you happen to drop by his house today?"

This was it. This was my opening to alert Ophelia to Cal's problems and wash my hands of the situation. It would be so easy to let someone else handle this situation. And it wasn't as if I didn't have enough on my plate. I had a complicated, high-maintenance business to run. I had Gigi to lead on the precarious path to functional adulthood.

But . . .

I breathed steadily through my nose. I could deny being there, but I'd left Cal's contracts on the counter. Besides, I was pretty sure that I'd left trace evidence all over that house. I didn't know if the Council had fingerprint analysts, but they did have psychic interrogators, and I wouldn't put using a few forensics geeks past them. Lying would only make Ophelia suspicious.

"Um, yeah, I got there just before sunset," I said. "I was running late. Mr. Rychek had some special issues for me to attend to, and it took me longer than expected."

"Diandra is making her triumphant return?" Ophelia asked. Through the phone, I could practically hear her eyes rolling.

"Yes. It took forever to work out her 'special dietary requests.' I had just enough time to drop the contracts off at Mr. Calix's and get out of there before the sun went down. You know I don't like getting caught in clients' homes after dark."

"And you didn't see anything unusual, out of place?" she asked.

Say, a six-foot-two Greek god of a vampire with a

pouty mouth and an acid tongue? He looked pretty out of place, sprawled unconscious on the kitchen tile.

"A couple of packing boxes. The house was pretty empty."

Notice that I hadn't actually lied. I just wasn't answering questions directly. I was raising a teenager and therefore familiar with the distinct difference.

"Is there a problem, Ophelia?"

"No, no," she assured me. "But I'm afraid Mr. Calix is going to have to cancel his contract. You will, of course, keep your retainer deposit, out of respect for your continued services to our local vampires. You should know that the access codes to Mr. Calix's house have been changed. You should not enter the house again. He is no longer your client."

"Well, I'm sorry to hear that," I said. My tone was a careful balance of detached, but sincere, regret. I would regret losing any client, but Ophelia knew that I wouldn't get hysterical over it.

"I'm sure you'll have another client to fill up his spot on your roster soon," she said in a tone that might have been considered reassuring from anyone else. "Speaking of which, have you managed to find the item I requested?"

"Yes, I found the doll," I said. "A pristine turn-of-the-last-century Clarenbault, with the original dress and bonnet. I only had to shamelessly flatter-slash-threaten the administrators of several obscure antique auction Web sites to obtain it. You owe my PayPal account a considerable sum."

"Send me an invoice," she said, her tone lifting. "I'm happy to pay any price."

I made a note about the invoice on my to-do list for the next day. And I knew better than to ask why a centuries-old vampire would want an antique porcelain doll. Ophelia frequently requested childish items such as bears, dolls, Mary Jane shoes, and sweet little dresses. Not to mention the obscene number of video-game controllers she went through every month. I was convinced that she was supplementing her income by posing for questionable Internet sites. But I didn't know how the video-game controllers came into play. I wasn't sure if I wanted to.

"If you happen to run into Mr. Calix, please let me know," she said. "We'd like to speak to him, but we seem to be unable to reach him by phone."

"Well, I doubt I'll see him," I said, keeping my voice deliberately casual as I tossed Cal's soiled shirt toward the laundry hamper. "You know me, I avoid face time whenever possible. But if I do, I'll give you a call."

"You do that."

Eager to get off the phone unscathed, I promised to drop the doll off at her office on Monday. I hung up and lay back on the bed. I'd chosen Cal. Why? I knew Ophelia far better than I knew Cal. I owed her some personal loyalty. She'd helped me get my business off the ground. She'd never tried to bite me. But I'd backed the guy who sort of threatened me and made me use animal-control techniques to keep him in line.

I'd given Cal my word. He seemed pretty keen to stay

away from the Council. And despite the regular flow of contract payments coming in, none of them would pay me $10,000 in one swift swoop. That had to purchase some sort of loyalty, too.

I sprang from bed and paced all over the house, a heavy, sour weight settling low in my belly as I straightened up the debris that resulted from teenage occupancy. I made a list of errands and tasks that needed to be completed over the next few days. Shopping for a week's supply of blood, meetings with two vampire brides, baking six dozen cupcakes for the high school's bake sale. I ran through all of the various ways this "vampire refugee" situation could end, and an alarming majority of those scenarios ended up with me broke or broken.

Finally, just before dawn, I sank into my bed, exhausted, and passed out.

I slept like the dead for hours, dark and deep. I dreamed of cool lips brushing over mine, down the line of my jaw, over my throat. My fingertips skimmed skin that smelled of sandalwood and leather. Rough hands slipped over my thighs, leaving burning trails of sensation. His tongue slipped against mine, pulling it into his mouth.

I was aching, hollow inside, desperately needing to be filled. I shifted my weight, rubbing against him and whimpering softly. He chuckled, sitting back and stroking his fingers down my face. In the dream, I sighed and gazed up at him with adoration. He bent his head to nuzzle my throat as he plunged between my thighs. Hot, crushing pain radiated from my pulse point as my skin tore like wet tissue—

I gasped as I bolted up, hands clawing at my throat. "No!"

The room was shadowed and cool. I was alone. My cool spring-green sheets lay crumpled across the floor, a sure sign that I'd kicked and flailed during my nightmare. The heady scent of sandalwood was replaced by that of the homemade chamomile and lavender sachet I kept under my pillow. I drew in a shaky breath. It felt so real. The soft, cool kisses. His hands on my skin. I could still feel hot, smooth pressure where . . . well, I hadn't felt much of anything lately. I was actually surprised when I pulled my hand away from my neck and found that it wasn't covered in blood. Part of me wanted to check under the bed to make sure my vampire client wasn't lurking among the dust bunnies.

I glanced at the clock. It was after five P.M. on Saturday. I'd slept almost twelve hours.

I immediately got up, pulled my laptop into my bed, and Googled "vampire dream hypnosis," but beyond the average crackpot Web sites, there was no evidence that vampires could diddle with my brain while I slept.

I checked my e-mails, put out a few bridal fires, and made arrangements to pick up some signed contracts from a new Council referral. If I found him passed out on the floor in a puddle of faux blood, I was taking Gigi, changing our name to Smooter, and moving to Tallahassee. Seriously, there's only so much vampire hijinks a girl can take.

I could hear light clanking noises from the kitchen

downstairs. I looked outside. The sun was still visible over the horizon. My vampiric guest shouldn't have been up and stirring yet. And Gigi's Beetle wasn't in the driveway.

I crept downstairs on silent feet. On the way to the kitchen, I snagged an ugly soapstone carving of a rabbit that we only kept around because Mom had been proud of it. Peering around the corner of the fridge, I couldn't see who was rifling through my kitchen drawers. I debated running out the back door and letting Cal deal with them. But instead, I jumped into the open, the statue held aloft over my head.

My little sister arched a dark, sleek brow at me while snacking on microwave popcorn. "I know you don't like it when I take the last bag of Butter Lovers, but I think this is an overreaction. It's not like I broke into your precious 'Do Not Eat Under Penalty of Death' chocolate stash in the freezer."

All of my breath left my lungs in a whoosh. I set the sculpture on the counter and threw my arms around her. "Gigi! What the hell are you doing home?"

"I . . . live here?" she said, her tone confused.

Gigi and I shared the same dimpled cheeks, stubborn chins, and eyes that our mother called cornflower blue. We had the same small, compact frame. But that's where the similarities ended. At seventeen, Gigi's looks were more refined than mine, like the difference between something that hung at the Louvre and something you hung on your fridge. I was simple lines and straight features, while she was all elfin curves and pert angles.

I couldn't have loved her more if she was my own child. But sometimes I considered shaving her eyebrows off while she slept.

For the sake of developing her character.

Moving on.

"I asked you to call before you came home," I said, hugging her as I set the sculpture on the counter. "Where's your car?"

Her mouth perked up at the corners. "I did call, several times. But you didn't pick up. And my car is in the garage. Did you know that you left the Dorkmobile parked out in the middle of the driveway? That's not like you." She took in my ragged hair and the circles under my eyes. She groaned and tossed a piece of popcorn at my head. "Aw, is Booty Call Paul here?"

Used to these theatrics, I ducked my head to the side and let the kernel sail by and bounce against the maple cabinet. My brow furrowed at Gigi's mention of my off-and-on, mostly off, somewhat boyfriend. "Why would you ask that?"

"You've got sex hair . . . or crazy cat lady hair. They're remarkably similar."

"If that's the case, I've always got crazy sex hair. That came out wrong," I conceded, gesturing to my bedhead.

Gigi shuddered delicately. "My point is that oversleeping and frizz usually mean that Napoleon has invaded once again. And then I find him in your bathrobe making frozen waffles in our kitchen."

I frowned. We'd talked about her none-too-subtle nickname for Paul, who tended to be sensitive about his below-average height. Well, I'd talked about it. Gigi had promised to "try" not to use it.

I'd started dating Paul Simms a few months after we moved to the Hollow. The assistant coach of the Half-Moon Hollow High football team, Paul was one of those good old-fashioned guys who believed in holding hands and having an actual conversation before engaging in sexual activity. We were exclusive for almost a year. We did all of the things couples on the "happily ever after" track did. I met his parents. I stopped wearing rose oil because it made his nose itch. He stopped cutting his own hair. We exchanged house keys and dresser-drawer space. I knew how he ordered his pancakes at the Coffee Spot. He knew not to touch the freezer chocolate stash, ever. He was a good guy, a keeper, one of those genuinely sweet men a girl dreams of building a life with.

But in the end, we wanted different things. He couldn't imagine living anywhere but the Hollow, whereas I could see keeping my geographical options open. Paul wanted someone who was going to cheer at his beer-league soft-ball games and really care about the outcome of the UK basketball season. I bought tickets to see a touring production of *A Midsummer Night's Dream,* and he looked like I'd suggested an evening of chain-saw juggling. He wanted a house full of kids, while I was tepid-to-undecided on the issue. And despite the fact that he worked around teenagers all day, he never quite warmed to Gigi. When he talked about our life together, discussion of cohabitation, marriage, and kids was always framed as "after Gigi leaves for college." There was something wrong about that.

So we parted ways, or at least, that was the plan. We had a cordial, friendly breakup, and we were proud of ourselves for handling it in such a mature fashion. Until a few weeks later, when Paul's grandmother died, and he came to me for solace. And a month later, on the anniversary of my parents' accident, he returned the favor for me. We developed a bad habit of turning to each other for comfort when we were sad, lonely, or just plain horny. The next morning, we'd realize what a huge mistake we'd made (again) and not speak for weeks, or we'd give dating another shot, only to break it off (again) a few days later and start the cycle all over again. It was a weird, naked trap that I couldn't seem to climb out of.

Three months earlier, I'd realized what a bad example I was setting for Gigi and slowly but surely whittled Paul out of my life. No phone calls. No texts. Blocked on Twitter. Defriended on Facebook. It was the social-media equivalent of an Amish shunning, although technically, he hadn't "wronged" me in any way. And he hadn't noticed for nearly three months, which in itself was a pretty good reason to stop sleeping with him.

"I just don't want to see you hurt, Iris."

"Geeg, there's no chance of me being hurt. Those sorts of feelings aren't involved anymore. Really."

"So you're having sex with him because he happens to be there," she said dryly.

"First of all, that hasn't happened in months. And second, consider some context, please. The way you're saying it sounds slutty and wrong. It's not like I'm jumping some poor unsuspecting UPS guy."

She snorted. "Yes, UPS occasionally delivers." When I shot her a bewildered look, she rolled her eyes and added, "If the orgasms were real, you wouldn't be so tense all the time."

"That's not tr—" I stopped when she leveled me with that wry blue gaze. I threw my hands up. "Two out of three, OK? Two out of three of them are real. That's not that bad. Meat Loaf even sang a song about it."

She leveled me with the patented, infuriating "I am Gigi, I see all" look.

I groaned. "Look, I don't have time to devote to dating. I have to work. I have to take care of the house and do my penance at the concession stand to fulfill my obligation to a certain someone's volleyball booster club. And I have to do my best parenting imitation so social services doesn't reassign you to some nice missionary family. Case in point, you seem to be eating microwave popcorn for dinner."

"Corn's a vegetable," she protested. "And butter's dairy, so that's half of a balanced meal."

"Well, that explains your C in health and nutrition," I muttered. "Anyway, the bottom line is that sometimes, I miss Paul. He was good to me, if nothing else. With him, I don't have to . . ."

"Make an effort? Expect to be treated like a girlfriend and not a convenient warm body?"

"That's not fair. I relinquished the title of girlfriend voluntarily. Why am I talking to you about this?" I spluttered. "I actually have something important to talk to you about. Something more important than my sad—"

"Pathetic," she interjected.

"Love life," I finished wryly. "You know, searing insight at your age just comes across as snotty, Gladiola Grace."

"Hey, hey, no using the birth name. That's a clear violation of the sisterly trust." She cringed, poking me in the ribs.

"Paul is not here, but someone is in the house, and until I'm sure that it's safe, I think you need to stay at a friend's."

"Well, that was a sudden shift in conversation," she deadpanned. "What do you mean, you don't know whether it's safe? Iris, what's going on? This cloak-and-dagger drama isn't you. You are Iris, patron saint of rational behavior."

"I know, I know. And I'm not trying to be dramatic. All I can say is that it's necessary."

"For how long?" Gigi demanded.

"I don't know."

She scowled. "You think I have friends whose parents will let me move into their houses indefinitely?"

"Not indefinitely," I assured her. "Just a week or so."

I heard a shuffling noise behind me. Cal was ambling through the living room, looking like he was recovering from a three-day bender. "Hangover" was still a pretty good look for him, all rumpled and rough. His hair was mussed, and his fangs were down. Snapping out of my ogling of the undead, I dashed to the window to pull the shades and pulled a packet of donor Type A from the fridge.

I shoved it into his hands while ushering Gigi toward the door. There was no way to get Gigi out without opening the back door and exposing Cal to direct sunlight. But if he lunged for us, I was willing to yank it open.

Cal barely paid any attention to her, instead slumping against the blue-tile breakfast bar and reluctantly slugging back the cold donor blood. Keeping Gigi behind me, I put another bottle into the microwave to warm it.

"What the—what's going on, Iris? Th-that is *not* Paul." Gigi spluttered.

"He followed me home," I said, deadpan. "Can we keep him?"

Gigi eyed the tousled dark hair and the broad shoulders. She smirked and opened her mouth to speak.

"Don't finish that thought, whatever it is," I told her, my finger in her face.

"Who is this person?" Cal asked, his voice sleep-roughened and gruff.

"This is my sister. Gigi, this is my client, Cal. Just Cal, like Cher, with fewer plastic parts. He ran into a little trouble last night and had to stay here. It's just a temporary situation."

"That you can't tell anyone about," Cal added hoarsely, his voice hovering on the edge of intimidation but not quite making it.

"That you can't tell anyone about," I echoed, nodding.

Gigi's eyes shifted between the two of us. "OK. Cal, can I ask what you've done to my sister?"

Now it was Cal's turn to splutter. "I haven't done anything to her!"

An impish light flickered in Gigi's eyes. "Well, then, I'm sort of sad for her." She ignored the indignant hiss from my side of the counter.

"How much to make her go to her room and stop talking to me?" Cal asked.

While I gaped at his rudeness, Gigi coughed a rather obvious "douchebag!" into her fist. I caught her eye and shook my head emphatically. Douche-coughing someone with superhearing was not a responsible choice.

Gigi rolled her eyes and cleared her throat. "I meant, how did you persuade my sensible, hyperrational sister to let you move in, even temporarily, without a plan or an end date or a chore chart?"

"Money," Cal muttered, sipping his blood. "I'm always surprised by what people will do for money."

Gigi's oceanic eyes widened in alarm. She whirled on me. "I thought you said we were doing OK!"

I shot a significant look at Cal, who was oblivious to the distress he'd just caused my anxiety-prone sister. "We are doing OK," I insisted. "This will just help us build a little cushion between OK and good."

Cal snorted, taking another drink. "It should be a bit more than a little cushion. I'm sure it will let your sister take care of all the little things she's been neglecting around the house." At my indignant gasp, he added, "It's nothing to take personally. Most start-up businesses don't show a profit before—"

"Gigi, would you mind going upstairs while I discuss a few things with our guest?"

My thin, forced smile made Gigi flinch. She turned to Cal. "You're in for it now. The last time she smiled like that, she told off Mary Anne Gilchrist's mom for piercing my ears without permission. I don't know what she said, but Mrs. Gilchrist turned white as a—"

"Gigi!"

She huffed and rolled her eyes. "You know I'm going to listen at the door, right?"

"Go upstairs and pack a bag."

Gigi sighed and stomped up the steps to make a point. The point being that she was a big, adolescent pain in my butt.

"Do me a favor," I said, rounding on Cal. "Keep your opinions about my house and my financial status to yourself. Gigi worries."

My icy tone made Cal's brows arch. I could see the protest forming on his lips, but instead of objecting, he said, "Excuse me. I wasn't thinking."

I nodded curtly. "How are you this afternoon?"

He sat heavily on a bar stool near the counter and leaned close to the giggling-caterpillar cookie jar. It struck me as a little funny, this big, manly vampire all docile and grumpy in our admittedly feminine kitchen. "Weak. Nauseated. Like I could fall back into my day-time sleep at any moment. I only came up to get more blood. The trip up the basement steps took an alarming amount of effort and concentration."

"I could put a cooler in your tent, if you'd like. It would save you some trouble. But are you sure it's a good idea

to drink more blood if you're sick to your stomach?" His
brow crinkled. Clearly, he didn't understand my question. I'm guessing it had been a while since he'd had a
tummy ache. "When humans are nauseated, they usually
avoid eating so they don't throw up."

"Yes, but I'm not human," he responded snidely, as if
the implication was insulting.

I ignored the haughty tone. "Did you sleep well?"

"Yes, considering the surroundings."

I chose to ignore that, too.

"What is this?" Cal inquired, looking up at the hanks
of herbs hanging from the ceiling to dry.

"Cuttings, from my garden. Lavender, chamomile,
mint. I like making my own herbal teas, sachets, pot-
pourri, that sort of thing. And Gigi gets heat rash sometimes. Lavender baths help."

His eyes narrowed at me. "You seem to know an awful
lot about plants."

I scoffed. "Yeah, that's right, *I* poisoned you. I'm part
of a mass antivampire conspiracy. And then, after I
tampered with your blood, I snuck back to the scene of
the crime, stumbled over your unconscious body, and
took you back to my house, all so I could become your
domestic servant. I am obviously the greatest criminal
mastermind since Ponzi."

He snorted but didn't say anything further. I let
the kitchen steep in silence for a few beats. Cal didn't
seem to be doing much better than the day before. His
hands shook slightly as they gripped the donor blood.

His shoulders were slack, as if he had trouble lifting the weight of his head.

"Do you feel strong enough to take a shower?" I asked. "There are still some, uh, red spots on your face. And your back. Plus, you kind of have a bedraggled-zombie thing going."

Cal frowned, surveying his wrinkled clothes and rubbing a hand over his equally furrowed face.

"If you think you'll have trouble standing that long, we could get you one of those shower chairs," I offered.

"You mean the kind that senior citizens fall off of, never to get back up?"

"Um, yes."

"I'm willing to risk standing," he said blandly.

We had a full bath on the ground floor, which was good, because despite the bottled blood, Cal seemed too pale and shaky to take another flight of stairs. After covering the windows with foil, I made sure he had fresh towels and waited outside the bathroom door while the water warmed up. I heard the shower curtain sling across the rod.

A few moments passed, and I heard him call, "I don't suppose you have soap that doesn't smell like fruit or flowers or some combination thereof?"

"Sorry, this is a girlie household. You're lucky there's not a Disney princess on the label," I said, glad that there was a door between us to keep him from seeing my snickering. There was a faint grumbling noise while the shower started up.

Gigi appeared at the end of the hall, her team bag slung over her shoulder. She was chewing her lip, eyeing the bathroom door like there was an army of evil winged monkeys ready to burst through it.

Gigi had *Wizard of Oz* issues.

"All packed?" I asked.

"Yeah. Sammi Jo said I could stay at her place for a few days. But I'm not sure about this, Iris. I mean, as cute as he is—in a haggard *Lord of the Rings* sort of way—you barely know this guy."

"Do you mean Gollum or Éomer?" I asked. "Because that's a pretty wide spectrum of haggard."

"Don't try to distract me," she accused, pointing her finger at me. "And he defies all hot Tolkien stereotypes. He's all rough-hewn intensity with a pretty mouth—"

"You came up with that description awfully quick," I noted. "And what sort of teenager says 'rough-hewn'?"

"You shouldn't leave those romance novels lying around," she shot back. "I'm a teenage girl. We mentally tag and categorize attractive male specimens within ten seconds of eye contact. And stop with the distractions. I mean, he's a *vampire*. You've always told me to be super-cautious around them, and now you've invited one to stay? I don't know if it's a great idea to leave you alone with him."

"So you would rather stay, just in case, so he can kill us both?"

She glared at me. "Iris! I'm serious!"

"So am I!" I exclaimed. "Look, I'm sure I'll be fine. But I think it would be a good idea for you to be elsewhere for a while, just until I have some idea how this is going to pan out."

"All right, but I want you to write down this guy's information and e-mail it to me, so I can offer the police some explanation for why my sister needs to be put on a milk carton."

"Nice," I muttered, smacking her arm.

"Child abuse!" she cried. Suddenly, she frowned and turned on me. "Is this all a very convincing act put on to get me out of the house so you can spend the weekend humping like deranged howler monkeys?"

My jaw dropped. "No!"

"Well, it would be clever of you."

"I'm not quite that devious," I said dryly.

She kissed my cheek. "I'm going. I'll call you when I get to Sammi Jo's."

"Hey, Geeg?" I called as she moved away. She turned. "Why would the howler monkeys have to be deranged?"

She grinned. "If you have to ask . . ."

"Get out!" I huffed.

"Call me every day," she said as she opened the front door. "So I know you're alive. Love you!"

"Love you, too!" I called. The door closed, and I sighed, leaning my head back against the wall.

"We should never have taught her how to talk," I mused. "I could have picked up sign language pretty easily . . ."

I closed my eyes and thought of the Twix bars I had stashed behind the encyclopedias upstairs. It was better than thinking about the fact that Cal was naked on the other side of the door. Cal happened to have a very nice body . . . and it had been about three months since Napoleon had "invaded."

A thud from inside the bathroom wrenched me out of my historically inappropriate musings.

"Hey!" I yelled. "Are you OK in there?"

There was no answer.

I jiggled the doorknob. It was unlocked, but I wasn't eager to open it unless I had to. "Cal!" No answer. I sighed. "I really don't want to do this."

After a few more beats of silence, I called, "If you don't answer, I'm coming in. Try to cover up!" I muttered, "Think of the money. Think of the money. Think of the money."

I slowly opened the door, billows of steam rolling toward me as I stepped through. Cal was sprawled on the floor, half in and half out of the shower stall. Suds laced over his dark hair like little tufts of icing. His eyes were closed, long lashes resting on his cheeks. With his lower half undressed, I could see everything I'd missed in his kitchen. Long legs. Flat stomach. Trail of dark hair that extended all the way to his perfectly proportionate—

"Oh, my gosh!" I cried, putting my hand over my eyes. "I'm sorry!"

But he was unconscious again and didn't seem to care that I was ogling him.

Despite his griping about girlie soaps, the steam and the heat seemed to intensify his natural woodsy scent, diffusing it throughout the room. I felt it seeping into my skin, marking me, as I knelt over him.

"Cal?" I murmured, shaking his shoulders gently.

"Wake up, Cal. I'm not sure what to do for an unconscious vampire."

As my fingertips grazed his cheek, his eyes snapped open. He popped up into a crouch, or at least, he tried to, but his limbs were too weak to let him maintain the position. He stumbled, falling against me, knocking me to the floor. His lips drew back over his fangs as a rumbling growl echoed through his chest. The vibrations spread from his sternum to mine, sending a strange electric shiver zipping over my skin. I might have leaned closer, if not for the whole "bared razor-sharp fangs" thing. He closed the distance for me, brushing the tip of his nose down my neck to my collarbone, purring in anticipation.

Shrinking back, I realized that until this moment, I'd been dealing with the civilized version of Cal. This was Cal stripped of all those pesky human trappings. This is how our kitchen encounter might have ended, with him poised above me, ready to strike, to drain the life out of me. Or throw up on me . . . which he did . . . twice.

I screamed, not in fear but in disgust, as Cal tossed up two bottles' worth of blood down the front of my shirt. He moaned piteously and collapsed on top of me, pinning me to the floor and squishing the breath from my lungs.

"Crushed by nauseated vampire" was going to be such an embarrassing cause of death.

I grunted, sliding my hands under his shoulders and thrusting my arms up with all my strength. I barely budged him, and when my arms gave out, he slumped down over my chest, making it even more difficult to breathe. And I'd just sent the one other person with the key to the house away for several days. I would die on my bathroom floor, covered in vampire vomit, crushed by a dead guy who didn't like me very much.

"I've got to find a new job," I grumbled.

4

Vampires are notoriously difficult to move once they are at rest for the day. So do not try to move them. Not even a little bit.

—*The Care and Feeding of Stray Vampires*

It took me an hour, a slightly sprained shoulder, and the defiance of several laws of physics, but I finally unwedged myself from under my undead guest.

I stumbled to my feet, sprawling across the floor as the blood flowed back into my tingling arms and legs. During my time on the floor, I learned a few things about Cal. One, he was as heavy as a sack of wet concrete. Two, even when he was all disheveled, he still smelled pretty good. Third, his hands had a bad habit of resting on the nearest breast, even when he was unconscious.

Dead or undead, men were all pretty much the same.

Finally free of my undead burden, I took greedy, gulping breaths. A dull ache in my side had me wincing with every movement. I wondered if he'd given my ribs compression fractures. I slowly sat up, propping myself by the sink so I could get a much-needed drink of water. I wiped the sweat from my face with a wet washcloth and carefully removed the fouled, sticky-stiff T-shirt. Fortunately, it was Gigi's T-shirt, a rather obnoxious "Coed Naked Volleyball" specimen that had nearly gotten Gigi suspended from school. Straight into the trash it went.

After calling Gigi's cell phone to make sure she got to Sammi Jo's house safely, I got a fresh shirt from the laundry room.

On my way back to my unconscious client, I passed my parents' ground-floor master bedroom. When we'd moved into the house, neither one of us could bear to open the door and face the room where my parents had slept. We couldn't face Mom's slouchy weekend gardening clothes or Dad's perennial bottle of Aqua Velva.

But a few months before, I'd managed to channel some "Paul trauma" energy into some postmidnight-insomnia cleaning. I'd tossed everything except photos and jewelry into boxes and sent them to the basement or to Goodwill. The room stood empty, except for the stripped bed and a nightstand. I stepped inside, blinking against the dust motes swirling on the currents of sunshine. The air was a bit stale and musty, but it would do until I could get Cal downstairs safely. I foiled the windows and made up the bed with fresh sheets. I somehow managed to get Cal rolled onto an old twin sheet from my childhood, and I dragged him down the hallway.

"Where's Mr. Wolfe when you need him?" I muttered, lifting him carefully onto the bed. "He hauled the bodies, cleaned up the mess, orchestrated embarrassing backyard prison shower scenarios . . . and I'm talking to myself . . . about *Pulp Fiction*, which is not a good sign."

I barely managed to haul Cal onto the bed, but he settled back down and was sleeping fitfully. I filled a bowl with warm water and snagged an old washcloth on my way back to my parents' room. In repose on the old bed, the sheet thrown haphazardly across his waist, Cal reminded me of some tragic marble statue, pale and frozen and oddly beautiful. I placed the bowl near his head and wondered what the rules were for sponge-bathing the undead.

I juggled the cloth between my hands nervously, unsure of where to apply it first. Although I'd known him for a short—though eventful—period of time, I definitely liked Cal better in this inanimate, unsnarky state. The man was just unsettling; there was no other way to put it. I couldn't seem to get my conversational bearings around him. And clearly, he had a negative impact on my decision-making skills, because I'd agreed to cohabitate with someone who was cranky, condescending, and prone to bouts of staggering insensitivity. If I'd wanted that, I'd get a cat.

Shuddering at the very thought, I bathed Cal's face, carefully wiping the skin around his mouth, the little divot between his lip and his nose. The bloody mess had trickled down his neck and his chest clear to his waistline, so I moved the cloth down his body in smooth, sure strokes. My fingertips tingled slightly from the friction of the warm, wet cloth over cold, hard muscle. The sensation spread up my arm, through my chest, and low and hot into my belly. Biting my lip, I adjusted my hand to put the cloth between my skin and his.

"Hold it together, woman," I muttered. "Or you're going to have to register on a special-offender list."

I tried to keep the ogling to a minimum, for my own dignity's sake. But his stomach tapered down from his hips into a solid V, something I'd only seen on the covers of those men's health magazines . . . which I read for the articles.

My eyes strayed south. A couple of times.

I'm only human.

My charge, however, was not human. And he would probably wake up soon either to vomit or to snack on me. So I needed to wrap up the sponge bath and go do some work that was not related to Mr. Sensitive Upchuck Reflex. I did have other clients, and I couldn't exactly tell them that I was neglecting their needs because I'd brought a stray vampire home with me. It might give them ideas.

I set myself back to my task, carefully scrubbing the drying blood from the strange little valleys between his abdominal muscles, the dip of his navel. His skin was feeling warmer, softer, nearly human, as I worked down his body. The blood clung to the little hairs trailing toward his hips. I lifted the sheet to wipe it away and squeaked.

Somehow I had forgotten that he was naked. Clenching my eyes shut, I dropped the sheet.

Think of the money, my brain scolded itself. *Wait, no, don't think of the money; that can't be right.*

I tucked the sheet around his hips and grabbed a towel to mop up the excess water. I pressed it to Cal's chest and felt a strong hand close around my wrist. A wry, rumbling voice said, "I don't know what exactly you expect from this arrangement, Miss Scanlon. But I have no interest in providing additional *services* in exchange for my time here."

I was confused. Did he just imply that I was some sort of predatory spinster? I was feeling less guilty about whacking him on the nose.

I yanked my arm out of his grip. I smiled acidly at him. "I'm sure you think this is a real treat for me, but let me assure you that I have no interest in you or your . . . vampire package."

I was proud that I was able to string together such a cogent, haughty-sounding rebuttal. But a tiny, insistent voice in my head noted that I was, in fact, interested in his vampire package; otherwise, I wouldn't keep looking at it.

He grinned, almost loopily, like a hausfrau who'd had too many glasses of wine at a book-club meeting. "Really? Because I detect a nice, tangy note of feminine arousal in the room. And I don't think it's coming from me."

I leaned closer than was probably advisable when dealing with an out-of-sorts creature of the night. I growled. "I know vampires are supposed to be the Space Mountain of the sexual carnival. But I have made it a point not to become directly involved in anything in your world, and that includes . . ."

"Behaving in the manner of a deranged howler monkey?" he offered blandly, cocking his head to the side and studying my face.

I dropped my head in defeat, groaning. "Gigi."

"Your eyes are such a lovely shade of blue," he said, tilting my chin so he could stare up at me. I blushed, busying myself with putting away the wet washcloth. And then he had to ruin it by squinting and asking, "Have you always had four of them?"

"Four what?"

"Eyes."

"Hey, are you OK?" I asked, placing a hand against his cheek. His skin felt clammy, damp, like my own after a fever had broken.

Vampires weren't supposed to get fevers.

"Cal?"

Waving his hand in front of his face, as if he'd never seen his own fingers before, he asked, "Where was I?"

"Howler monkeys."

He gave me a lopsided grin. "It was the last thing I heard before I . . ."

"Passed out," I supplied.

He frowned. "Vampires don't pass out."

"They do if they've been poisoned and severely weakened."

He narrowed his eyes at me. "You enjoy pointing that out, don't you?"

I smirked, and his own lips curled at the sight of it. "A little."

When Cal inevitably dozed off again, I checked my calendar. I had a few deliveries to make the next day, not to mention picking up Ms. Wexler's dry-cleaning and meeting the contractor who was installing a sizable blood chiller in Mr. Kraznov's kitchen pantry.

I had three missed calls from clients, not to mention an obscene number of e-mails. Working my way through the requests, complaints, and demands, I took notes and filed them in my day planner. I made lists and a to-do spreadsheet.

Still, if he didn't improve, I wasn't comfortable leaving Cal alone in the house while I went to work. He wasn't well. What if he got worse or threw up on something irreplaceable? I doubted he would be amused if he woke up unattended. He would probably consider it a violation of our verbal contract.

I was going to have to call my backup—Jolene Lavelle, a friend of Jane's who sometimes filled in for me. Jolene, a stay-at-home mother of twins, was happy to have a reason to leave the house during the day. And riding around in the car was the only way she could get her babies to nap in the afternoons. It was a win-win.

Crap.

Jane.

I'd planned Jane Jameson's wedding to her sire, Gabriel Nightengale, the year before. A recently turned librarian who'd opened an occult bookshop, she was a handy reference for new vampires in the area, and it was always interesting to see what sort of mess she'd created for herself.

For instance, on the night of her wedding, she was kidnapped by an angry redneck bent on revenge. I spent several hours coaxing her family into staying at the wedding site by opening the bar early, creative use of charades, and finally, hiding as many purses as I could within the depths of Jane's house so they couldn't leave. I endured passive-aggressive insults, threats of an "ass whipping," and several attempts to recruit me into selling Tupperware. And that was just from Jane's cousin Junie.

When she found out about my "heroics" in dealing with her relatives, Jane pledged her eternal friendship to me—which takes on a whole new meaning when it's coming from a vampire. Funny, brilliant, and just awkward enough to make my job interesting, she was one of the few brides I actually wanted to maintain contact with after the ceremony. I went into her shop, Specialty Books, on occasion just to touch base. And there had been a few movie nights, a disastrous excursion to a night spa, and a failed attempt to start a book club. We never managed to get the book discussion going because Jolene got distracted by the snacks.

And because Jane had signed on as one of my day-walker clients, I'd delivered a case of Faux Type O to her house a week before. Jane, her husband, Gabriel, and her recently turned teenage protégé, Jamie, drank it on a regular basis. Cal said that most of the affected bottles had been reclaimed by the Council, but what if a bad one got mixed in with her delivery? What if she drank it around her very human friend Zeb? Or Jolene or their twins? Or God forbid, her living family members? I couldn't risk my friend getting hurt or hurting someone she cared about over something as stupid as vampire PR.

On quiet feet, I crept toward the far side of the house. Glancing down the hallway and listening for sounds of stirring from Cal's room, I surreptitiously dialed Jane's number. On the other end of the line, I heard a yawn and a string of curses while Jane bobbled her cell and dropped it on the nightstand before finally putting it to her ear. "Yello?"

"Jane, it's Iris."

"Iris?" she mumbled. "Did you get the Q-tips out of the VCR?"

"Jane, wake up!"

"M'wake," she muttered. "I feel the urge to reach through the phone and smack you, which means I'm awake."

"Right back at you. Look, I can't really talk right now, but I need you to do me a favor. Don't drink any synthetic blood. Throw anything that you have in the house away. Tell Dick and Andrea to do the same."

"You know, you're the second person this week to give me dietary advice," Jane said, yawning loudly.

"What do you mean?"

"Well, you know Jamie's dating Ophelia, from the Council? She came by the house with a whole case of donor blood the other day. Said she wanted Jamie to eat better and was worried that synthetic blood wasn't fulfilling his dietary needs. That's not unusual, because she frequently implies that I'm not properly parenting him. What was weird was that she insisted on dumping out my entire supply of Faux Type O down the drain." Jane paused for a long yawn. I could hear Gabriel murmuring in the background. "I take it this is not just a conspiratorial campaign to keep me from getting all chunky post-marriage?"

"I can't say."

"Well, if I've learned anything since being turned, it's that when people offer you cryptic, half-assed advice for your own good, you should follow it to the letter," she said, snorting loudly.

"Just promise me you won't buy any more. Stay on donor blood until further notice. And I know you're not really a live feeder, but maybe you should consider contracting with a blood surrogate for a while. I have contact information for a couple of them in the area, very discreet, healthy—"

"Can we stay away from arrangements that sound like you're engaging in human trafficking for me?"

"Jane."

I could hear her voice muffled by the pillow she was burying her face in. "OK, I'm going back to sleep now. I will follow your vague, unhelpful advice, as is my lot in life. I'll call Andrea tonight."

"Good girl. Sleep tight." I hung up the phone and felt a bit better about my participation in these bizarre vampiric shenanigans. I was contemplating a cup of chamomile tea when I heard a voice behind me.

"You're not very good at following instructions, are you?"

I turned to find Cal standing behind me, leaning heavily against the door frame. He looked exhausted, drained, but I supposed that sleeping in such a weird pattern for the last day had screwed up his internal clock.

As it was, he was barely standing but still looked irritated enough that he could take my head off with little provocation or physical effort.

He was wearing a pair of navy sweatpants that barely covered his hips, hugging that well-defined V that I'd found so fascinating just a few hours before. Now I could barely look at it, look at him. His eyes were trained so intently on me that I was afraid I would freeze, like a mouse in front of a stalking cobra. The crown molding was suddenly downright captivating.

I stepped back against the counter as he stumbled into the room, glaring at me. His skin was still pale but tinged a dull pink. His eyes were glassy and bright, as if a fever was raging through his system. He stopped just in front of me, lurching forward, bracing his hands on the countertop on either side of my hips.

He snarled. "I told you not to tell anyone. Did you think that meant 'except for the people you deem special enough to tell'?"

I fought the instinct to shrink back like a caged animal. I stood ramrod-straight, eyes trained on his. "My friend Jane lives with two other vampires, so there's quite a bit of bottled blood circulating through their fridge. She works in a shop where humans visit every day. She has contact with her family. Would you rather she hurt someone she cares about? That would leave you with a considerable PR mess on your hands, wouldn't it? I'm doing you a favor."

"The tainted blood was quietly, quickly tracked down and accounted for. There are no more tainted bottles on the shelves. You would have known that if you'd asked."

"So why did Ophelia switch out Jamie's blood?"

"Ophelia's paranoid and overprotective of her boy-friend." He growled, bristling at my admittedly prissy tone. "So next time, instead of using your own judgment, I would rather you do what I ask you to, particularly when it was such a reasonable request. I would like to be able to trust you."

I snorted. "Oh, like I'm able to trust you?"

"You trust me enough to bring me into your home, which I am absolutely sure is a first for you."

"You don't know anything about me."

"Has any other vampire seen the inside of this house?" he demanded. When I bit my lip and crossed my arms over my chest, he smirked. "I didn't think so. You know, it's rather hypocritical to work for vampires but think that you're too good to be 'directly involved' with our world."

"I don't think I'm too good!" I exclaimed. "I've just found that with a few rare exceptions, like Jane, you aren't trustworthy. Vampires put their own interests first, no matter what the cost. If it came to a question of my well-being versus your survival, I would be drained faster than you could say 'collateral damage.'"

"As opposed to humans, who are so generous and selfless."

"I'm not saying we're perfect, but at least we don't *eat people*."

He muttered something under his breath.

"What was that?"

"I said, some of you do!" he exclaimed. "Humans are

just as destructive and selfish and shortsighted as we could ever think to be."

"Well, you used to be human, so—so, suck it!" I yelled, flustered and sputtering.

He arched an eyebrow. "Suck it?"

"Not my most mature comeback," I conceded, before adding hastily, "or an invitation."

He smirked again. "You don't strike me as the type that plays hard to get."

I seethed. "Well, I can arrange striking you very soon."

"Has anyone ever pointed out that you tend to use violence to solve problems?"

"Has anyone ever pointed out that your moods are about as dependable as cheap panty hose? It makes it extremely difficult to spend time around you."

"Do you think I would be here unless it was absolutely necessary? You think this is easy for me?" he demanded. "Do you think I like needing humans? All I want to do is finish this job and get out of this backwater burg so I can get my life back!"

"Trust me, you've made it absolutely clear how you feel about being here!" I shouted back. "You've treated me and my home with nothing but disdain and condescension ever since you got here. Well, news flash, I *don't care* what you think of me. The possibility of me being embarrassed by you pretty much ended when you threw up on me."

He stopped, the irritation draining from his face as his mouth slanted into a grin. "I threw up on you?"

"A lot."

He burst out laughing, chuckling so hard that his abused stomach muscles clenched and doubled him over, nearly toppling him against me.

"I'm so glad that my ruined clothes and personal trauma amuse you. Are we going to argue like this about every little issue?"

"I hope so. I feel a little bit better every time we do. And it's . . . interesting to see you in the heat of the moment."

I gasped indignantly. "Are you *provoking* me into arguing with you?"

"I wasn't at first, but I can't help it now. You're just so pretty when you get upset. Your cheeks get pink. And your eyes turn this beautiful sharp blue, like lightning about to strike. And your mouth—"

"There is something very wrong with you."

"There it is again." He chuckled. "Pink cheeks and all."

"If you continue to quote-unquote 'charm' me, I'm going to punch you in the throat," I told him.

"You could try," he shot back. Before he could elaborate on my flimsy human fighting abilities, he stood and listened, his head cocked to the side like a curious canine.

"What's the matter?"

"There's a car coming," he said. He crossed to the window and cursed in what sounded like Greek. Really dirty Greek. "It's a Council vehicle!"

I shot to my feet and peered out the window. I couldn't see anything but the faint light of headlights at the end of my winding driveway. "Are you sure?" He gave me a withering look. "Well, I don't have superhuman hearing!"

"Don't panic. It will be fine."

I whirled toward him. "Don't panic? I went from having no vampires in my house to having one in the basement and an unknown number in the driveway, and you don't want me to panic? Why can't you just talk to them now?"

"Because I'm just as weak and sick as I appear to be. And if the one who poisoned me is among the Council officials, I might as well paint a target on my back."

I sighed. I was so close to just waving the approaching Council members into the house and letting them cart his blood-spewing butt home. Cal flustered me. And he insulted me, regularly, with laser precision. But he honestly seemed frightened, and I could tell that was not a comfortable emotion for him. So I nodded slowly, my mouth set in a grim line.

His fingers wrapped around my arm, squeezing it gently. "I'm going downstairs. I'll wait there until they leave. I doubt they'll search the house. They probably just want to ask you a few questions. Answer them honestly, and don't try to make up an elaborate story. You'll be fine."

"Won't they be able to smell you in here?" I asked.

He considered it for a moment. "Take them to the garden. Offer them lemonade and iced tea."

I exclaimed, "They don't drink lemonade or iced tea!"

"But they'll appreciate the 'humanity' of the gesture. And people with guilty consciences generally don't take the time for beverage service."

"I don't have a guilty conscience. Other than taking you in, I haven't done anything extraordinarily evil or stupid lately," I hissed as he headed for the basement door. "And don't go back downstairs; go upstairs to the alcove. You'll be able to hear what's being said if you crack the window. I don't want to have to relate the conversation to you later."

He shrugged and changed directions, heading toward the stairs. I opened up the junk drawer and rummaged around for the old clipping shears with the green plastic handles. Cal paused to watch.

"Why are you looking through old takeout menus and batteries?" he asked.

"I'm going to go out there and prune a bunch of geraniums," I said, brandishing the shears.

He stepped out of range, hands raised. "I know I told you to be a nice hostess, but I don't think this is the time for flower arranging."

"Geraniums are chock-full of essential oils that stink to high heaven. If I go out there and stir a bunch of it up, maybe they won't smell you."

"Good idea." His hands dropped, and his posture changed. He relaxed, as if he was so surprised by my saying something sensible that he forgot about the doom on wheels rolling up my driveway.

I exclaimed, "I don't need your sarcasm right now!"

"No, really, it's a sound strategy."

"Well, then, I'm not sure how to respond to that," I said, running my hands under the tap and scrubbing off the traces of his scent.

"The customary response to a compliment is 'thank you.'"

I grumbled, "I'm working up to it."

5

Vampires do not share emotions readily. Questions
to avoid: "Why?" "Why not?" And "No, really, why?"
—*The Care and Feeding of Stray Vampires*

By the time the Council reps unloaded themselves
from Ophelia's black SUV, I'd scrubbed my hands and
face again, snagged a clean shirt from the laundry basket at the foot of the stairs, and clipped dead ends from
a half-dozen geranium plants hanging from baskets on
the porch. I crushed the leaves and flowers between my
fingers, sending as much of the bitter green scent into
the air as possible.

Offering a guileless smile, I waved like a polite little
country girl. I'd only interacted with the Council members at the office. They were intimidating individually,
but faced with them en masse on my home turf, I was
practically twitching with nerves.

The first out of the car was a blond lady with a slight
British accent, who went by Sophie. Despite the fact that
even the most ancient vampires had adopted some form
of last name to put on government paperwork, she just
went by Sophie. She had a Barbie-doll type of beauty, un-

lined and unpainted, with a weird plastic sheen to her skin.

Sophie was a walking truth serum. If she was touching bare skin, she could yank the truth out of you like a loose tooth. I'd spent several unpleasant hours in her company during the Council's screening process for humans who planned to work with vampires. That's when I learned that you don't refer to Buffy, the Winchesters, or even the Frog Brothers from *The Lost Boys* in front of Council officials. They do not have a sense of humor about that sort of entertainment.

Then there was Peter Crown, who, as far as I could tell, had never smiled. His special vampire talent seemed to be maintaining a really bad mood for centuries. Mr. Crown didn't contract with my service, because, as he told me, he didn't trust a human to get his dry-cleaning right, much less his complicated blood selection.

I didn't like Mr. Crown.

A Colonel Sanders look-alike improbably named Waco Marchand was possibly the only person on the Council who didn't creep me out entirely. He was a kind, grandfatherly sort of man, who just happened to have fangs. He smelled pleasantly of hair tonic and carried peppermints in his pockets. I was 90 percent sure I recognized him from a Confederate memorial statue downtown.

And last but certainly not least, Ophelia Lambert. The willowy brunette was wearing a red cardigan and plaid kilt that made me think of wildly inappropriate schoolgirl uniforms. She usually dressed a bit more outrageously, in carefully themed costumes. Her theme was most often "jailbait." But since she'd started dating Jane's ward, Jamie, she'd tried to appear a bit more like a nice girl. The femme-fatale bit made Jamie uncomfortable.

Council members were assigned to their precincts regardless of origin, so Ophelia's and Sophie's "Continental" presence was unremarkable. I could only guess that Peter's grumpiness had gotten him kicked out of all of the other Council regions.

As they approached the porch, I took a deep breath and tried to focus on keeping my heart rate even. I smiled sweetly. "Hi, Ophelia, how are you? Sophie, Mr. Marchand, Mr. Crown. What brings you here?"

"How are you on this lovely evening, Miss Iris?" Mr. Marchand chuckled, bending over my hand and kissing it. He had lovely old-fashioned manners, reminding me of my great-uncle Harold.

"Fine, thank you." I barely resisted the urge to curtsy. It was a near thing.

"I see we caught you in the middle of yard work." Mr. Crown sniffed, surveying my ratty clothes and the crushed foliage in my hands.

"Well, with my schedule, I have to fit it in whenever I can," I said pleasantly, although the dismissive tone in his voice set my teeth on edge.

Ophelia cleared her throat. "We need to ask you a few questions, Iris."

I kept my expression blank, except for a slight frown. "Sounds serious."

Mr. Marchand patted my hand. "Oh, no, dear, just strictly routine."

"Well, it's such a nice night. Why don't you all have a seat on those benches in the side yard, by the roses? Can I offer you something to drink?"

"No, thank you," Mr. Crown said, looking bored as he scanned the windows of my house. I bit my lip, unsure of what to say next. Ever the social buffer, Mr. Marchand made a few polite comments about the clever arrangement of the garden. I nodded absently, praying that Cal was smart enough to stay out of sight. I didn't think I'd be in physical danger if the Council found out that I was lying to them, but my business would definitely suffer. My hands began to sweat, the warmth of my skin intensifying the aroma of geranium oil in the air. The smell seemed to distract Mr. Crown, who wrinkled his nose and stepped away from me.

Ophelia cleared her throat again. "We've come to ask you about one of your clients, a Mr. Calix. Have you met him?"

"No, not face-to-face. I usually don't meet my clients in person. It's more comfortable for both sides. Is Mr. Calix in some sort of trouble?"

Mr. Crown lifted an elegant black brow and sneered at me. "He's missing."

"Oh, no!" I exclaimed, hoping that my distress came through as concern for a client. "That's awful."

"It's nothing to worry about, dear," Mr. Marchand said, taking me by the elbow and leading me to the grouping of cedar benches that my dad had installed around a stone fire pit near the rosebushes. Ophelia was watching me carefully as I sat down, hoping to catch some nervous twinge or tic. But I was the picture of clueless composure. If anything, the complexities of my job taught me to keep my poker face even when faced with the bizarre, the alarming, the odd naked human who can't seem to remember why he woke up in a vampire's living room with a splitting headache and a new tattoo. The only exception was Cal, who seemed to make my equilibrium all wonky just by looking at me.

"When was the last time you were in his home?" Sophie asked, her eyes drilling tiny holes into my forehead, as if she expected all of my secrets to come spilling out from her sheer concentration. Sadly, most of my secrets were pretty lame, with the exception of the one currently cowering under a window seat upstairs.

"Friday," I said, looking to Ophelia. "Didn't you ask me this on the phone the other night?"

"It's not your place to question the Council; it's the Council's place to question you," Mr. Crown spat crossly.

I lifted the corners of my mouth, smiling mirthlessly. "I think you'll find that my place is being polite to the Council for the sake of friendly cooperation. I don't actually have to answer any of the Council's questions, since I'm not governed by vampire laws. I'm a living, breathing United States citizen. I have all kinds of annoying civil rights."

Mr. Crown huffed. "Just have Sophie examine her. An adjustment of attitude is certainly in order."

I fought to keep a straight face as a ripple of fear zipped up my spine. Sophie would drag the truth from my mouth. And then Cal would be dragged from my house. And then my business would fail, I'd lose the house, and Gigi and I would be dragged onto the streets. There would be an exhausting amount of dragging.

As quick and lethal as a cobra, Sophie slithered toward me. I closed my eyes, concentrating on the scents around me: the spiced tang of geranium, the heady sweetness of honeysuckle and roses. Because passing out under scrutiny would not scream "guileless, innocent bystander" to the vampires clustered around me.

"Are you sure that's necessary, Ophelia?" Mr. Marchand asked, frowning as I let Sophie step well within the acceptable social-space bubble.

Ophelia was staring at me, considering. I was afraid to show any fear, any hesitation, because I didn't want to tip my hand. Innocent people didn't protest telling the truth, even if compelled through abusive psychic means.

After some consideration, Ophelia nodded at Sophie, who didn't do me the courtesy of looking me in the eye as she wrapped her long, cold fingers around my hands. I winced, knowing that the burning pain of her talent would start singing through my skin at any moment. But other than mild discomfort in the areas where she was touching me, I didn't feel much. Sophie and I shared a moment of perplexed hesitation. Her hands seemed to slip uselessly over mine, unable to get the grip she wanted. She frowned, grasping my hands so tightly that I whimpered under the pressure.

Was it the geranium oil? Did it have some unknown properties beyond being a stinky natural bug repellent?

Nope. Wait. Blinding, disorienting pain. *Sophie's filter-crippling powers are a go.*

"Ow!" I shrieked as Sophie's handprint seemed to sear into my skin. I sank to my knees on the grass, limply wrenching my hand away from her.

"Look into my eyes," Sophie commanded, her voice stripped of all pretense of charm. Breathing through the pain, I met her gaze. Her irises flared to black, and I was plunging through bottomless space. My head seemed so heavy, too heavy to lift. Images of the vampires standing around me, the house, swirled around my head like jetsam in a tornado.

The sting from Sophie's grip was venom spreading through my system, scorching from my arm to my chest. Hot iron claws dug into my throat. At any moment, they would begin scraping words from my tongue . . .

Or would they? Unlike in previous "interviews" with Sophie, I felt a strange sort of detachment from the proceedings. Don't get me wrong, it burned like the dickens, but I was able to think around it, like a strange little detour in my brain that gave me time to think before I spoke. I blew through the pain like it was a labor contraction, forcing myself to concentrate on Sophie's questions, on the words coming out of my mouth. I could think clearly with some distance between my brain and the throbbing heat of my skin. I couldn't prevent myself from telling the truth, but I could keep myself from sharing unnecessary details. I could work around the compulsion to spill my guts.

I heard myself repeat the barest possible account of

my visit to Cal's house, how I'd arrived a little before sunset, how nothing had been out of the ordinary when I'd
arrived. And nothing had been, really. My visit hadn't
gotten weird until I'd walked into the kitchen.

It turned out I was quite the agile liar. That could be
considered a skill set, right?

"Had you had any previous interactions with Mr.
Calix?"

"It was my first day with him. I was dropping off the
contracts. He hadn't even called for any supplies yet," I
said.

"So you didn't see anything amiss at the house?"

"Other than the moving boxes, not much," I said.

"Do you know where Mr. Calix is now?"

Although I'd expected the question, the urge to respond honestly surprised me. The words were like an air
bubble trapped in my throat. I could feel them stretching the tissue of my larynx, forcing their way out. *Don't
tell them he's upstairs,* I commanded my brain. *Tell them
he moved to Pacoima to start a commune for vegetarian
vampires. Tell them he's looking into getting a sex-change
operation and renaming himself Lulu Pleshette.* I glanced
up at the window, but I couldn't see Cal. "I—I don't know
where he is." I said.

I blew out a wheezing breath as Sophie relinquished
her grip on my hand. It was the truth. I didn't know exactly where he was. He could have been in the alcove. He
could have been in the bathroom. He could have been
in the basement. It was all about semantics . . . maybe
I needed to look into law school once this was all over.

Sophie eyed me speculatively, like she didn't quite believe me. I would have smiled guilelessly, but I couldn't control all of the muscles in my face yet.

"See?" Mr. Marchand said, offering me a handkerchief to wipe the drool from my chin. "She doesn't know anything about Mr. Calix's whereabouts. There's no reason to subject her to any more questioning."

"Always the soft touch, Waco," Sophie murmured.

I cradled my arm against my chest and smacked my dry lips against each other. My mouth tasted like old pennies and Gigi's volleyball kneepads. I felt a hand at my elbow, leading me to one of the benches so I could sit. I was surprised to find that it was Ophelia, and she was gazing at me intently.

I nodded weakly and smiled at Mr. Marchand, handing him his square of crushed linen. There was a *W* embroidered on the corner and a strange little white-on-white flower. I would remember to ask him about it, once I could produce all of the vowel sounds.

"This is the last time we'll discuss this matter," Ophelia told me, her voice official and louder than was probably necessary. "Do not discuss Mr. Calix with anyone outside of the Council office. Do you understand me? Continue with your business as usual."

Mr. Crown and Sophie left without another word to me—surprise, surprise. Mr. Marchand gave me a little bow before turning to the car to argue with Mr. Crown about the proper etiquette involved in calling shotgun.

Ophelia lingered, her eyes glued to the upstairs window. Without looking down at me, Ophelia said, "If you should stumble across Mr. Calix, let him know that we are looking for him. But he should stay where he is."

While the use of the word "stumble" was eerily accurate, I kept an untroubled expression on my face. Behind Ophelia, Mr. Crown had lost the shotgun argument and was currently glowering at me from the backseat. Ophelia threw on a mask of smug indifference, which was her usual expression. Turning to the car, she tossed her hair and sauntered away.

When the SUV was safely speeding down the drive, I called over my shoulder, "Did you get all that?"

There was no answer from the upstairs window.

"Cal?"

Still nothing. I sank my head into my hands and sighed.

"If he's thrown up again, I'm going to leave him outside and let the sun sort it out."

A dark blur popped up to my right. I shrieked, picked up another of my mom's soapstone sculptures—a squirrel—and brought it crashing against Cal's head. Or I would have, if he hadn't managed to duck at the last minute. The momentum of the swing carried my arm through the arc, and the statue was slung across the kitchen. Off-balance, I stumbled into Cal with an "uhff."

I shrank back, sure that this would be enough of an excuse for Cal to sink his fangs into my neck and cease my attempts to brain him with ugly wildlife statuary. But instead, he seemed to think it was adorable that I had tried to drop him like panties at a KISS concert. He grinned down at me, leaning close and running his nose along my hairline. He murmured, "You're a vicious little hellion when cornered, aren't you?"

"No, *you* just seem to bring it out of me."

"I like it. I do have a question for you, though."

Cal took my elbow and led me to the little reading alcove near the top of the stairs. My dad had built a special window seat for my mom, who had always dreamed of a place where she could "think and meditate"—also known as hiding from us all.

After culling through most of their paperbacks and secondhand-bookstore finds, I'd filled the shelves with my old college textbooks, the family's old botany books, the encyclopedias Dad had bought one letter at a time from the local Kroger. Cal was folded up in said window seat, poring over our copy of *Rare Plants of Kentuckiana*.

"Why do you have these books?" he asked me.

"Because my mom was an avid gardener. And I studied botany in college," I said. "And my dad liked yard sales."

"Why didn't you mention that before?"

"Because you were being an enormous asshat?"

He scowled. "An enormous what?"

I ignored the instinct to clap my hand over my mouth at the use of such a naughty word. I shook my head, crossing my arms over my chest. "No, I don't think I'll be explaining that. I will enjoy your situational ignorance."

"It didn't occur to you that these books might be helpful to me?"

I smiled thinly. "Oh, no, it did."

"Resourceful and resentful," he muttered.

"Only toward asshats. Look through the books as much as you want. Though I don't know how helpful they'll be. None of them was written with the supernatural in mind."

I turned toward the shelf and looked for a particularly battered tome covered in red cloth. It was an estate-sale find that my dad had teased my mother shamelessly over: *Metaphysical Aspects of Botanical Aromatherapy.* He'd told her that no matter how much she searched, she wouldn't find a legitimate spiritual reason to return to her hedonistic college pot-loving ways.

I prayed that he was just kidding. My mom firing up a water bong was not a mental image I needed.

I flipped to the index and looked up geranium oil. I read it to myself: *Thought to affect the users primarily in matters of romance and open communication, geranium is also a powerful protectant that forms a psychic boundary between the anointed and sources of negative energy.*

So, conversely, if someone didn't want open communication with a vampire who was trying to force a connection, could geranium oil cause some sort of psychic static? Note to self, roll around in geranium oil the next time I met up with Sophie. And Jane, who had occasional psychic flashes into my mind. And Jane's friend, the vampire Dick Cheney, because it just seemed like a good idea to give him static in any way possible.

Reaching over Cal's head, I located a bag of Sour Worms that I'd hidden in one of those hollowed-out dummy books people typically use to hide jewelry or liquor. I perched on the opposite side of the seat and opened to the first chapter of the book, wondering what other helpful little nuggets lurked inside. Maybe there was a plant that could keep vampires from insulting or vomiting on you.

"You're just going to sit there and read?" he asked, incredulous. "You don't want to talk about the frightening interaction with Council officials?"

I bit a blue-and-orange gummy worm in half and shrugged. "Nah. You heard what they had to say. The only thing we learned is that the Council isn't that great at investigating missing persons. And I'm pretty sure Ophelia knows where you are but thinks you're safer with me. The less time I spend talking to you one-on-one, the less time you have to be a jerk. "

Given Cal's nauseated expression as I bit into another worm, he seemed far more concerned about my choice of candy than any offense he might be causing. "It would seem Ophelia suspects something is amiss within the Council offices, too. She wouldn't be able to make accusations without proof," he said. "And if she's found to be building a case against her fellow Council members, it could cause serious political problems for her. It would seem she's embracing willful ignorance, and we're on our own."

"Or she's the one who poisoned you, and she wants you to stay put so she can come back to finish the job."

"How do you maintain such a sunny, cheerful outlook on life?" he asked, scowling at me.

I shrugged blithely and returned to my book, reading about cedar oil's aura-cleansing properties. "I believe in the power of positive thinking," I told him. "I am positive that this is going to come back and bite us in the butt."

6

No matter how much you try to protect your household's schedule, it's inevitable that a vampire's presence will disrupt it. The best course of action is to make small changes over time, rather than resisting it altogether. Resistance is futile.

—*The Care and Feeding of Stray Vampires*

Cal and I settled into an uneasy stalemate. Now that his nausea had finally eased, it was as if healing took up all of his energy. He slept, rising only to feed and then go back to the master bedroom. After the vomiting and the inappropriate touching, I didn't have the heart to send him back to the basement. I stayed close to the house, asking Jolene to do the actual daytime running for me while I made as many arrangements as I could over the phone.

The distance I'd put between us seemed to have forced him into a slightly snarky, but polite, persona. He didn't make inappropriate jokes, but he wasn't exactly friendly, either. I couldn't help but feel that we'd lost ground in terms of cordial relations.

My replacement BlackBerry arrived the next morning, heralded by a loud thump against the door. Joe Wallace, our mailman, did extra-speedy deliveries so he could finish his work early and fit in a few hours of fishing. He seemed to see "Fragile" stamps as a personal challenge.

Sipping coffee, I went outside to retrieve my dented box and immediately started to sneeze violently. I groaned, wiping at my watering eyes.

Pine pollen.

I could stand the scents and sheddings of almost every flower out there. But every spring, when the pine pollen blew so thick it formed a sickly yellow film over every standing surface, I went running for the Benadryl. It was supposed to be particularly bad this year because of high winds. I was adding allergy meds to my mental shopping list when I turned back to the door and paused. Just outside my front-porch window, there were two shoe prints outlined in yellow dust. I turned to look at the window opposite the door, and there were two more prints under it.

Had Joe tried to peek in through the windows to see if we were home for the delivery? That wasn't like him. He generally just tossed packages against our door and ran.

I shook off the sense of foreboding that rippled up my spine. I was being silly. I had my phone back; almost 75 percent of the things in my world were right again. Shaking my head, I plugged the new phone into my bedroom charger and dialed the activation code. It rang almost immediately, a dull, robotic buzzer noise, rather than my personal ringtone, "Flight of the Bumblebee." I was going to have to reprogram it. Frowning,

I hit the call button. Before I could get the receiver to my ear, I heard, "Where the hell have you been? I've been worried sick!"

"Gigi?" Before-school volleyball practices had created an obnoxiously alert early bird in my sister. How she was able to function, much less perform coordinated acts of athleticism, at this hour had always been a mystery to me.

"You were supposed to call me!" she cried. "Days ago! Your cell's been useless. And every time I call the house, I get the machine. Are you OK? Did he hurt you? Did he bite you?"

"No, I'm fine. I'm sorry. My schedule has been so screwed up."

"Not good enough. Remember that time in St. Louis you caught me sneaking back into the apartment after Shelley Pearson's party and you yelled so loud that Mr. Baker came running over because he thought you were being murdered? It's time for payback."

"I'm sorry, Gigi."

"Well, why don't you address that to 123 Suck It Lane, in care of Mr. Shushy McShoveit," she retorted.

"Remind me why I didn't send you to boarding school. One of the scary ones with knee socks and hazing."

"I worry about you, too, you know," she grumbled. "It's not a one-way street."

"I know."

"When can I come home? Sammi Jo's mom is understanding, but she's making comments about starting a tab for me. That can't be a good sign."

I mulled that over. If Gigi continued to stay with Sammi Jo's family, people would start to talk. Besides that, if the Council members returned and found that Gigi had essentially moved out, Ophelia would know that something was wrong. Better that Gigi return home and continue her schedule as normal. Besides, it didn't seem as if Cal was going to be a threat to her safety. He'd had plenty of time to attack and drain me, and so far, his advances were of a more "naked" nature. He seemed to view Gigi as some sort of annoying accessory.

"I think Thursday should be OK. How's school? Did you get your AP history test back yet?"

She huffed. "Don't think you're going to act like everything's all normal and use my AP history test—which I aced, by the way—to distract me from the wounded hunk of hotness you're 'nursing back to health.' How's it going? Are the howler monkeys howling? I could put off coming home for a day or so if you make it worth my while . . . say, two weeks without dishwasher duty?"

"Gigi."

"Hey, I just want to make it clear. I'm happy for you and all, but I do not want to hear any UNFs coming from your room. I'm a young, impressionable girl."

"UNFs?"

She snickered. "Yeah, universal noises of fu—"

"How do you even know words like that?" I yelped.

Gigi cackled like a madwoman on the other end of the line. "I know what your substitute curse words really mean. I know what you're capable of."

"In other words?"

"I learned it by watching you!" she cried, in a bad imitation of a drug-awareness campaign that was popular when I was a kid.

"I'll see you on Thursday, smart aleck. Love you."

"Love you, too."

I hung up the phone, got dressed, and padded down the stairs. I was surprised to find Cal sitting at the breakfast bar, typing on his laptop. He had several notebooks and scraps of paper spread out in some order that I'm sure made sense to him.

His skin was pale but without the waxy pallor of the last two days. His eyes were bright and clear. He was wearing jeans and a T-shirt extolling the virtues of the Who, which fit so well that it could be considered pectoral porn. He was sipping blood from a mug that Gigi had painted for me on Mother's Day the previous year. It was covered in little bumblebees and said, "I Heart My Big Sister."

I was getting used to having another adult in the house at an alarming rate. Even if I was technically taking care of him, it was sort of nice having Cal around. I felt like the burden of being the designated grown-up had been lifted from my shoulders a bit. I'd been on my own for so long, making all of the decisions. I liked the fact that if the water heater exploded or the zombie apocalypse started, I would have someone who would take my survival scenarios seriously.

And yes, I do realize that was a broad range of scenarios.

Cal glanced up but didn't stop typing as he murmured, "Morning."

"Morning. Going to bed?" I asked, feeling blindly for the coffee supplies.

"Just about," he said, stretching his arms over his head.

"How are you feeling?" I asked as I heated a packet of Type A for him in the microwave.

"I thought we agreed that you won't start every conversation like that."

"I don't know how else to start conversations with you. All other subjects lead to veiled insults and the threat of projectile vomiting."

His lips twitched, and he set aside his laptop, giving me his full attention. "I am feeling much stronger, strong enough to continue my investigation. I've spent the last few hours going through your books, writing e-mails to contacts in the medical field, and inquiring about my symptoms and what botanical compounds could be responsible."

"There are vampire doctors? Isn't it sort of a moot point for you guys?"

He crossed the room and leaned against the kitchen counter while I assembled my morning cup of "liquid stupidity tolerance." He said, "There are vampires who used to be doctors in their human days. Their input is very valuable."

"That makes sense," I said, glancing over his shoulder at the pictures stacked in front of him. A woman's body flayed in horrific Technicolor glory, her face so mutilated she barely seemed human. I shrieked, stumbling back against the counter. Cal started, closing the file over the bloody images, and turned to me. His hands gripped my arms, keeping me upright.

I closed my eyes and breathed deeply, willing unwelcome images to leave my brain. Cold, gray cement-block walls. Polished stainless-steel tables dully reflecting fluorescent lights. The sound of Gigi weeping softly outside the swinging hospital door. My mother's dark hair glittering with broken glass. The morgue attendant had to cover her left side with a sheet. As the scent of bleach and disinfectant seeped into my lungs, I ended up on my hands and knees, retching over the wastebasket.

Standing on shaking legs, I reached into the junk drawer for a handful of M&M's. My hands shook as I popped them into my mouth, meaning that I lost a few to skitter across the floor under the stove. The crackle of the candy shells against my teeth drew me back into reality. I swallowed past the lump in my throat and let the sweetness of chocolate coat my tongue.

Blowing out a breath, I tried to focus on anything else. "Is th-that what—w-was she attacked by one of the poisoned vampires?" I stammered as his face swam in front of mine.

"I'm sorry," he said softly, shoving the folder into a stack of papers. "I didn't want you to see that."

"Who was it?"

He tucked the stack of paperwork into his laptop case. "A blood surrogate named Katie Rigsby. She was the first attacked. I don't believe the culprit had the dosage quite right yet. You can see the hesitation marks in the bite wounds. The vampire in question didn't want to do this, tried to stop. But eventually gave in."

I glanced away, wiping at my cheeks. "Wait, Katie Rigsby? I knew her, in passing. I saw her at the Council office once or twice. She was a nice girl, one of those naturally sunny personalities. Wait, Katie died in a car accident last spring. The newspaper said she fell asleep at the wheel, driving home from a party. I took a potato casserole to her mother at the visitation!"

Cal nodded. "After documenting her condition, the Council's 'public relations committee,' led by Mr. Crown, made it appear as though Ms. Rigsby died in a car accident. This is what they do to cover up a problem within the vampire community. You should know as much as anyone that vampires can be brutal and cruel."

"But you're not that way," I insisted. "You could have hurt me, several times, but you haven't even tried."

"I can be just as bad as any of them, Iris. I've killed people, many people over the years. The young, the old, the rich, the poor, sinner and saint. That's who I am, Iris. Whatever emotional attachment you may be forming to me, it should stop now. It's not good for you, and it will mean nothing to me if it keeps me from getting what I want."

I straightened, shrinking back from him, the taste of chocolate turning bitter in my mouth. So, that's how it was. Clearly, my help didn't mean anything to him. The rapport I thought we'd established, the time we spent together, didn't even make us friends. I was, apparently, cannon fodder, destined to be used as a human shield if Cal was in danger. Mortification flushed through me, warm and watery. I'd become so lonely that I looked to an uninterested vampire for friendship. How sad was that?

I cleared my throat, clenching my teeth against the tremble in my voice. I steadied my hands against the counter, shying out of his grasp. "Don't let Gigi see that, OK? Keep the files somewhere she won't be able to find them."

"I will," he said, pulling back at my clipped, business-like tone. "I'm afraid I'm going to need further assistance from you."

"How do you mean?"

"I don't have all of the information I need here. I grabbed what I could on the way out the door. I need you to go to my house later today and pick up some of my files."

I frowned. "I've got a full day scheduled already. I've got to make up for the time I've already missed at work."

He leveled his gaze at me. I swear, the only thing that could have made his stance closer to my secret naughty boss fantasies was a loosened necktie and collar. I shook my head, hoping to rid my traitorous brain of those use-less sentiments. "I think I am paying you enough that I can comfortably command your attention for a week. Whether that attention is at home or in more remote locations."

"I don't know if you're aware, but references like that make me sound . . . less than virtuous."

"Few prostitutes are paid twenty-five thousand dol-lars a week for their services," he said, rolling his eyes.

"Clearly, you've never been to Vegas," I retorted. He shot me a withering glance, which I blithely ignored. "Why can't you just go yourself?"

"Because I prefer not to burst into flames?" he retorted archly. "The house is probably being watched, and I don't want anyone to see me. If you're seen going in, you can explain it away, say you lost something at the house while you were dropping off the contracts and needed to retrieve it."

"I don't like it," I grumbled.

"I don't, either. If there was any other way, I would suggest it."

We stared at each other, stalemated. It wasn't a terribly unreasonable request, really, unless the house was being watched and I ended up in vampire jail. And refusing could mean mucking up Cal's investigation and stretching his stay at my house past a week. While he hadn't exactly been a nightmare guest, I wanted him gone. I wanted my quiet, predictable, pre-Cal life back, with schedules, routines, and a lack of confusing sexual tension. I wanted to be the normal, non-risk-taking non-vomit-target I once was.

I blew a breath, ruffling a hank of curly hair that had fallen in my eyes. "How much longer do you have until you have to go to sleep for the day?"

He closed his eyes, as if checking some internal gauge. "About twenty minutes before I start to feel fatigued. At full strength, I'm a bit better at staying up during the day than I used to be. It takes age and practice. And for some of the young ones, large amounts of caffeine. But honestly, unless it's a dire emergency, there's no real point."

"I'll go by the house in the afternoon, when you've had some time to rest. I'm going to talk to you on my phone the entire time, so if I have trouble finding your files, you can help me look . . . and so I don't get home only to have you tell me you just remembered that you want your bunny slippers. Will you actually wake up, or will you pull the typical male 'oh, babe, I guess I didn't hear it ring' thing?" I asked, frowning at him.

"I take it Booty Call Paul is a heavy sleeper?" he asked, smirking at me. It was nice to see him smiling from simple mirth. Of course, it was mirth at my expense, but I was willing to let that go for now.

"There's blood in the fridge, and my numbers are on a list by the phone. I'll be back before you wake up tonight," I told him. "I'll call you when I get to your house."

The corner of his mouth lifted, revealing the barest hint of a dimple on his cheek. "Try not to trip over any of your clients today."

"I'll do my best," I muttered as I walked out the back door.

As usual, I ran the errands scheduled for the day—a case of blood at Mr. Rychek's house, cat food for Ms. Wexler, a meeting with a photographer who was thinking about expanding into vampire ceremonies.

And I deposited some of the rather large wad of cash Cal had given me as a "retainer." That was unusual. I felt like I was walking around with a target on my back, carrying that much money around. There was a possibility that the Council was watching my accounts following their visit. So I put half of the money into Gigi's college fund, which was in her name, and made a double payment on the home-equity loan. The loan payments were reasonable enough that making several increased payments over time wouldn't raise too many eyebrows. The rest would be kept in my sock drawer for emergencies . . . or to lure Chick Webster to the house the next time we had a midnight plumbing disaster.

"I don't think I've ever seen this much cash at once, Miss Iris," confessed Posey Stubblefield as she counted out five thousand dollars in hundreds for Gigi's tuition fund. A recent hire, Posey had been fired from her job at the Half-Moon Hollow Public Library for setting the reference room ablaze with a badly planned Halloween display. Lit jack-o'-lanterns and newspapers were, apparently, a dangerous combination. With this in mind, I kept my very flammable stack of money close until it was absolutely necessary to hand it over.

"I've been saving up here and there for a while," I told her quietly. "Sort of a cookie-jar savings account."

"Must have been one hell of a cookie jar," she muttered. "Do vampires really tip that well?"

I chuckled. To most humans who worked for them, vampires were notoriously horrible tippers. Most of them had been turned long before the practice became popular and seemed to resent the idea of rewarding humans for "doing their jobs properly." But instead of bursting poor Posey's bubble, I just nodded and signed the slip for Gigi's deposit.

"Do you need any extra help at Beeline, Miss Iris?"

Thinking of the many jobs Posey had lost because of mysterious workplace fires, combined with the general flammability of my clients, I shuddered. "Sorry, Posey. I'm just starting out. I don't need anyone else just yet."

Posey shrugged and grinned good-naturedly. "Oh, well, but keep me in mind, will you?"

I booked it out of the bank lobby before Posey managed to ignite her nameplate.

Eager to make up for missing the day before, I was meticulous in my attention to detail. I double-checked invoices and triple-checked blood types. I entered my clients' houses carefully, straightened area rugs, and left each place tidier than I found it.

I was not looking forward to going into Cal's house later. I had a weird sense of foreboding, like a black spot hanging over the end of my day. I chalked it up to anxiety over the bank deposit and whether Posey would flap her gums about my "tips." Anyone who knew vampires would see through that ploy right away.

I tried to think of something else, focusing on the tasks at hand. But finally, just around four, I pulled into the driveway four doors down from Cal's house. I dialed my home number on my cell and actually hoped that Cal wouldn't pick up, so I wouldn't have to go in. But damned if he didn't pick up on the second ring, sounding somewhat coherent.

Silently mouthing curses, I tucked my earpiece into my left ear and got out of the car. I pulled a slip of paper and a blue plastic card out of my purse. I punched the code into the keypad near the door. But the light over the buttons flashed an uncooperative red.

"I told you, the Council has changed your door code," I said, checking the paper and retyping the code listed.

"That's why I gave you that blue card," he said, yawning.

"What does it do?"

"I can't tell you."

I cocked my hand on my hip and glared toward the earpiece as if he could feel my irritation through the cell connection. "I get really tired of that answer."

"Place the card between the wall and the lockbox, and shove it until it's between the metal plates. It will interrupt the signal to the lockbox without alerting the alarm company."

I was about to follow his directions, but I withdrew my hand from the keypad. "Will that shock me in any way?"

I heard him yawn again. "It shouldn't."

"Also not a great answer," I told him dryly as I slipped the card into place. The indicator lights flickered once and turned green. I yanked the card out and stuffed it into my pocket. The house was dark. The sunproof shades were down, and I didn't think it would be a good idea to raise them or turn on the lights. I stilled, blinking rapidly to let my eyes adjust to the darkness.

"Cal?" I whispered into the headset. "Are you awake?"

"Barely," he muttered. "Why are you whispering?"

"I really don't know." I allowed my voice to rise to a normal level. "Where do I need to look?"

"My office," he said. "Top of the stairs, first door on the left. There should be a white cardboard file box on the desk."

"Seriously, you just left your files out on your desk?" I asked, climbing the stairs.

"No, that's my decoy box. I just want to see if they took it."

"Your mind is a dark, scary place," I murmured as I turned into the hall.

I looked into the office. The room was practically sanitized. The spare black console desk had been stripped clean. The filing cabinet had been emptied, its drawers standing open. I was surprised the Council had left the desk lamp behind. "They took your decoy box."

He snickered.

"What was in it?" I asked.

"I hand-copied about a year's worth of *Penthouse Forum* letters into steno notebooks."

"Ew."

"In Serbian," he added. "By the time they figure out what they have . . ."

"They'll think you stole a bunch of notebooks from a perverted Serbian," I said. "I'm not sure whether to be impressed with you or concerned. Where are the real notebooks?"

I could hear him rolling over on the bed, the sheets rustling against the phone. This called to mind images of Cal naked and barely covered by sleep-rumpled sheets, which was not good for my powers of stealth and concentration. He cleared his throat, as if he could sense my indecent thoughts through the phone connection. "Front bedroom closet, in a box marked 'Receipts 2009.'"

"Vampires never save receipts."

"So it should be easy for you to find," he retorted.

I stepped into the hallway. I heard a strange sort of shuffling noise downstairs, then a light thud. I stopped.

"Iris? Your breathing's changed. What's happening?"

"Shh," I whispered, listening.

"What's wrong?" he demanded, his voice suddenly sharp.

The house was silent. When I didn't hear so much as a creaking floorboard, I shook my head, stepping toward the bedroom. "Nothing. I thought I heard something."

"Get out," he commanded. "Get out of the house, right now."

I listened for a moment, wondering what happened to "no emotional connections" and using me as a human shield if necessary. "No, it's OK. It's nothing."

"Are you sure?"

"Yeah," I said, approaching the closet near the front window of the bedroom. "I'm probably just being paranoid. B and E isn't exactly an everyday occurrence for me."

"If you feel uncomfortable, I want you to leave."

"It's fine." I closed my fingers around the closet door and opened it. It was completely empty. Not so much as a dust bunny.

"Cal—" A hand closed over my mouth. I shrieked, inhaling an unpleasant combination of woodruff and lime that stung my nose. I was pulled back against a solid, hard body. The rough fingers stretched across my mouth, the taste of his skin making me gag.

"Iris!" I heard Cal's voice yell from the earpiece, which was now dangling from my collar.

I took a deep breath, but before I could scream, the hand closed over my throat, cutting off my air. The earpiece clattered to the ground, bouncing across the carpet. The only sound I could make was a strangled croak. Another hand slipped down my ribs and pressed hard, squeezing me back against him.

"Sweet little thing." The cold, rough voice slipped down the side of my neck. I tried to shrink away, but he just pulled me closer. He ground his hips against my butt, letting me know exactly how much he was enjoying toying with his food. Hot, humiliated tears gathered at the corners of my eyes.

"Iris?" Cal called, his voice small and far away. "Iris, answer me right now!"

I whimpered as his grip tightened on my mouth. Fangs dropped, sounding like a knife being unsheathed. I felt the points scrape against the flesh of my neck.

"What are you doing here, pretty thing?" he whispered, his lips clammy and wet against my skin. "You woke me. No one is supposed to be here."

His voice slithered around in my head, constricting, smothering. My head felt so heavy, full and numb, like an overblown bloom on a weak steam.

"Do you work for him?" he asked. "Do you know where he is?"

"Wh-who?" I stammered, whimpering when he wrenched my neck.

"Don't play stupid with me, pretty thing."

"I work for Ophelia," I whispered. "For the Council. I came to close up the house."

"For the Council?" He chuckled. He sniffed my neck. "You're untapped. No one's ever taken a bite out of you?" I shook my head frantically.

Please, please, please, just let me get out of this "untapped," I prayed. *Gigi is too young to be left alone. I haven't filled out her Free Application for Federal Student Aid yet. And she still doesn't understand that the "check engine" light is more than just a sparkly greeting from her car.*

His voice was flowing over me now, pulling me under an oily surface. I couldn't breathe. I couldn't think. He murmured, "I'm so hungry, and you smell just mouthwatering. I think I might keep you with me so I can drink you all up. You don't mind, do you? After all, it's the neighborly thing to do."

The hazy brain-fog cleared enough that I found that I didn't mind giving him my blood. It didn't seem like such an unreasonable request. It seemed rude somehow not to offer him something to drink. I tilted my head so he would be able to access my neck. He chuckled, pressing a smacking little kiss over my jugular before sinking his fangs into me.

A stuttering gasp rippled through my chest as he broke the skin over my vein. Pain, a bright, hot, pulsating flower, bloomed through my nerve endings. I felt a trickle of blood soak through the neck of my cardigan. He moaned, making loud slurping pulls at my skin. I whimpered at the burning, tugging sensation of my blood being drained away.

His enjoyment of my blood was so complete that he wasn't even bothering to hold my arms. My eyes rolled back, and I fought the need to pass out. Breathing deeply, I snuck my hand into my pocket and wrapped my fingers around the silver handle.

I inhaled sharply, jerking the silver pie server out and shoving it over my shoulder. There was a horrible screeching noise as the pie server met a little resistance, sinking into the vampire's flesh. The pressure at my neck slipped away.

I stumbled out of the closet and toward the window, pressing the button that released the sunproof shades. The room was flooded with sunlight, temporarily blinding me as the vampire screamed in rage. I turned to face him, a canister of silver vampire spray in hand. I couldn't make out his face, just the smoking outline of a very angry vampire.

The smell of burning popcorn sizzled through the air as the combination of silver and sun burned his flesh. Wrenching my shoulder, he shoved me back toward the open closet, cursing and sputtering. I pressed the spray button, aiming for eye level. He screamed, growling viciously as I added another layer of pain to his suffering. Howling, he threw me back into the open closet. Flailing, I caught the doorknob with my sleeve, inadvertently slamming the door behind me.

For a second, I panicked, thinking he might be in the closet with me. I kicked and struck out, swinging at nothing but air. Lunging for the rattling doorknob, I held it in a death grip as he yanked on it from the outside. Although the strain on my arms burned, exposure to the sunlight had obviously weakened him. I held on, despite the guttural stream of graphic, anatomically impossible death threats he threw at me.

The growling and shaking stopped suddenly, but I kept my grip on the door for another minute. I only let go when my legs gave way. Slumping against the wall, I sucked in huge, gulping breaths, closing my eyes and willing the panic to die down. My stomach rolled, and I pitched to my knees, praying that I wouldn't vomit on the floor in Cal's closet.

Though, clearly, I owed him a few yarks.

I pressed my fingertips into my eyes, willing myself to wake up if this was a nightmare. Because this couldn't be the way Iris Scanlon departed this earth, huddling in a closet, waiting for the angry, weakened vampire outside to recover enough to swoop in and devour her. At this sad point, my options were:

1. Go charging out of the closet, screaming Xena-style, and hope that the vampire was weakened by the sunlight or doubled over laughing at my weak attempt at overpowering him.

Likely result: Death or, at the very least, humiliation.

2. Duck out of my closet just long enough to grab for my purse, hoping that the vampire didn't catch me, and then call 911 . . . and carefully explain to the police what I was doing in a vampire's home where I had no legitimate business.

   Likely result: Three to five years for breaking and entering. Which was inconvenient, because I looked really washed out in orange.

3. Hide in this closet overnight until sunrise.

   Likely result: Being yanked out of the closet and drained as soon as the vampire recovered.

I split the difference between options 1 and 3, waiting until I had the nerve to crack the door open and scan the room for Gropey Groperson. All was quiet in the bedroom. I couldn't see the silver pie server. I wondered idly whether it was still stuck in the vampire's chest.

From the other side of the door, I could hear the faintest impression of Cal's voice calling. I waited several long minutes, listening for any sound of the injured vampire. I grasped the can of silver spray firmly in front of me and kicked open the door. The well-lit bedroom was empty. And my mom's silver pie server was gone.

I was so glad she wasn't around to ground me for this one.

"Iris!" Cal yelled, his voice tinny and remote from the earpiece on the floor. "Answer me!"

"I'm fine." I wheezed, putting the module back in my ear. "I'm fine."

"What happened?"

"I, uh, I just got spooked," I told him, carefully poking my head into the hallway and flicking on the light switch. I didn't see any evidence of a smoking vampire's trail, but there was no way he had gotten out of the house in broad daylight. I went to the window and pushed the button to lift the shade. A breath I didn't realize I'd been holding rushed out of my chest.

"I heard the growls and your screams."

"I'm fine," I insisted as I blazed a path through the house to the door, turning on lights and opening windows until all of the rooms were sunlit.

"Don't lie to me. You're frightened. I can hear it in your voice," he insisted. "What happened?"

"There was someone in the house, but I'm fine," I said, bolting for the front door. My car was down the street, untouched. I jumped in and pulled out into the street without bothering with a seat belt. I did, however, manage to find the lemon drops in my center console.

"What do you mean, someone in the house?" he demanded. "Are you all right?"

"I'm fine."

"You keep saying that, but I don't believe you."

I didn't answer, crunching my teeth through the citrusy hard candy instead. A few houses down the street, I forced myself to pull over. I took a few deep breaths, leaning my head against the steering wheel. I had nothing against the guard at the booth. I didn't think it would be nice to run him down. "I'll be home in a few minutes. I'll explain then. Just let me get out of here. I just can't—I can't talk right now."

Breathing. I focused on breathing, on keeping my hands steady on the wheel and distinguishing the gas pedal from the brake. My losing track of the pedals would surely upset the other drivers.

"Start talking to me," Cal said, his voice like a gentle caress against my ear.

"About what?" I asked. I sniffed, wiping at my eyes and pushing the car back into gear.

"Anything. It occurs to me that I've entrusted my entire existence to you, but I know very little about you. What's your favorite color?"

I scoffed. "Really?"

"It's to get your mind off of your state of panic. So, favorite color?"

"Blue."

He prompted, "What kind of blue?"

"The kind that's not red or yellow," I deadpanned.

"There are hundreds of different shades of blue."

"Cobalt." I huffed. "My mom had this vase when I was a kid, cobalt glass. I used to sit on the floor and watch the sunlight coming through it."

"Where is it now?"

"Gigi broke it when she was five."

"When did Gigi start living with you?" he asked.

"We went from favorite color to custodial issues?"

"I've wanted to ask for days but couldn't find a way without sounding inquisitorial. How is it that you're raising Gigi?" he asked as I turned onto County Line Road. "Where are your parents?"

"They died a few years ago. Gigi was twelve. They were coming back from a New Year's Eve party, and they were struck by a drunk driver."

He said, "I'm sorry." And for once, I was sure he was sincere. "What were they like?"

"My dad worked at the phone company. He loved York Peppermint Patties and Conway Twitty. Mom was a teacher. She was all about her garden. You'd probably figured that out already, since she named us Iris and Gladiola. Even now, something happens every day—whether it's Gigi saying something really funny or some crisis with the house—and my first instinct is that I should call them and talk to them about it. And then I remember that I can't, and it's like losing them all over again."

"I'm sorry that they passed when you were so young."

I shrugged. "We were lucky that Gigi wasn't with them. She was staying with a friend that night."

"Where were you?"

"I was home for the holidays, sleeping off stress from finals. I had just finished my degree in biology, a semester early, and started a graduate program, plant biology at Washington University in St. Louis."

"I've been meaning to ask," he said. "Why plants?"

"Why not plants?" I shot back.

"It just seems like a sheltered, lonely field, especially when you consider that you clearly have a gift for customer service. You know what someone wants and how to get it to them. What did you plan on doing with your education?"

"I was torn between research and commerce. I didn't know whether I wanted to find new uses for plants in pharmaceuticals or open a shop where I sold herbal shampoo. I thought I had time to figure it out."

Talking helped me focus. I managed to slow down to a safe speed, remember to use turn signals, and not follow other drivers so closely that I could read which brand of pine-tree air freshener they were using.

"Somehow I thought it would be easier, better for Gigi, for her to leave the memories behind and come stay with me in St. Louis. I don't know what I was thinking, believing I could work, go to school, and take care of a teenager. Gigi was my parents' late-in-life surprise. She was used to being the center of their world. She missed her friends. And she was used to a smaller, rural school environment. She didn't adjust very well. She made friends with the wrong kids and started getting into trouble—fights at school, skipping classes, that sort of thing. I realized that what I was doing wasn't working and wouldn't work, no matter how much I wanted it to. So I made a change, quit school, moved back here, and made her needs my priority.

"We tried to rent or sell the house, but we never found a buyer. A few months after we moved back here, I was still looking for a permanent 'breadwinner' sort of job and failing miserably. A high-school friend's sister had been turned into a vampire and asked me to take care of the flowers for her wedding. Beautiful sprays of gardenias, very dramatic without the cliché of using calla lilies. She liked the way I organized the flowers. And since she couldn't go out during the day and didn't trust her mother with the other details, I ended up taking care of the cake, the bar order, the tuxes. Before I knew it, I'd planned her whole wedding for her. That's how I got my start working with the undead."

"You didn't think to work in a nursery or for a landscaper?" he asked.

"It was a while before I could work out in the garden and not get weighed down, I guess, by memories of my mom. And in the long run, I think I'm better suited to not working with plants, because it would have become a job instead of something I loved. Working with vampires was a perfect solution for me. I needed a job that was daytime-oriented and flexible, for Gigi. I wasn't qualified for much. I couldn't sell a life vest to a drowning man. But I'm organized. I'm a multitasker, and I knew a few people who worked at the courthouse. Vampires had come out of the closet a few years before, and they still were having trouble setting up hours so the newly declared undead citizens could come in and pick up the paperwork they needed to straighten out taxes and property. I figured vampires are busy, just like everybody else. And they have an even smaller window of time to get out and about . . . and frankly, some of you are kind of lazy when it comes to the details of everyday life."

"Undeadist," he muttered.

I ignored him. "I volunteered to run the paperwork out to their houses during the day, while they were sleeping. I built up a list of contacts, got to know the vampires at the local Council office, and everything just sort of went from there. I'm thinking about adding a transport service. You know, for vampires who don't like to fly? It will be a while yet before I can afford it. But it's nice to have a plan."

There was a long pause from the other end of the line. Finally, he cleared his throat and said, "You are a very clever girl."

I snorted. "I know."

Han Solo, eat your heart out.

7

Remember that after endless years, some vampires are immune to emotional responses such as sympathy or affection.

—*The Care and Feeding of Stray Vampires*

Cal kept me talking, asking mindless little questions about my parents, Gigi, birthdays and holidays and vacations. I told Cal about spending weekends and summers in the garden with my mom when I was a kid, about my pride in transplanting my first windowsill bean plants grown in a plastic cup to the sacrosanct backyard soil. I talked about my pseudo-naturalist phase, which ended after I gave myself a homemade facial and got a horrible rash in reaction to turmeric. Mom had told me she loved me, but from then on, I had to buy Noxzema at the drugstore like a normal girl.

By the time I pulled into the driveway, my breathing was even and my hands steady. I walked up the porch stairs, the strong rays of the late-afternoon sun warming my back.

As I approached the darkened door, my stomach tumbled. Outside was safe. The sunlight was safe. The idea of trapping myself in another house with a vampire, even if it was my own house, made me want to retch. I took a deep breath and turned the doorknob. The door lurched forward, dragging me inside the house with its momentum. My stomach pitched, and I lost all sense of up or down. I was plummeting, falling through space. Steely arms closed around me, pulling me into the darkness of the shaded foyer. Instead of fighting Cal's grip, I sank into it, my breath rippling out of my lungs in racking little sobs.

I opened my eyes. Cal was leaning against the hallway wall, his face drawn and tired as he looked me over. He lifted my hair from my neck and growled when he saw the bite mark. The silver on my sweater made contact with his skin, but he didn't flinch from the sizzle and smoke as he pulled me to the floor and cradled me in his lap.

"Why are you covered in silver?" he asked, his voice low and hoarse as he unbuttoned my sweater. He pushed the offending cardigan from my shoulders, leaving me in a slate-blue camisole and a pencil skirt. "And what's that smell?"

"It's a new perfume," I retorted. "It's called Residue of an Icky Groper. Do you like it?"

"You're going to tell me what happened," he said sternly. "Every detail."

"I talked too much already on the drive over here. I just want to sit here and be quiet for a while."

Cal nodded, holding me until the sun shifted in its descent, sending a beam of dying sunlight across the maple

floor toward us. It was a struggle for us to get to our feet.
He was still weak, and I was shaky. But we finally un-
twisted ourselves from our person pretzel and pushed
ourselves up along the wall, out of danger. Cal pulled
me down the hallway toward the master bedroom. He
pushed me down to the mattress, yanking off my shoes
and pulling the clean sheets under my chin. He loped
around the bed, silently sliding under the sheet next to
me. He wrapped an arm around me and pulled me close,
tucking his chin over my shoulder.

For the first time since walking through his door, I felt
safe. I closed my eyes and concentrated on breathing, on
the sensation of his hands rubbing circles on my back.
After a long while, I was able to speak again.

"So, clearly, there were some unexpected develop-
ments at your house," I said into his shirt. "There was
a vampire in your closet. He seemed to think he could
chew your whereabouts out of me." He nodded, pulling
my hair away from my neck to inspect the wound again.

"I didn't tell him anything," I added quickly.

"I knew you wouldn't," he assured me. "I'm sorry this
was done to you. I wouldn't have asked if I thought you
would be hurt. Do you think he could have followed you
home?"

"I don't think so," I told him. "It was still broad daylight when I left, and I took a pretty good chunk out of
him with a pie server. It slowed him down."

"Do you think he's still there?" he asked, a dangerous
glimmer of anger lighting his dark eyes.

"You're not going back there," I told him, gripping

his arm. "Besides ruining your 'cover,' you're not quite at full strength yourself. You have no business getting into vampire fistfights right now, even if I did soften him up for you."

His eyes widened as he caught my meaning. "Why would you take the risk of fighting back? There's no way you could win a close-contact fight with a vampire."

"I kind of did win, since I walked away without a pie server sticking out of my person."

"Good point."

"Besides, what happened to 'no emotional attachments'?" I asked him pointedly, though I didn't pull away. "I'm just a human, after all."

"I shouldn't have said that." He hesitated. "I find myself . . . more attached to you than I previously believed. It's particularly strange considering I've only known you a few days. Perhaps it's like Stockholm syndrome."

"I don't think that's the way Stockholm syndrome works."

"Well, I can't explain it. It's been so long since I was human. I can't ever remember being sick or weak. But when I was ill and miserable, it was your scent, your voice, that drew me out. I can't lose that right now."

That would have been such a sweet moment if he hadn't added "right now."

"I knew the moment the door closed that I shouldn't have asked you to go," he said, shifting my weight against him and running his fingers along my spine. "I could hardly sleep today. And when I heard you scream over the phone . . . You have wormed your way under my skin,

Iris. I find myself very concerned about your well-being. I want to be near you, to listen to you speak, because I need it somehow. It's uncomfortable."

"I'm sorry to put you out," I muttered, leaning my head against his collarbone. I felt him drag the clips from my hair, letting it fall loose over my shoulders. My fingers curled around the fabric of his shirt, twisting it, pulling him closer and giving me something to concentrate on other than the effort not to cry. I closed my eyes, willing myself to take deep breaths, to relax, starting with my toes, then my legs, and working my way up to my arms and shoulders. The scent of his skin, that mellow woodsy aura, helped considerably.

His fingers slid down the length of my spine, settling over my hip. I could feel his eyelashes fluttering against my temple. I could hear him swallowing, over and over, and I wondered if the scent of my blood was bothering him—and whether he was going to yark on me again. He pressed his face to my hair and breathed deeply. The tip of his nose slipped down the curve of my cheek, along the skin of my neck, settling just over the bite wound.

My spine stiffened. My shoulders closed in, and I pulled away. He gave me a sheepish look as his fangs snapped back up. He loosened his grasp on my hips, ghosting his hands over my face, my hair, my arms. "I think we're going to need to renegotiate the terms of our agreement."

"Were there terms?" I asked. "I thought it was a pretty standard 'accept my money to shelter me, or I track you to your house and kill your family' deal."

"I said I was sorry about that. Look, it's clear that I'm going to have to continue to look into this matter from a remote location. I need to stay underground, so to speak. And considering the encounter at my house, I would feel better knowing there's someone in the house with you and your sister. There's no better way than to continue staying here. I think we've come to an understanding. And we work well together when you're not being prickly."

"Prickly!"

He smiled at finally hearing some force in my voice. "Like a cactus. I will double my offer if you let me stay another week. If I haven't resolved my situation at that time, we'll renegotiate."

I chewed my lip. "For fifty thousand dollars, I suppose you can stay in one of the family rooms upstairs. Considering that you haven't eaten me yet, I guess I should trust you."

His eyebrows arched, but he was still grinning, amused by my greed. "Fifty thousand? There's no prorated, special guest price available?"

I looked down toward the bruises forming on my arms, daring him to question the price. "Give me flak about it, and it will be seventy-five."

He none-too-tenderly pressed my head against his collarbone with a thunk. "Apparently, you know more about negotiating than I give you credit for."

I chuckled against his shirt and stayed burrowed there. We remained quiet as my breathing slowed. I tangled my fingers in his dark hair, winding it around my fingertips. His soft, cool lips rested against my forehead, and his arms pulled me tight against his solid chest. It would be so easy to imagine that he really cared, that we were a normal couple, cuddling up after a long day. But he didn't care. He barely knew me. He was just clinging to the only person he knew who was willing to shelter him. And I was going to have to learn to prevent this sort of closeness if I was going to survive after he inevitably blew out of town.

I would have to invest in some Godiva, because that was really going to suck. But for now, it felt really good to share any sort of connection with another person, breathing or not.

He rubbed his hands along my arms, my back. My pulse evened out, and my eyelids drooped. And the incredible heaviness of ebbing adrenaline sucked the strength from my limbs. I was on the point of dozing off when Cal said, "Go take a shower. I'll make you something to drink for a change."

I nodded, wiping at my sticky, drying cheeks. "Something with vodka."

I shampooed four times before realizing that I'd completely zoned out under the hot spray. Even with leave-in conditioner, the next morning was going to be a rough hair day. When I finished my shower, I drew back the curtain to find two fingers of vodka on the rocks waiting for me on the bathroom counter. I chose not to think about the fact that he'd been in the bathroom with me while I was naked. After all, I'd seen him "indisposed" often enough in the last few days.

I grabbed for my fluffy pink robe and slugged back the drink in one gulp . . . then immediately regretted it. I wheezed in a croaking gasp, my windpipe burning in the fumes of the ice-cold alcohol. "Holy Lord, it's been a long time since I've had a grown-up drink."

I bent over the counter, breathing out of my nose to lessen the sting. I was out of practice at this particular skill. Being a single pseudo-parent seriously screws with one's alcohol tolerance.

I eventually emerged from the bathroom, wet hair combed and teeth brushed. Cal wasn't in the master bedroom when I came out. I went upstairs to my room, determined to find the least attractive pajamas I owned. Standing in front of my dresser, I dropped the robe and opened the top drawer.

I heard a throat being cleared behind me.

I shrieked, turning around to find Cal standing in the doorway, holding another vodka and a bag of Jolly Ranchers that he must have found in the vegetable crisper. "Cal! Get out!"

"You saw me naked," he noted, his voice irritatingly untroubled.

"This is why you're not supposed to be on the second floor!" I cried, yanking my robe over my shoulders.

"Because you walk around nude?" he said, smirking. "You have nothing to be ashamed of, Iris. You have a lovely body. Shapely calves, high, firm breasts, a sweet heart-shaped little—"

"Easy," I said, glaring at him.

"Don't be upset." He waggled the glass at me. "I

struggled all the way up the stairs to bring you this. You rewarded me handsomely."

"If I hear you say the words 'tit for tat,' I am not above repoisoning you."

Cal smirked. "But you feel better now, don't you? Now that righteous indignation has replaced your fear?"

"Not really, no." I tied the robe tightly at my waist and sat heavily on my bed. I scooted against the headboard and clutched an embroidered green pillow to my stomach. Cal put the drink on my nightstand and carefully sat on the end of my bed, on the opposite side. I appreciated that he was trying to give me some space, but it was still very strange to have a vampire perching on the blue log-cabin-pattern quilt that my grandma made for me. I dropped two green-apple Jolly Ranchers into the glass to flavor the vodka, a trick I'd learned when I'd outgrown wine coolers in college.

Sipping my drink, I told him in more detail about my walk through his dark house, about the empty front bedroom and being felt up by a randy, hungry vampire. He examined the bite mark at my neck, his face hardening, but he remained quiet.

"I don't understand where he even came from," I said, draining the glass. "Would the Council have left someone sleeping in your house? Like a guard?"

I cut my eyes toward his face, and the room spun a little. Perhaps I shouldn't have had two stiff drinks on an empty stomach after blood loss. I blinked rapidly, and his frowning face wavered a little before my eyes.

"If they did, they certainly wouldn't send someone

who would bite an intruder. You would have been taken directly to the Council office for questioning. You would have cracked under their tactics and revealed my whereabouts in about an hour."

"Thank you for your faith in me," I deadpanned. "So I guess it was a good thing, then, that it was some rogue vampire squatter who molested me and fed from me against my will."

His face softened. I closed my eyes to that pitying, guilty stare and felt a cool hand stroke my bare ankle. "I've never been bitten before," I said, running my fingers over the raw red mark at my neck. "I didn't care for it."

There was an incredulous note in his voice now. "Never?"

"Never," I repeated. "I work for vampires. I don't fraternize with them."

"I am sorry," he said. "It can be very enjoyable for the . . ."

"Victim?" I asked dryly.

"I was going to say donor," he corrected me. "If there is an understanding between the vampire and the human, the vampire can make it very pleasurable for him or her."

"So why not do that all the time?" I asked petulantly. "Why make it violent and painful if it doesn't have to be?"

He shrugged and looked down at my foot, the foot he was still trailing his fingers over. "Because the vampire doesn't care to take the time or enjoys taking the blood by force. A good number of us prefer our meals that way.

A touch of fear can make the blood that much sweeter. And sexually—"

"Enough," I said, raising my hand to cut him off. "Disturbing bite wounds aside, there were no files anywhere to be found."

"Damn it," he grumbled. "The Council operatives are notoriously lazy. I thought they'd see the decoy box and stop looking."

"So basically, we're back at square one?" I asked.

"If square one is somewhere behind our starting point, where we've tipped our hand and my adversaries now know that a comely human is helping me, then yes. We are at square one."

I slumped against the headboard, deflated. Cal reached for me, just as the opening notes of "Flight of the Bumblebee" blared out of my BlackBerry. Cal heaved an irritated sigh and rolled back to the mattress. For the first time in a long time, I considered not answering. Surely, there were more pressing issues in my life than Mr. Dougal's custom-embroidered handkerchiefs or the order of plasma due at the Wyatt house the next morning. But Cal would be leaving soon. And my business had to survive after he was gone. Missing calls was not a good way to keep it going. And I would just worry about the numerous possible reasons for the call, like a dog gnawing a bone, until I drove myself crazy. Better to answer the phone and cut out the interim mental gymnastics.

I pulled myself together enough to press the send key, take Mr. Rychek's order for a new batch of *gluten-free* organic almond milk for Diandra, then close my day with a few phone calls. Because he was incapable of picking up human social cues, Cal amused himself by sprawling across my bed, picking through my collection of embarrassing romance paperbacks. He snickered and read portions of *Lord of the Rogues* aloud, while I arranged a tasting of specialty bloods for Mrs. Dunston, who couldn't seem to get out of the habit of throwing dinner parties after her recent turning. I arranged a carpet-cleaning appointment for Mr. Crown, who had never contracted with my service before. He insisted that no one accomplished "menial tasks" like I did, which I tried to see as a compliment. I narrowly avoided having to go to his house and oversee the cleaners myself, claiming a scheduling conflict. The very idea of entering another vampire's home so soon after being mauled in one was nauseating. Mr. Crown huffed that he *supposed* a half-done job would have to do, and I ended the call as quickly as possible without actually hanging up on him. Jerk.

At last, I crawled into bed next to Cal and collapsed into a pillow.

"It's very interesting, the number of topics you cover in your phone calls," he said, lazily stretching his arms over his head. "It's a bit like the women of my time. They had to run the households while we were away at war. They had to know a little bit about everything. They had to delegate, organize. I always thought it was a bit like juggling."

I cocked my head to the side as I rolled over to stare at him. "Would it be rude to ask you how old you are?"

"Do humans think this is an appropriate question?"

"From men to women, no." I shook my head. "From women to men? It's allowed."

He chuckled. "Strange double standard."

"Well, women have made what progress we can over the years." I snorted. "Where do you come from?"

"I was born in what was known as Mycenae."

"As in ancient Greece?" He nodded.

I made a mental note to hide the copy of *300* that I had tucked into my "Lonely Nights" DVD collection . . . and to stop picturing Cal in the *300* leather warrior underwear ensemble.

I cleared my throat. "How ancient?"

"I have lived long enough that I don't keep track of exact years."

"Why can't you answer a question directly? It's like living with the Riddler." I groaned. A factoid from some long-past World Civ class floated to the surface of my memory. "Wait, didn't Paris steal Helen of Troy away from Mycenae, to get away from her husband?"

He rolled his eyes. "Yes, two royals acting like children brought ten years of war and misery down on our heads." He held up my romance novel, then let it flop to the bedspread with disdain.

I did some quick mental calculations. If he meant "our heads" literally, if he meant that he'd lived during that time, that would mean that Cal was an antique.

I goggled at him, looking so comfortable in jeans and a faded T-shirt. How did he stand it? The constant changes. The blaring technology. The crowding. The increasing selfishness of every generation. How could someone stand the monotony of a million nights and still enjoy mocking my stupid little romance novel?

"You're counting the years in your head, aren't you?" he asked, without looking up at me.

"I'm sorry. I can't help it. Why don't you have more of an accent?"

"It became easier, over the years, to learn the modern languages. It's been a long time since I thought in Greek, ancient or otherwise. It makes me a bit sad that I've lost touch with that part of myself. But keeping a bit of mystery, keeping my enemies from knowing exactly how old I am, has its benefits."

"How have you managed to live so long? Don't you get bored? Frustrated?"

He shrugged. "Honestly, the world didn't change so much until the last few hundred years. And then, suddenly, the last century, it feels like everything is on fast-forward. I'll admit that even I worry that the end of everything is near."

"But everything you must have seen, it's—I can't even imagine it. Did you meet Gregor Mendel? George Washington? Elvis?"

I was on my knees now, crouching on the mattress in front of him, bouncing and demanding answers like a schoolgirl. He seemed amused by my reaction, chiding me gently. "You do realize that just because I lived during a certain time period doesn't mean that I had access to celebrities?"

"You had a better chance than most people," I retorted.

"I met Abraham Lincoln once," he said, smiling up at me. "I bumped into him as he was coming out of the gentleman's lounge . . . at Ford's Theatre."

I gasped. "No!"

He nodded. "Mr. Lincoln seemed like a very good man, especially for one with so much power. But he was obviously troubled."

I protested, "But you could have, I don't know, followed him to his deathbed and turned him."

"You think a six-foot-four bearded vampire in a stovepipe hat with a striking resemblance to the recently assassinated president could have gotten around unnoticed?" he asked.

"I hate it when you make sense. So, did you have a family before you died? Children?"

"My wife was expecting our first when I sailed away. My son was half grown by the time I would have returned from war."

"Would have returned?"

"How do you get me to talk so much about myself?" he wondered.

He plucked at the bedspread with his fingers. Most vampires didn't reveal this sort of information to humans, preferring to keep exactly how old (read: powerful) they were close to the vest. But it seemed that he couldn't deny me. He rolled onto his back, fiddling with the binding of my paperback. "Vampires cannot resist a good battle. There's too much confusion to notice when a man goes missing, never to be heard from again. Humans regard wars with regret or reverence. Some vampires remember them as particularly enjoyable feasts. As the war lagged on, we heard rumors of battalions being picked off from the far reaches of the battlefields, of bodies disappearing from the aftermath while the surgeons searched for survivors. By the Night of the Horse, we'd attracted quite a swarm of the undead. The realization that the battle was coming to a close whipped them into a sort of 'last call' frenzy. They took all stragglers, anyone who had his back turned. I survived all those years of war, only to be dragged into the bushes while I was relieving myself after the gates of Troy were breached."

I gasped in horror. That was almost as bad as the story of Jane's turning, which involved her being stranded on the side of a dark country road, mistaken for a deer by the town drunk, and shot.

"I don't know why my sire chose to feed me his blood rather than simply leave me to die. I only remember waking up, buried in sandy soil, and clawing my way to the surface. I ran rather wild that first year, slaking my thirst wherever I could, feeding on some of my former brothers-in-arms as they attempted to march home. If another vampire hadn't tracked me and taken me under her wing, others might have destroyed me just to prevent me from calling attention to myself. "

"Did you ever see your family again?"

He shook his head. "I thought about going back to visit after I adjusted to my new life. But I didn't want to take the chance that I would hurt them. Years later, I learned that my son was healthy and strong, married, with three sons of his own. My wife had remarried and had more children. They were fine without me."

"I doubt that's true."

"But I prefer to think of it that way. It's easier than picturing them suffering."

"Sounds like being a vampire sort of sucks, if you'll pardon the pun."

"We're in a dangerous situation, Iris." He was plucking at the bedspread again, choosing his words carefully. "You saw that today, I think. Next time, you may not be so lucky. I will do everything I can to protect you, but you could be hurt. If you were in a condition from which you could not recover, I need to know whether you would want to be changed."

I blinked owlishly at him. I'd never been able to come up with a definitive answer to the question every human had asked himself or herself since the Great Coming Out. *Would you want to be turned?* Clearly, there were advantages—immortality, near-indestructibility, and, let's face it, increased hotness. But could I survive on blood for eternity? Did I want to live that long? What about Gigi? What about my business? Could I stand only seeing my gardens in moonlight?

And there were considerations besides Gigi and how she would be affected. Because so many humans said yes when asked whether they'd want to be turned, the Council had established a strict protocol for turning that required mutual consent, sire fostering, and about a dozen safeguards. If the Council decided that the transformation was done too hastily or that the sire wasn't giving the newborn the proper supervision, it could "take custody" of the newly risen vampire. The sire could be fined heavily or, in cases where turning was forcible, subjected to the Trial, the vampire definition of overkill. If the Council decided to retaliate against Cal for his less-than-aboveboard dealings with them during this escapade, it could decide to destroy both of us.

Cal seemed insulted by my pregnant pause. "You've never craved immortality?" he asked, tilting his head as his eyes swept over my face. "You spend your life serving vampires, and you have no desire to become one of them?"

"I don't serve vampires," I snapped. "I provide a service for them. There's a difference."

"Fine, you spend time in the company of vampires, but you have no urge to live as one of them? Aren't you afraid of growing old? Getting sick? Dying?"

"I'm supposed to do all of those things. It's natural."

He asked, "But what about Gigi? If your time came, would you leave her alone?"

"So, it would be better to put her in danger while I'm a newly minted vampire, trying to figure out my bloodlust? Besides, if I was a vampire, I could lose her. And then, if by some miracle she stays with me, I get to watch her grow old while I stay the same . . . If something happens to me, do your best to save me. If I rise, don't leave me alone with Gigi until you're absolutely sure I'm in control. Even if she has to go live with Jane and Gabriel for a while."

He muttered, "Good to know that you don't find my condition so objectionable."

I chuckled, eager to change the subject. "You do realize that there are some people who don't believe that the Trojan War actually happened, yes? They think that Homer made the whole thing up to hawk his poems. Can you imagine what you could do to set history straight with just a magazine interview? Are there many vampires out there as old as you?"

"Yes. Homer, for instance, is almost as old as I am," he said, bemused laughter edging his voice.

"You're telling me that the guy who wrote the *Iliad* is a vampire?"

"Yes, and he has been writing all these years. He makes a very nice living out in Los Angeles, working on television shows."

"If you tell me that Homer wrote for *Two and a Half Men,* I will throw myself out of that window."

He chuckled. But I noticed that he did not answer.

"So, where will you go, after you finish here?" I asked.

"What do you mean?"

"Where do you live? Where's your home?"

He pushed an unruly strand of hair from my face. "I don't have a home. I move from place to place, wherever I'm needed. I've lived all over the world."

"Isn't that sort of lonely?" I asked.

"I happen to like my life," he said, rather haughtily. "I

like living in places where a greasy spoon isn't considered the hub of local commerce and social interaction. I like being able to walk out after ten P.M. and know that something besides a gas station will be open. When I'm done here in this wretched little armpit of a town, I will leave and never look back."

"You know, we tried putting 'Welcome to our wretched little armpit of a town' on the city-limits sign, but we couldn't get approval from the Chamber of Commerce," I drawled, nudging him with my elbow as I swallowed the last of my drink. I winced at the biting burn of vodka slipping down my throat.

He burst out laughing, so loudly that I almost didn't hear the muffled knock at the front door. But Cal's ears pricked up, and his head swung toward the stairs. The next knock was louder, more forceful. I peered over at my alarm clock. It was almost ten. Only one person would be knocking on my door this late on a weeknight.

I groaned. I forced myself up from the bed, but Cal hopped up with surprising speed, considering his week. "I don't think you should answer that. What if you were followed home after all? That vampire might have followed your scent if it was strong enough."

"I have a pretty good idea of who it is, and trust me, it's better if I just go get rid of him quickly," I said. Cal's brow folded in confusion. "I just need you to stay up here, out of sight."

"You know, you need to make a decision regarding which areas of the house I am allowed in," he said dryly. "Your indecision is very confusing and could lead to more incidents in which I see you gloriously naked."

I rolled my eyes as I stalked toward the door. I stopped and smirked at him over my shoulder. "Gloriously?"

"Spectacularly. Deliciously. I can come up with several more adverbs while you're downstairs."

"You're just trying to distract me from the continuing crappiness of this day." Rolling my eyes, I cursed the existence of confusing, flirty vampires while I trod downstairs. "I will be watching from up here!" Cal stage-whispered.

"Not necessary!" I whispered back.

"At least look through the peephole before you open it!"

I opened the door, and when I saw that lazy, confident smile stretched across my former lover's face, I groaned. Paul was here now, after months of radio silence, when I had a vampire in the house. I must have been a serial killer in a previous life to deserve this. Or one of those people who invites you to dinner but will only feed you after giving an Amway sales pitch.

"Paul." I opened the door, just halfway.

"Hey there, how's my Petal doin'?" Paul said, giving me a sweet, crooked grin. I groaned again. He was using the "I was hoping I could borrow a cup of sex" voice. He knew I had a hard time resisting that voice. He was not playing fair.

The use of "Petal" had me wincing. Gigi would give me hell if she heard him use that nickname, which, sadly, had worked on me once upon a time. Since Cal was staying put, I squared my shoulders and faced Paul full on.

I had to be strong. I had to put a permanent end to this weird thing of ours. I had to keep Paul from seeing the smirking vampire hanging on my stair landing.

"Paul—"

"I've really missed you," he said, tilting his head and giving me a crooked grin. "I've been thinking about us a lot lately."

"Paul—"

"Haven't you missed me?" he asked. "Aren't you goin' to invite me in?"

Why was he not noticing that so far, I'd only said his name?

"This isn't a good time," I told him.

"You've said that before." He chuckled as he tried to step past me over the threshold.

"No," I said, putting my hand on his shoulder and holding him in place. It was a far more effective tactic with Paul than with Cal, since Paul didn't have super-strength. "I can't. I told you, it's not a good time."

He caught the way I glanced over my shoulder toward the stairs. He slid his hand around my wrist, his fingers shockingly warm after my having dealt with Cal for the last few days. My arms relaxed by degrees. "Are you OK? What's goin' on?"

"Nothing," I insisted, stepping back out of his reach. "I told you, it's just not a good time."

"Are you sure nothin's wrong?"

"Fine," I promised. "I'm just working a lot, tired, you know?"

"You always have worked too hard." He chuckled. "I

could come in, make you one of my famous cheese omelets."

"They're famous because they're the only thing you know how to cook." I laughed, remembering the breakfast attempts that had resulted in Cajun-style "blackened" waffles. "And no, thanks. I appreciate the offer, but Gigi's gone out with friends. I've got the house to myself, and I'm just going to go straight to bed."

Paul's eyes lit up, and I realized that I'd taken the exact conversational route I should have avoided. He thought I was about to issue an invitation. Oh . . . fudge.

"Well, that's good news," he said, taking another step inside the doorway, backing me inside. "Because I was hoping we could 'catch up.'"

"Catching up"—another Paul code phrase, meaning "panties optional."

I was spluttering an excuse when I felt a wintry hand slide around my waist. I tensed, and Cal's smooth, honeyed voice said, "As a matter of fact, she's busy at the moment. And if you don't mind, we'd like to continue where we left off."

I turned to find Cal smirking down at Paul. And he was shirtless. Shirtless, barefoot, with the top button of his jeans undone. Between that and my rumpled pajamas, it looked like Cal had just rolled out of bed to see why it was taking me so long to bring back the whipped cream and the padded handcuffs. It took all the dignity I had not to slap my palm over my forehead.

Suddenly, I wished I'd consumed a lot more vodka.

"Who the hell are you?" Paul's tanned face flushed

beet red. His wide brown eyes narrowed at me. "Iris, who is this?"

I stammered. "I—that is—uh, I—"

"I'm Cal." The vampire grinned and slipped his arm from around my waist to extend his hand to Paul. I noticed that he didn't drop his fangs . . . and he had adopted a softer version of our bluegrass drawl. His body language had relaxed, and he seemed to be intentionally moving at a slow, almost jerky pace. He was playing human bumpkin—pale human bumpkin but human all the same.

Looking at Cal's hand as if he'd been offered dead squirrel à la mode, Paul spluttered, "Iris, honey, what the hell is going on?"

"Paul, I told you, it's not a good time."

"You're seein' someone else?" he exclaimed. "But you didn't tell me."

"Technically, I'm not seeing you," I said, reluctantly adding, "right now."

His cheeks flushed, as if he had just realized that this whole thing was playing out in front of a shirtless stranger.

"Paul, I'm sorry."

"No, no." He grimaced. "That'll teach me not to call first, I guess. Really, I'm lucky this hasn't happened before."

It took me a moment to absorb his full meaning, before I cried, "Hey! That's not fair!"

"You're right," he mocked, his hands up in a defensive position. "I'm just a little upset. I mean, it's not every day you come over to your girlfriend's house to find out she's shacked up with a caveman."

I scoffed. "Girlfriend?"

"Caveman?" Cal repeated, equally offended.

I pulled at the door before Cal could lumber after him. "I think it's time for you to go."

"Iris, can we talk about this?" he asked. "Just tell me what's going on."

"Go home, Paul." I closed the door without another look at him.

"Wha—Iris! You call me if you need anythin', you hear?" he shouted as the door swept his foot out of the way. Through the door, I heard him yell, "Hey, jackass, I'm calling tomorrow to make sure she's OK. You hurt a hair on her head, and I'm calling the cops!"

I called, "That's a little bit of an overreaction, Paul!"

"I don't like the look of him, Iris!" Paul yelled back.

Cal turned toward the door, eyes narrowed. I had to hook my arm through his to keep him from grabbing for the doorknob. Weakened though he was, Cal still had all that vampire strength, so my shoulders took the brunt as Cal's forward momentum drove me into the door. I shoved back, hooking my foot around his calf and throwing my weight against him. My hands shot to his shoulders to keep my balance, but my other foot slipped, and I ended up wrapping the other leg around his waist to keep from falling on my butt.

I heard Paul's truck spin out on the gravel of my driveway, the Southern male equivalent of flouncing away. Struggling between his desire to get through the door and my climbing him like a particularly fetching tree, Cal snapped the knob from the door. He pulled it loose and stared at it incredulously.

For some reason, the sight of my big, bad vampire boarder standing in my foyer staring at my broken door-knob like it was an artifact from some alien civilization struck me as really funny. I roared with laughter, bending at the waist until my head thunked against Cal's collarbone. I laughed until big, fat tears rolled down my cheeks. As I shook and keened, I became acutely aware of my legs wrapped around his hips, my weight centered over his zipper. And the more I squirmed around, the more that zipper bulged under me. I watched my tears make a watery trail down Cal's collarbone, down his white skin, and onto my pajama pants. Tense little lines formed around Cal's mouth as he tried to shift me away from his, er, growing problem.

Desperate to quell the silly, girlie giggle that threatened to bubble up from my chest, I pressed my lips together and pinned them with my teeth. Cal was starting to look uncomfortable . . . and tired. Even a man with superstrength couldn't support my weight for any amount of time.

"Kill me now," I grumbled. I felt Cal's head duck closer to my throat. I shoved away, whacking my head against the door. I exclaimed, "Poor choice of words! I don't have an actual death wish."

"Well," he quipped. "I can certainly see why you're so attracted to him. It must be so convenient to have a companion you can stow away in your handbag."

I groaned, swiping my hands over my eyes. "Why did you do that?"

Cal frowned, glancing down. "Well, you're not an *unattractive* woman. It's a natural reaction even for the undead."

I burst out laughing. "No, not your, er, problem. Why did you come out here and act like we—like you're my—why did you make Paul think we were together?"

He glowered at me, but there was no real heat in it. "Did you think I would just stand aside and let you go upstairs for . . . what did Gigi call it, a booty call?"

I poked his chest, his skin cool and silky against my fingertip. "First, I wouldn't have done that with you in the house. And second, if I did, it wouldn't be any of your business. My personal life is personal. This is a business arrangement, not a friendship."

Cal frowned at this, his eyes scanning my face for a long moment before saying, "I didn't like the way he talked to you. His attitude toward you, it's condescending, disrespectful."

"You talk to me with condescension and disrespect all the time," I retorted.

"It's different when I do it. You know I don't really mean it."

"No, actually, I don't know that!" I exclaimed. "You're all over the place. You sneer at me, but you kiss me. You have no attachment to me, and then you're concerned about my well-being. It's very confusing!"

Cal tilted his head, shifting me so that his hands cupped my cotton-covered ass. He gave me a jiggle, his tone teasing. "Oh, come now, are you really that upset? Gigi said your relationship was over a long time ago."

"I do not like being used for your amusement," I spat. "And don't pretend you were doing it out of some urge to stick up for me or protect yourself. What happened to keeping a low profile? Not letting anyone know you're here?"

"Does your Lilliputian ex-paramour have any contacts in the vampire world?" he asked.

I threw up my hands, which caused the support I held against his shoulders to disappear. He adjusted, pushing me against the door. I could feel the warmth pooling between my thighs as I slid down his length. My breath caught, and I braced my hands against his arms. I cleared my throat, searching for a steady voice. "Again with the short jokes."

"Does he?"

I sighed. "No, Paul doesn't have anything to do with vampires. He didn't like that I worked with vampires. He was always worried that I would get hurt. By the way, slumping your shoulders and adopting a hick accent does not amount to a 'human impersonation.'"

"It's worked before."

"It's insulting."

Cal pursed his lip, his eyes twinkling. "Are you sure you're not upset because I made Paul think you're unavailable?"

I jabbed my finger into his bare chest. "You know, I was completely happy before you showed up. My life wasn't much, but it was mine. And when I'm no longer useful to you, you're going to leave. And you'll forget that I even existed."

This would have been a really good time to walk away. But it's really difficult to storm off when you're straddling someone.

I tried to wriggle my way to my feet, but Cal held me fast against the door. He leaned closer, and I shied away. His mouth closed over mine, taking the air from my lungs. He pinned me to the door with his hips, and his hands slid up to my face. His rough, cool palms cradled my cheeks.

He tilted his forehead against mine. "That's what you think?"

Before I could answer, his tongue glided easily over my lips, teasing them open. His mouth was cool and surprisingly fresh, although there was a subtle undertone of copper in his kiss. My knees sagged at the soft, insistent pressure that pulled my tongue past his lips. His hands slipped into my hair, pulling my face higher and closer to his as he pressed me back against the wall. Biting gently on my bottom lip, he nipped and nuzzled down the line of my chin to my ear.

I'd never kissed a vampire before. The lips were firmer and cooler, and the absence of breath against my skin was odd. I worried that I was too human, too weak, too plain. But soon even that thought evaporated into the ether, and every cell in my body fired for the sake of keeping me upright and attached to Cal's mouth.

The slide of cool flesh against mine and the rasp of teeth against my lip were soft and affectionate. He was coaxing a response from me, teasing me into relaxing against him. He pressed a kiss to my chin. His hand slid under my shirt and over my ribs, up to cup the weight of my breast in his palm.

I was trying to figure out how to reach for his zipper in this position when I heard an exaggerated throat clearing behind me, from the kitchen door.

"So, are we still claiming that we're just business acquaintances?"

8

Vampires are wily, seductive creatures. Even if you think you are resistant to their charms, you are most likely thirty seconds from losing valuable undergarments.

—*The Care and Feeding of Stray Vampires*

Cal turned, with me still attached to him like a human barnacle, to find my sister leaning against the frame of the kitchen door, struggling to hide the look of smug triumph on her face.

"At least this time the hair is deserved," Gigi said, gesturing at the tumbled mess on top of my head.

Cal snapped out of his lustful haze and set me on my feet. He carefully adjusted his jeans and fastened the top button. Vampires were incapable of blushing, but if Cal had had the blood flow necessary to tint his pale cheeks, he would have been roughly the color of a fire hydrant. He kept his back to Gigi and seemed unsure of how to stand. Taking pity on him, I stepped around him and stood as a sort of human shield against upsetting mannipple exposure.

"Aren't you early?" I asked.

"Well, where's the fun in showing up when you're supposed to?" she asked. "You don't see nearly as much. By the way, was that Paul's truck I saw pulling out of the driveway?"

"Gladiola."

She blanched at the use of her proper name. "Sammi Jo's grandmother dropped by for a surprise weeklong visit at dinnertime. I had to get out."

I gave her a sympathetic little smile. "The one who tried to baptize you with bottled water?"

"Is that common practice now?" Cal asked quietly.

Gigi heaved a dramatic sigh and stretched across the couch. "Grandma McCuen says I'm a bad influence on Sammi Jo because we don't go to church regularly."

"Well, Grandma McCuen is a closet drinker who lost her car title at the bingo hall. I wouldn't worry too much about her opinion."

Gigi snickered and nudged me with her hip.

"This is Cal, by the way," I said, pointing over my shoulder. "I'm not sure whether you were properly introduced last time."

Cal nodded stiffly. "Teenager."

Gigi gave him a mocking little salute. "Shirtless wonder."

And there we went with the vampire nonblushing again. I would have corrected my sister, but frankly, if she was teasing Cal, she wasn't teasing me. It was like having a human—well, vampire—shield against adolescent disdain.

"So, you're a vampire. What's that like?" Gigi asked, ignoring Cal's indignant glare.

He parted his lips, his fangs dropping dramatically. "Like being a human, only better and for much longer."

Gigi laughed, despite the dental display. And I couldn't help but marvel at her ease with the walking national treasure of Greece. Why was it that my sister cowered when confronted by long division, but bared vampire teeth fazed her not one bit? I supposed that next to SATs, classroom queen bees, and constantly evolving body parts, the undead probably weren't all that intimidating.

Apparently finished with risking suicide by sarcasm, Gigi turned on me. "I'm starved."

"You're always starved."

"Dinner at Sammi Jo's was sort of skimpy. Grandma McCuen believes that girls should be served half as much as boys at mealtimes because boys 'work so hard.'" Gigi rolled her eyes.

"Don't Sammi Jo's older brothers stay home all day playing Xbox and smoking weed?"

"Apparently, it's very hard work." She made doe eyes at me and fluttered her lashes. "Elvis pancakes?"

I pursed my lips, surprised that Gigi was willing to bend her stance on sweets. It must have been a very stressful week at Sammi Jo's. "I thought Elvis pancakes were verboten after the Great Carb Embargo."

She put her arm around my shoulders, nudging my hip again as she jutted her chin toward Cal. "Well, I thought you didn't bring work home with you. Rules were made to be broken."

* * *

I didn't know how Gigi did it, but somehow she managed to get Cal to (a) put a shirt on and (b) join us in the kitchen while I cooked a completely unhealthy late-night snack. He tried to leave several times. His feet were pointed out the door and in motion, but she was just so damn sweet, asking detailed questions about how to heat a packet of donor blood and offering to put it in a fancy wine glass for him, that he couldn't find a way to back out of the room without feeling like he was kicking an adorable adolescent puppy. If he wasn't careful, he'd wake up in the morning to find that she'd painted his toenails sparkly pink.

Scooting closer to me so that he could put distance between himself and my sister, Cal asked, "So, what separates Elvis pancakes from all other inferior pancakes?"

"Peanut butter and bananas," I told him as I mixed Bisquick with milk.

He grimaced as I mashed two bananas and creamed them with the batter. "That doesn't sound terribly healthy."

"Hey, I used to prep the griddle with bacon grease until Gigi started counting calories." I chuckled, stirring peanut butter ice-cream topping into the batter just before pouring three small pancakes onto the griddle. She frowned at me, reminding me that we'd agreed not to discuss her frantic "I can't button my jeans!" episode.

I snickered and blew her a raspberry kiss as I flipped the pancakes. "She also makes me use *light* syrup."

Cal took a sip of the blood. I plated the pancakes and slid them across the counter. He blanched at the sight of the dripping flapjacks. "How does one stumble onto this treasured family recipe?"

I watched as my sister dolloped knobs of butter onto each flapjack, then drizzled lacy loops of syrup over her handiwork. Sliced bananas and more ice-cream topping followed as a final touch. "Gigi's school had a dessert fundraiser a few years ago. And Gigi insisted that we try to make banana pudding for two hundred people. It was hell—sticky, messy, banana-flavored hell. We ended up with half a mashed banana stuck to the ceiling and about ten bunches of leftover bananas. We made banana bread, banana pancakes, banana milkshakes. Anything to get rid of the bananas. I thought that adding peanut butter to the pancake batter would make it even better, because, well, I was flipping sick of banana. And thus, Elvis pancakes were born."

"Hey, you were just starting off. You hadn't grasped the concept of bake-sale-scale cooking yet." Gigi chuckled, spearing a bite of pancake.

Cal's brow furrowed. "Starting off?"

"As my parent and/or guardian."

I beamed as Gigi pushed her plate toward our guest. "You wanna try some?"

Cal shrank back from the plate. "I'm pretty sure those would look disgusting even if I was human."

"They're delicious," Gigi said, her cheeks puffed slightly with syrup-soaked pancake.

"They will make me vomit."

Gigi swallowed loudly and gave him the stink-eye. "Well, that's rude."

And for the first time, Cal actually seemed concerned that he had offended a lowly human. He shook his head and explained. "No, no. Vampires lack the enzymes to digest solid foods, which is part of the reason we instinctually shy away from it. It smells rotten to us and tastes worse. If I were to take a bite, I would be overwhelmed with the scent and taste of something like roadkill, and I would throw it right back up."

"Thank you for describing that. Vomit talk always gives me a big appetite," Gigi said, rubbing her stomach. I burst out laughing, which made Gigi giggle. And as Cal looked on, perplexed and irritated, the pair of us sat at the table and cackled like a couple of hyenas.

"What's wrong?" I asked him as Gigi snickered on.

Cal frowned. "You're laughing at me."

"But not in a serious way. We're just teasing you. You have no problem teasing me when it's just the two of us," I reminded him.

"I guess I'm not used to being mocked by more than one person at a time."

Gigi reached over to pat his arm while stabbing more pancake with her other hand. "You'll get used to it. That's what families do. Families are the people who will always call you on your crap and will laugh at you no matter how serious the situation. Because you know they don't mean it."

The little lines etched in Cal's face deepened. I could

tell that he was trying to find some graceful way to remind Gigi that he wasn't family. He wasn't even a friend, really. He was just the guy sleeping in a tent in our basement. And honestly, I was grateful to him for not just blurting it out, so I said, "I've been telling her she should stitch that on a sampler, but she doesn't like handicrafts."

"Needles intimidate me," Gigi admitted.

Cal snickered, and the little lines smoothed back out. Gigi proved to be quite the conversational buffer, peppering Cal with questions and observations about his vampire status. She'd never met a real "live" vampire before. I'd made sure of that. And now that she was face-to-face with one, she wanted to know whether he fed on live donors, what his sleeping arrangements were like at home, where he'd traveled. It was the best possible way to avoid the postmauling awkwardness. Except that Gigi's questions seemed to be giving Cal a headache. His eyes were glazing over, and the corner of his mouth was starting to twitch. But instead of giving in to his tendency to be grumpy and taciturn, he turned the tables on my sister. He asked about her classes at school, her friends, her previous run-ins with Sammi Jo's grandmother. He basically talked her into the ground, until she was practically dropping off over her plate.

"That was impressive," I told him as Gigi bid us good night and trod up the stairs. "I've never seen Gigi out-talked by anyone."

"She seems to be a level-headed, good-natured girl. I think you're past the worst of it."

I dunked a tea ball full of my own rosehip-and-raspberry tea into an "I Heart My Big Sister" mug. "Worst of what?"

"Adolescence," he said, shuddering. I chuckled. "She's a lucky girl, to have you taking care of her."

"I'll rest on my laurels when she's thirty, living independently, and not working a job that involves a webcam," I muttered, blowing over my tea.

He gave a violent shudder and backed toward the basement door. "And on that note, I bid you good night. I've got some paperwork I need to go over before I turn in at dawn."

"Where are you going?"

Glancing at the stairs, he said softly, "With Gigi here, it would be better if I were to go back downstairs. But I appreciate your offer to upgrade me to a 'family room.'"

That set me back on my heels. He was right, of course. What did I expect? That we would continue what we'd started in the foyer while my baby sister slept twenty feet away? I cleared my throat and tried to school the edge of disappointment from my features. "Do you have everything you need down there?"

He pursed his lips, his eyes shining mischievously. "Well, not everything I need . . . but yes, I'm comfortable. Are you going to be all right? No lingering feelings after what happened earlier?"

Was he talking about my assault by his mysterious vampire intruder? Or Paul's visit and the subsequent kissing? Because one had my nerves in an uproar, and the other was just damned annoying. Now, if I could only decide which was which . . .

Unable to answer that question aloud, I nodded, keeping my eyes glued to the sink full of dirty pancake dishes that I'd resolved to wash in the morning. The awkward silence hung heavy between us, and I wished I could find something clever to say about his technique. But the encounter at his house, the vodka, and the late hour had taken their toll. I was too tired for sarcasm.

He cleared his throat. "If you have trouble sleeping, you know where I am."

I did have trouble sleeping. Exhausted, I tossed and turned, unable to find a comfortable position, the right angle for my pillows. The blankets were too warm, but the sheet was too cool. And there were moments during that lonely time between two and four A.M. that I seriously considered toddling down the stairs to the basement and crawling into Cal's tent. But my apprehension was twofold. First, Gigi would hear me, and the teasing would be excruciating. And second, Cal had me all wobbly and off balance. And crawling into his tent after he'd seen that mortifying scene with Paul, after the way I'd mounted him against the door, felt like a concession.

Instead, I took advantage of the whatchamacallit in my nightstand.

I was not this woman, this ill-tempered, impulsive bimbo who resorted to nightstand candy in the face of a little stress and writhed all over clients just because they happened to be present and shirtless. I was a level-headed, responsible single-parent figure, who had responsibilities and bills to pay and no time for ill-fated dalliances with the undead. Instead of sleeping, I made a mental list of reasons that starting any sort of personal relationship with Cal was stupid on the level of alligator wrestling or electing a member of the *Jersey Shore* cast to public office.

By sunrise, I had a list of 268, including "Stockholm syndrome be damned, you have to serve as a good example for Gigi" and "Vampires do not date 'the help.' They eat 'the help.'" But most of them applied to vampires in general, not Cal, whose only flaws so far were snark and emotional unavailability.

I dragged my butt out of bed, flinging myself out the door at first light without benefit of coffee or refined sugar, and began my workday as usual . . . after a stop at Walmart for one of those tacky Vampire Home Defense Kits.

Vicki Stern, who was used to seeing Faux Type O and Fang-Brite Flouride Wash in my cart, did a double take at the red polyester gym bag emblazoned with a Count Chocula look-alike with little Xs over his eyes.

"It's a gag gift," I told her, rolling my eyes, tossing an Almond Joy onto the register belt. "One of my clients has a weird sense of humor."

Given the way she was yawning, I'm guessing that Vicki's interest waned pretty quickly.

I entered each house that day with liquid silver hidden in my hip pocket and a stake in my sleeve, despite the fact that spotting me with anything like that would have resulted in the loss of my contracts with the Council. I slipped through every front door like a cat burglar, silver spray at the ready, and completed my tasks with my back against a wall at all times. It made work tedious and stressful, but at least I was able to restock Ms. Wells's blood supply without my hands shaking.

I rushed through my tasks, sure to leave the last client's home long before sunset. I came home to find Gigi had gone to study at Ben Overby's. Ben, a classmate of Gigi's at Half-Moon Hollow High, was a sweet boy who bagged groceries at the Super Saver and drove his grandmother to church on Sunday mornings. He had big puppy-dog eyes the color of new moss and dark hair that sort of flopped over his forehead. Lanky, lean, and clean-cut, he actually went to class and cared about what he did while he was there. He was a nice boy, the kind you could count on to show up on time, to call when he was supposed to. You could trust that he wouldn't drop mind-altering substances into your soda if you left it unattended around him. He was not exactly Gigi's type, which ran toward the bigger, jockier, "I could bench-press you if I wanted to" variety. I hoped that Ben's presence was a sign of her having some sort of dating epiphany.

Cal was sitting at my kitchen table, curtains drawn tight against the setting sun, typing something on his laptop. He looked up at me and smiled. I sensed some saucy opening line coming my way. For some reason, "Making any progress?" slipped out of my mouth.

Right then, right to business. No talk of grinding against door frames or slippery fingertips. Internally, I slapped a palm to my face and called myself a coward.

Cal's shoulders sagged under the weight of . . . disappointment? Insult? Hell, maybe he was hungry. I couldn't read this guy if he had bold print on his face. He recovered quickly and shook his head. "I hate to harp on this point, but I still need my files. You're sure they weren't in the front bedroom?"

"Well, I did spend some quality time in that closet. I think I would have noticed a big white file box."

He sighed. "If the Council claimed the files from my house, they will be stored in my office or Ophelia's— most likely Ophelia's, since she wouldn't trust anybody else with it. And there are few items on my desk that would be helpful."

"How could someone who has secret cash and an emergency weekend bag stashed in his kitchen not keep his files on a flash drive?"

"I do have a flash drive . . . at the Council office. I have some digital scans of the important documents saved on my hard drive here, but other reports and some samples were left at the house. If they're at the Council office, I need them back."

"And calling Ophelia to tell her what you need is out?"

"Do you think I haven't thought of that? Do you think it hasn't crossed my mind every waking moment? But I can't do that now, not after you were hurt in my house. Clearly, someone on the Council is trying to hurt me, even if they have to do it through people who are only loosely connected to me."

Loosely connected? What the hell did that mean? I turned my back on him, heating water for a cup of tea. It gave me an excuse not to look at him and ample time to mull over how quickly my thrall had dissipated.

"You can't re-create them?" I asked, rinsing out the tea ball. Cal grunted, which I assumed was a negative response. "Well, I guess I'm going to have to visit the Council office."

"No." He went into the living room, snagged his laptop bag, and rifled through it for some random piece of paper.

"Why not? You didn't have any problem sending me to your house when you needed information."

"That was before—before I thought it was possible that someone could be lying in wait to hurt you. They weren't supposed to be able to do that, Iris. They weren't supposed to be able to get into my house. I had to sit there and listen while you were—It won't happen again. I won't have it."

"You won't have it?" I shot back. "You won't *have* it? Where in your contract did it say, 'Cal the vampire makes all decisions for Iris Scanlon?' Have you ever seen me at the Council office before, Cal?" I asked.

He ground his teeth, which I took as a no.

"And why do you think that is? I mean, I have to stop by the office on a regular basis to collect paperwork, drop off invoices and deliveries. The offices are only open at night. How do you think I conduct my business without being seen by anyone but Ophelia? I'm like a ghost in that place. You spend enough time around people who are hardwired to see your kind as prey, you learn to move quickly and quietly, to stay in shadows and behind doors. I know how to stay as unobtrusive as possible."

"To drop off paperwork, yes," he said, rolling his eyes. "Not to break into Ophelia's desk."

"I'm not going to break into anything," I protested. "Ophelia hates to file. All of her papers are kept in stacks on the table behind her desk. And she's rarely in her office, unless she's expecting me, so it should be easily accessible. And as for your workspace, if your house is any indication, there's hardly anything there. It should be easy to sift through *your* desk, too."

"I said no."

"And that would matter if you were my daddy. But since you're not—Look, the sooner you have your information, the sooner you can finish your investigation and the sooner you can get out of my house and leave my little armpit of a town. That's what you want, right?"

"Not like this, I don't."

"I just want to help. How am I supposed to sit around the house, watering plants and balancing my checkbook, knowing that you've toddled off to that nest of vipers, weakened and not quite at your stealthiest, to get yourself even deeper into trouble?"

"Weakened?" He growled. He hauled me against the wall with his hand gripped around my throat, squeezing lightly. I was pinned by his hips again, scrambling for purchase as I fought gravity and an irritated vampire. I flailed my limbs and ended up wrapped around him like a climbing vine. He glared at me, his fangs down. "This is what matters. Strength. Even *weakened* as I am, I would be able to hurt you, Iris. It has nothing to do with gender or how intelligent you are. Is it better for me to treat you as an equal, as someone with thoughts and opinions and feelings as important as my own? Yes, but at the end of the day, the only way to stay alive is strength."

"What is your deal with walls?" I demanded, shoving his hand away from my throat. He grunted and trapped my wrist over my head. No matter how I tensed the muscles, I couldn't pull away. I was caught, pinned like a butterfly. I hissed out a breath, glowering at him . . . which he seemed to find amusing.

"Why can't you be afraid, like a normal woman would be?" he sighed, exasperated, fighting the upward motion at the corners of his mouth. "For God's sake, you were attacked and bitten by an angry vampire a day ago. Why aren't you afraid of me?"

"Because you wouldn't hurt me."

Eyes narrowed, he lunged for me. I tensed and squeezed my eyes shut, waiting for the inevitable plunge of fangs through my skin, but instead felt a cool, insistent pressure at my mouth. Cal's tongue slipped past my lips to claim my mouth. He kissed my chin, the little indentation above my lips, my throat. I clung to him, clutching at his faded navy work shirt. We slid down the wall, sinking to our knees on the floor.

Cal threaded his hands through my hair, pulling me close, pressing my breasts against his rough shirt. I rose on my knees, giving his hair a gentle tug back as I rolled my hips over the rigid bulge in his lap. He shuddered, throwing his head back as I rode up and down. My heart stuttered as I moved, sending wondering fluttering sparks from my belly to my thighs.

"Is this your idea of hurting me?" I asked, my lips curling up. He dove, cutting me off by closing his mouth over mine, cupping my face between his hands. Swallowing a giggle, I attempted to scoot away, but he anchored me with a hand splayed across my back. He moved my hips in a circle, trying to re-create that delicious grinding pressure.

I tilted my head, running my lips along the rough line of his jaw, nibbling the point where the bone met his throat. Cal slid his hand up my spine, dragging my bra straps down my shoulders. He nibbled from my collarbone down to the swell of my chest, tracing the top of each soft swell of flesh with his tongue. I ran my fingertips along the ridge of his stomach muscles before dragging the shirt over his head.

My bra clasp snapped, leaving my breasts to fall forward into his waiting hands. At the sight of them, high and firm and plum-tipped, he growled again and shoved me back against the wall. He eased the skirt down my thighs, pulling my legs free. He dragged his mouth along my bare ankle, tickling the delicate bone with the rough pad of his tongue.

Twisting his neck at inhuman angles as he moved, he nibbled my shin, my kneecap, the back of my knee, my inner thigh. When he reached my panties, he pressed a kiss to the fabric just over my heated flesh. He gently bit the soft skin just below my belly button, moving up to take one nipple into his mouth as he kneaded the other in his hand. I sighed, arching into his mouth as I threaded my fingers through his dark hair.

I rolled over him, settling my weight on his hips, easing his zipper down. I shook out of my little cardigan sweater, dropping it to the floor. He dragged his mouth across my throat, nipping on the sensitive area just below my ear. His hands stayed busy, fingers tracing and touching and testing. He slid two fingers inside me, plunging in, twisting up to nudge at that elusive spot inside me. I yelped and threw my head back as I convulsed around those cool digits, whacking my head against the wall. His thumb circled, using the right amount of pressure to tease. He spread my thighs farther, hitching my free leg over his hip as he entered me in one swift stroke.

I pressed my hands against his chest, stilling as I adjusted to him. He glided his hands over my face, his eyes sweeping over me as I slowly squirmed over him.

Cal kissed my lax mouth as he moved again, thrusting gently at first, then building as I angled my hips in time with his. I dragged my nails down his back, sliding my hands around his butt as the muscles clenched and released. I felt the pressure coiling inside and knew I was close. I raised my hips so he could slide against that spot and cried out when he struck home.

He nuzzled my neck, his fangs scraping the skin over my jugular. I tilted my head, offering up my vein, but he trailed kisses down my chest. He worried the skin above my left breast. I guided my hand around his head, pressing his mouth against my neck.

"It's OK."

The whispered words seemed to echo across the empty room. His dark eyes locked on mine, he pressed a kiss over my heart. Then he sank his canines through the skin. I gasped, a pulse of pleasure rippling through me as the blood welled into his mouth. He drew at the wound, and it felt like a pleasantly rough little string linked my core through my belly to the wound, chafing and tugging with every pull. He timed his thrusts with each tugging sip, increasing his pace. My legs tightened around him as the first flutters of my orgasm began.

I thought he would follow. I was waiting for it, for quite some time, relaxed and happy as he manipulated my body into different angles and positions. In fact, I was waiting so long that kisses were exchanged, buttons were pushed, and I ended up falling over the edge again. My muscles tensed to the point of pain, clutching him close as a low purr built in his throat.

Clearly, this was why so many humans were having sex with vampires.

He gave a hard thrust, breaking his grip on my neck to shout out in a language I didn't understand. I tipped my forehead against his as my own release settled over me.

He slipped his hand up my neck and cupped my jaw. I took his thumb into my mouth and sucked hard. Cal yelped, and I grinned at him. He thrust one last time, and I bit down on his thumb. He gave an exaggerated frown and tugged his hand away.

I snickered as he lowered my back to the floor. "Hey, you bit me first."

"Yes, but my bite was finessed and served a purpose."

He growled, nuzzling the mark he'd left on my chest. "Your bite was meant to tease me and to remind me how I've ignored your apparently talented mouth."

"Teasing implies that I wouldn't follow through," I reminded him, pressing my teeth against the skin just over his nipple.

"You're going to be the death of me, woman." He sighed as I wrapped my hand around his neck and pulled him down to me. "The final death of me."

I woke up feeling weak-kneed and sore, which made a certain amount of sense. I'd been drained of blood and treated to a vampire sex marathon. A stay at a four-star spa it was not.

Cal was likewise sprawled on the floor in some sort of postcoital coma. I had ridden him and wrung him out like a sexy washcloth, a thought that made me giggle ridiculously. He looked so big and male, but not out of place, naked on my living room carpet.

Maybe that's why he didn't want me going to the Council office on his behalf. So far, this whole ordeal had been pretty tough on Cal, as a vampire and a man—particularly one raised in his time period. I understood that it stung to rely on me so completely, but honestly, why did he want to do things the hard way? The longer his investigation took, the more people would be in danger. He was at risk, and so were Gigi and I. It made more sense to get all of the resources he needed as quickly as possible.

I glanced at the clock. It was only nine-thirty. Gigi

was still studying at Ben's. The Council office was open until two A.M. And if the blissed-out, slack condition of Cal's face was any indication, he was going to be out for a while. He probably wouldn't notice if I slipped out . . .

Better to apologize than to ask permission, I mused. I could get into the office more easily than he could. And I could probably get back before he woke up. I grabbed my purse from the table and stepped silently toward the door.

I looked down at my nakedness and did an about-face toward the stairs. First, I needed pants.

9

When vampires manage to form emotional attachments, they tend to be very intense. Be prepared
for possessive behavior and sexual attentions that
keep you from contacting the outside world for
days at a time . . . That's not really a drawback.
Just an observation.

—*The Care and Feeding of Stray Vampires*

I decided to complete this mission without the Blue-
tooth. I didn't want Cal to be able to call and yell at me
while I was trying to be all covert. I was, however, carting
the largest "Beeline" tote bag I had, which Gigi assured
me was the largest mom purse she'd ever seen. But the
Council employees were used to me acting as my own
sherpa, so no one batted an eye as I lugged it through the
staff entrance.

The Council offices used to be housed below a Kinko's
just after the Coming Out, before the upper echelons
of the Council were sure that the locals wouldn't torch
their facility. Ophelia had recently moved to a low-key
office building in the Half-Moon Hollow Industrial
Park, between an insurance claims office and a company

that made garden gnomes. Nothing about the building screamed "vampires work here," which meant that few Hollow residents even knew it was there.

I moved down the gray-carpeted hallway on quiet feet. The halls were empty. Vampires tended to be task-oriented, so they stayed in their offices—it wasn't like they had to go to the bathroom. And Ophelia wasn't about to put security cameras in the halls. They might *record* something.

I started to relax a little as I moved around the familiar space. The soft gray walls were blank, undecorated, except for the bulletin board displaying employment-law information. It could have been any office for any company in the country. The only difference was the suspicious "questioning room" down the hall . . . and the break-room vending machine that dispensed packets of donor blood.

I crept past the cubicles of the "underlings," the lowest of vampire administrators who handled meaningless paperwork and ordering office supplies. In general, they were newer vampires who were either desperate to move up in the Council hierarchy or had done something to publicly embarrass the undead community. There were four of them jammed into the little office, which I suspected was Ophelia's way of winnowing her employees down to the strongest and most cunning.

Cal said that his office was the last on the left in the "visitors" wing for vampires on temporary assignments. It was locked, but Cal was helpful enough to leave his keys in his laptop bag. I popped the door open and snapped it quietly shut behind me.

Even in the dark, I could see that Cal's office was devoid of personality. There was nothing but a desk, a desktop computer, and a stack of file folders. I flicked on the desk lamp and reached under the lip of the top desk drawer, where there was a flash drive duct-taped to the underside of the desk. I tucked that into my shirt pocket. The file folders went into my tote bag. There were some sample vials and few other odds and ends that I thought he would need, so I snagged them, too.

I turned off the lamp and listened at the door, then eased into the hallway. Cal's office was the easy part. Ophelia's office, the last door on the end of the hallway? Not so much. She rarely sat at her desk, but knowing my luck, she was having some sort of meeting in there, and I was going to interrupt a PowerPoint presentation on vampire recycling efforts.

I stood outside the door, my hand on the knob, debating whether I should go in. Did Cal really need those files?

"Suck it up, Scanlon," I said to myself, sighing. "You've come this far."

I stepped inside and once again was unnerved by the number of Hello Kitty accessories Ophelia had, from the stapler to the mousepad to the phone. It never failed. Even after working with vampires for years, this setup was the creepiest thing I'd ever seen.

Shuddering, I crossed the room and slid into Ophe-

lia's black captain's chair. I'd never seen her desk from this
angle. I glanced at her computer . . . Hello Kitty glared at
me from the screen. The only thing that didn't fit the bizarre theme was a small portrait of a sweet little girl with
gray eyes and golden curls. Her cheeks were as white
and smooth as ivory. She was wearing a little red sweater
and a plaid dress. One adorable little ringlet hung in the
middle of her forehead. But either the artist hadn't liked
the little girl, or he was really bad at painting eyes. They
were cold, calculating, a patch of ice on a lonely country
road, waiting to trip up unsuspecting prey. I shook off
the little shiver that rippled up my spine.

I turned to the stacks of file folders neatly arranged
on the table behind Ophelia's desk and narrowed down
which of her "file piles" I needed. I found files marked
"Calix" and "Blue Moon Incidents." I pulled out the
small, portable scanner Gigi had given me for Mother's
Day the year before. It was one of those digital wonder
devices meant to save space by eliminating the need for
paper records. You moved the wand over the document,
and it quickly scanned a copy into a memory card.

Gigi had run out of good gift ideas for me sometime
around eighth grade.

I methodically copied each page, placing them back
in order so they wouldn't seem rifled through.

Hearing a thump down the hall, I froze. I heard a muffled male voice and then a closer thud. I tried to shuffle
the folders into the right order, but my hands wouldn't
move as fast as I needed them to. I stood and moved
away from the desk. Scanning the surface, I looked for

anything out of place. I heard another thud, and the voice was farther away this time, fainter. My hands seemed to relax, to still, and I was able to draw my tote over my shoulder.

And when I turned, my bag knocked another pile of files off the table.

"Shoot!" I hissed, falling to my knees to gather the dropped papers. They were neatly stapled and clipped, so it wasn't difficult to sort which papers went into which folders. I found another file folder marked "Blue Moon, Analysis" and "Vee Balm—Testing." Another file was marked "Calix."

On the bottom of the stack, in the very last folder, marked "Beeline," was a neatly typed dossier. I read the top page aloud: "*Iris Scanlon, 29, owner of Beeline daytime concierge service. Owns home and acreage at 9234 Olivet Drive. Marital status: Single. Children: Custody of a minor sibling, Gladiola, age 17. No clear religious ties. Debts . . .* What the hell is this?"

I skimmed over the handful of pages, which included a credit report, my college transcripts, my (blank) criminal record, my personnel history with the Council, and a picture of me unloading blood from the Dorkmobile. The final page was labeled "Observations."

No good could come of reading that.

My hands shook as I closed the folder. Cal knew me. Or at least, he knew about me. All of those questions he'd asked me about Gigi, my parents, my background—he'd already known the answers. But for some reason that I couldn't begin to fathom, he'd pretended otherwise. From the moment I found him on the floor, he'd been lying to me.

Why? Was he testing me? Playing with me? Was my personality profile be so boring that he simply forgot who I was? I glared down at the folder in my hand.

"Screw it." I whipped the folder open again and flipped to the final page, where I saw Cal's now-familiar bold block handwriting. I huffed an unsteady breath before reading: *"Observations: No lasting romantic attachments per Ophelia. Dress: Conservative to the point of chastity belt. Spinster? Lonely? Financially unstable. Looking for an escape from sad little life? Likely starving for any sort of attention, male or otherwise. If confronted, turn on charm. Not a threat."*

My mouth went dry. My throat was too swollen and tight to swallow the lump growing there. Is that what he really thought of me? Is that what he'd been thinking of me the whole time? Was he laughing at me, sneering inside at the poor, pathetic loser he could manipulate with a few flirty suggestions and a pity lay?

Biting my lip, I willed away the hot tears gathering at the corners of my eyes. At least Paul only showed signs of emotional indifference. With Cal, I'd slept with a man who seemed to disdain me actively before even meeting me.

"You will not cry in the middle of the Council office," I ordered myself with a growl. "You will not cry here. You will not cry in the car. You will finish up here, go home, and shove a stake up his ass. Sideways."

Boiling rage, like lava rising from the pit of my stomach, consumed every cell in my body. It was comforting or, at least, more comfortable than the crushing weight of self-doubt. How dare he? How dare he make those "observations" about me without even meeting me? What was he basing this on? Secondhand accounts from Council officials? Had he watched me from a distance like some creepy stalker? Because using a telephoto lens was a great way to sketch someone's character. And my clothes were not *that* conservative!

Grinding my teeth, I had shoved the file folder into my bag, followed by the scanner, when I heard a voice outside the door. Terror replaced my righteous spinsterly anger.

Yeah, I was going to have a hard time letting that one go.

Ophelia was berating some poor underling for "not knowing her ass from the sparse collection of cells between her ears." I scrambled to restack the files on the table. Should I hide? Should I try to crawl under the desk?

I slipped around the desk to the black leather armchair decorated with zebra-striped pillows. I dropped the tote on the floor and crossed my legs, as if I'd been waiting patiently. I concentrated on my breathing, trying to slow my pulse.

Please don't let me be sweating right now. Pit stains would both tip off and offend Ophelia.

The door clicked open behind me, and I turned, smiling as Ophelia walked through.

She arched an eyebrow. "Iris, we didn't have an appointment."

Reaching carefully around the scanner, I pulled the shoe-box-sized carton out of my tote. I smiled, easily feigning excitement thanks to nervous energy. "I know, but I couldn't wait to drop off the Clarenbault!"

For a moment, an honest expression of delight passed over her eyes. She looked like the schoolgirl she pretended to be. She held out her hands and took the box from me, opening it to find a sweet-faced porcelain princess in an intricately embroidered peacock-blue gown.

"Oh, she is a beauty." Ophelia sighed. "I am very pleased, Iris."

"Wonderful, but I'd be more comfortable if you didn't look at the receipt while I'm in the room."

She smirked at me, crossing her office to sit in her desk chair. "You know what I find interesting about you, Iris?"

"My puckish sense of humor?" I suggested, my voice cracking slightly on the last syllable.

She tilted her head, resting her chin on her hand. She eyed me, her gray eyes twinkling with some mischievous glee. "You've never asked why I ask for dolls and toys and frilly dresses."

I cleared my throat and answered shakily, "I figure that's your business."

"You're not wrong," she said, glancing down at the framed portrait. "You have a sister, yes? Gladiola. How old is she now?"

"Seventeen going on forty," I muttered, grateful to have something to think about besides the numerous ways I could kill Cal and get away with it. The sideways ass-staking was definitely in the lead.

She snorted. "You have no idea how apt that description can be. I have a sister, too. Georgina. I was nine years older."

My brows rose. Did she say "have"? I peered at the gray-eyed little girl in the portrait but decided it was in my best interest not to comment.

Ophelia continued, "Our parents brought us over on one of the crossings just after the *Mayflower*. It was miserable. Hot, cramped, and smelling to high heaven. At night, I would go aboveboard just to get a breath of fresh air while everybody else was asleep. And I found that there was a vampire stowed away on the ship, feeding on rats and trying to stay under the radar. He didn't threaten me or try to bite. I think he was just lonely."

I sat stock-still, afraid that Ophelia would realize how much she was sharing with me. This marked two very old vampires spilling their guts to me in as many days. Clearly, I had some sort of invisible sign on my forehead that said, "Deposit origin story here."

"When we landed, I expected him to forget me, but he stayed near and watched. I think he knew how hard life would be in Massachusetts. There was rarely enough food. We had to work constantly just to scratch out the barest existence. He turned me before I could die of what was probably the flu.

"I rose just in time to find that Georgie had taken ill. I couldn't stand the idea of letting her be buried in an unmarked grave. My friend and sire, Joseph, ordered me not to turn her, but she was my sister. I broke with my sire and turned Georgie. He had no choice but to take me before what served as the Council in those days. They decided that they would let Georgie live but that I would be responsible for her for the rest of my days."

"And Georgie?" I asked. "I take it she's the proud recipient of frilly dresses and antique dolls?"

"She has beautiful taste," Ophelia said. She leaned forward on her elbows, staring at me. "It's difficult being the older sister sometimes. Making the sacrifices we have made to make sure that our younger sisters survive, if not thrive. That survival may not come in the form we would hope, but we do the best we can."

Cryptic, thy name is Ophelia.

In the face of my blank stare, she frowned, the classic frustration line forming between her downy black brows. She cleared her throat and tried a different tack. "I've always appreciated your discretion when it comes to Georgie's special orders. Very few people know about her existence."

I nodded. "So why are you telling me about her?"

"A show of good faith," she said. "I want to level the playing field, so to speak. You're a person who knows how to keep information to herself. You're someone who realizes how easily misplacing that information could hurt other people. People who are important to you and to the vampire community."

Ophelia shuffled some papers on her desk, looked through a page in her calendar. "Sometimes the things we know can put us in danger, particularly if other people are aware of what we know. No matter who we are or what our positions are, we have to keep in mind that someone is always listening, always watching, so sometimes we can't act the way we wish we could."

I glanced down at my tote bag.

"If you ever need help keeping that information private, you let me know," Ophelia said. "I may not be able to intervene directly, but I am able to prevent you from being bothered by those trying to find that information. You'd be amazed how I can work behind the scenes. It's a talent I think the two of us share."

I nodded slowly. "I understand."

She beamed. "Good. Now, Georgie is mad for a first-edition copy of *The Secret Garden*. She had one, but she put her thumb through the spine."

I shuddered, imagining what this vampire child could be capable of with an actual human spine. I didn't think I wanted to meet Georgie. Ever.

I smiled, a cheerful professional through and through. "No problem."

As I pushed myself to my wobbly legs, a thought occurred to me, a question that, frankly, I was embarrassed I hadn't thought of earlier. Ophelia had already lost interest in my presence and was playing FreeCell.

"Actually, Ophelia, I have a question."

She didn't look up.

"Regarding that private information," I added. She glanced up through her long sable eyelashes, looking vaguely interested. "I was thinking about expanding my services to the Council. I noticed that new vampires get a welcome basket when they arrive in the Hollow. I could deliver them when I drop off the new-client contracts."

Ophelia lifted a brow. "I'm afraid that wouldn't work. The point of the baskets is to give the Council an excuse to make contact with recently relocated vampires. Would that I could assign you the task. The Council representatives take turns making the deliveries, and it's increasingly tedious sending them reminder notes. They try to weasel out of it—shameless, really."

"Really?" I smiled. "Well, that's too bad."

"Yes, the lack of whining would have been a refreshing change of pace," Ophelia muttered.

I stepped away from her desk but turned back on my heel toward her so I could reach the point of this line of conversation. "Just out of curiosity, who was assigned to deliver Mr. Calix's welcome basket?"

Ophelia gave me a stony look. "You mean the client you never met and who no longer contracts your services?"

I nodded. "I was just curious. They left a bit of a mess, and I had to clean it up. I thought you'd want to know."

Catching the potential double meaning, Ophelia clicked a few keys on her keyboard. She frowned. "There's no name on the schedule."

"Well, that's interesting," I said in an intentionally bland tone.

"Indeed," she said. "I'll look into this. Thank you for bringing this scheduling issue to my attention, Iris."

I wrapped the tote handle around my fingers and wondered how soon I could bolt without being rude.

"Run along now," Ophelia said with a dismissive wave of her hand.

Asked and answered.

I stepped out of Ophelia's office, tucking the bag under my arm like it was a treasured infant. I rushed around blind, heedless of whether I would be seen as I ran through the maze of hallways. I mulled Ophelia's revelation, worrying it like a loose tooth. Cal said that the tampered blood was delivered to his house before he arrived, which was clearly a break in the usual Council protocol. If Ophelia could track down who was assigned to the task, maybe we could figure out—

I ran smack into a wall of cold, unyielding man, bouncing off of him and into a wall.

I let out a stunned huff as I pitched forward. My nose was pressed into a stiff suit jacket that smelled of woodruff. The scent made me want to gag, reminding me of something unpleasant. I shook my head, rubbing gingerly at the spot that had whacked against the wall.

Peter Crown glared down at me, his hands curled around my arms in an iron grip. "I suppose it's too much to ask you to show some decorum when it is absolutely necessary for you to be here?"

I nodded, looking down at my shoes. As angry and upset as I was, now was not the time to show an inordinate amount of spine. "Yes, sir."

"Why are you here, anyway?"

I shrugged, and his hold on my arms tightened. "Just checking in with Ophelia."

He sniffed. "I never have understood why she lets you gallivant around this office like it's your own personal Chuck E. Cheese's."

A smarter person probably wouldn't have laughed at that.

"While our fair leader seems to think of you as some sort of pet, please remember that the rest of us expect a minimum of comportment. I would hate for you to stumble into a situation that you can't handle. *Ophelia* would very upset if you got hurt."

As soon as they landed, the words chilled me to the bone. I *had* stumbled into a situation where I'd gotten hurt—recently, in fact. Did Mr. Crown know about that, or had he just made an unfortunately timed conversational gaffe?

He rolled his eyes at my nonresponse and pointed an imperious finger toward the nearest exit. "Leave now, before you manage to topple some lesser vampire, you silly thing."

I nodded again, scurrying toward the back door with Cal's files cradled safely against my chest. *Slow down,* I commanded my legs. Running would make me seem guilty and frightened. The fact that I was guilty and frightened was neither here nor there. I needed to get home, to process Ophelia's cryptic suggestions and Mr. Crown's derisive, yet insightful, insults.

I stopped, glancing back to see if Mr. Crown was still

watching me. But he was gone, off to cow some other human with his undiluted contempt. Was it wrong to wish spontaneous combustion on someone? What if you only wished the flames to affect one area of the body, say, the zipper of his pants?

Still wrong, I supposed.

Probably.

I really needed some M&M's.

10

We cannot emphasize enough our warnings against trying to get vampires to share their feelings.

—The Care and Feeding of Stray Vampires

Despite the fact that she'd been "studying" at Ben's, Gigi was sitting at the kitchen table, her homework spread around her, when I walked through the door. Cal was sitting with her, holding a case file in one hand while he argued with her about the known facts of the Trojan War. The vampiric target of my wrath was indignantly rejecting Gigi's textbook's assertions that Helen's "abduction" led to the war. When Gigi called Helen "the face that launched a thousand ships," Cal was downright offended.

"Helen was acceptable," he insisted. "Nothing more. Personally, I thought my own wife was prettier, but I might have been biased. Helen was a spoiled, silly girl who was unhappy with the way her fate had twisted. Honestly, she wasn't that important in the grand scheme of things. Agamemnon would have used any excuse to attack Troy. A perceived insult to his family honor was a convenient ploy. Humans love attaching sweeping romantic notions to history, because they need to see order in it, reason. The truth is that events that shape history are rarely black and white, reasonable. They rarely make sense until we can see them in hindsight."

Gigi was doing her Pied Piper thing, leading Cal deeper into the conversation without his realizing it. I really had to figure out how she did that. "How close were you?"

"What, to the machinations of war?" he asked. "I was a common soldier, but my captain, Palamedes, helped organize the troops in the early days. I was clever and loyal, so he trusted me with errands and messages and to guard his back on the field. So I was witness to hundreds of bizarre little dramas. You see, Menelaus demanded that all of Helen's old suitors fulfill their oaths that they would assist him in defending her honor. Removed from the lure of Helen's pretty face, those suitors had regained their senses, and many of them had no desire to join his fight. Odysseus pretended to be insane until my master tricked him into admitting that he was sound. The king of a small Cyprian kingdom promised Agamemnon fifty ships for the Greek fleet, and he provided them—but only one was a real vessel, commanded by his own son. The rest of his armada consisted of clay toys."

"And did the Trojans really fall for the wooden-horse gag?"

"Nearly ten years later, yes. And it wasn't a gag. There was a horse, a small one, beautifully carved from a single tree. And it was left outside the Trojan gate, surrounded with the entire army's store of wine. Believing that we'd abandoned the field in despair, the Trojan army used it for their celebration, and after they'd drunk themselves into oblivion, the gates were rather easy to overtake."

She frowned. "I feel like everything I know about history is a lie."

"Most popular history is. It's all very romanticized and clean. Real life is very rarely like that. It's hard to spot the real heroes, the real villains."

"Well, you can hardly expect them to walk around wearing name tags," Gigi muttered. Brightening, she grinned at him and added, "I'm so going to ace this AP history essay."

Cal scratched his chin in an effort to cover the fond little smile quirking his lips. *Do not be dissuaded by someone else potentially appreciating Gigi as much you do,* I told myself. *He is a bad man who thinks you're a desperate, horny loser. Granted, he's only wrong on one count . . . Never mind which one it is.*

Moving on.

"Is it considered cheating to use a witness to the historical event as a source?" I asked. Cal gave me a little nod of greeting, which I returned with a cold stare.

"Not if we don't tell anybody, it's not," Gigi singsonged.

I held up a takeout box from Pete's Pies. My sister's face lit up with delight, and she lunged for me.

"Pepperoni and pineapple?" she cried, opening the box and doing a happy dance.

"That sounds revolting." Cal shuddered.

"It is," I assured him dryly.

"Iris always orders plain cheese," Gigi told him, halfway through her first slice. "Booooo-ring."

"I need to talk to you," I said, while Gigi dragged plates and cups out of the cupboards.

"Oh, I need to talk to you, too." His expression shifted to livid while my sister's back was turned. "Gigi, would you excuse us?"

"Sure," she said, waving us away as she returned to her pizza.

Cal's fingers wrapped around my arm just as my fingers caught my tote bag. He dragged me down the hall to my bedroom and shut the door behind us. Given my current mood, I rather welcomed the manhandling. It gave me an excuse to stomp on his toes. He grunted and lost his grip on my arm, spinning me rather unceremoniously toward the bed. I bounced off the mattress.

"Have you lost your mind?" he demanded. "You took off without a word, without waking me up. Do you know how stupid that was?"

I crossed my arms, meeting his rage with stone-faced indifference.

"Let's not even explore how humiliating it is to be awakened naked, on the floor, by the screams of a hysterical teenage girl, demanding to know *why* I'm naked and what I've done to her sister. Or the fact that I had to comfort said hysterical teenager and assure her that I had not, in fact, murdered you but had no clue where you were or when you would be home—all the while unable to reach my pants because they were across the room. But for now, let's focus on the fact that despite my telling you not to out of concern for your well-being, you went to the Council offices anyway! I won't allow it, Iris. I will not cower behind a woman's skirts while she runs off to—"

"Get the information you need without incident?" I supplied in a tone so saccharine that it should have tipped him off that his testicular health was in serious peril. I reached into the bag and waved the scanner at him. He scowled at me, so I crossed the room, popped out the memory card, and inserted it directly into my laptop. I opened the drive and selected "Print all files," and the printer began spitting out the reports Cal needed. As I dropped document after document into his hands, I let him absorb the information. I even gave him a moment to be pleased with me. And then I moved in for the kill.

"But you know what I really found interesting?" I tossed the "Beeline" file with my background information at him. The folder flapped open like a drunken bird, the loose sheets hitting his chest before fluttering to the ground. He watched as the papers floated down, eyes widening when he recognized the handwriting. "It's not shocking, I suppose, that you did a background check on someone who would be coming into your home, Cal. But why act like you'd never heard my name before? Why ask me all of those questions about my background? Why pretend to be interested in my 'stupid little life'?"

"Because it helped you relax around me," he admitted quietly. "It made you feel a connection to me. And I was curious about how much you would share with me."

"So sleeping with me, was that just part of forming a

connection? Or were you just curious about whether I would spontaneously combust from sexual frustration?"

"Iris, no—"

"I want you out of my house." I snarled, poking my finger into his chest. "I got your files. You're clearly feeling better. It's time for you to go. I'm sure someone with your resources will have no trouble anonymously renting a hotel room. I don't want you anywhere near me or Gigi."

"I can't leave now," he insisted. "For one thing, there's the matter of my investigation. I need a solid, discreet base of operations. We agreed on a week. I need the full week. And don't pretend that you can do without the rest of my payment, because we both know that you were just scraping by. There's also the small matter of the person hell-bent on killing me. And the vampire who attacked you at my house. You may not believe me, but I won't leave you and Gigi unprotected."

"Yes, I feel supersecure with a lying, untrustworthy vampire skulking around my house."

"You can trust me. You're just a little angry with me right now," he said, ducking deftly out of the way as I lobbed the soapstone rabbit at his head. It bounced off the wall behind him with a thunk, leaving a basketball-sized dent in the drywall.

"Oh, I'm not a *little* angry. I'm fricking furious with you!" I shouted. "The things I told you, I don't tell people. I haven't even told Paul. I don't know what's more disturbing, the fact that you can lie to me and not even change the expression on your face or the fact that I didn't pick up on it. You're a vampire. That sort of thing comes naturally to you. I should expect it. I mean, were you really even poisoned? Was this 'defenseless, wounded vampire' thing just an act so you could con me into providing an off-the-grid hiding spot? You did your homework. I'm sure my profile suggested that poor Iris Scanlon would do anything for money. And hey, if you throw her a bone and sleep with her, she'll be so grateful that she'll let you get a meal straight from the source!"

I pulled angrily at my collar, revealing the bruised bite wound on my chest. His expression shifted from defiance to sympathy, and the look of pity made me exponentially angrier. So I grabbed another figurine, a chipmunk, and slung it at him.

"Where did your mother *buy* this concussive menagerie?" he yelped as he sidestepped airborne statuary. In answer, I threw a fawn and a cardinal and a raccoon in rapid succession. Cal ducked through the field of flying woodland creatures and grabbed my arms. We struggled for control of the final figurine, a matching cardinal.

"I didn't mean to lie to you. I didn't know you'd be—I didn't know that I would want to know who you are. That you would be worth so much more than just safe passage and survival. I know you, Iris. I may not have met you in childhood. I might have missed the awkward adolescent 'flower child' stage. But I *know* you."

Please note that he didn't say he liked what he knew about me.

"I wouldn't do anything to bring you harm," he murmured. "I need to know that you're safe before I leave. Please don't send me away now."

I refused to look up at him. I wouldn't let him see me cry. I'd already done too much to show him how much he'd hurt me.

"You're gone in three days," I said, my voice quiet and flat. "I don't want to see you. I don't want to talk to you. I was safe passage for you. Now you're a meal ticket to me, nothing more."

I brushed past him, returning to the kitchen. Gigi was pretending to work, her fingers anxiously shredding a paper towel. I squeezed her shoulder and gave her a little half smile. Behind me, I heard the cellar door slam, indicating that Cal had retired for the evening.

"What gives?" Gigi asked, nibbling on a pizza crust. "Does our vampire have PMS?"

"I don't understand living men," I muttered, picking at a slice of pizza. "Do you think I understand undead ones?"

Gigi's reply was cut short by the opening bars of "Flight of the Bumblebee." I reached for my phone, not missing the disappointed eye roll she gave me. Grimacing, I hit send and accepted the call, dutifully taking down an altered floral order for the upcoming Carver-Owen nuptials. The bride's living uncle insisted that he was allergic to roses, which meant a complete change of theme. I offered several alternatives, and we agreed to substitute bold pink stargazer lilies. But I completed the call in a brisk, businesslike manner, lacking my usual enthusiastic flair. And it had Gigi nervously chewing at her lip. When I hung up the phone, she asked, "Iris, is everything OK?"

I cleared my throat and gave her my best reassuring smile, although I felt none of it. "Nothing that won't be fixed in three days."

I managed to avoid Cal for two days by waking up after he went to bed for the day and shutting myself up in my room at night. Gigi said that Cal was friendly if they happened to cross paths in the house. Apparently, her finding Cal naked on our floor was some sort of bonding experience.

Cal stayed in the basement and read over the Council reports whenever I was home. I appreciated the effort to make me comfortable, although I still considered whacking him in the face with a shovel if I was ever given an opportunity. Over and over, I considered going downstairs to discuss my conversation with Ophelia and the weird implications of Mr. Crown's comments in the Council hallway. But I couldn't bring myself to walk down the basement steps. I didn't want to help Cal in the slightest way. I didn't want him to have any reason to believe that I'd forgiven him, that I was interested in doing anything *besides* smacking him with the aforementioned shovel.

I was well versed in carrying on detached relationships after sex. If he thought I was going to cling all over him, he was sorely mistaken. I was tired of being jerked around by emotionally unavailable men, pulse or no pulse. Going into the Council office on my own, I felt like I was finally regaining control over my life after a week of uncertainty and chaos. Even though it involved some rather painful revelations, it was a gamble that had paid off. I hadn't had too many of those lately.

And frankly, it was sort of a relief to return to our regular routine. Gigi and I left the house during the day. I was able to return all of my attention to my job and get mired in all of the fantastically mundane details of my clients' lives.

I returned to my garden, forcing myself to get home before sunset or before Gigi came home from school, so I could throw myself into what had been left undone during Cal's crisis. I replenished my candy stores and found new hiding places. I clipped the deadheads from the plants and cut back the climbing roses. I pulled weeds and scattered pulverized eggshells along the flower beds. I threw out long-overdue bouquets from the living-room vases and replaced them with experimental arrangements of lilies and ferns or roses and rosemary. I attended one of Gigi's volleyball games, sold popcorn at the boosters' concession stand, and put up with passive-aggression from the über-competitive mothers of Gigi's teammates.

There were no repercussions from my "visit" to the Council offices, so I was back to remote dealings with clients who didn't want to feed from me or live with me. I delivered cases of blood. I received shipments of tacky Vegas-themed furniture. I sent a cleaning crew to Mr.

Rychek's house to remove the gastrointestinal evidence of Ginger the hypoallergenic cat's distaste for his wallpaper.

The lowlight of my day was an early-morning brush with creepy Mr. Dodd, a lower-level Council employee who was getting a bit too familiar in his communications with me since signing his contract three months before. I made the mistake of arriving at his house too early to accept delivery of a painting that was being shipped on a six A.M. flight from Chicago to the Half-Moon Hollow Municipal Airport.

I'd been working for weeks to secure this painting, an example of Renaissance portraiture that apparently resembled Mr. Dodd's first "lover." Hindsight being what it is, I should have known to stay on my guard around someone who could use the word "lover" without shuddering in discomfort.

The sun was barely over the horizon as I pulled into the driveway on Deer Haven Road. I needed to drop the portrait off as soon as possible. Otherwise, I'd be toting a very expensive, delicate painting in the back of my unsecured van all day. I slipped through the front door as quietly as possible and left the portrait in Mr. Dodd's bedroom closet, as agreed. He wasn't in the room, which wasn't unusual. Most older vampires were unaccustomed to the idea of sleeping in a bed, so they created little light-tight cubbyholes elsewhere in their homes.

The house was quiet and still, darkened by sunproof shades. I hooked a left through the kitchen to check on Mr. Dodd's blood supplies. I was almost to the front door when a hand shot out from the hallway and caught my arm.

I shrieked, yanking my arm back, but the grip was too strong. I was pushed back into the kitchen, against the counter, the handle of the utensil drawer digging into my back. I hissed in pain, knowing that it would leave a bruise. The stove light popped on. In front of me stood a tall, lanky vampire with shaggy dark blond hair. He smirked down at me, sizing me up and down with cold blue eyes before drawling, "So, you're the busy little bee who keeps me fed."

"Iris Scanlon, Beeline. I hope you're Mr. Dodd." I managed a prim professional smile while I gave a final tug on my arm. He finally loosened his hold but stepped even closer, cornering me against the counter.

"I have been very pleased with your . . . services," he said, his eyes sweeping down meaningfully. "I'm thinking I'm going to have to expand my contract. I'm going to need more of your attention."

I had a can of silver spray in my pocket. As creepy as he was, Mr. Dodd hadn't done anything to deserve a face full of corrosive chemicals. So far, he was just displaying the oily, overaggressive charm that came as second nature to vampires who'd had one too many human groupies tell them how mysterious and powerful and seductive they were. They got used to playing women a certain way and couldn't seem to break out of that role in everyday interactions.

He was like a vampire peacock. A lot of show but basically harmless.

Mr. Dodd leaned closer, his hand braced against the lip of a drawer left slightly ajar. I straightened, my arms at my sides, and hip-checked the drawer closed, snapping it on his digits. He hissed out an annoyed breath, and I sidestepped while he was distracted.

"We have several expanded-service packages," I told him, stepping around the decorative, but unnecessary, kitchen island. "Just check the contracts and decide what you're comfortable with."

"If I wanted to contact you directly, how would I do that?" he asked, looping around the island and following me to the door. I snagged my purse from the foyer table. I kept my hand in my pocket, fingers wrapped around the spray canister, because Mr. Dodd's predatory pacing was starting to make me nervous.

"Just call my cell phone and leave a message. Or you can e-mail the address on the card."

He'd sped around me by the time I reached the front door, stepping in front of me as I wrapped my free hand around the doorknob. He smirked, his voice low and deliberately sultry. "And if I wanted something special? Something more personal?"

"Call my cell phone and leave a message or send me an e-mail," I repeated.

He leaned his weight against the door, leaving me to tug futilely at the handle. "But what if I want to see you in person?"

"I don't do that." I grunted, pulling harder on the door. Because clearly, this whole door situation had nothing to do with his vampire strength. I just needed to pull harder.

"But you're doing that right now, aren't you?" he said, leering down at me.

"I don't normally."

"I'm the first vampire client you've met?" he asked, eyeing me carefully.

"You're the first vampire I've seen in months," I lied, smiling pleasantly. "I tend to keep daytime hours. If you'll excuse me, I've finished here. It's time for me to leave."

He ignored me, moving closer and closer with every passing second. The doorknob pressed into my back as I strained away as far as possible. "You smell just mouthwatering. Hasn't anyone ever told you that?"

A frisson of fear bubbled up in my throat. As a matter of fact, someone *had* told me that, at Cal's house, just before he sank his fangs into my neck.

I cleared my throat, breathing carefully out of my nose. "No, actually, no one has ever told me that."

"Do you have any plans later?" he asked.

Yes, I planned to introduce him to the joys of a colloidal silver facial in about four seconds. Four seconds counted as later, right?

"I'm leaving. Now."

He chuckled. "You think so?"

Dodd slithered into the space between me and the door. He smirked down at me, his face alarmingly close to mine. His lips parted, and he leaned down, either to kiss me or to sink his teeth into me.

Stepping to the side, I jerked the door open and let the weak morning sunlight flood the little entryway. Stumbling back into the shaded living room, he seemed amused by my antics. His lips curled back in a leer as he dragged his gaze up and down my form. "Oh, you are an interesting little thing, aren't you? I'll be in . . . touch, soon."

Just before slamming the door, I shot back, "Consider our contract canceled."

I ran to my car, hands shaking as I tried to stick the key into the ignition. I leaned my head against the steering wheel and took a few deep breaths. What was wrong with me? Why hadn't I just shot that moron in the face with silver spray and run out of there? Was I so afraid of losing business that I was willing to put myself in danger to keep some psycho happy? It was time to reevaluate my business model.

What exactly was the protocol here? Should I call Ophelia to complain about Dodd's inappropriate behavior? Should I mention that based on the "mouthwatering" comments, it was possible that Dodd had attacked me at Cal's house? Then again, how exactly would I do that without explaining what I was doing at Cal's house after the Council closed it up?

I missed my old life. I remembered fondly when my biggest worries were Gigi getting a bad grade on her Spanish midterm or the looming demise of our water heater. I'd carefully constructed a quiet little life for myself, and it had taken just a few minutes in Cal's kitchen for it to derail. Now I was wrestling vampires in blandly decorated foyers and having angry sex against walls with an ancient Greek boarder.

To whom I was not currently speaking.

Damn it.

I didn't tell Cal about my run-in with Mr. Dodd. First, because I would have to seek him out in the basement to tell him, and I wasn't ready for that. And second, because I wasn't sure whether Mr. Dodd was the vampire who attacked me at Cal's house or just a horny vampire with a poor choice in colloquialisms. But I did call Ophelia at sunset and explain that her subordinate's contract was canceled and why. The cold, steely tone of her voice when she assured me that "the matter would be addressed immediately" made me want to crawl under my bed in the fetal position with a blankie and actually made me feel a little sorry for Mr. Dodd.

That didn't last long.

After I worked the Dodd-related adrenaline out of my system, I could almost forget about everything that had happened in the previous week. Except at night—after I'd gone to bed ridiculously early—when Cal moved quietly around the dark house. I could hear him warming up blood in the kitchen, typing on his laptop. After a few hours of work, he seemed to fall into a pattern of moving between the front and back windows, prowling. I wanted to go downstairs and talk to him, to demand an explanation for his jackassery. But it was so much easier to stay curled in my bed with chamomile tea, pretending that he wasn't there, pretending that I wasn't watching the door to my room for any sign of him outside.

And as if I needed more testosterone-based drama in my life, Paul started calling again. Those calls were the few I was comfortable sending straight to voicemail, but some sick part of me couldn't help but listen to them. He just wanted to make sure I was OK, he said. He missed me. He missed us. He wanted to go out to dinner so we could talk. His voice grew more strained with each message.

So I took on a new mission: evasion. If I could avoid Paul and Cal for the next few days, I could collect a handsome fee, put some distance between my family and financial disaster, and perhaps regain a little self-respect. OK, maybe just collect the handsome fee.

My luck ran out on Friday night. According to her Facebook page, Gigi was planning to leave for some vaguely described "party" after she got home from school. To avert disaster, I came home early, while she was still getting ready. I found that the element of surprise was an essential part of parenting.

I walked into the bathroom, following the roaring of Gigi's high-powered blow-dryer. My sister executed a perfect little hair flip, popping up from her awkward bend with shiny, smoothed locks. She grinned at me, shutting the dryer off long enough to spray herself with a coat of hair shellac.

"What's the plan for tonight?" I asked.

She watched me in the mirror as she coated her lips

with shiny raspberry gloss. "I'm just going to hang out with Kristen."

This caught my attention. Kristen Duffy was a nice enough girl, a teammate from the volleyball squad, but her parents worked a lot and left her to her own devices. Sometimes those devices included the contents of the family liquor cabinet and poorly thought-out photos posted on Facebook. I'd encouraged Gigi to spend time with her other friends, without outright forbidding her to see Kristen. Teenage friendships were dramatic enough without adding a *Romeo and Juliet* element to them. I made a circulating gesture. "And?"

"We're meeting Kristen's brother and some of his friends at the state park for a sort of bonfire."

"Kristen's brother who's in college?" I asked, arching my brow. "Which would mean said friends are also in college?"

She nodded.

"And I take it Kristen's parents won't be chaperoning?" I cocked my head to the left, asking dryly. "I'm sorry, did I unwittingly ingest the enormous portion of controlled substances it would take for me to agree to this scheme?"

Gigi huffed. "No."

"Then you call Kristen and tell her you are declining her generous invitation, because there is no way this is happening while I'm still breathing."

"Iris, nothing's going to happen!" Gigi cried. "I'm not stupid."

"I would never say you're stupid," I assured her. "But

older boys plus a dark, unsupervised area plus the beer I know will be there—honey, you do the math."

Gigi sighed but didn't respond.

"It's not that I don't trust you," I assured her.

"Thank you."

"I just don't trust anyone else," I added, pinching her cheek.

She grumbled. "OK, so I can't go to Kristen's. Can I go out with Ben?"

The sudden change in conversational lanes caught me off guard. That idea came up way too quickly. Gigi never just assumed that a boy would be available to go out. Sometimes she stressed all week about not having weekend plans and then got even more agitated if the expected invitations came from the wrong boys. I shot her a speculative look. "Did you already have plans with Ben?"

She twisted her hands at her waist. "He might have mentioned going to the movies tonight. Please can I go, Iris? He's so cute, and even you would have to admit that he's a nice guy."

I bit my lips to keep from snickering. "So you invented this beer-fueled forest orgy so a trip to the movies with Ben would seem reasonable and innocent. Well played, young Padawan. Very sneaky."

"Well, I haven't figured out how you keep track of my chemistry average, so clearly, you're no slouch, either."

"I will not reveal my secrets until I see midterm reports," I told her. "Tell Ben he has to pick you up here. You know the rule. All dates must be prescreened and patted down. And willing to sign the release form for a background check."

"No!" she hollered. "Iris, no one else's parents make them do that!"

"Well, three of your classmates are going to have to order maternity graduation gowns, so I think we'll stick to my archaic, unreasonable policies. Look, Gigi, I won't ask him for a blood sample. I just want to meet him."

"Ugh, why can't you just be the cool parent figure who wants to be my friend?"

I shrugged apologetically as "Flight of the Bumblebee" rang from my phone. "I bring home vampires. How can you get cooler than that?"

Gigi turned on the blow-dryer, covering the crude response that I could barely make out in the bathroom mirror. I smiled sweetly and blew her a kiss as I answered my phone and took an order for three kinds of bath salts from three different boutiques for Ms. Wexler.

Then I trotted downstairs and ran smack into Cal as he walked out of the kitchen. I rammed headfirst into his chest, bouncing off him like a pinball and colliding with the countertop.

"Mother of fudge!" I yelped, cradling a hand over my aching hip. Cal grabbed my arms to stop my mad ricocheting about the kitchen. My hair flopped into my face like a dense, unmanageable veil.

"Are you all right?" he asked, pulling my hips parallel with his so he could check for bruising.

"Fine," I ground out, pushing his hands away and shoving my hair out of my face. I turned away from him, rummaging through the spice drawer for the package of Laffy Taffy that I kept there.

Cal frowned at my bizarre choice of candy storage. "Why do you have candy there—" I lifted an eyebrow. He stepped back. "Never mind."

Ripping into the package, I stared at the artfully faded collar of his denim work shirt, the same shirt he'd worn the night of the "incident." Its presence wasn't helping with my frame of mind. Somehow seeing it made me really angry for reasons that my rational mind couldn't seem to pin down.

"Is there anything I can do to make the last day of your stay more comfortable?" I asked, my tone flinty. His sable eyebrows rose as I glared up at him. "Leave your bags by the door? Pack up your leftover blood in a doggie bag? Launch you off the front porch with a catapult timed for sunset?"

"Can we go outside for this discussion?" he asked, looking pointedly upstairs, where Gigi was singing some obnoxious bubble-gum pop song with the word "boy" in every other phrase. I nodded and followed him to the backyard. I stopped near the back door, but he continued out into the garden, between flanking beds of fragrant white and purple irises, their delicate, waxy petals fluttering slightly in the breeze.

I let him walk ahead. He would not touch me. I was out of his reach. At least, that's what I told myself. "I understand why you're so upset. Reading what I wrote, it . . . When I wrote those things about you, I hadn't met you," he said softly. "You were just another nameless, faceless human, so small and apparently harmless that I barely deemed it necessary to look into your background."

I snorted. "Oh, yes, it's so much better to make hasty, hurtful judgments about someone you don't know."

"I'm sorry. I'm sorry that I didn't think about you beyond what you could do for me or to me. I'm used to thinking of humans as a means to an end. It's not an excuse, it's just the way it is. And I didn't know you would turn out to be . . ."

His heavy silence started to grate on my nerves, so I threw up my hands. "What?"

He scrubbed a hand through his dark hair, leaving it wild and tousled. His eyes were eerily black in the dim light, no pupils. "There aren't words to do you justice."

"Find some."

"You shame me, Iris."

I frowned at him. "Find some different words."

"Do you have any idea how difficult it is to thank you for going out and risking yourself to protect me, to take care of me? Despite the blustering to the contrary, you are generous and gentle. You have devoted your life to taking care of other people, even when it means giving up what you want. Even when it could mean putting yourself at risk. You shame me. And I haven't felt shame in a millennium.

"The hardest part is that a year ago, a month ago—hell, last week—I wouldn't have cared. If some little human had volunteered to help me, leaving me free to finish an assignment faster, I wouldn't have blinked an eye. If she put herself in danger, well, that would be unfortunate,

but I would make sure that she knew the risks involved
and then let her go on her merry way. I'm objective, logi-
cal, focused. That's how you manage to survive walking
this earth for a few thousand years." He paced over the
grass, brushing past flowers, leaving trails of silvery dew
on his jeans. "But you, you just creep in and—a few days
in your basement and a blissful encounter against your
living-room wall, and I become *emotionally involved*."
He spat the words as if they tasted foul. "You make me
weak, Iris. You keep me from being able to do what's best
for me."

"I'm having a hard time understanding why you're
blaming me for something that isn't a problem."

"This is a real problem!" he shouted. "I don't make
commitments. I don't form attachments. I do not court
locals. I do my job, collect my fee, and then move on to
the next assignment, wherever it may be. That's my life,
and I love it. When this is done, I will be leaving. Nothing will change that. Not even this bizarre hold you seem
to have on me."

"Well, who asked you for a commitment?" I shot
back. "Have I asked you for a promise ring? I didn't have
a commitment to the last man I was with. I 'courted' his
brains out for years. If you feel any sense of obligation
to me because we happened to see each other naked,
don't bother." I turned on my heel to leave, only to swing
back and jab my finger into his chest. "And by the way,
I'm sure it's awfully fulfilling, being able to pack your
whole life into a cardboard box and move from one
sterile condo to the next. So, once you're done here, feel

free to traipse around the globe doing whatever strikes your fancy, living in the moment like some spontaneous world-traveling sex pirate!"

Now it was his turn to put his finger in my face, which was probably a safer option, since I was not, in fact, an angry vampire. "Don't even try to compare me with the Pygmy. What the two of you were doing was not 'courting.' If it was, and he had a single firing brain cell in his head, he would be here right now, not me. You are not the kind of woman a man loves once and then walks away from." He stopped suddenly, staring at me, his eyes narrowed. "Did you just call me a 'sex pirate'?"

"I was hoping you wouldn't notice." I sighed, rubbing my hands over my eyes. "I don't even know what that meant."

A good, honest laugh burst from him. He straightened, gripped my upper arms, and dragged me toward him. He held me, pressing my face against his chest, where I inhaled the comforting scent of leather and sandalwood.

"I don't know what to tell you," I said, pulling back from him. I stepped away, warding him off with raised hands to prevent further contact. "I'm sorry if I interfere with your ability to be a detached, rational vampire. I'm not going to change. If that makes you uncomfortable, maybe you should leave."

"You know I can't," he said.

"Oh, that's right. You have no other options," I grumbled.

"Indeed." He cleared his throat, and all mirth was

leached from his voice. The bluish moonlight gave his face a more skeletal, otherworldly shape. I was reminded of Hades, god of the Underworld, lurking in the shadows . . . I needed to knock off the Greek mythology books before bedtime. "The situation is becoming more serious, Iris. I saw on the news today that there was a fire in a college dorm near Seattle. Four people are dead."

"And what does that have to do with you?"

"I looked up the story online," he said. "The school boasts a state-of-the-art sprinkler and alarm system. All of the other residents managed to evacuate, but somehow four people in a single room died of 'smoke inhalation' and were burned beyond recognition. This is the Council's work. They're covering up another attack. The question is: how were the vampires in this case poisoned if all of the tainted blood was recalled?"

I shuddered, forcing the images from my mind by cataloguing the various chores I needed to complete around the garden. Mulching, weeding, pruning, training. I toyed with the idea of putting a vegetable garden in the far corner of the yard, a particularly important project if Gigi persisted with her threat to become a vegetarian. I could see the rows of zucchini and squash. And, like most of my neighbors, I would never be happy with my tomato plants—

"Iris?" Cal nudged me. "Iris, focus, please. I need more time here. I need to stay off the Council's radar, and the best way to do that is to stay still, to stay somewhere they've already looked for me. Will you let me stay? Until I decide it's best for me to leave?"

I nodded slowly, rubbing my hands over my arms, warming them, despite the balmy spring evening. "How many more times do you think they'll get away with covering up attacks before the human government starts to notice?"

"Not many. And if that happens . . . it could be worse than it was just after the Coming Out. The delicate peace that we've reached with the humans will be shattered. The human press will demonize us. There will be protests and convenient fires that somehow claim entire houses full of vampires. Iris, if that happens, I'm going to have to disappear. No good-bye. No exchange of e-mail addresses. It will be like you never met me," he promised. "Most of the older vampires will do the same. Hell, some of them haven't come out of hiding since the last time the humans turned on us. It would be better for you that way. None of your neighbors would know that you had a vampire living with you. You wouldn't be snubbed by your community."

I crossed my arms over my chest, glaring at him through hair that had flopped into my eyes. "Yeah, that makes a lot of sense . . . with the exception of the part where I will be broke and jobless because all of my vampire clients went underground. Not to put any pressure on you, but are you making any progress?"

"I'm finding lots of interesting little pieces to the puzzle, but so far, none of them fits," he admitted. "I've made lists of possible suspects, of vampires who would be bold enough to break into my home and attack someone connected to me. But the list keeps expanding, and I keep going around in circles. The good news is that the files for Vee Balm have proven to be very useful. Vee Balm appears to be some sort of combination preventive vaccine and cure for the poisoning. The national Council has just completed safety testing and deemed it safe for use. Council offices all over the country will be ordering it in massive quantities, to protect the vampire population from this 'previously unknown vulnerability.' The whole endeavor has involved some significant financial approvals from the international office."

"What's in it?"

"I have been studying this report for two days, and I have to say . . . I really don't know. It identifies multiple botanical compounds. I've been trying to track them by chemical trace, but that's very time-consuming. And it's only helped me narrow down a list of suspects, so to speak. If only I knew someone with a background in botanical studies."

I snorted. "Why didn't you just ask me for help?"

"You made it clear that your door was closed to me."

"And you've never heard of knocking?"

"Vampires aren't used to . . . knocking." He tensed at my side, cocking his head as if listening for some noise in the distance.

I frowned at him. "Are we still talking about knocking, or does 'knocking' mean something else?" When he was unable to answer, I sighed. "Can we talk about this later? I have a teenager to scar psychologically." I heard a car pull up in front of the house. I nudged him with my elbow. "Relax. It's just Gigi's date, Ben."

Cal's face went blank and then drew into a fierce scowl. "Date?"

Cal apparently forgot the part where he wasn't supposed to be seen at our house. He followed me into the living room and stood at my heels while I let Ben in through the front door. Ben stood awkwardly in the foyer, its sunny yellow paint reflecting none of its intended warmth as Cal stood, arms crossed, staring him down.

"Hi, Miss Iris," Ben said, his apple cheeks blushing red.

Ben was tall for his age, but he still only came up to Cal's shoulder. Cal took full advantage of this, glaring at him with the hardened stare that had probably made ancient soldiers piss their leather skirts. Fortunately, Ben played a lot of violent video games, so he was immune to that sort of thing.

I rolled my eyes. Honestly, why didn't Cal just break out a shotgun and clean it in the living room?

"Um, hi," Ben said, squeaking slightly but stretching his hand out for a manly shake. "I'm Ben."

Cal arched a brow, glancing down at the outstretched (sweaty) palm as if Ben was trying to hand him a pair of sweaty gym socks. I none-too-subtly nudged his ribs with my elbows. Cal cleared his throat and finally deigned to shake hands. "Cal."

"Are you a friend of Miss Iris?" Ben asked carefully.

Cal smiled, his teeth white and sharp and not exactly friendly. "A very close friend of the family."

"Oh, well, that's nice," Ben said, relaxing but shifting his body away slightly.

"Tell me, Ben, what are your plans for the evening?" Cal asked, smoothly leading Ben over to the living room and pushing him into the Report Card Chair. Cal stood over him like a mob enforcer in a Scorsese movie. Ben cleared his throat and wiped his hands on his jeans. I stood behind Cal and tried to make calming gestures.

"Um, Gigi made the plans," he said. "I think we're supposed to go to the movies and then get some ice cream at the Dairy Freeze."

"And when you drive Gigi to and from your destination, you will, of course, obey all traffic laws, both written regulations and common sense," Cal said. Ben nodded dutifully. "And you will drive directly to and from your destination, without even pausing along the way?"

"Yes, sir. I mean, no, sir . . . which answer means I won't be stopping to take Gigi to Half-Moon Point?" he asked, flushing even redder.

"I didn't mean to fluster you, Ben," Cal said, clapping a hand over Ben's shoulder. "But Gigi's health and safety are very important to me. Should she come home in any condition other than the one in which she leaves the house, even if that condition is mildly disappointed, I can only say that I would feel very sorry for the young man who let her down."

He bent low and murmured something into Ben's ear. I couldn't hear all of it, but I made out "back roads" and "shovel." The redness drained out of Ben's cheeks, leaving him a sick chalky color.

And suddenly, I was very glad that Ben didn't know that Cal was a vampire. He might have soiled himself.

Gigi descended the stairs wearing formfitting jeans, a black T-shirt with a deep V neck, and a pretty pink floral scarf knotted at her throat. She smiled sweetly when she saw him. "Ben!"

Ben relaxed slightly, as if having one more witness in the room made him feel safer. "Gigi, you look great!" Cal shot him a hard look. Ben stammered, "I—I mean, really pretty. Um, very attractive, in a completely respectable, nonpervy way."

Gigi turned to me, a confused expression marring her carefully made-up face. I shrugged. "You all set?"

Ben's happy grin nearly cracked his cheeks, but I wasn't sure whether it was my sister's influence or the idea that he was getting away from my "friend." Gigi asked, "Can I borrow your gray jacket? The theater's always cold."

I nodded, ducking into the kitchen to grab it for her. I felt a hand close around my arm and yank me back. "Yipe!"

Stupid vampire speed.

"What are you doing?" I whispered, shrugging Cal off as he skulked behind the refrigerator door and watched Ben's every move. The poor kid could hardly produce a sentence without stammering or blushing. And Cal was staring at Ben like the boy was directly responsible for the discovery of karaoke.

"I don't think I like that boy." He growled, glaring for effect, just in case I hadn't figured out his oh-so-subtle interpersonal cues.

"He's a sweet kid," I insisted, folding the gray blazer over my arm.

"He's a teenage boy," Cal said, his dark eyes narrowed. "They're all sexual deviants under the surface. I should know. I was a teenage boy once."

"Thousands of years ago," I countered.

"Times may change, but testosterone does not."

"I'll be sure to write that on Gigi's Affirmation of the Day Calendar." I snickered, closing my refrigerator door and starting for the living room. Cal hooked his arm through mine and dragged me back.

"OK, this is becoming annoying." I huffed, reaching into the fridge for a ginger ale.

"You know, in my time, girls Gigi's age were already married and bearing their second or third children. Girls didn't 'date.' Their marriages were arranged by their families. Personally, I think we should go back to that system."

"Yes, taking away their right to choose whom to spend the rest of their lives with would be a huge step in the right direction," I retorted. "This is so not the subject for you to expound on. No matter what you say, you're bound to piss me off."

"I should distrust any young man who thinks he's good enough to court her." Cal touched my arm again, lightly this time, his voice quiet and steady. "She's a good girl with a sweet disposition. I wouldn't want anyone to take advantage of that. I don't think I'll rest easy tonight until she's safe at home, maybe under lock and key."

I tugged on his shirt, pulling him close and giving him a brief hug.

When he was gone—because he would leave the moment he could; he'd made that much clear—I would be alone again. But for that moment, it felt so good to have someone to share my family with. Yes, he was obnoxious and high-handed, but he was also decent and very good to Gigi, when he didn't have to be. He made me laugh, which was something previous lovers hadn't bothered with. And he listened when I had a good idea.

Of course, he pitched a fit if those ideas put me in harm's way, and he'd written some really hurtful things about me. I was going to have to let go of that if I was going to survive the next week or so. Cal didn't know me then, and now he did. And I think he was aware that if he said anything like it again, he was in for a whooping.

"And if I happened to imply that should anything happen to Gigi while in his care, it would take every law-enforcement resource available in this backward little hellhole of a state to determine what I've done to his body, well, that might just lessen the chance of his doing something regrettable."

"See, you took a nice moment, and you took it too far." I sighed, burying my face in his shoulder.

Gigi stuck her head through the doorway. She snickered and said quietly, "Iris, dismount the vampire and get out here."

I straightened, holding the jacket out to Gigi. "Ixnay on the ampirevay," I muttered, glancing toward Ben.

Gigi smirked. "You know that pig Latin went out with scrunchies and Smurfs, right?"

I warned her, "Easy."

"We're leaving."

"Back by eleven," I reminded her, then cut her off at the first sign of a groan. "Complain, and it will be ten-thirty . . . and if you're not in that door on time, I'll show up at the Dairy Freeze in my bathrobe, yelling your full legal name."

"You wouldn't." She hissed.

"Try me. Now, have a good time." I kissed her fore-head. Gigi snatched the jacket from me, pulling Ben by the collar as she bustled out the door.

"Good night, Miss Iris," Ben called as Gigi yanked him along.

Cal cleared his throat. "Remember what I said, Ben."

Ben flushed red, then white, as he disappeared into the shadows of the porch.

11

You should set up a deadline for your vampire guest to depart your house. Vampires are creatures of habit. Unless you specifically order them off of your couch, they will not leave.

—*The Care and Feeding of Stray Vampires*

"Must you torture the boy?" I asked, turning on Cal as we heard Ben's car engine start.

"Yes, it's a rite of passage," he said, nodding emphatically while I flopped onto the couch. "Your threat to show up at the drive-in wearing your bathrobe was particularly inspired."

He sat on the opposite end of the couch, relaxing into the cushions. It struck me as odd that we hadn't shared this room since his first night in the house. It seemed so long ago that I was staring down at a pale, gaunt stranger whom I didn't quite trust.

I wasn't sure I trusted him entirely now.

I cleared my throat and slipped my feet into his lap, hoping that maybe treating him like furniture would make him less intimidating. "For a teenage girl, fear of embarrassment is far more powerful than fear of consequences. Gigi didn't believe I would do it until last year, when I actually pulled into the Dairy Freeze parking lot twenty minutes after her curfew. I didn't even have to get out of my car. My mere presence was enough to make her jump into Sammi Jo's car and beg her to floor it."

"Were you wearing the bathrobe?"

I nodded, grinning. "Over my T-shirt and jeans."

"You're going to make a fantastic mother someday," he said, chuckling.

"I think taking care of one so early in life may have scared me off of having more. I have a child," I said, nodding toward Gigi's school bag, slung across the foyer table. "I've raised her, just as much as my parents raised me. I've loved her, lost sleep worrying about her, taken care of her when she was sick, suffered through embarrassing but informative anatomical conversations. If that doesn't make her mine, I don't know what would. And at least I got to skip the messy-diaper-and-two-A.M.-feeding phase."

Cal seemed to be mulling that information carefully, so I added, "Now that we've hashed out my numerous issues, what are you doing tonight?"

Cal frowned. "More research. I've been trying to track Blue Moon and its various dummy fronts. Whoever set this up knows exactly how to put up as many paper shields as possible."

"What about the employees at the synthetic-blood plant? Surely they didn't just agree to put experimental additives in their product without so much as a meeting."

"The arrangements were made by one employee, Margaret Rimes, Nocturne's director of product development—not unusual considering it was a relatively minor change to the formula. Her notes show that she met with the Blue Moon representatives at their offices."

"The abandoned office park?"

"Most likely dressed up with rented furnishings," he agreed. "Ms. Rimes seemed pleased with the company's work. Her supervisors stated nothing seemed amiss about her reports."

"What does Ms. Rimes have to say about it?" I asked.

"Nothing. Ms. Rimes died in a car accident a month ago. She lost control of her car. It flipped and rolled one hundred yards down an embankment, then caught fire."

"Let me guess, this took place late at night on a remote stretch of highway? Because it's sounding less and less like an accident."

"Convenient car accidents can solve a lot of problems."

"Later, I'm going to Google how to check my brakes for tampering," I muttered. "Give me the lab results. I had to take a lot of organic chemistry in college, so there's a good chance I'll understand some of it. It might help to have fresh eyes."

"Please, take it." He shoved the files in my direction unceremoniously. We sat there, sprawled on the couch, reading paperwork. I'd broken out several of my mother's books to try to interpret the different lab reports. And then I broke out some Twizzlers, which Cal insisted I put away, because seeing me "orally toy with sucrose-based whips" was too distracting.

I told him he should be happy I didn't go for the Blow Pops.

He made me face in the opposite direction.

Despite this refreshing change of perspective, I couldn't make much sense of the lab reports. The analysis of the poisoned vampire's blood showed compounds I'd never heard of and chemical traces that didn't make sense. For instance, there were healthy amounts of silicic acid and saponins, consistent with extract of lungwort. But lungwort had astringent properties used to treat lung infections. Then there were traces of thymol, a natural antifungal that served as the active ingredient in most mouthwashes. Apparently, our culprit wanted the vampires disabled with healthy, minty-fresh breath.

I could not think of any possible reason for lungwort or balm plants to be used in a poison that was supposed to drive vampires crazy. The chemist who came up with this was either brilliant or brilliantly disturbed.

I flipped to the last page of the report and zoned in on one word. Aconitine. Huge amounts of aconitine. My first botany professor spent three days talking about the elegant "Queen of Poisons" derived from aconite, also known as wolfsbane or monkshood.

Dr. Bailey had been a big murder-mystery fan. He went on and on about the various people who had tried to bump off loved ones and not-so-loved ones with aconitine . . . Victims experienced numbness and tingling in the extremities, and if the dose was large enough, they felt burning pain followed by paralysis, then lung and heart failure. Dr. Bailey used aconite as an example of why we had to respect all plants, even the pretty ones, because they could be the deadliest.

Some ancient cultures used aconitine in battle to tip their spears and arrows, a sort of double whammy for those who survived wartime impalement. Cal should have found this interesting. But he seemed to be concentrating awfully hard on tax paperwork for Blue Moon, and if I interrupted, he might try to explain it to me.

Shudder.

After a few hours, my eyes started to cross over the tiny text. I stood, cracking my stiff neck and stretching my arms.

I wondered if Jane had this sort of thing in her shop, Specialty Books. She had an alarming range of titles, including werewolf relationship guides, biographies of the "real" Sasquatch, and remedial books for poorly trained witches. The copies of *World War Z,* a treatise on surviving the zombie apocalypse, were shelved in the nonfiction section under "self-help." When I asked whether that was a joke, she sort of chuckled nervously and didn't answer.

The problem with Jane is that I can never tell when she's kidding.

"This is all starting to look the same." I moaned. "I think we're going about this in the wrong way. I'm looking up each chemical on the ingredients list to pin down which of them could cause specific symptoms. But botanical compounds work together. It may not be a one-to-one effect."

"What if you looked up the individual symptoms and worked from there?"

"That's a good idea," I replied. "Except for the part where all of my resources refer to human symptoms. I would imagine that vampires are affected differently, since you're . . . um, well, there's just no other way to put it—you're dead."

"I hadn't thought of that," he admitted.

"I am your detail girl," I said, yawning widely. "I think I know where I can get some more relevant books. I could go online, but frankly, I don't want to trust this to some wacko running a blog out of his mama's basement."

Cal growled and tossed his paperwork aside. Under the cursing and muttering, I could make out "clever bastard" and "goddamn invisible." I shrank back into the couch cushions. When he saw me moving away from him, he closed his eyes. He stretched his hand out tentatively and stroked it up my calf.

"Why don't you go up to bed?" he said. "You've been up all day, and you've spent the last three hours staring at chemical nonsense. You must be exhausted."

"I want to stay up and wait for Gigi. And I don't want to leave you unattended, in case you get ideas about ambushing Ben in the driveway."

"The damage wouldn't be permanent!" he protested.

"You're not used to this level of frustration, are you?"

"No," he admitted. "I won't say that the answers I need fall out of the sky into my lap, but I'm used to having the full resources of the Council at my disposal. I'm used to working out in the open. I'm not used to being frustrated. I'm not used to feeling weak and indebted."

"You're not weak." I scoffed, nudging him gently again. He shot me a scornful look. "OK, for a vampire, you're not in top shape. But compared with me, you're still practically Superman . . . or at least Aquaman."

"I noticed that you didn't tell me I wasn't indebted," he said.

"Well, you still owe me about forty thousand dollars."

"Ah." He chuckled. "How could I forget?"

"I won't let you, trust me. You're not the only one who can track people down."

"Why does it sound so intriguing when you say it like that?" He leered at me, leaning closer. I angled away, not quite ready for close contact yet.

Just then, the door swung open, and Gigi came barreling through, flushed and happy. When she caught sight of her sister in some sort of smoldering staring contest with our houseguest, she rolled her eyes dramatically. "Is all of this unresolved sexual tension going to become a thing with you two? Don't make me get the hose."

I straightened, attempting to look like the respectable adult I was supposed to be. I crossed to the front window, where I saw Ben sprinting for his car like his shoes were on fire.

Cal cleared his throat and straightened his shirt, trying to keep some semblance of respectability. "We could have this discussion, Gigi. Or we could talk about the fact that I heard Ben's car pull into the driveway at least fifteen minutes ago." His lips twitched. "What have you been doing all that time?"

Mouth agape, I turned to Gigi, who looked stricken.

Clearly, vampire hearing could be very helpful in parenting.

"Well, I'm suddenly very tired." Gigi pantomimed a huge yawn and broke for the stairs. "Good night, all! Happy straddling."

"You are really getting the hang of this whole teenager thing," I marveled.

"It's all about elimination by escalation." He sighed. "You humiliate them before they can humiliate you. They seek shelter elsewhere."

"Lao Tzu?"

He shook his head, holding up one of Gigi's magazines. "*Cosmo Girl.*"

12

Just because advice comes from an older vampire doesn't mean it's good advice. Sometimes ancient vampires survive on pure dumb luck.

—*The Care and Feeding of Stray Vampires*

Sighing heavily and hauling my butt out of the Dork-mobile, even I had to pause and admire Mr. Marchand's sweeping plantation house. Given that he was additionally immortalized as a Civil War memorial statue downtown, I could only assume that he'd been living there for several hundred years. While Jane's place, River Oaks, was more English farmhouse than Tara, and Gabriel had taken the time to update his place with all of the modern conveniences of rain gutters and aluminum siding, Mr. Marchand had perfectly preserved his little piece of prewar heaven in the true Georgian style—tall white columns, a porch complete with a cupola, freshly whitewashed walls. Except for the elegant little sedan parked in the pea-gravel drive, it would have looked like a sketch from one of Mr. Jameson's history books.

I'd never actually seen Mr. Marchand's house. He usually asked me to drop anything he needed by the Council office. And it was highly unusual for me to visit a vampire's home after dark, but I needed his signature on a Council form ASAP.

Earlier, at sunset, Ophelia had called to inform me of a paperwork snafu in the Council's finance department, where there always seemed to be paperwork snafus. Mr. Marchand was head of the finance committee. If I didn't get his approval on an expenditure form and mail it by the next day's post, I wouldn't be able to invoice the office for about six months of work. I'd actually secured his signature a few months before, but the form listed him as head of the budget committee, which—believe it or not—was a pretty important typo. And the World Council just *loooooooved* to find reasons not to pay their bills based on technicalities. It gave them a sense of superiority over us lowly humans.

Since Mr. Marchand wasn't working at the Council offices, I dropped by his house on the way home from a PTA meeting. Ophelia had said she would have delivered the paperwork herself, but she had plans with Jamie, and this "wasn't her problem." I really didn't mind. I liked Mr. Marchand. He was one of the few vampires I'd ever met who still treated me like a person and not a Happy Meal on legs.

I knocked on the front door but didn't get any response. There were lights burning in the house. And the car was in the drive; surely, he was home.

"Around back!" a twangy, accented voice called. After rounding the corner of the house, I stopped in my tracks, struck dumb by the scope of Mr. Marchand's backyard.

He'd arranged his flower beds in islands randomly floating on the lawn, so that no matter where you stood, there were arrangements of plants at varying heights, creating layers of color on the horizon.

The yard was surrounded on all sides by ginkgo trees, with their delicate green, fan-shaped leaves. They would turn a beautiful, vibrant gold this fall, and I imagined it could be bright enough to look like a sunrise, even at night.

I found Mr. Marchand on his back porch, stretched out in an old cane rocker, reading a leather-bound copy of *The Prince*. He stood, smiling warmly at me. "Miss Iris, how are you, my dear?"

"Very well, thank you, Mr. Marchand."

"What brings you out my way?"

"I'm so sorry to bother you at home, Mr. Marchand. I'm just bringing by the paperwork we talked about."

He smiled, guiding me by the elbow to an elegant little chair. "You're never a bother. Can I offer you something to drink?"

"No, thank you." He sat next to me and used a fancy enameled pen from his pocket to check and initial the numerous lines required for the approval. I had nothing to do but admire the lovely grounds. I rose, examining the line of ground-cover plants that edged his porch.

"I love what you've done with your garden, Mr. Marchand."

He didn't look up as he crisscrossed and signed. "Oh, thank you, my dear. How kind of you to notice," he said absently.

"Clever of you to plant night-blooming flowers, so you can enjoy them. Particularly the night-blooming daylilies, which I always thought was sort of oxymoronic," I said, bending to press the faintly lemon-scented petals of hardy commuter daylily to my nose.

"I have a clever landscaper," he said, his tone dismissive enough for me to know that it was time for me to move the conversation along. "I've never had luck with plants. Everything I touch dies. If I didn't have such a talented landscaping staff, there's no telling what this place would look like."

I ambled about the yard while he double-checked the paperwork. I stopped in front of an impressive collection of rosebushes ranging in every color from white to peach to red. My mind wandered to my mother, and Mr. Marchand appeared at my elbow, startling me. He gave me an apologetic little smile and handed me the sheaf of papers.

"Flowers are such delicate things," he said, plucking a full white bloom from a rosebush and examining the perfect petals. "There are so many things that break them, damage them, take the life from them. There are things out there that set out to hurt flowers—disease, pests, and the like. A smart gardener puts barriers, protections, between the blooms and the things that could hurt them."

Well, that was a random statement. Darn subliminal-messaging vampires.

He pressed the bloom into my hand and held me with a stern, serious gaze. "I enjoy your company, Miss

Iris. You're a nice girl, with pretty manners and a good head on your shoulders. I appreciate what you do for our community. But it's important that you remember who you're dealing with."

I kept my face schooled, still. Was he referring to Cal, or had he somehow heard about my problem with Mr. Dodd? Or was he ignorant of both situations and by some bizarre conversational coincidence had managed to home in on a subject that made me uncomfortable? I gazed at his face, my expression open, as if I didn't have a clue what he was talking about.

After a long, silent moment, he gently patted my hand. "I don't want to see you hurt because of your involvement with us. I know that you're . . . I won't say close, just—familiar, with Ophelia. But if there's anything you need, call me, please."

He smiled, a kind, grandfatherly expression, and then lightly pinched my cheek. I nodded, smiling without any real force of feeling. And I barely managed to escape the house with a potted African violet that he claimed needed to go to a good home.

Citing his plant-killing ways, Mr. Marchand persuaded me to consider taking the plant an act of goodwill to another life form. But I managed to avoid taking the geraniums he said were hanging on by a thread. Overall, it was a fulfilling but confusing visit. I got the forms I needed to get paid, which was good. But I'd broken my own rules about vampire visitation to do it, which was bad.

Mr. Marchand was on my side. He was trying to give

me helpful advice, but I couldn't tell if he was telling me to withdraw from the Cal situation or from the vampire world entirely. And he was a plant murderer but still had a nicer garden than mine. So, in addition to everything else going on, I had yard envy.

Sick of researching blind, I stopped by Specialty Books on my way home. I loved Jane's quirky little shop, which had belonged to Gilbert Wainwright, Jane's deceased employer. Working at the store was Jane's first job after she was turned, and when Mr. Wainwright willed the shop to her, she'd expanded, remodeled, and turned the chaotic rat trap of an occult bookstore into the little gem of oddball charm that it was today.

The scent of coffee and old paper greeted me at the door. I passed the antique leaded-glass and maple counter with its old-fashioned register and a large display of Jane's cornerstone product, *The Guide for the Newly Undead*. The wide coffee bar matched the shiny maple shelving system, Jane's pride and joy. Any customer could walk into the store and find any book on any subject—from Sasquatch to Santeria—purchase it, and then safely navigate his or her way back out of the store. None of these conveniences was encouraged by the previous system, according to Jane.

The interior was a mix of the mystical and the quirky. I had searched the Home Depot high and low, but I'd never been able to find that same restful shade of midnight blue on the walls. Andrea Byrne-Cheney, Jane's assistant manager, had mixed several different colors to come up with it, then added a sprinkle of twinkling silver stars to keep the place from being "too serious."

A handful of customers sat in comfy purple chairs near the back, arguing over John Harwood's *The Ghost Writer*. Jolene sat at the bar, sipping a cappuccino and wolfing down a croissant the size of my head. Andrea was mixing synthetic blood in some sort of frozen coffee concoction, which I did not think would work out well. Jane sat at the counter balancing ledgers, exuding that typical newlywed glow, all dewy and bright-eyed and annoying. Her face lit up with a happy grin when she saw me, and she circled around the counter to envelop me in a hug.

Yep, newlywed vampires were huggers.

"What brings you here?" she asked. "Oh, my gosh, did I not pay this month's invoice?"

"Nope, we put you on automatic withdrawal, remember? After you made up for one missed payment with two payments, duplicated by Gabriel's payment, because he didn't think you paid me."

"We're still working on the joint-accounts thing," Jane muttered sheepishly.

I chuckled. "Those sorts of mistakes I can handle." I pulled out several extra-large sachets stuffed with rosemary and lavender from my garden, combined with bay leaf, cloves, and cedar chips. "I've been meaning to bring these by. You said you needed something extra-powerful to cover up the smell of Jamie's sneakers?"

"I do not understand how someone who technically does not sweat can have swamp feet!" Jane exclaimed, clutching the sachets to her chest like a shield. "It's starting to permeate the second floor!"

I squeezed her shoulder as she pressed the sachets to her nose like they were an olfactory lifeline. "Welcome to life with a teenager. Dealing with weird smells will occupy a good portion of your time."

Jane stashed the little cloth parcels behind the bar while Andrea brought the espresso machine roaring to life. "I was afraid you were here to give me more cryptic messages about my food supply and then not follow through with an explanation. You know unanswered questions drive me nuts," Jane said.

"I'm sorry about that," I told her.

"Thanks for calling me and including me in your one-woman recall, jerk," Andrea muttered.

"I told Jane to call you, too!"

"You know she doesn't remember anything until she's awake for at least an hour!" she grumbled. "Don't play with my well-being all willy-nilly."

"I'm sorry."

"Well, are you here to tell me why I tossed out an entire case of Faux Type O, other than that it amused you and Ophelia to jerk me around?" Jane asked.

"No." I mouthed a quick thanks as Andrea set one of her delicious cappuccinos in front of me.

"Oh, did you try to attend another chamber meetin'?" Jolene snickered. "Because I want to hear about it."

"I had to try it once!" I insisted. "Despite your many,

many . . . many warnings. I'm a local business owner. I had to at least try to join the Chamber of Commerce."

Much like Jane, I had been summarily tossed out of the Half-Moon Hollow Chamber of Commerce, a semi-productive civic group infested by perky women named Courtney. But while Jane had lasted several months, I was asked to leave after one meeting. When the Courtneys found out that my business was catering to vampires, they couldn't get me out of the meeting house fast enough. In fact, after the Head Courtney found out that I was a friend of Jane's, they'd done everything they could to cause problems for me in town. I'd tolerated their attempts to get my business license pulled. I'd even laughed when they tried to get my suppliers to black-list me . . . because they didn't really know my suppliers well and ended up offending them and rallying them to my side. But when they approached the teachers at Gigi's school to determine whether my sister was a "disruptive influence" on the other kids, Jane visited the Chamber office . . . and would not tell me what was said. All I knew was that Head Courtney couldn't look me in the eye when I saw her at Walmart.

"I'm not one to say I told you so." Jane sighed. "But I'll sing it. I tooooooold you soooooo!" She finished on one knee, fanning her fingers dramatically.

"The jazz hands are completely unnecessary," I told her. "Especially since I am here as a customer. Do you have any books on plants and the supernatural?"

"First of all, jazz hands on a vampire are rare enough to be appreciated under any circumstances," she said, popping up from her position at a speed that would have caused permanent damage in a human. "And yes, we have a whole section on gardening." She led me to the front of the store, between an old rack of *Tales from the Crypt* comics and a large framed picture of Jane and Mr. Wainwright at the old counter. Jane had added several "family" photos in the last year, spread here and there throughout the shop with a careless touch, giving it a feeling of familiarity. There was a picture of Jane and her human best friend, Zeb, who also happened to be Jolene's husband. Another showed Andrea and her husband, Dick Cheney, arguing over the espresso machine, which Andrea protected with the fierceness of an agitated mother bear. There was a group shot from Andrea's annual "Ugly Christmas Sweater" Holiday Party. This one included Jane's darkly handsome husband, Gabriel, who seemed less than thrilled to be sporting a sweater vest crawling with bell-wearing elves. Although she didn't have much retail experience, Jane had an eye for setting up the sales space. Everything drew the customers in, made them feel connected and comfortable.

I felt a bit envious of their little family. They were perfectly welcoming anytime I saw them. But I didn't have much time to spend with them. I didn't have much time for friends. I'd never made the transition from pooling pizza and beer money with my roommates in the dorm to Girls' Night Out and Sunday brunch. It was a sad, strange realization to know that a seventeen-year-old was your only real source of companionship.

What was I going to do when Gigi left for college? I

would come home every night to an empty house. There would be no volleyball games, no last-minute rushing to buy supplies for procrastinated science-fair projects, no midnight pizza or dramatic reenactments of high-school soap operas. A bizarre hollow sensation had me gripping the nearby shelf for support.

"Are you looking for something in particular?" Jane asked, nudging me gently.

I blew out a breath, nodding shakily. "I'll know it when I see it."

Jane grinned at me. "My kind of book shopper."

She piled several books into my arms, from recent softcover editions to old linen-covered tomes. I wobbled under the weight of them, so she helped me toddle toward the coffee bar. I took a seat at the bar, where my cappuccino was waiting for me, and tried to determine which books I needed.

"So, you're taking your gardenin' to a whole 'nother level?" Jolene asked as I immediately eliminated a leather-bound hardback called *Man-Eating Plants of the Amazon.*

The reading group had adjourned, promising to read something a little more romantic next month. I used their noisy, happy departure for an excuse not to reveal too much about Cal. But as soon as the shop door closed, Jolene was back to looking at me expectantly.

"Just a little research for a friend," I said, picking up *Botanical Aromatherapy and Psychic Abilities.* "He doesn't know anything about botany, and he's trying to find some information about which plants have effects on vampires. Like garlic, for instance. I've noticed that it does not, in fact, burn you alive, contrary to what *The Lost Boys* would have us believe."

"Well, that's what you get for getting your vampire survival tips from Corey Feldman," Jane said archly.

"It's more of a stinky-breath issue," Andrea added.

"How'd you get close enough to Corey Feldman that you know what his breath smells . . . oh, never mind." Jolene chuckled.

Jolene was an odd duck. She was beautiful in a fierce, exotic way—auburn hair, flashing green eyes, sharp white smile. Jane told me that she was once bitter about being replaced as Zeb's "best girl" by someone with a clear genetic advantage . . . but then she consoled herself with the fact that Jolene's braying backwoods twang could peel paint. It was a small consolation, especially when she was such a genuinely nice girl.

I opened a copy of *Bizarre Botanicals and Their Uses*. I muttered, "Devil's claw. Bloodwort. Marrow root. Why do they insist on giving these plants such scary names?"

Jane shrieked. "Augh!"

"What?"

She shuddered and slammed the book shut. "I just got a look at eyeball plants."

"Jane has a thing about eyeballs," Jolene said, rolling hers.

This started a good-natured argument about the group's various obscure phobias, including Jane's fear of clowns and puppets. After a few minutes, I narrowed my choices to *Imperfections of a Perfect Creature* and *The Natural Versus the Supernatural*, a guide to the plants, metals, and minerals that had physical effects on supernatural creatures. And *A Guide to Ancient Poisons*.

"You would tell me if you were planning to use something I sold you to kill someone, right?" Jane said, clearing her throat. I waggled my hand as if I might consider it. She threw a novelty voodoo doll at me. At least, I thought it was a novelty doll.

"I'll take them," I told her. I pulled out my purse, but Jane snapped it shut and pushed it back into my hands. "Oh, your money is no good here."

"Jane, one of these books looks like an antique," I said, holding up *Ancient Poisons*, with its weathered green cloth cover.

"You helped me survive wedding-dress shopping with my relatives," Jane countered. "And you managed to distract my mother during my reception so she was unable to force-feed me cake. You don't pay here, ever."

"Thanks, Jane," I said, hugging her.

"So, I was thinking," Jane said, squeezing me gently, "that we need to go out for drinks sometime. You know, a Girls' Night Out. I feel like we don't get to spend enough time with you. With Gigi leaving for school, you need to get used to 'adult time' again."

I narrowed my eyes at her. Sometimes it was a pain in the butt hanging out with a mind reader. She arched an eyebrow at me.

I thought, *Heard that, too, huh?*

She nodded.

Know-it-all psychic.

She grinned cheekily.

Meanwhile, the spoken conversation around us continued, our companions unaware of Jane's mental maneuverings.

"I don't like your Girls' Nights." Andrea pouted. "One of us always ends up questioned by the authorities."

"Well, who told you to dance on that cop car?" Jolene countered.

"You're the one who dared me to do it!" Andrea snapped.

"It was in motion!"

Andrea cried, "I borrowed Jane's bad-decision dress. I had no control over my actions!"

"We're burnin' that dress," Jolene muttered.

Jane smiled serenely, as if there wasn't a live production of *Jerry Springer* occurring behind her. "So, this friend that you're doing the research for, how long have you been . . . seeing each other?" she asked delicately.

I gasped, hoping that Jane hadn't seen much of Cal inside my head. I doubted that she'd take the information to the Council, but I didn't want her to get into trouble with Ophelia on my account. The problem with spending time with Jane was that the minute you realized that she could be listening to your thoughts, you automatically started thinking of all of the things that you shouldn't think about in her presence. When I was embarrassed over a minor account-balance hiccup with the bank three months before, I learned to recite lists of plant identifications in my head when she was around. It took her a week's contemplation to ask why I was mentally cursing at her in Latin.

"We're not dating so much as spending a lot of time together."

Andrea's lips quirked at my disaffected tone. "And you don't seem very happy about it."

I groaned and dropped my head to the counter. Jane chuckled and patted my back. When I looked up, she'd pulled out the little pink crystal-encrusted flask I kept for bridal emergencies and was waving it in front of my face. She flipped the cap open, and I could smell the alcohol fumes rolling over the lip.

I scowled at the little yellow crystal bee winking at me from the corner of the flask. "I don't know if vodka is going to improve this situation."

"Would it make you feel better if I mixed it into your coffee?" Jane asked sweetly.

Behind her, I heard Andrea whip out a little pocket digital recorder and murmur quietly, "Consider adding alcoholic coffee specials to the menu. Investigate licensing issues with the state."

"OK, so if you won't drink, you might as well spill," Jolene said. "Jane's gonna drag it out of you anyway. She has . . . evil ways." She shuddered.

"Fine. I will admit it. I am spending time with a vampire. And sometimes he's so funny and sweet . . . and, guh, sexy as hell. But then there are times when he just makes me so angry I could stake him out for the sun to handle. He makes all of these decisions for me, like I'm not even there!" I exclaimed in a tone that had Andrea and Jane sharing a look of amused recognition. "It's like he thinks he can protect me from the whole world just by—what are you smiling at?"

Jane and Andrea snickered simultaneously. "OK, the mind-meld thing is becoming a little unnerving," I complained.

Andrea gave me a smile that I hadn't seen since my mother gave me the "birds and the bees and your changing body" lecture. "Welcome to life with a male vampire."

"The most dangerous of all boyfriend species," Jane intoned solemnly. "You're being Nightengaled."

"Most dangerous." Jolene huffed and said something along the lines of, "Clearly, you never hung out with my pack." Which didn't make any sense.

"He's not my boyfriend. He's just a client."

Jolene pouted prettily. "But you are havin' sex with him, right?"

I knocked a clay, acorn-shaped plaque from the bar, only to have Andrea pluck it from midair before it hit the ground. Vampire reflexes would be so handy to have.

I stammered, "Wh-why would you say that?"

Jane tsked. "You have that 'I'm having the best sex of my life, but it leaves me emotionally conflicted' look. We're familiar with that look."

"I lived that look for the first six weeks after Dick moved in," Andrea said in a tone so candid that I expected to see a blush on her pale, undead cheeks.

"Until about two months before the wedding," Jane said, raising her hand.

"Does it get any better?" I asked.

Jane grinned. "The sex?"

"No!" I exclaimed as Andrea cackled. "The emotional conflict. Pervert."

Jane shrugged, pouring another cup of coffee for Jolene. "That depends on you and your friend. Honestly, it's difficult having a relationship with a man who thinks he needs to leave you out of the loop to protect you and is generally unfazed by threats of murder. Trust me, I nearly lost Gabriel because of his pigheaded protectiveness. And there's not much you can do, except refuse to put up with it. Fight back. If your friend is anything like Gabriel or Dick, he wants you to challenge him."

"To a duel?" I asked.

"No, in the bedroom—and everywhere else. Stand up to him. Assert yourself. You'll feel better about the relationship, and he'll respect you more," Andrea insisted. "One of the reasons Dick liked me was that I was the first girl to turn him down for anything since he was human."

"And a good fight always leads to . . ." Jane chewed her lip, as if she wasn't sure I was ready to hear that.

Andrea sighed dreamily. "Makeup sex."

I chewed my lip, tinkering with a blue embossed Specialty Books napkin. "Technically, we don't make up; it's more like declaring a ceasefire."

"Does he make you sign a treaty? Is that your twisted form of foreplay?" Andrea asked, her perfect brow furrowed. I tossed the frayed napkin at her. She snickered and danced out of the way.

"Now I'm curious," Jane said conspiratorially. "I never

had sex with a vampire as a human, and I refuse to hear any details from Little Miss Disturbing Penis Nicknames over there." She jerked a thumb toward Andrea. "What's it like?"

"I'm not telling you that!" I exclaimed.

Jane whined, "Oh, come on, be a sport."

"Why are we friends?"

"Do it, or she'll talk about her first time with Gabriel again," Andrea grumbled.

I ducked and hopped off the stool to avoid answering. My eyes landed on a glossy soft-cover book featuring a gaunt, weary-looking vampire sprawled across a Gothic four-poster bed.

"Hey, what's this?" I asked, pulling a copy from the pile. "*The Care and Feeding of Stray Vampires.* A comprehensive guide to safe, loving treatment of the injured undead."

I flipped through the book and found nutrition guides, feeding schedules, an appendix on skin care after minor sunburns. "This would have been useful a week ago," I muttered.

"Wait, he's injured? Your vampire is injured? Iris, you didn't pick this guy up while he was hitchhiking or something, did you?"

"Yes, Jane, I did. In fact, he was holding a sign that said, 'I need a ride, and I'm probably going to end up draining the moron who stops for me.' But I figured, hey, what's the harm?"

"All right, all right," Jane grumbled. "I'm used to mothering now. I worry about Jamie constantly. Suddenly, I have a whole new respect for Mama."

Behind her, Andrea gasped. Jane whirled on her, eyes narrowed. "If you ever tell anyone I said that, I will deny it, and then I will tell Dick all of the access codes for the adult channels on your cable box."

"You wouldn't." Andrea hissed. "We'd never see him again."

I turned to the redhead behind the bar. "Jolene, how do you put up with these two?"

Jolene yawned and turned a page in *The Drama of the Half-Were Child*. "I'm just here for the comic relief."

Armed with enough books to keep me busy for weeks, I stopped by the Dairy Freeze on the way home to pick up the traditional Tuesday-night cheeseburgers. Joe Brooks, who'd been manning the grill for almost forty years, was sure to put extra grilled onions on Gigi's, just as she liked it. That, combined with the crispy Tater Tots in the bottom of my grease-spotted brown takeout bag, guaranteed a happy evening at home.

"See you next Tuesday!" I called over my shoulder. Joe Brooks grinned and waved his spatula at me.

I hurried toward my car. I had about twenty minutes to get home before the cheese on the burgers lost ideal elasticity.

"Iris!"

I turned to see Paul jogging across the parking lot from his truck. Damn, there went my guaranteed evening of domestic felicity.

"Hi," he said cheerfully, kissing my cheek.

"What are you doing here?" I asked, making the expected smacking noise, without any real enthusiasm. Paul hadn't darkened the Dairy Freeze's door since he'd gotten sick on a bad chili cheese dog in high school. He was about as likely to try his luck at snake handling as ordering one of Joe Brooks's specials. Paul's light hair reflected a corona of sea-green light from the streetlamps. His eyes twinkled as he nodded toward the greasy bag.

"You're always here on Tuesday nights," he said. "It's cheeseburger night. How are you? Are you OK? I've been calling."

"I know," I said, wincing. "I'm sorry, I've just been so busy."

"With your new guy?" he asked, and although his tone was bright and even, there was a tinge of hurt around his eyes, an unhappy turn to his mouth.

"Sort of," I said, awkwardly opening the door and shoving the takeout bag onto the passenger seat.

"So, where did you and Cal meet?"

"Through work," I said.

"Is it serious?" he asked.

"He's usually pretty serious, yes," I muttered.

"Wait, you met him through work? He was so pale, and his eyes . . . Aw, man, he's a vampire?" He groaned. "How's a guy supposed to compete with that?"

"It's not a competition," I reminded him gently. "You and I don't work, Paul, remember? Not in the long term."

The corner of his mouth tilted. "And I guess dating somebody who won't die is pretty long-term, huh?"

"Paul—"

"Iris, I think we should give it another try. I miss you.

No one makes me laugh like you. No one understands the way I think like you do. I think we *can* make it work long-term. We could get married, have kids, the whole deal. We could, Iris. We just have to try a little harder."

"I want that. I want that just as much as you do, but we shouldn't have to try so hard, Paul. It should just happen. We don't have that . . . spark. That thing that makes you want to scream at someone one minute and kiss him the next. The thing that keeps life interesting."

"OK, what if we got back together and we didn't try at all?"

I laughed. "This feels like some sort of relationship trick."

"I don't do tricks. I don't play games. You know that," he said, squeezing my arm gently. "We may not have a spark, but what we have is the real thing. We're friends, Iris. I can't think of any better way to start a life together."

He was right, of course. He didn't play games. He was always very up-front with me, even when he knew it would hurt me. "No, Paul, thank you, but no. I don't want to try again . . . with or without trying."

"Are you sure you don't want to go out to dinner some night?" he asked. "Just as friends? I just—I miss talking to you, Iris. I miss you."

I closed my eyes and breathed deeply. I honestly missed my old friend. I missed the simplicity of being with him. No drama. No danger. Pulses all around. I hadn't been involved in a life-or-death struggle once while dating Paul.

He was there at the Dairy Freeze because he knew me.

He knew my habits, my routine, my likes and dislikes, because he knew me. Not some dossier in a file that declared that I was a pruned-up spinster, ear-deep in debt, but the real me. Why couldn't I make something relatively easy work? Why did I have to be such a personal train wreck?

Height jokes aside, Paul was a good-looking man in a small town, where the dating pool was limited. And there were a lot of reasons he was a viable candidate.

1. He had a steady job.
2. He didn't expect me to cook for him, clean for him, or be his mommy.
3. He had no problematic tendencies such as drinking, drug abuse, or spending all waking hours playing World of Warcraft.
4. He was generally considerate and remembered my birthday every year without prompting.
5. I could count on him not to take inappropriate pictures of me while I was sleeping and post them on Facebook, which was more than I could say for one of the guys Andrea dated.

I didn't want to play at relationships anymore. I wanted something I could hold on to, something that held on to me. Even if that thing was sort of dangerous and occasionally, and quite literally, bit me on the butt.

"It's just not a good idea, Paul. I'm sorry. I miss you,

too. But we can't go on like this. This constant push-and-pull. It's not healthy. We're never going to meet the people we can have actual relationships with if we're pseudo-dating."

"But we can be friends, right? And friends go out to dinner all the time."

"Yes, but friends don't have sex afterward," I deadpanned.

"Good friends do."

"Paul."

"It was worth a shot. But you're OK, right?" he asked. "You're not mad at me? Or dating some vampire to try to get over me?"

"I think *you* should try to get over you," I shot back.

"That did sound a little douchey, didn't it?" He chuckled. I nodded emphatically. "OK, go home before your cheeseburgers get cold. Tell Gigi I said hi."

I bade Paul good night. He shut the door behind me as I started the car. As I pulled out of the parking lot, I watched him in my rearview. In the three years I'd known him, this was the first time Paul had mentioned Gigi without being prompted. Was he growing up or just hoping to convince me that we could still "work"? Why did he only decide to miss me after seeing me with someone else? And why did his hints of jealousy brighten my day?

I sighed, turning the car away from town. "Having feelings for a living ex while wrestling with the romantic stupidity of a potential vampire beau. You've got a real wacky sitcom of a life going, Scanlon."

13

Vampires, particularly older vampires, do not enjoy reminiscing about their pasts. It reminds them of what they have lost over the years. If a vampire voluntarily shares this history with you, you should treat the disclosure with the respect it deserves.

—*The Care and Feeding of Stray Vampires*

I did not mention Paul's visit to Cal when I returned home and spread the cheeseburgers out on the table. He was sitting there surrounded by research, frowning at his laptop. I warmed up a bottle of blood to serve him while Gigi and I ate the burgers, because it seemed rude to do otherwise.

"Gigi!" I called upstairs. "It's cheeseburger night! Come and get it!"

"She's not here," Cal said. "She said she had to study with that Ben boy again. She said she called you and left you a message."

I made an indignant little noise.

His plump bottom lip twitched, and he added, "If we'd taken the boy out of the equation when I suggested it, this wouldn't be a problem."

"Yes, murdering a teenager is a far more rational step than imposing a stricter curfew." I grumbled softly as I checked my voicemail. Gigi had indeed left me a message while I was in Jane's shop, otherwise occupied. I frowned. Gigi knew the rules. No school-night outings unless approved by me. Face-to-face, not via voicemail. Was she bending the rules because she thought I was too distracted by Cal to watch her properly? Or was she so crazy about Ben that she would risk grounding and sisterly wrath?

Gigi was in for a *looooooong* talk when she returned home tonight. Or I was going to have to pull some sort of Machiavellian parenting maneuver that kept her guessing about my next move and questioning my motivations. My last effort had involved a dummy Twitter account and a rented pickup truck.

Sigh. I really didn't have time for Machiavellian brilliance right now. The best I could come up with at this point was sticking her bra in the freezer. I didn't think that would get my point across.

"Well, now I'm left with an extra cheeseburger and an undead guest who can't eat it."

"Would that I could," Cal mused, sniffing delicately at the wax-paper bundles on the table. He poked one with a fingertip and moved back as if he expected it to move in response. I chuckled, snatching my dinner out of his reach.

We sat at the table together, him with his blood, me with my calorie-laden bit of beefy goodness. It was oddly domestic and distinctly uncomfortable without Gigi as a social buffer. Cal's eyes stayed trained on my mouth, the way it moved, the way my lips wrapped around the straw of my milkshake. But he didn't speak.

Most awkward dinner date ever.

I finished as quickly as possible without choking, went outside to set up the sprinklers to water my herb beds, then headed up the stairs to the book nook. I tucked the *Care and Feeding* guide away behind the encyclopedias just as Cal was climbing the steps behind me. Somehow I thought that he would find an instruction manual for his species condescending.

I ducked into my bedroom to change into some comfortable yoga pants and a jade-green "Camp Half-Blood Hill—Demeter Cabin" T-shirt. Jane had gotten Gigi hooked on the *Percy Jackson and the Olympians* series, and Gigi had found the T-shirt on a particularly devoted Etsy fan site last Christmas. Unfortunately, it had been washed a few too many times and had shrunk a bit. But it was soft and comfy, and I wasn't going to slink around the house in a silk teddy in my downtime.

By the time I emerged, Cal was settled on the window seat, looking through my new titles. His eyes scanned the Greek-style letters stretched tight across my chest. "Demeter? The goddess of harvest and plenty? That's fitting. You do look particularly . . . bountiful in that shirt."

"It was a gift," I told him tartly, climbing onto the window seat. Cal's legs were stretched toward me, his back propped against the wall. I copied his pose, careful not to let our feet touch. "Gigi bought herself a Hermes Cabin T-shirt. We wear them when we make s'mores."

"Hermes." He frowned. "God of thieves?"

"God of athletes," I reminded him.

"He was never my favorite," Cal said, shrugging. "There was an altar to the gods in my home, although my wife paid particular attention to Ares and Athena, to bring me strength and wisdom in battle. Anything to bring me home safely. I put a little something extra to pay tribute to Hestia, to help my wife along as she learned to cook. But she noticed, and the maelstrom that followed wasn't worth risking it again."

"Your wife was a bad cook?"

"Terrible." He laughed, his face softening to a contemplative smile. "She made bread you could use as a discus. She just never got the knack of it. But her parents loved her too much to tell her how unappetizing her efforts were, so she left their house believing that she was quite the capable housekeeper. I don't know how she managed it, but she burned a pot of boiling water once. The hem of her dress caught fire, and she ran out of the kitchen, stripping the smoldering material away. The pot boiled dry and cracked. She ended up standing in our courtyard, as naked as a plucked goose! I tried so hard not to laugh. But she was so indignant, standing there, arms crossed, mouth set in a firm little line, while she glowered up at me. And when I wrapped a spare cloak around her shoulders, all she said was, 'Thank goodness we don't have servants!' And then she swept back into the kitchen to finish the meal."

"And how was it?"

"Barely edible," he said, shuddering. "But we laughed

over it, eventually. We didn't have many times like that. I haven't thought about that day in . . . far too long. I'd almost forgotten about it."

His eyes had a faraway look, as if he was scanning his internal banks for more memories of his wife, his family. His brow creased, a straight little line forming between them. Was he upset that he had to try so hard? Could he not remember what she looked like? In another thousand years, would he struggle to remember my name? Would I qualify for a spot in his recollections? It seemed unlikely that he could forget someone who tripped over his half-dead body and smuggled him away like a thief in the night. But Paul had only remembered me when he had no other options. This did not bode well.

Depressed by this train of thought, I asked, "What was her name?"

"Euphemia," he said, smiling.

"Euphemia and Cletus?"

"Don't start, woman."

I nudged him with my foot. "It's a sweet story, Cal."

He smiled at me, catching my foot by the ankle and squeezing it gently. "Thank you for reminding me."

I nodded, pleased that he seemed happy for the moment. Chewing on a strand of licorice, I dug into my new books and searched for any information on plants that had a paralytic effect on vampires or encouraged their bloodthirst. But this was a new field of plant research for me, and the work was slow. I took notes, made a little chart to cross-reference, and eventually threw it out when it started to look like a tiny inked-up patchwork quilt.

Frustrated, I crumpled up the paper and threw it into the wastebasket. I turned back to the shelf, letting my eyes wander over the gilded titles. I needed inspiration. I needed something that would connect all of the little bits of information floating around in my head. There was something itching at the corner of my brain, something I was missing, something I should know—

"Oh!" I exclaimed, launching myself at the window seat. I balanced one foot on the edge—right between Cal's thighs—as I strained to reach a book on the far top shelf.

"Can I help you?" he asked, eyeing the position of my foot warily. I ignored him and jumped to the floor, *A Guide to European Wildflowers* in my hands. I opened it, grinned widely, and showed him a picture of vibrant blue blossoms.

"You, my friend, were poisoned with a combination of wolfsbane and bittersweet nightshade!" I exclaimed.

"That's a poetic combination. What are you basing this on?"

"Pure conjecture," I deadpanned. When he rolled his eyes, I explained, "OK, so we've discussed the fact that aconitine showed up in the Blue Moon poison, yes?" He nodded. "Aconite is another name for wolfsbane."

"I thought we'd covered the fact that I'm not a were-wolf."

"According to this, aconite is sort of a catchall supernatural plant. It's sort of funny that humans got this one right. Botanists believe that early Europeans attributed the plant's supernatural quality to the unearthly blue color. Anyway, according to *The Natural Versus the Supernatural,* the plant contains an enzyme that basically opens up vampire neurotransmitters to constant stimulation. Your muscles, your nervous system, your vascular system are all wide open. If someone were to combine the plant's effects with another compound . . ."

"I take it that's where the bittersweet nightshade comes in?"

I opened *The Natural Versus the Supernatural,* pointing to the relevant passage. The illustration showed a climbing vine plant with strange purple flowers. The blooms hung from the stem in an arch, puffing out like a sultan's cap over a distinct yellow stamen.

"Bittersweet nightshade contains a glycoalkaloid poison called solanine."

"Do you know what a glycoalkaloid is?" he asked suddenly.

"I happened to perform very well in chemistry, thank you, so yes."

"That is far sexier than I anticipated," he said, chewing his lip thoughtfully. "Have I mentioned that I adore your little blouses and pencil skirts? I've never worked fulltime in an office, but I think I would enjoy chasing you around my desk in the outfit you wore to work today."

"Why am I the secretary in this scenario?" I asked. "I could be your boss."

"Fine, you could chase me around your desk." He sighed. "I would enjoy it either way."

"Stop sidetracking me with premeditated sexual harassment," I snipped. "Now, in humans, this causes dizziness, fever, intestinal chaos—the descriptions of which I will spare you—and sometimes paralysis. But vampires don't get dizziness, fevers, or the intestinal pyrotechnics. Instead, you just get the paralysis. That might not be so bad, except, thanks to the aconitine, all of the little transmitters in your brain are wide open, so it's a total shutdown of your systems."

His face darkened, and my triumph at having found the answer was diminished. Someone had tried to tear him down completely, to make him defenseless, helpless, so they could sneak into his house and finish him. I couldn't find the words to comfort him or to help him see that ultimately, it didn't matter, that he'd outmaneuvered them anyway. So, I just kept talking.

"The only treatment for the poison is feeding, flushing it out with fresh blood," I said, pointing to the page. "Unfortunately, in you, this seemed to trigger the emetic aspects of the solanine, and you vomited. A lot. On me."

"Message received. I will stop vomiting on you," he grumbled. I grinned cheekily and nudged him with my elbow.

I thumbed to an index of each plant's ideal growth conditions. It was a concise little chart with color photos and a handy little map illustration with each entry.

"I think we can safely assume that whoever is diddling with the blood supply is the same person who poisoned you. If we could just figure out where this person is growing this stuff, it might help us figure out what they're using for the mass poisonings." My finger traced down the index, stopping next to a cluster of small white flowers with yellow centers. "That's weird," I mumbled, flipping through the pages for the plant's full entry. I hopped up to grab *The Natural Versus the Supernatural,* finding the plant bolded in the index under "highly dangerous."

I studied the illustration in Jane's book. I murmured, "Glossy green leaves, white flowers, spots on the . . . how many plants could there be that look like that?"

"Is this a private conversation, or can anyone join?" Cal asked dryly.

"Cute." I pulled a face at him and showed him the illustration. "When I was looking at the lab reports before, I couldn't figure out why chemicals found in lungwort were showing up in the poisoned vampire's blood. This plant in Jane's book, fangwort, would be very similar in structure and chemical makeup. Jane's book says it 'fires the bloodlust of vampires to a painful degree; they will recognize neither friend nor foe.' It's supposed to grow in hot, humid areas of the Iberian Peninsula—you know, modern-day Spain, Portugal, a little tiny bit of—"

"I know where the Iberian Peninsula is, Iris."

"I know, I know, you probably built the first road or furrowed the first wheat field ever sown there."

"Brat."

"Cradle robber."

"Grave robber."

When I couldn't come up with a sufficiently snarky insult, I went on. "Fangwort is supposed to grow in the warm, humid areas of the Iberian Peninsula. But I swear to you, I've seen it before. I remember spotting something like that on one of my mom's hiking expeditions. She used to take me on these hikes through the woods to find interesting plants for her garden. We'd cut a sample to dry and another to plant. She loved using wild, uncultivated flowers in her beds. She said it kept her gardens honest. And in general, they were heartier than what you buy at a nursery. And I remember seeing something like this weird-looking plant on one of the last trips we took before she died. Mom liked it, but we'd already taken so many that day that she didn't want to be greedy. But—"

I hopped up, dashing to the bookshelf. I ran my fingers along the spines until I found the spiral notebook I was looking for.

"What are you doing?"

"Looking for my mom's cutting journal."

"What is that, exactly?" he asked. "Was your mother a particularly violent woman?"

I shoved at his shoulders absently as I searched the shelf. Mom's journal was a thing of beauty. A smooth canvas cover embroidered with little spring green leaves, hand-stitched by Gigi as a Girl Scout/Mother's Day project. Inside, Mom had catalogued every interesting plant we'd seen on our hikes, by date, including the latitude and longitude, the size of the bed, a description of the environment, and a sketch of a sample. My mother's neat block print brought a strange longing sensation that I hadn't expected. I missed her so much. I missed the way she teased a laugh out of us when we were upset. I missed the way she cheated at Monopoly and tried to make us think that we'd just forgotten that she had hotels on Boardwalk and Park Place. I missed knowing that we were safe and that Mom and Dad had everything in hand.

I flipped to the end of the book, to June 2005: *Found a rather sizeable plot (6m by 4m) of this strange root plant today in an area off County Line Road. It's clearly a "wort" plant, note broad flat leaves, and small white flowers with greenish-yellow stamens. Similar to an illustration of bloodwort,* but leaves seem too different. I didn't take a cutting because it just felt, well, wrong somehow. There was something very off-putting about the plant, a bit like approaching poison ivy and knowing you're about to do something that will bring about itchy misery. Iris wasn't keen on it, either, so we left it alone. *Illustration found on page 233 of "An Illustrated Guide to the Flowering Plants of Europe."*

I opened the book to show Cal my mother's sketch, which bore a striking resemblance to the illustration in the book. "My mom wouldn't have had access to books like Jane's; otherwise, she might have known what she was looking at. So, how are all of these obscure foreign plants finding their way here to rural Kentucky? I mean, other than the warm, humid climate, the two places have nothing in common. And why is there a patch of it growing in a field in the middle of nowhere? There are no houses in that area near County Line Road. I don't know if there ever have been, so it's not like it's some remnant of a Civil War era garden."

"Where is it?" he asked, pulling out a map of McClure County.

I compared my mom's notes, which included a meticulous notation of the exact longitude and latitude of the location, with the county map and pointed. "Right there."

"Do you think the patch might still be there?"

"Anything's possible," I said, shrugging.

"You have been a tremendous help," he said, kissing my forehead. He bounded off the couch and was down the stairs in a flash. By the time I reached the ground floor, he was reaching for the front doorknob.

I called, "Where do you think you're going?"

"The location mentioned in your mother's cutting journal."

"It's the middle of the night. It could take us hours to find the right place and hours more to get the information you want, which could leave us stranded in the middle of the woods at sunrise. That would not be good for your complexion."

"I could be there in far less time if I went alone," he said, casting me an apologetic look. "I would move faster without you."

"But you wouldn't know what you're looking for," I countered.

"I am capable of following a map and your field guide."

"But short of a little sign that says, 'My name is (blank)

and this is my poisonous plant farm,' which is doubtful, you won't be able to interpret what you see there. You need me."

"How many more reasons are you going to give me to delay until tomorrow?"

"As many as it takes. I'm good with lists," I said, innocently batting my eyes. Cal growled in frustration. I nipped the tip of his nose and smirked at him. "Admit it, honey, you need me. Rescuing you from kitchens. Stealing valuable documents. Personal forest tours. I provide a comprehensive, invaluable service."

"I do need you," he said quietly. Without finishing that thought, he sighed, resigned, and slumped up the stairs to the reading nook. Snickering quietly to myself, I heard him mutter, "Should have been in the Athena cabin."

A hungry vampire is a dangerous vampire. Have alternative blood sources at the ready at all times.

—*The Care and Feeding of Stray Vampires*

The next sunset found me strapping on the hiking boots and the Jansport backpack I'd been using for these little excursions since high school. After massive apologies for her unauthorized school-night outing, Gigi announced that she had plans for the evening. Despite her assertions that she'd been at Ben's so he could help her with a PowerPoint presentation for her final AP history project, my initial instinct was to ground her.

But Cal insisted that it was a good idea for her to be out of the house for the night. In fact, he was so insistent that I bit back my irritation at his interfering. Cal was worried, whether it was some unseen menace he felt coming or the idea of leaving Gigi unchaperoned in the house where Ben could come by for a "visit." So Gigi was heading to Ben's, where both parents were present and had a "the bedroom door stays open at all times" policy.

"Are you sure you're up for this?" I asked, double-lacing my boots as we prepared for our outing.

He seemed insulted by the question. "I am stronger every day."

I was a bit disappointed that he didn't flex his arms to prove his point. (Don't judge me. I like arms.) He was getting stronger, strong enough to leave the nest, so to speak. My time with him was coming to a close. I could feeling it slipping away like a clock winding down. I cleared my throat, eyeing his battered motorcycle boots, which would be pretty damn uncomfortable after a few miles. "I'm just saying, you don't seem like the outdoorsy type. Do you even ride a motorcycle?"

"A few of them over time. There happens to be a motorcycle in my garage at this very moment," he retorted. "And I slept outdoors for almost ten consecutive years."

"I know you hate when I point this out, but that was a while ago."

"You know you two sound like the Bickersons, right?" Gigi giggled, bounding down the stairs and settling between us on the couch.

"When does the movie start?" I asked.

"Seven-thirty," Gigi said. "Ben's meeting me there. He's got baseball practice. I will be home by ten-thirty, unless we stop for ice cream. And if we do, I'll call you."

"Good girl," I said.

Cal cleared his throat. "And do you have the, er, item I gave you?"

I arched a brow at Gigi, who gleefully reached into her purse. "Cal got me Mace!"

"Aw!" I grinned at him. "That was thoughtful of you."

"And a Taser!" Gigi exclaimed, whipping the pocket-sized device out of her handbag.

"Are you insane?" I cried at my vampire, who was making "cut it out" gestures toward Gigi behind my back. "Why not just get her an Uzi?"

"Because Uzis don't come in pink!" Gigi added, pulling the candy-colored stun gun out of its holster. She fired it up, giggling as an arc of light jumped between the two metal probes.

I shot an incredulous look at Cal. "How did you even get that?"

"Internet," Cal mumbled. "I just want Ben to watch his step. A well-placed touch of the Taser can help keep someone on his best behavior."

"You cannot take that to school, Geeg. I'm going to get phone calls," I told her.

"I know," she said, rolling her eyes. "Cal ordered a special mount for my car, so I can store it under the driver's seat. He showed me how to fire it and which areas of the body work best. And if I Tase someone just to see if it works, he will take it away. And on that note, I'm going. I'll call you."

"Do not get that stuff out of your purse unless you feel uncomfortable," I told her. "People have very little tolerance for accidental electrocution."

Cal nudged her shoulder and told her, "Remember." Then he began an odd sort of dance in which he gestured to his neck, his armpits, and his groin. She rolled her eyes again and slung her arms around him. He froze, and I was about to warn her off, but he awkwardly patted her back. She gave me an absent wave and bolted out the door.

"What the hell?" I demanded, doing a bad impression of the dance he'd just performed.

"I was just reminding her of the most painful places to be Tased," he said.

"You know, I'm going to forward the calls to your cell phone the first time she zaps some hapless classmate's junk because she's having a bad day."

"It's a risk I'm willing to take," he said solemnly. He pulled a little box from behind the couch.

"What's this?"

"I got one for you, too," he said as I pulled out a frightening-looking box proclaiming the make and model of my very own Taser. It was green, with a floral-print holster.

"Wow, Cal, I don't know what to say."

Really. How *do* you respond when someone gifts you with nonlethal law-enforcement equipment? If I was a rational person, I would thank him and turn it down. But considering the rate at which I'd been accosted, attacked, or just plain annoyed over the last few weeks, I thanked him politely and stuck it in my purse.

"Just say you'll read the instruction manual," he said sternly. "I think Gigi only skimmed it because she knew I was going to quiz her."

He was really, sincerely, worried about her. I could see it written all over his face: the furrowed brow, the tense mouth. I saw that in my reflection more often than

I cared to admit. Cal wasn't just worried about this un-known entity targeting vampires. He wanted Gigi safe from everything, and just like me, he realized that plac-ing her in a hermetically sealed habitat wasn't possible. Not to mention that it was cost-prohibitive.

For so long, I'd been the only one worrying about Gigi. To share that weight, however willingly I'd taken it on, was a sublime thing. Touched by his inappropriately applied concern, I kissed his mouth with a resounding smack. His arms wound around me, pulling me close. The tension seemed to melt away from my body.

"What was that for?" he asked, pushing waves of hair back from my face.

I rested my forehead against his throat and sighed. "No reason."

As expected, Cal barely disturbed the limbs as he wound his way through the trees, as lithe and smooth as spilled mercury. I felt like a clambering elephant by contrast, clomping around, leaving footprints and damaged foli-age wherever I went.

Two people hiking through the woods with flashlights would seem suspicious if we were seen from the road, so we had to rely on Cal's considerable night vision. I'd never hiked at night before. The leaves were a silvery ashen green, fluttering in a warm breeze like verdant lace. The night sounds—crickets chirping, birds calling— quieted as we passed, the animals sensing a predator com-ing close. It was also very dark. I had to hold on to his arm to stay upright on a couple of occasions.

There was no trail, but I hadn't thought there would be. Mom and I used to just wander, keeping mindful of private fence lines and hunting stands. We were always careful not to go out during peak deer and turkey seasons, because that would be an embarrassing way to die.

Just ask Jane.

The site we were looking for was about three miles from the road. We stayed quiet, moving as quickly as we could. Cal seemed tense, constantly scanning the horizon, tracking every noise. I knew we'd both been through a lot, but I doubted that the poisoner was lurking behind a tree somewhere just in case we happened to wander by.

I kept my eyes on the ground, watching for the distinctive leaf patterns. This meant that I didn't see Cal stop short, and I plowed into his back.

"Ow," I grumbled, rubbing my bruised nose. "Stupid vampire stealth. Why'd you stop?"

Cal pointed to an oddly inorganic shape, nestled in a little clearing among tall pines. The prefabricated metal walls reflected dull grayish mint green in the light of the full moon, covered with an artfully shredded green tarp, made up to look like leaves. This was a new building, well maintained. And judging by the closely trimmed grass surrounding the concrete pad, it had been visited recently. In fact, most of the ground in the surrounding area was cleared. It had been harvested. Something had grown there in neatly furrowed rows. I couldn't estimate the size of the plot, because of the darkness, but it had been sizable.

"That . . ." I said, squinting at the heavily draped out-building. "Seems out of place."

I checked our exact coordinates. "We're just a few degrees off of the location Mom and I found before." I pulled out my county map to determine our location in reference to roads. "And we're about twenty miles from the nearest house. This could be a hunting shack. Some guys around here lease a plot in the middle of a farm or old homesteads so they can hunt in peace."

He gestured to the windowless little cube, which lacked the charming little touches hunters used to mark their territory. License plates from long-defunct trucks, wind chimes made of beer tabs, deer skulls sporting sunglasses and trucker hats. "Does that look like a hunting shack to you?"

"No. You don't have to wait for a warrant or anything, do you?" I asked as we circled to the nondescript metal door. "Just in case we find something?"

He snorted, dropping to his knee to examine the door. It was fitted with a standard Master Lock, which Cal ripped off like it was some cheap papier-mâché decoration. "Ophelia's more of a 'solve the problem by any means necessary, and we'll worry about paperwork later' sort of administrator. You watch too much *Law and Order*."

I grasped the door handle, and Cal grabbed my wrist. "It could be rigged."

"What sort of moron would rig a booby trap on the inside of the building where he couldn't reach it when he needed to open the only door?"

"Good point," he admitted.

"You watch too much *Burn Notice*," I told him primly as I pulled the door open. Since we did not, in fact, blow up, I stepped inside to find drying racks, planting tables stocked with terra-cotta pots, organized shelves of pruning shears, spades, plant-food mixers—all the tools needed to run a remote operation like this. Unfortunately for us, there was no helpful sign on the wall saying, "This evil botanical lair belongs to . . ."

"I need pictures," Cal said, taking out his digital camera. "Could you look around, see if you spot anything unusual or particularly interesting?"

"Well, the fact that this guy isn't growing weed is pretty interesting," I retorted as I studied the peat pots sprouting tiny seedlings.

Cal gave me an amused look, which I took as a prompt to continue.

"Why do you think our green-thumbed friend took so much time to camouflage this building? The chances of someone stumbling here on foot are pretty slim, but the state police do regular helicopter circuits, checking for marijuana patches. Growers who aren't sophisticated enough to buy grow lights and hydroponic sets will sneak out at night and put in plants in the middle of nowhere. Sometimes farmers have a quarter acre of pot growing in some remote corner of their property and have no clue."

"How do you know so much about the habits of marijuana farmers?" he asked.

I waggled my eyebrows at him. "Misspent youth."

"Really?"

"No, I watch the news. I thought you were supposed to be a truth seeker. Dork."

"I offer her the world, and she calls me a dork," he muttered.

"I don't recall being offered—"

The door slid shut behind us, an internal mechanism locking with a resounding snick.

We both turned toward the noise. Cal hissed, his fangs bared as he threw me behind him and crouched defensively. A metallic pinging, the sound of another padlock being looped through the outside brackets.

We could hear footsteps outside, shuffling. A vent opened over the door, above our heads. I could hear the faint electric whir of a fan. Air-conditioning seemed like a strangely thoughtful gesture for someone who was locking me into a small enclosed space with a vampire.

"Hey!" I shouted. "Whoever that is better open the door quick or . . ."

Before I could come up with a threat violent enough, a strange yellowish-gray dust began circulating from the vent in a swirling billow. I sneezed mightily, waving my hand in front of my face to ward away the pollen. The footsteps outside stopped. Either our host had wandered away, or he was waiting for something.

"This can't be good." I grunted, yanking at the door handle. "I couldn't budge it a millimeter. "You want to help me here, Mr. Superstrength?"

Cal nodded slowly, as if his head was fuzzy. He ambled toward the door. The moment he touched the handle, he hissed and yanked his hand back. The skin of his hand was sizzling and gray, like badly cooked meat. "Silver." He hissed. "The handle is very pure silver."

He stumbled back, holding his burned hands up as if to keep me away. "Well, who the hell would put a silver handle on the inside—" I grumbled. "Hey, are you OK?"

He shook his head. "I feel strange."

"What can I do?" I stepped toward him, but he fell back against the drying racks, scrambling away from me.

"Stay away." He growled, his voice guttural. His eyes were strange, flashing almost yellow, before the pupils flared and nearly overtook the irises entirely. "Iris, get away from me."

"Cal!" I yelped, rattling the handle behind me as he advanced. His shoulders were hunched in a predatory crouch, the muscles bunching in a way that reminded me of a jungle cat.

"Cal, it's me!" I cried. "Cal, please snap out of it. I know you don't want to hurt me."

His lips were pulled back from his fangs in a feral snarl. I bit my lip to keep a whimper from escaping as he lunged closer. His throat rumbled. His nose grazed my cheek as he inhaled deeply. His fangs scraped across my jugular, leaving tiny pinprick scratches that only hinted of blood.

As he continued to lick my throat, I slipped my hand toward the worktable. There was a stack of little gardening plaques with sharp wooden stakes attached. I wrapped my fingers around one, sobbing lightly as I wound my arm around his shoulder. He didn't even notice the awkward posture as he feasted on the skin just over my pulse point. I pressed the stake against his back, just over his heart.

"Please, please, I don't want to do this to you," I whispered. Cal's ears seemed to perk at the sound of my voice, and his head snapped toward my mouth. The blacks of his eyes were bottomless, soulless. There was nothing of my Cal there. This was the monster. I whimpered, my bottom lip tearing under the pressure of my teeth. I could feel the blood welling into my mouth.

Not good.

I pressed the tip of the stake into his back as he lunged. He claimed my mouth, lapping at the blood, pulling it from my torn flesh in deep drafts. Each pass of his tongue seemed to inflame and calm him at the same time. He purred, tugging my bottom lip into his mouth and pulling me flush against him. I scrambled against the door, winding my legs around his waist to keep from falling.

The slick, metallic taste of my blood didn't bother me as much as I thought it would, the flavor adding a primal element to an already wild struggle. I tugged at his hair, trying to force his face away, but he only growled. I pulled harder, and his head snapped up, eyes wild and lost.

Palms up, submissive, I traced his cheeks with my fingertips. His dark eyes narrowed, blinking wildly as if trying to remember the identity of the silly human pinned under him. I tried to lower my legs to the ground, but he growled, and I froze immediately. Unable to stop the trembling of my hands, I clenched them into fists, my nails biting little half-moons into the flesh of my palms. I felt blood trickling into my palms. *No, no, no. Not good.*

My breath came in a ragged gasp as he loosened his hold and skimmed the length of my throat with his mouth. The scrape of fangs against skin sent a frisson of fear up my spine. The arm behind him tensed to strike. Instead of sinking those teeth into my throat, he caressed it with his tongue.

I stilled, every cell of my being focused on that small patch of skin. He ran that smooth feline tongue along the strained tendons of my neck. His fingers slithered down my rib cage to cup my rear, grinding his hard length against me. He nuzzled his nose against my cheek, purring softly, whispering kisses along my jaw. The stake clattered to the cement floor.

Snagging my right hand, he pressed the fingertips into his cool mouth, sucking the reddened digits lightly, drawing them in. Ripples of pressure, zipping straight to my dampening core, had me clinging to his shoulders. I ground against him, riding out the burning, delightful pressure. Purring, he pulled me closer, nipping my bottom lip. It felt like he was consuming me from the inside, pulling everything I was into his mouth, accepting me as no one ever had.

I freed him from his jeans, running my fingers carefully under his length. He ripped my shirt over my head, turning us toward the potting table.

I whined in protest when he set me on my feet. He tugged my jeans down my thighs, then pulled my leg over his hip and thrust forward, balancing my ass on the edge of the table. Seedlings hit the floor. I vaguely registered the sound of terra-cotta breaking. Lips curling back into a wicked smile, he rolled his hips, teasing me, rubbing just at the edge but not thrusting home. Whacking the back of my head against the table, I matched his movements, seeking some sort of friction as he slowly inched his way inside me.

His faded shirt gave way under my hands. Dropping the rags to the floor, I dragged my fingernails over his rippling skin. He thrust inside me, and I screamed out. My legs scrambled against his ass, trying to hold on under his thrusts. The rough table bit into my back as it slammed into the wall.

He bent his head, taking my bloodied fingertips between his lips. He looked up at me, eyes boring deep into mine as he licked and sucked at the digits. My orgasm burst through me like a thunderclap, loud, deep, and fierce.

Chuckling darkly, he crawled up my body, running his nose between my breasts, to my throat. The slip of fangs into skin was so quick I barely felt it. I sighed, sinking against the table as his movements sped up with each draw at my skin. I felt limber and happy as Cal shouted out his release and slumped against me. His mouth stayed latched at my throat, taking deep pulls of blood long after the last tremor.

"Cal," I whispered, nudging at his shoulder.

He growled, clasping my jaw in his palm while he drank from me. My blood ran in a warm line down my chest, soaking into my bra. This was different from the drainer at Cal's house. Cal wasn't hurting me, but he was taking too much. My hands were cold and becoming too weak to push him away.

"Cal!" I yelled in his ear. He didn't even flinch. I was using the "wake up Gigi on Monday morning" tone, and he was still snacking on my neck like it was a Baptist pot-luck. My hand fumbled along the table, finding a heavy terra-cotta pot. Using all of the strength left in my arms, I raised it over my head and brought it crashing down on him. He raised his head, his lips red and wet. His mouth drew into a frown before his eyes rolled back and he collapsed on top of me.

I slumped under his weight, unable to summon the strength to sit up. His knees gave way, and he sagged to the floor, pants around his ankles.

"Oh . . ." I groaned, hissing at the various pains as I sat up. "He is *not* going to be happy about that."

I cleaned up the best I could, using some Wet Wipes in my backpack to erase the evidence of Cal's nearly drain-ing me dry. By the time he woke up, pants still around his ankles, I'd dressed, rehydrated, and taken samples and pictures of everything I could find. And I'd discov-ered that whoever designed this outbuilding clearly did not have escape of accidental prisoners in mind. There was no way out of the place, except for the door, which I wasn't strong enough to yank open and Cal wasn't able to touch.

This was like one of those *Saw* movies . . . only a little sexier.

Cal stirred at my feet, groaning softly.

"What happened?" he grumbled as I helped him sit up. He tilted my head gently to examine my bite mark and winced. "The last thing I remember is kissing you . . ."

"I'm OK."

"I'm sorry," he said, checking me over for other wounds. "I remember wanting your blood so badly. Then I got just the smallest taste of it. But I was able to pull myself out of it. I remembered it was you. I could hear your voice, smell your skin. And that seemed so much more important than being angry or hungry."

"Actually, other than the whole 'mortal peril' thing, it wasn't that bad." I sighed. He pulled his shirt over my head and covered my blood-soaked bra. "I'm OK."

"I—"

"Don't," I told him, tapping my finger against his lips. "Just get us out of here. I need some juice and a cookie."

"Blood-donor jokes are not appropriate right now." He growled.

"It's my blood loss, and I will joke about it any way I please," I said, slumping against the wall as Cal tried the door again.

Several failed experiments later, we discovered not only that the handle made it very difficult for Cal to open but also that there was something holding the lock in place from the outside. Cal rolled up the leg of his jeans and ripped a black canvas holster away from his leg. He unsheathed what seemed to be a short bronzish sword, broad and flat, shaped a bit like an oak leaf. It was the perfect length to wear against his calf, just less than two feet. It looked worn, old, but cared for. It shone in the dim light as he tapped it against the door, looking for a weak point in the lock mechanism.

"What—what the hell is that?" I spluttered.

"It's my sword."

"I can see it's a sword. But how long have you had it?"

"When I tell you these things, they tend to send you on conversational tangents."

"Cal."

"A long time," he admitted. "I carried it into battle as a human. It's not as impressive as some of the other specimens I've collected over the years, but it's the one I'm most comfortable with."

"Are you telling me that all this time, you've been walking around with a *sword* strapped to your leg?" I yelled.

"I never leave home without it," he said.

"How do you get through airport security?"

He grinned, shoving the blade through the mechanism holding the door shut and twisting it viciously. The innards of the lock tinkled to the cement pad like broken toys. He wrapped his shirt around the handle and yanked the door open.

Cal burst out of the building in full vamp mode, expecting whoever had shut us inside to be waiting for us. But the clearing was empty, quiet, oddly removed from the blood scene inside the shed.

I took deep lungfuls of the clean, cool air, feeling suddenly dizzy. I'd come very close to dying. Again. It was a habit I seemed to have picked up since meeting Cal. And the idea that I could have been killed in some bizarre vampire sex accident scared me. The idea that I could have left Gigi alone, to fend for herself, scared me. But none of these things scared me nearly as much as the fact that some dark, perverse side of my nature was screaming at me to drag Cal back into the shed and do it all over again.

I was going to need serious therapy if I survived this.

I looked up to find that Cal was watching my every move and expression, as if he expected me to burst into hysterics at any moment. I wasn't 100 percent sure that he was off base with that. I reached into my backpack and pulled out a pack of Skittles. I needed blood sugar, and I needed it quick.

"You feeling OK?" I asked, deflecting.

"Oddly enough, yes," he said, stretching his arms over his head. "I feel energized, better than I have in weeks."

Now would not be the time to mention that the energy most likely came from snacking on live, human me. Instead, I chewed my fruity candy, slumped against his bare chest, and leaned my head against his collarbone.

"Good." I sighed as he lifted me. "You can carry me home."

15

⁓◦∘◦⁓

If you choose to let your vampire guest feed from you, keep a heavy silver object handy. Also, remember to take vitamin and iron supplements.

—*The Care and Feeding of Stray Vampires*

I managed to get back to the house before collapsing completely. Cal propped me up on the couch, forcing as much orange juice into my system as possible and covering me with a soft blue fleece blanket. He tried to make me some toast but nearly set my kitchen on fire. So I settled for valerian tea and lemon drops.

I was going to need serious therapy *and* a new toaster.

As far as we could tell, whoever was running the grow operation had returned to the site and seen us rooting around in the shed. But their decision to eliminate the problem "naturally" by dosing Cal with pollen from the fangwort plants left us with even more questions. Did they know what we were looking for? Did they know that one of us was a vampire, or had they just assumed and hoped for the best? Did they know that they'd dosed Cal, specifically? I guessed that they probably didn't. If so, I said, they probably would have stuck around to see the job finished.

Cal seemed to find that insulting.

I hadn't quite processed the whole thing. I was tired and weak and really wanted the "mortal peril" business to stop. I had wanted Cal, wanted him desperately. But that sort of encounter was very different for me. It didn't feel wrong, but the idea that I had that sort of passion in me, that sort of violence, scared me.

There was no reason for fangwort to have this effect on vampires. I couldn't find any chemical or physiological reason for the plant to make Cal all bloodthirsty. I found that frustrating to the point of throwing one of Jane's books across the room. Unfortunately, Cal was in the way at the time and took my books away for the rest of the night.

He also said, for the safety of his cranium, that I should just chalk the strange vampire reactions up to "general mystical forces" for now.

Another irritating mystery was Cal's ability to pull back from bloodlust and settle for plain old lust. From what we'd read, the vampires affected by the poisonings were so overwhelmed by thirst that they tore their victims apart indiscriminately, even if those people were close friends or lovers. And if I tried to ask him about it, he found creative ways to leave the room.

It was doubly upsetting to Cal, knowing that a vampire of his age had lost control so quickly and that the substance was capable of affecting vampires in airborne form. He'd been lost, he said, to the call of my blood, even though he knew it was wrong and he didn't want to hurt me. The possibility of it being used as some sort of aerosol weapon against vampires, and therefore the humans around them, seriously concerned him. But considering Cal's ability to "pull himself out" of his bloodthirsty state, we assumed that the inhaled pollen was less potent than the ingested version. That made sense, as much as any of this made sense. A vampire's digestive system was a bit more active than his respiratory system.

Once I'd convinced Cal that tearing through the Council offices like a wrecking ball, searching for the person who'd locked us in, wasn't a good idea, he finally settled down enough to sit still and drink a bottle of clean donor blood. Cal had worked too hard to get the answers he needed to risk exposure through a bloody, destructive tantrum. Besides, if anyone was going to have the stakey hissy fit all over Mr. Evil Pollen, it was me. The courts were more lenient regarding human-on-vampire violence. I could get away with it.

I was afraid that Cal would distance himself from me, either because I was pushing him or because he was afraid he'd hurt me. But rather than shutting down and shutting me out, Cal seemed afraid to let me out of his sight. From the moment I walked through the door, Cal was with me. He helped Gigi cook before I arrived home, to make sure I would eat. When I got into the shower, he joined me and scrubbed my back.

It felt like home. It felt like having a family. It felt . . . a little claustrophobic.

OK, the shower thing I didn't mind so much.

But when he tried getting up before sunset so he could "have dinner" with us, I blew up.

"What is going on with you? What if we didn't happen to have the kitchen blinds closed? Is this because you're trying to make up for the, uh—" I looked toward Gigi, who was applying herself to her last-minute math homework with too much earnestness to be genuine. "The incident? I told you, I'm fine. It's no big deal."

Cal put his reading aside and cast a sidelong glance at my sister. "Gigi, would you mind going into the office and getting a file marked 'Blue Moon Financials'?" he asked.

"I know when I'm being sent out of the room, you know," she said, frowning into her salad.

"Good, then you know I'm doing it to avoid being rude to you, which is a mark of respect," he countered.

She growled and launched a grade-A flounce from the room. "I hate when logic works against me."

"I told you, I'm fine, nothing a few iron supplements couldn't take care of," I whispered, knowing that Gigi was listening outside the door. "If you're trying to prove to yourself that there aren't any aftereffects of the pollen—"

"It's not that," he said, stroking the still-raw bite mark I'd hidden under a collared Beeline shirt. "I can feel something coming, Iris, something that's going to resolve this mess. It's a sort of tickle at the edge of my brain telling me I'm close to a solution. My time here is coming to a close."

"Oh." I slumped back against the couch. "Oh."

I hadn't thought of Cal's leaving in days. He was enmeshed in our home now, our lives. I forgot that he only considered it a temporary situation, and an inconvenient one at that. Cheeks pink, I averted my eyes and wanted the floor to swallow me.

"I don't want to waste what time I have left with you," he said softly.

"Oh."

Why couldn't I stop saying "Oh"?

He smiled, affecting a cheerful tone of voice. "The good news is that I will be exacting bloody, anatomically detailed revenge on the person who nearly killed you—twice. And, of course, you'll have your life back."

My expression must have been hurt, because when Gigi walked back in with the file, she faltered a bit. I recovered, smiling. She frowned and handed Cal the file.

Cal flipped through the file, sending a pile of papers sliding into my lap. It was the Vee Balm Inc. Articles of Organization. The papers were filed three years before, in Delaware, a state known for its leniency toward vampire businesses. The papers outlined the initial statements required to form a limited liability company and helped the state track the company's officers, inventory, and property. I glanced over the papers before handing them back to Cal.

"Hey, what's this?" I stooped to pick up a battered yellow Post-it half stuck to the third page of the document I was holding. I peeled the note from the page and handed it to Cal.

"It's just copying instructions," Cal said, reading the note aloud. *"Copy 2x, one to 1420 Hillington Drive, one to PO Box 0609, both Half-Moon Hollow KY 42002/1—PO BOX—SECOND REQUEST—was pissed on phone."*

I took it from him. "Let me interpret for you. It means someone else in the Hollow requested a copy of Vee Balm's company charter paperwork before you did. And apparently, they had to ask for it twice and were not happy about it. Also, the office staff is careless about where they leave sticky notes," I said, looking the Post-it over. "Why would someone from the Hollow request a copy of the company's charter? Was it sent to the Council's PO box?"

Gigi shook her head. "No. All Council office boxes start with a double zero. It's a special designation through an agreement with the postal service to get free postage. This is a standard box number." Cal raised his eyebrows. "What? Sammi Jo's mom works at the post office."

Cal stared at us for a long, drawn-out pause, his expression thunderstruck. A wide grin split his face, and he sprang up from his seat. He clutched Gigi's face between his palms.

"You, my sweet girls, are brilliant," Cal said, giving her cheek a smacking kiss before lunging for me and giving me a long, wet kiss.

Gigi, who was used to casual contact with Cal now, shrugged. "I've always said so."

Cal pulled open his laptop and opened a Web site I didn't recognize. He tried a reverse lookup of the PO box by number, but it came back as "private." He bolted out of the room and came back with his jacket and Gigi's keys. "I need to borrow your car, Gigi."

She lifted an eyebrow. "Where are you going?"

"I can't tell you."

"When will you be back?" I asked.

"I don't know."

"Well, by all means, please take my vehicle," Gigi muttered. "Is this my reward for being a genius?"

"I'm sorry. I would borrow Iris's car, but it's a little . . ."

"Conspicuous?" I suggested.

He nodded, eyeing me carefully. "You could say that a vampire driving a canary-yellow minivan is conspicuous, yes. I'll bring it back with a full tank, Gigi."

"Do you have liability insurance?" Gigi asked in an airy tone, clearly enjoying herself.

Cal narrowed his eyes at her. "She gets this from you," he told me.

Gigi sighed, the picture of teen martyrdom. "OK, but only because the idea of you squishing those long legs behind the wheel of a VW Bug amuses me," she said. "Oh, wait, I'm going to go get the little bud-vase attachment for the cupholder."

He groaned as she scampered out of the room.

"Are you going to break into the post office?" I asked.

"Don't think of it as breaking in, think of it as liberating information."

"In a way that involves breaking windows and several federal laws."

He shrugged. "I've done it before."

I cried, "Don't tell me that!"

"Really, all post-office door codes are the same."

"Don't tell me that, either!" I exclaimed. "I'm sure that just knowing that is some sort of felony. Look, I don't think this is safe. You don't think it's a wonderfully strange coincidence that this Post-it just happened to end up stuck to your copy?"

"No. In general, that's the way my gift works, some random happenstance that leads me to what I'm looking for."

"So it's not so much a gift as blind stinking luck."

"Don't think of it that way. Think of it as serendipity." When I rolled my eyes, he nuzzled my neck. "It led me to you."

"You're not strong enough yet!" I cried. "Let me come with you."

"No. I've learned my lesson, Iris. And after what happened in the shed, don't even think of arguing," he said. "I want you and Gigi to be seen out in public, somewhere with lots of people."

"Yes, thank you for including me in this decision that affects me. I am so glad my opinions and considerations were taken into account."

"Trust me, your needs were taken into account, which is why you aren't going," he said, slipping into his jacket. "I shouldn't be gone for more than a few hours. If you come home and I'm not here, if anything seems wrong, I want you to call Ophelia. Tell her the information she needs is in graphite under petal."

"Is that considered English?"

"She'll understand eventually."

"So was this the big 'moment' you were waiting for?" I asked.

He shook his head. "No, but it's a step in the right direction. It's coming, Iris. And when it does—"

"All set!" Gigi crowed as she bounced back into the room. "I even put a Britney Spears CD in the stereo for you."

It took the concentration of every single cell in my body to keep from bursting out laughing at the expression on Cal's face.

"I'll be back soon," he told me, kissing me softly. Gigi made requisite gagging noises until Cal walked out the front door. We watched as he folded himself into the little green car and drove away.

I tried to tamp down my disquiet. He was just running to the post office. People did that every day . . . in broad daylight . . . when it was open. Still, it wasn't as if someone was going to be lying in wait there just in case Cal caught a misdirected Post-it. But why had Cal given me the weird instructions? Why did he seem so worried?

And when he kissed me, why did it feel like good-bye?

When the brake lights cleared my driveway, I turned on Gigi. "What do you want?"

Her brow creased, and her blue eyes widened to the point where she looked like an animé character. I knew something was up. "Why would you assume that I want something?"

I crossed my arms and gave her a speculative once-over. "June 2007, you wanted your ears pierced a second time. Your grades improved to a three-point-four average without a lecture from me on responsibility or buckling down. November 2008, you wanted an iPod for Christmas. Without preamble, the garbage was routinely taken out without my nagging, and the laundry pile mysteriously disappeared from the office couch. June 2009, you wanted a car. The recycling miraculously sorted itself. History shows that your sudden willingness to share your car, which you've never even let *me* drive, has to be connected to some sort of personal goal."

She winced, wringing her hands and bouncing on the balls of her feet. "I might have told Sammi Jo and Braelynn that I would meet them for ice cream tonight at ten."

Excellent—mundane details to distract me!

"At ten? On a school night?" I exclaimed.

"They're both in rehearsals for the spring musical," she said, her tone tipping toward wheedling. "They won't get out until ten. I haven't seen them in weeks. Please, Iris, please! I've got all of my homework done, and I don't have any tests tomorrow. I'll be home by eleven."

I checked my watch. It was around seven-thirty. Cal had told us to go somewhere public, with lots of witnesses.

"I tell you what, you and I will go see a movie, and I'll drop you off at the Dairy Freeze on the way home. Can Sammi Jo give you a ride?"

"Yes!" she cried, hugging me. "Thank you, thank you!"

"Don't thank me yet," I told her. "I get to pick the movie."

"Oh, no." She moaned. "Come on, Iris, I can't suffer through an Iris pick on a school night!"

"My movie taste isn't that bad," I protested as she grabbed her purse.

She snorted. "Says the girl who paid top dollar to see *The Bounty Hunter* in the theater."

"I have an inappropriate loyalty to Gerard Butler," I grumbled, shutting the door behind us.

"OK, but did you have to buy it on DVD?" Gigi chuckled.

"It was a Christmas gift. Uncle Clark grabs the DVD with the silliest cover and wraps it," I shot back, climbing into the driver's seat of the Dorkmobile. "I am willing to admit that Gerard Butler has single-handedly murdered the romantic comedy."

Gigi snickered. "Gerard Butler took the romantic comedy to an orgy, accidentally strangled it during an air game, panicked, and dumped its body in the woods."

I stared at her, gobsmacked. "That may be the funniest thing I've ever heard—" I spluttered. "How the hell do you even know what an air game is?"

Gigi preened. "Just because you put the parental locks on HBO doesn't mean I can't get around them."

Gigi and I attended a showing of the Bollywood version of *Pride and Prejudice* at the Palladium. The once-great theater had fallen into disrepair over the years, becoming the local "throwback dollar movie" theater during the last decade. At Jane's suggestion, Gabriel had bought the theater, refurbished it to its former glory, and turned it into a "nostalgia house" showing old black-and-white movies, eighties classics, and the like. Every Thursday was Jane Austen Night, to honor Jane's fetish for all things Bennet and Darcy.

Having expected to see something loud and stupid at the multiplex, Gigi was not pleased with this turn of events.

"Why didn't you ask Miss Jane to come with you?" Gigi asked as I bought tickets for *Bride & Prejudice*.

"Jane won't do movies with me anymore. I went to her house for *Sense and Sensibility* night. And when I pointed out, quite rightly, that Marianne was a twit and Colonel Brandon would have been better off marrying Elinor, Jane turned gray and started yelling."

"There better not be subtitles," Gigi groused, leading me to the candy counter, where I was already eyeing a box of Goobers in the display case.

There were very few subtitles. The movie was a nice blend of Hollywood glamour and Bollywood flair, with just enough snarky humor. Gigi even giggled a few times. I relaxed back into my seat, pushing aside for a moment money problems, Cal, mortal peril.

I forgot sometimes what it was like just to be lazy. Not to run, run, run, checking through the list of things that had to be accomplished that day or the sky would fall down around my ears.

I was content to sit there with my large popcorn, soaking up the revamped romanticism, but Gigi was up every twenty minutes to go to the bathroom. After the third trip, I started worrying about her kidneys. When she bounced out of her seat during Darcy's disastrous proposal, I waited a minute and followed her out to the lobby.

Unfortunately, the other movie had just let out, and a crowd flooded the lobby. Apparently, a lot of people wanted to *Sense and Sensibility* that night. I searched the flow of faces, looking for Gigi. I turned the corner around the concession stand and saw Mr. Dodd leaning against the wall, scanning the crowd. Dropping my popcorn, I ducked into the crowded ladies' room. There was a line, of course, and I subtly glanced under the stall doors for Gigi's turquoise striped sneakers.

"Gigi?" I hissed.

No response, other than concerned or irritated looks from the other ladies in the bathroom.

"Gigi Scanlon, if you're in here and ignoring me while I make a jackass out of myself, I am going to be very pissed."

Other than a few feminine snickers . . . nothing.

I stuck my head out through the door and checked for Mr. Dodd. I didn't see him, but I did see my sister, ducking in from an exterior door, looking all flushed and happy. She was tucking her phone into her pocket and looking around the lobby. She turned her back to me while peeking down the corridor. I snuck up behind her and tapped her on the shoulder, all the while watching out for Mr. Dodd.

"I know exactly what you're up to, sister."

She shrieked and whirled on me. "Iris, I—I'm so sorry!"

"I see how you are, skipping out on valuable sisterly bonding time to secretly text Ben." I scowled at her. "You'd rather exchange xoxo's with your supercute boyfriend than watch a girlie movie with me."

"No one xoxo's." She laughed, her cheeks flushing. "I'm sorry, Iris. It's nothing personal. But the 'Snake Dance' sequence was just too much for me."

"It's—" I turned to see Mr. Dodd across the lobby. A cold, watery sensation seeped through my chest, surging to an all-out tidal wave when the crowd parted enough to let me see the long, lean frame of Peter Crown stepping from behind Mr. Dodd. Mr. Crown whispered furiously to Mr. Dodd, who was pointing in our direction. Crown turned, his steely eyes locking with mine. He mouthed something along the lines of "Get them out to the car."

I grabbed Gigi's arm. "It's fine. We're leaving."

"Because I took too many trips to text?"

I looked over my shoulder as a steady stream of people moved between us and the vampires, preventing them from inconspicuously crossing the lobby. I did, however, hear Mr. Dodd growling, "Get *out* of my way!" as he tried to move through the clumped concession line.

"We just have to go," I told Gigi, pulling her through the front door, staying tucked within a large group moving toward the parking lot. I pulled her behind me, forcing her to walk faster.

"Iris, why are you being all weird?"

"I'm naturally weird," I said, breaking into a sprint and tugging her along. "Come on. You can get to the Dairy Freeze a little early, get some chili cheese fries before Sammi Jo and Braelynn show up and start talking about diets."

"Ugh." She groaned as I unlocked the car. I kept an eye on the door of the theater, watching as the vampires moved across the pavement toward us. "I hope no one sees me riding around in this."

I was suddenly very much on board with Gigi's arguments against driving around in a bright yellow van. This was not the vehicle you drove when you wanted to be incognito. She slouched down in her seat while I pulled out of the lot.

I was able to relax a little once we were safely on the main drag through town. Vampires or no, Crown and Dodd weren't going to abduct us from a street in front of dozens of other drivers. I pulled my phone from my purse and saw that I had a voicemail waiting. Gigi raised her eyebrows when I punched in my access code and listened. I was usually the one giving her "distracted driving is the moron's equivalent to drunk driving" lectures. But I figured that fleeing from disingenuous vampire administrators called for a special exception.

The voicemail was from Ophelia. It was brief and cryptic, like most conversations with Ophelia. "Iris, I thought you'd want to know I finally tracked down a hard copy of that delivery schedule we discussed. Peter

Crown was assigned to that task. Keep that in mind. Keep the information close to you. Stay where you are. I will talk to you soon."

Mr. Crown had delivered the poisoned blood to Cal's house? Not surprising. Ophelia managed to find this information *after* Mr. Crown chased us out of a Jane Austen movie? Well, that was decidedly unhelpful.

Which was also in line with most of my conversations with Ophelia.

I dialed Cal's cell phone, but he didn't pick up. I dialed Ophelia's number, but I got sent to voicemail. I left her a message saying that I'd seen the gentleman we'd discussed before at the movie theater, and I hoped she'd catch up to him.

Gigi gave me a suspicious look. I offered her a grim smile but checked the rearview mirror every few minutes to see if we were being followed. Annoyed with my antics, Gigi was overeager to get out of the car when I pulled into the lot of the Dairy Freeze.

"Free at last." She sighed.

"Have fun," I said. "Stay here at the drive-in. Stay with the other girls. Call me if your plans change."

"I always do," she said.

"Hey!" I called as she closed the door. She yanked it back open. "Love you."

"Weirdo," she muttered, slamming the door shut.

I watched as she walked into the restaurant and took a booth to wait for her friends. I felt myself relax slightly. As long as she stayed around witnesses, Gigi was safe.

Whatever strange sense of foreboding I felt now had to be defused by the knowledge that she was secure. My mind raced as I calculated my options. I waited for a few minutes and pulled out into the street. I dialed Cal's number again but was directed to his voicemail.

"Hey, Cal," I said. "Um, I hope I'm not blowing your cover as you're crawling through the air ducts. I don't know what you're doing. But I'm really hoping you're on your way home. Because it is your home. I know you've spent a good portion of your time avoiding emotional complications, but I do have them—emotions, that is. Um, if you run into Peter Crown from the Council office, I'm pretty sure he's the one who poisoned you. I don't have any proof, of course, but it's a pretty good hunch." I glanced into the rearview and saw the lights of a car staying a careful twenty yards behind me, as it had been for a few blocks. "I—I've got to go, but I hope I'll see you soon. I love you."

I tucked the cell phone into the console and commanded my hands to stay still and steady on the wheel.

"No big deal, Scanlon," I told myself. "Sure, you're being followed by a creepy vampire client and an undead bureaucrat who may or may not be involved in a string of vampire poisonings. And your pseudo-boyfriend is MIA. You just entrusted the safety of your baby sister to another seventeen-year-old with a history of night-vision problems. Nothing can go wrong here."

Ophelia had told me to stay where I was. I could only

assume that she thought I was at home. So I turned left onto County Line Road. The car behind me didn't turn, leaving me alone on a proverbial dark country lane. Apparently, I wasn't being followed.

"Shoot," I grumbled. "I probably shouldn't have said my first 'I love you' in a voicemail."

16

Their survival instincts honed from centuries of intrigue, vampires tend to be self-interested creatures. Do not overestimate their loyalty toward you. You will be disappointed or seriously injured.

—The Care and Feeding of Stray Vampires

Remembering Cal's instructions, I slipped my cell phone into my pocket as I trod up the porch steps. The house was just as we'd left it, living-room lights on, front door locked. I locked the door behind me and dropped my purse onto the foyer table. I'd just reached the landing when I heard someone bumping around in the living room. The footfalls were heavy, booted, the rhythm too masculine to be Gigi's light step.

"Cal?" I called, stepping carefully down the stairs. I turned into the living room to find a strange teenage boy rifling through my writing desk. The living room had been tossed, a hurricane path of damage stretching from the door to the kitchen.

"What are you doing in my house?" I asked, carefully moving toward the door. I fished my phone out of my pocket. There was a flash of movement, and the vampire was standing nose-to-nose with me. He slapped my phone out of my hand and sent it flying. The shattered pieces of black plastic rained down at our feet.

Vampires were not kind to BlackBerrys.

He was just a boy, really, turned at eighteen or so. He was a lithe, whippet-thin kid with pale blond hair artfully arranged into stylish chaos. Everything about the pale storm-gray eyes and elegant features spoke of menace. He leaned far too close for comfort and inhaled deeply. His intense, hungry expression had me backing toward the door.

He purred. "Miss Scanlon, I need you to stay calm."

"Who are you?"

"You can call me John. I'm just a courier, really, Iris. May I call you Iris?" he asked, offering me an ingratiating smile. Hesitantly, I nodded, but I refrained from taking the slim white hand he offered me. A ripple of disappointment flashed across his face before he settled his features into a polite mask. "It's lovely to meet you . . . face-to-face, so to speak."

He snickered as if he was enjoying some private joke. The sly laugh sent a nauseating echo through my belly.

"I need you to come with me, quickly, quietly, and without a fuss." His voice wound its way around in my head, like cotton soaked in some sweet, cloying medicine. I couldn't breathe. I could barely keep my head up.

"Why?" My head felt heavy. My thick tongue made it hard to form words, and I just wanted to close my eyes. Numb, I slumped against him, and he gently pushed me into a nearby chair.

"I finally caught up to your Mr. Calix. I've been watching your house off and on for a week, and this is the first time he's left it alone." He knelt in front of me, pulling at my chin so I was forced to look him in the eye. He grinned wickedly. "It was luck, you see, stupid luck. The night your vampire disappeared, I followed your scent from his place to yours. There was no sign of our Mr. Calix from the outside, not even his scent. All I got was the maddening smell of all those flowers in your garden. So I went back to Deer Haven and waited." He trailed his fingers down my throat, to the long-healed bite mark he'd left on my skin. His fangs dropped, and he licked his lips. "And then, to stumble onto you when you returned to his home—his scent on you was so strong. I was sure he was at your house. But you were so careful to be home before dark. I couldn't get information from you or about you. I was perplexed for days. And then, one night, I was out at a high-school football game. Large crowds are good places to find prey. And I found that scent again. Like lavender with just a hint of iron.

"Your sister was so sweet, so eager to please. And delicious. Both of you have such a delicate bouquet. It's as if spending so much time in the garden has steeped flowers into your very skin. Every time we met, I asked her more questions to gauge how your guest's investigation was progressing. And she was just so, mmm, accommodating."

My mouth dropped open. What had this freak done with my little sister? When had he had time to see her? Had he fed from her? Had he hurt her? Taken advantage of her? Hot, boiling rage bubbled up in my throat, freeing my tongue enough to let me say, "I'm going to kill you. A lot."

His grin seemed to stretch even wider at my slurred words. "There's no need to be rude, sweet thing. Especially since we're going to be spending so much time together after my employer takes care of your Calix. You and Gigi are going to be a sort of bonus, you see. I was afraid, after you stumbled onto the grow operation, that I'd lost you. I didn't want to lock you in that shed with him, but I couldn't risk him making it to the Council before I'd had a chance to collect from my employer. It pained me, the thought of wasting your blood in such a stupid, pointless manner. Leaving before I was sure that he'd finished the job was a mistake, but I just couldn't bear to listen to you being destroyed. I would have made do with just Gigi, but . . . but it's all worked out for the best, hasn't it? You and Gigi and your delicious blood are just the sort of treat I deserve for a job well done. And when I've tired of feeding from you—though I can't imagine that will happen anytime soon—I'll turn you. And then we'll be together forever, one big, happy family."

The leering, dreamy quality to his voice gave me an idea of the bonding activities he had planned for that happy family. That thought was sobering enough. I pinched my arm, letting the pain bring me into some sort of focus. I shook my head and tried to concentrate on the words he was speaking, rather than his voice. "When I kill you, it's going to involve injuries to your crotch."

He chuckled and pinched my cheek, as if I were a charming toddler. "Well, I would love to hear about any plans you have for that particular area of my body, but my employer is eager to see you. I strung him along for weeks, lying about my progress. I wanted him to be desperate for the information about Mr. Calix. I wanted him to pay top dollar. So giving him hints was quite profitable. And Gigi proved to be so amusing I wanted it to last and last."

He was doing something extra now; there was a musical quality to his voice. My head drooped, a heavy bloom on a weak stem. My chin touched my chest under its weight.

"Now," he said, patting my head, "if you would wait here, I need to retrieve Mr. Calix's files. You don't move from this spot, do you understand? If you move or make a noise, I will be very, very upset. You wouldn't want that, would you?"

I shook my head. It didn't seem like such an unreasonable request, really, sitting at my own kitchen table. I smiled and folded my hands in my lap, as still as stone as he moved up the stairs. The farther he moved away, the clearer my head became, but the strange numb weight kept my arms in my lap.

I heard a car pull up outside. I wanted to call out a warning to Gigi, to spring up from the chair and run out to her, but I couldn't move. My fingers wouldn't even twitch. If I moved, the world would end. The ceiling would come crashing down on my head. I couldn't even draw the breath to squeak. I just sat there, my hands clamped together.

I heard Gigi clomp through the front door. "Iris, is everything OK? Why is the living room all messy?"

I looked up, unable to produce any sounds beyond heavy breathing. I had to stand, had to get up. I had to tell Gigi to get out. Lifting my arms to put my hands against the table took all of my strength. I imagined all of my energy gathering in my palms, pushing against the scarred pine surface.

"Iris, are you all right?"

"Geeeee," I whispered, my eyes pleading with her. *Run. Leave, run away, and never come back.* Her pale, frightened face swam in front of mine.

I heard footsteps on the stairs. I couldn't even turn my head to see the vampire boy trotting into the kitchen. He dropped Cal's laptop bag and a box of files on the table.

"Gigi?" he said, giving her a charming lopsided grin.

"John!" she cried, shooting a significant look at me. "Um, what are you doing here?"

Oh, right, my sister had been dating our burglar. Behind my back. The last tendrils of fog seemed to clear from my head. I narrowed my eyes at her and demanded, "Gigi, who is this?"

She blanched and looked down at the hands twisting in her lap. "Um . . ."

"Spill it," I ground out.

"That's John," she said, giving a nervous little chuckle. "He's sort of my boyfriend."

"I thought . . . Ben?" I mumbled.

Gigi's face sort of crumpled into that weird "there's something I don't want to tell you" origami expression. "Every time I was supposed to be going out with Ben, he would drive me to meet John."

"Wh-why did Ben agree to that?" I asked, struggling over the syllables.

She shrugged. "Because he really likes me."

"Gigi!"

"Shut up, both of you!" John yelled, exasperated. "This is not the time for girl talk."

We both shrank back into our chairs, chastened.

"Both of you, just be quiet," he said, his tone stern but not unfriendly. "Gigi, I'm very glad to see you. Now that you're here, you can help me."

The smooth, velvety tenor of his voice seemed to curl around her body, making her relax and sag into the chair. A dreamy smile tilted the corners of her mouth, and she leaned into the caress of his voice.

"Don't you want to help me, Gigi?" he asked, his lips nearly touching her ear. She nodded, smiling shyly. "Just close your eyes and sit there quietly," he whispered.

With his focus aimed elsewhere, I was able to move again, to concentrate. Gigi's eyelids drooped, and her head dropped to her chest as if she'd suddenly decided to take a nap at our kitchen table.

"Hey!" I stood up from my chair, flinging it behind me. "What are you doing to her?"

He turned on me, that winsome expression firmly

in place, although his eyes were as dead and blank as a shark's. "Sit down and be a good girl, like your sister."

Although I fought against the urge to obey, my arms reached out of their own volition and righted the chair. I sat heavily, gripping the edge of the table and praying for the strength to push up and stand again. But the urge to stay seated seemed to be the only thing that kept me breathing. If I stood, something terrible would happen. John hummed a tuneless ditty as he opened the back door and disappeared into the house. His absence let me flex my hand enough to reach out to Gigi. But then he came back, and the music clogged my thinking.

The humming continued while John wrapped duct tape around our ankles, secured our wrists behind our backs, and put us into the trunk of his car. The humming was so soothing, so calming, that my limbs were too limp and heavy to push John away. Hell, I even tilted my head helpfully so John could tie my blindfold more easily. I was only able to move and think freely after the trunk slammed shut and the humming stopped. Even in that small, cramped space, it felt easier to breathe.

It took a few long, agonizing miles for me to focus enough to rub my face against the carpet of the trunk. I worked until the blindfold slipped from my eyes and around my neck.

"Gigi," I whispered, my tongue heavy and thick. She didn't stir, so I kicked her shins. She jerked awake, head rolling wildly around in the little space.

"Iris, what—where are we?"

"Deep breaths, Geeg," I told her, shaking the last foggy remnants of John's influence from my head. I leaned forward to tug the blindfold down with my teeth.

Head lolling, she blinked against the harsh red light of the brake lights. I cleared my throat.

"What the *hell* has gotten into you, Gladiola Grace?"

"Wow, you sounded exactly like Mom just then."

"Don't flatter me." I growled. "Why did you lie to me? Did you think I would forbid you to date him? Did you think I wouldn't understand that you wanted to go out with a vampire? I would never judge you, because clearly—pot, kettle, black, hello?"

Gigi squirmed uncomfortably. "Vampire?"

"John is a vampire."

She scoffed. "No, he's not."

"Are you telling me that you did not notice that your boyfriend doesn't have a pulse?"

"Well, it's not like I was feeling around on his wrist."

I closed my eyes and bit my tongue, because I did not want to know where she *had* been "feeling around." Instead, I asked, "Have you ever seen him during the day?" She shook her head. "Have you ever seen him eat?"

The two of us smacked our heads together when the car hit a bump. She winced. "I thought he was a little cold."

I groaned and promised myself that if we lived through this, my sister would be sent to a convent school.

"He came to a football game at school. I knew he wasn't the sort of boy you wanted me to date, so I had Ben cover for us. He was mysterious and perfect and charming."

"If you tell me that he wooed you by reciting passages

from *Twilight* as if they were actual conversation, I'm going to have to bludgeon you with that tire iron."

"You promised you wouldn't judge!" she exclaimed.

"I promised I wouldn't judge, not that I wouldn't mock. I don't suppose you managed to sneak your phone in here with us, did you?"

"It's in my back pocket," she said, her eyes alight with excitement. It took a few tries for us to roll over, with our hands bound, then get my hands lined up with her pockets.

"No, not that one," she said as I blindly patted her cargos.

"Seriously, how many pockets do you need in one pair of pants?" I grunted. "Shift your butt."

Gigi shifted as John turned a corner. Just as my fingertips found the solid, square weight of the cell phone, the turn sent Gigi rolling across the floor of the trunk, her head thunking into mine.

"Ow!" I yelped, wincing as the bruised spot on my head grazed the tire iron and Gigi's head-butt landed. I closed my eyes, clenching my teeth as the pain radiated through my head. The scent of Gigi's shampoo—lavender, wisteria, and jasmine—wafted up to my nostrils. It was a calming scent. It reminded me of the relative safety of our bathroom at home, of sitting out in the garden with a glass of lemonade. And something else.

The car slowed. I patted Gigi's pockets, frantically trying to manipulate the phone out of her awkwardly wrinkled pocket. I had no idea how I would dial it or talk, but it had to be better than lying there like a hog waiting for slaughter.

"You got it?" she asked.

The car stopped completely.

Gigi whimpered. "What's going to happen, Iris?"

"I don't know, Geeg," I whispered back, still working the phone out of her pocket. "We're going to be OK."

I heard her sniff. "You don't know that."

"No, but I'm the big sister; it's my job to lie."

The trunk popped open, and John's face appeared overhead. I pulled my hand away from the phone and pretended that I was trying to comfort my sister. He tsked indulgently, pulling the cloths back over our eyes. "Naughty, naughty. What have you two been up to back here? I could hear you talking, you know. I've always wondered what two sisters talk about late into the night. I'm definitely going to keep you around long enough to find out . . ."

Ugh. Evil, creepy teenagers.

John hauled us out of the trunk by our elbows and set us on our feet. He cut the tape away from our ankles and then linked his arms through ours, like he was escorting us to a garden party.

"Step carefully, my pretty things," he said, helping us down a long, uneven path as he hummed a happy tune. He pushed us gently onto a bench, the cool metal un-yielding against our awkwardly positioned hands. I heard a low, threatening growl to our left. Gigi shrank into my side. I shushed her. "Now, you two just sit there and look appetizing. No funny business."

There was silence. I assumed that John had stepped away. The humming had stopped, and my head cleared.

We were surrounded by pleasant earthy scents. A strange sensation niggled at the corner of my mind. Something I should be remembering. Wisteria. The light citrus of commuter daylilies. Mulch . . . no, ginkgo. The sour "earthy" scent of ginkgo. Where was I when I'd last smelled ginkgo?

"Oh, sonofabitch!" I yelled.

Gigi gasped at my right. "Iris, you said a cuss word!"

"And I'm about to say a few more. Sonofabitch!"

"No, that's the same one," she reminded me.

"Wisteria, ginkgo, crepe myrtle. Those weren't black-thumb plants!"

"Have you been drinking?" Gigi asked.

"His garden is chock-full of temperamental wonders." I continued to rant. "He has flipping Mexican heather. Do you know how temperamental Mexican heather is? I'm astonished that he could keep it alive. Our winters are too cold. Our summers are too hot. If you let the soil dry out the least little bit—"

"I get it, I get it. You're a big plant geek," Gigi said. "What the hell are you talking about?"

"Mr. Marchand. He said he had bad luck with plants when I visited him last week. He acted like he didn't know anything about gardening. But I don't care how good your landscapers are, unless they're sitting outside your house twenty-four hours a day with a hose, Mexican heather is going to die without constant, focused care. The kind of care that might go into growing large batches of rare plants used to drive vampires into a frenzy."

"What does that mean?"

"Mr. Marchand is the guy, the guy growing all of the ingredients for the vampire whammy potions. It's more than likely he's the guy brewing and selling them. And I owe Mr. Crown a large apology."

"Awesome, you figured it out," she said. "What now?"

"Nothing. It doesn't really help us."

"Shoot," she grumped. "I really thought you had something there."

"Well, it does show what a gift she has for botany." A new voice sounded to our right. We both jumped at the dulcet baritone. Gigi cowered at my side, ducking her head against my neck. Cool hands peeled down the blindfolds, and the smiling face of Colonel Sanders's evil twin appeared in my line of vision.

Mr. Marchand greeted us cordially. "Ladies, thank you so much for visiting us this evening. I can see the blindfolds are no longer necessary, Miss Iris, since you are so very clever."

We blinked as our eyes adjusted to the dark, fragrant recesses of Mr. Marchand's garden. This was a section I hadn't been shown before, a quiet little alcove near the west end of the porch. A gorgeous hydrangea bloomed to our left. A fountain—a woman pouring water from an earthen jar—burbled cheerfully near a little table and wrought-iron chairs. Little red Japanese lanterns swung from a line overhead. It would have been an elegant, peaceful setting, if not for the whole "hostage" thing and the fact that Cal was gagged and handcuffed to one of the wrought-iron chairs with his laptop open in front of him.

"Cal!" I yelled. "What the hell?"

Mr. Marchand smiled cordially as John stood near Gigi, playing with the dark strands of her hair. Although he spoke with the same genteel tone, all of the amiable manners of the Council official I'd known were gone. This Mr. Marchand was cold, nearly reptilian in his movements, as his gaze bounced back and forth between his new guests and Cal. "Your friend, Mr. Calix, has been most unhelpful in resolving a little administrative matter. It might have something to do with injecting debilitating poison into his gift blood. Some people hold grudges."

Dark with hate, Cal's eyes were narrowed on Mr. Marchand, tracking his every movement. His lips curled back into a snarl as he struggled against the cuffs. Each movement of his wrist made his skin blacken and burn as he came into contact with the cuffs. Silver cuffs. Mr. Marchand had been torturing him with silver.

Bastard!

My own lip curled back into a snarl. If I lived through this, Mr. Marchand was going to be in a lot of pain. And you'd better believe I was going to cancel his contract.

"You have been a very naughty girl, Miss Iris," Mr. Marchand chided. "I never would have guessed you were such a talented little liar. I believed you when you said you'd never met Mr. Calix in person. I defended you to the other members of the Council, did you know that? Mr. Crown and Sophie wanted to drag you into the detention center for questioning, and I said, 'Oh, no, not Iris Scanlon. She's as trustworthy as the day is long.' How did you ever manage to fool Sophie's filter system? She would be so upset if she knew. She considers herself to be foolproof."

I stayed quiet but eyed the pots of geraniums hanging from hooks on the porch railing.

"I have to admit it was foolish on my part to hope that Mr. Calix had simply scurried off like a sick animal. After taking the trouble to volunteer for Crown's delivery duties and replace Mr. Calix's gift with my own special blend of bottled blood, not knowing whether it worked was so frustrating."

He laid a hand on my shoulder, a sort of friendly pat from your neighborhood undead sociopath, as he added, "John was able to find all of Mr. Calix's files at your home, and his backup drives. But, industrious little squirrel that he is, your vampire backed up every document and note onto an online storage service. Can you imagine the liability of all of those documents just floating out there in the ether? We can't allow that. But we can't seem to get him to share the password with us so we can delete the account. I thought perhaps the presence of you and your sister might persuade him to be more accommodating."

He slipped behind me, squeezing my shoulder affectionately. His lips were at my ear, the bristles of his mustache tickling the skin. "You see, if he doesn't hand over the password and delete every single file, I'm going to rip out your little sister's throat. And I'm going to make you watch. Imagine how much it will hurt him to see you suffer that. And then, as much as it pains me, I'm going to let John do every depraved, twisted little thing he's talked about nonstop since meeting you. And your Mr. Calix will have a front-row seat for it all."

Despite the fact that every word turned my insides to water, I kept a still, serene expression in place. I kept my voice friendly, sweet, as if we were all sitting around in this garden scene waiting for mint juleps and petit fours to be served. "I think there's been some misunderstanding, Mr. Marchand. Hurting me isn't going to bother Mr. Calix. I'm just his employee."

"I think you're a bit more than that, dear. Your Gigi gave John a lovely picture of the domestic life you've built together. It was charming, really, to hear it from her perspective. Imagine, an ancient like Calix falling in love with a little human girl from the Hollow."

Cal wouldn't look at me—couldn't, I supposed, if he didn't want to see my face as Mr. Marchand gave his secrets away.

I cleared my throat, pushing past the hot, tight sensation of it closing. "Fine. If you think I mean so much to him, it's not necessary for Gigi to be here. Let her go."

"I don't think you understand how negotiations work," he told me.

"You're not the first to say so. Look, I will be a very cooperative hostage if you let my sister go."

"You'll be a more cooperative hostage if the imminent threat of your sister's death is hanging over your head."

"Damn, that's a good point," I admitted.

He chuckled, patting me on the head. "Now, Mr.

Calix, have you reconsidered your stance? Surely the well-being of two innocents outweighs the considerations of such a minor administrative matter."

"It's hardly a problem with ordering office supplies," I said. "People are dead. Vampires driven mad. You did all that, for what?"

He shrugged amiably. "I wish I could claim some great philosophical motivation. But honestly, I'm in it for the money. I devised the Blue Moon compound knowing how it would affect vampires and knowing that I was the only person who could provide a preventive treatment. I arranged for the 'accidental' release of the altered synthetic blood to the market, took care of the loose ends at Nocturne, and waited for reports of attacks. I was just as shocked and appalled as any vampire when I heard about the violent killings. Imagine the chaos if the poison was distributed on a larger scale, I told the other Council members. And when the time was right, the manufacturers of Vee Balm made contact with the Council offices."

"You made Vee Balm?"

A shrewd look seeped into his icy gray eyes. "Technically, a company in South Bend, Indiana, makes Vee Balm. I just happen to own that company. Well, the subsidiary that owns that company. And another company that supplies the botanical ingredient necessary to make Vee Balm. The same company that just struck a rather lucrative deal to provide Vee Balm to Council chapters in each state. Overall, those contracts will add up to a tidy little nest egg to keep me flush through the next millennium.

"Now, Mr. Calix, have we come to a decision? This is a time-sensitive offer. Your password in exchange for guaranteed safe passage for the Scanlon sisters. The clock is ticking."

"Cal, don't let them get away with this," I told him. "He's bluffing. John's got some disturbing agreement to keep us as his pet blood donors after this is over. I think I can safely say that a quick death would be preferable."

Cal's lip curled back into a snarl. Perhaps my being used as a human bargaining chip was not the best point to bring up. I really did suck at negotiating.

"Tick-tock, Mr. Calix." Mr. Marchand purred, leaning close to Gigi, fangs bared.

My lungs seemed frozen. I couldn't do anything to stop him. He was going to hurt Gigi. I'd failed. I'd failed to keep her safe. Failed to see her grow up. I'd brought this on us with this stupid, pointless business.

"She's so lovely," Mr. Marchand murmured, pulling Gigi's dark hair away from her neck. She closed her eyes and whimpered as he wound it around his hand. He pulled her head back to bare her throat. "I do so enjoy the young ones. They're so . . . unspoiled. John here assures me that our Gigi is a very good girl. Pure as the driven snow. So even if you don't cooperate, I am anticipating a very nice meal and a show. I win either way."

"This isn't the way it's supposed to play out," John protested.

"Gigi," I whispered, whimpering when Mr. Marchand's fingers tightened around the back of Gigi's neck with crushing pressure. "I'm so sorry."

"Screw them sideways." Gigi had gone from sniffling softly at my side to glaring at Mr. Marchand and John with more heat than I thought possible. "They're going to kill us anyway. If John's going to do something creepy and awful to us, I'd rather go sooner than later."

I gritted my teeth, barely able to move my head enough to look Cal in the eye. "Do the smart thing, Cal."

Mr. Marchand moved to strike. I clenched my eyes shut, tucking my head into my shoulder.

"Petal!" Cal shouted. "The password is Petal."

Cal's password was Paul's booty-call nickname for me.

Mr. Marchand's grip relaxed. I sighed. "Not funny, Cal."

"It's a little funny," Gigi muttered, wincing when I elbowed her.

Gigi slumped against me, shrinking away from John's coos and assurances that she would be just fine now.

Mr. Marchand swaggered over to the laptop and tapped the keys. A little bell tone indicated success. He grinned widely. "Excellent."

A few more taps and clicks, and Mr. Marchand was even more pleased with himself.

"Thank you very much." He chuckled. "You have been very helpful. But I am afraid that you're about to meet with an unfortunate accident."

"Well, I, for one, am shocked," John said smarmily.

Mr. Marchand pulled a packet of donor blood from a little red Coleman cooler by the table. He chose one of several carefully labeled syringes arranged on a white cotton pad, then jabbed it into the packet and shook it thoroughly. "I made a special purchase of AB negative for you. I wouldn't want your last meal to consist of synthetic blood." Mr. Marchand shot a sympathetic look at Gigi and me. "Well, I suppose it won't be your *last* meal."

"No." Cal growled, shrinking away as Mr. Marchand held the packet to his lips. Mr. Marchand gripped his hair and shoved the bag into Cal's mouth. He struggled, trying to spit the blood out, to wrench his mouth away, but Mr. Marchand was pouring it down his throat, forcing it down.

"Oh, this is bad," I murmured as Cal spat and coughed.

"What? What's bad?" Gigi asked.

"What are you doing?" John demanded shrilly. "You promised I could keep the Scanlon girls."

"The Scanlon girls are about to fall victim to the unfortunate poisoning-related attacks," Mr. Marchand said blithely, as if describing our lunch plans for the next day. "I stumbled upon him attacking these poor young ladies on the side of the road after Ms. Scanlon's van broke down. I had no choice but to stake him. No loose ends, John."

"No! I will not allow it!"

Mr. Marchand sniffed. "Don't you talk back to me, boy. Don't forget who you're talking to."

John shot back, "Don't forget that I'm four hundred years older than you."

"And yet you act like a petulant child denied a treat."

"Don't call me a child!" John yelled, stamping his foot. While they argued, I felt a gentle tug at the tape behind my back. There were warm, steady hands quietly cutting through the tape and peeling it away.

I looked over my shoulder. Ben Overby held a finger to his lips and shushed me.

"What?" I shrieked as Gigi clapped a hand over my mouth. We all glanced over at the arguing vampires, who hadn't noticed my surprised squawk.

Gigi's tape was already removed. She was subtly rubbing the circulation back into her wrists. When my hands were free, I slowly sat up, watching Mr. Marchand and John arguing.

"What are you doing here?" I whispered as Ben freed my hands. "How did you find us?"

"Not important right now," he whispered, eyeing the vampires warily.

Pushing Gigi behind him, Ben helped me to my feet. Moving faster than I should have on wobbly, cramped legs, I grabbed handfuls of geranium leaves and crushed them, rubbing the oil over my hands and face.

"Here," I said, pulling more leaves loose and rubbing them over Ben's and Gigi's perplexed faces. "Ben, I want you to take Gigi and get to an area with a lot of people. Take my phone out of my bag and dial the number marked 'Ophelia.' Tell her to get to Waco Marchand's place as soon as possible. If that John prick tries to talk to you, I want you to think of anything but what he's saying. Think of geometry formulas, lines from *Avatar*, anything but the bullshit that's coming out of his mouth."

Gigi protested. "I'm not leaving you."

"Yes, you are. Now, get out of here."

"But—but," she spluttered. As she stalled, I saw John's eyes narrow at us over Mr. Marchand's shoulder. He tried to push past Mr. Marchand, to stop the kids, but the older vampire grabbed him and shoved him back into place with a thundering "Listen when I'm talking to you!"

"No buts." I shoved her toward Ben. "Get her out of here now. Gigi, I love you, move it."

Gigi hesitated, but Ben dragged her away. Her stiff, achy legs caught and stumbled, and he helped her to her feet. Mr. Marchand and John were full-on grappling now, with John yelling, "The younger one's getting away, you fool!" I crept carefully over to Cal's slumped form. One of the syringes stuck out from the cooler bag at an odd angle, the label catching my eye. VEE BALM. I snatched, snagged another capped needle, and jammed them into my pocket.

I bent to examine Cal's cuffs, moving slowly so I wouldn't attract the other vampires' attention. The restraints were held together without locks, a rather ingenious but cruel invention. I just had to slide solid pins of silver out of the cuffs to release his wrists. Cal could have freed himself easily, if he could bear to touch the metal.

"What are you doing?" he asked, slurring softly.

"Getting us out of here. Can you walk?"

He nodded, then bent to unwind the wire around his ankles. I pulled out the syringe of Vee Balm.

"I'm sorry about this," I whispered, jabbing the needle into his neck and pushing the plunger. Cal hissed, glaring up at me as the chemicals spread through his bloodstream. I grimaced and showed him the syringe label. "It's going to help."

I knelt and patted his calves, feeling for his sword. "Where's the holster?"

"They took it off of me the moment they captured me," he said, his voice hoarse and tired.

"Now?" I squeaked. "We're in an actual combat situation, and you don't have your sword *now*?"

"You're not in a combat situation," he told me. "You are in a running-and-hiding situation."

"I won't leave you," I insisted, echoing Gigi's stubborn belligerence.

Standing on unsteady legs, he forced me to my feet and cupped my chin in his hand. "Yes, you will."

"Don't make me—"

"If you love me at all, you will leave right now."

"That's not fair, Cal."

"It isn't," he agreed. "But you'll forgive me eventually. Now, go."

I nodded, digging my fingers into the bloodied material of his shirt and yanking him to me so I could lay a hot, desperate kiss on his lips. The metallic tang of polluted donor blood clung to his mouth, but I pressed close, drank him in, unsure of whether I would see him again, feel him next to me. His freed hands locked around my face, caressing my cheeks, tracing the tear tracks he found there.

"Go," he whispered, pushing me away.

And in a flicker of movement, he was gone, running

across the lawn toward the arguing vampires. Swiping at my eyes, I ran around the house, ducking behind an arbor when I sensed movement in the trees. I crept through the long, purple shadows, keeping my back against the house. I wondered if Gigi had made it to Ben's car. I wondered if I could sneak into Marchand's house to use his phone or steal some car keys or if it would be better just to stay there, hiding in the dark . . . which seemed to be the direction that the weak, numbed muscles in my legs were leaning toward.

Outside was better, I told myself. In the house, I could be trapped, dragged into closets and small spaces. Outside, it was harder to sneak up behind me. I rounded a corner of the foundation to find John hovering over me, smiling sweetly.

Sneaking up in front of me, on the other hand, seemed to be pretty easy.

Sidestepping me in a blur of motion, John wrapped the length of my hair around his fist and yanked me close, nuzzling the place where my neck and shoulder joined and leaving a cold, wet spot on my skin. Inhaling deeply, he leered down at me, then dragged me off to a remote corner of the garden, under an arch of wisteria. Settling near a worn stone bench, he spun me, pinning my hips with his hands as he pressed against my back. It would have been quite a romantic spot if I didn't have a clear view of Mr. Marchand destroying Cal's laptop with a shovel.

My heart sank. Having already received the same

treatment as his laptop, Cal was sprawled across the grass. John's nimble fingers plucked at my shirt as he ground against my ass.

"Marchand has what he needs. Your friend Mr. Calix is as good as dead. I thought you might want to enjoy the show before we start our fun and games."

"You are such an *asshole!*" I hissed.

"I like you *so much.*" He sighed. "Where did your sister skip off to, the little minx?" John chuckled. "Never mind, we'll track her down later. You two are going to be so much fun. But first, I want you to run. Anywhere you like, into the woods, into the house, to the road. Just scamper off. I'll be along any minute."

"No," I spat, eyeing the shovel lying abandoned on the ground, at least twenty feet away.

"Now, Iris, our games will be so much more fun if you just give yourself over to them. I don't want to waste our precious time together disciplining you for your petulance. Run," he ordered. "I loved it when you struggled with me at Cal's house. Come on, pretty thing. Give me a challenge."

"No."

"Oh, come on, Iris," he cooed, and that strange, detached cotton-headed feeling crept in at the edge of my brain. "Be a sport. I only want to play a little."

I planted my feet, staring him in the eye—a big no-no when dealing with a predator. "You know what I think? I think you never learned to fight. I think your vocal talent meant you never had to learn. You just hum your little tunes, and people do whatever you want. I think I could probably kick your skinny, over-hair-gelled ass if I wanted to. And I think I mentioned earlier that I definitely want to."

"Do you really want to fight me?" John asked, his musical tenor lilting sweetly. "You're just a silly human. You don't know anything about fighting. And I'm so much stronger than you."

My arms felt like lead, like lifting them would take a crane. He chuckled as I struggled to move my feet toward him. I groaned.

"Why don't you just sit down, Iris?" he asked. "Just sit down and wait for Marchand to kill your little boyfriend. And then you and I will make another game out of finding your sister."

His cold, cruel laugh brought the memory of that day at Cal's house hurtling to the surface of my brain, his icy-cold, slimy hands on me and the vicious bite at my throat. I thought of the time he'd spent with Gigi and how easily he could have hurt her and how hard it would be for her to trust boys after this. He could have killed her, arranged it so she never came home, and I would never have known what had happened to her.

Anger as hot and consuming as any blaze spread through my chest, loosening my arms. And what really pissed me off was his confidence. He was so sure of my inability to strike at him that he didn't move when my arms flexed, not even when I did run, loping across the lawn like an overcaffeinated cheetah. I slid across the grass, diving for the kind of home base that meant more than "not it." I snagged the shovel, turning to see that

John had finally moved. He was sauntering toward me with the widest kid-in-a-candy-store grin I'd ever seen. He was enjoying this, the thrill of the chase, the taste of my fear. This was his game.

Well, olly-olly-oxen-free, asshole.

I stood, planting my feet wide. When John finally moved close enough, I swung the shovel handle like a bat toward his neck. Grunting with the effort, I landed it flat across his throat. He sank to his knees, clawing at his neck and making strange honking gasps.

I yanked his hair, stretching his neck back and making it even harder for him to speak. I whispered, "I don't know anything about fighting. But I do know it's hard to talk when you've been hit in the throat with a shovel."

I swung again, splintering the wooden handle across his back. John fell to his hands and knees, honking all the way. I raised my arms over my head and plunged the jagged end through his back, pinning his heart in its descent into the dirt. John seemed to disintegrate in a wave. His skin turned gray and began to flake away to reveal his musculature, then a bare skeleton that exploded in a cloud of particles, leaving only a wavering wooden fragment sticking out of the ground.

With a triumphant cry, I looked up to see if anyone had seen me dispatch a vampire with a badass bon mot.

Of course not.

Having pushed himself back to his feet, Cal was too busy fighting off Mr. Marchand. The two of them were circling like feral dogs, searching for weaknesses, testing each other with random swings and swipes. They kept changing position, so that neither could get a grip on the other. Mr. Marchand was surprisingly agile for an older guy, ducking and sidestepping every blow with a toe dancer's grace. Although I supposed the whole "vampire reflexes" thing was an unfair senior-citizen advantage.

Cal was less smooth. He took every shot he could, swinging wildly. He didn't retreat; he only advanced. He was fighting angry, which was not good. Unfocused vampire fighting usually led to staking. I yanked at the shovel handle, but in my zeal to stake John, I'd apparently used that supernatural "mother lifts a car off her toddler" strength you only read about in tabloids, because I could not pull that sucker out of the ground. I leaned against it, changed my grip, tried kicking it at the base, but nothing worked.

"Damn it."

What were my options? *Think, Iris,* I commanded myself. *Think!*

1. Running. Running as fast and far as my little feet could carry me.

   Likely result: Escape to a dark country road, where, knowing my luck, I would be kidnapped and murdered by a drifter. Also, Cal would probably die because it looked like he was losing the fight.

2. Finding a pointy tree branch and jumping into the fight.

Likely result: A much faster and bloodier death than option 1.

3. Calling 911.

Likely result: Dead Cal and injured cops. Also, I would have to run inside to find a phone, and the possibility of getting trapped in Mr. Marchand's house of horrors was not appealing.

Wait.

I patted my pockets for other potential weapons and found the syringes. The first needle I pulled out was marked "Calix, Batch 1." Was this the poison that left Cal incapacitated? If John hadn't shown up with the lovely Scanlon sisters bait package, had Marchand planned on giving Cal another dose to persuade him to give up the information he wanted? Was this the stuff that made him weak and ill and immobile?

Because that I could use.

I jumped onto a nearby wrought-iron chair, waiting until they moved close. I uncapped the needle and held it like a dagger, poised behind Mr. Marchand's neck. Or the area near Marchand's neck if he had been standing less than ten feet away from me. Cal saw this and shook his head violently. I mimed stabbing, which made Cal growl. I assumed that meant no.

Seeing me seemed to help Cal focus. He concentrated on keeping Mr. Marchand's back to me, which kept his movements controlled, his anger in check. He swung, connecting his fist with Marchand's nose. The old man's head snapped back, and he stumbled. He snarled, advancing and kicking Cal's legs out from under him. Cal landed on the grass with a thwump. He rolled as Mr. Marchand scissor-kicked down, just missing Cal's solar plexus. But as he rolled, it shifted Mr. Marchand toward me, his back still turned.

When he was within leaping range, I launched myself at Mr. Marchand's back. I wrapped my arm around his neck and my legs around his waist, clinging to him like a koala on crank.

Cal yelled, "Iris, no!"

Mr. Marchand roared indignantly and sank his fangs into my forearm, tearing viciously into my flesh. I screamed, pulling uselessly at the arm caught in his teeth.

"This was stupid! This was *so* stupid!" I yelled as he bucked and dodged. I used my good hand to stab the syringe into his neck and push the plunger.

All of this was enough to make Mr. Marchand shake me off of his back and throw me. I went flying, soaring through empty space and crashing into a thick oak tree. My shoulder bore most of the impact, with my injured arm flopping forward and hitting the bark with a distinct snap. With a wet shriek, I slid to the ground. My arm hung limp and useless at my side, the pain in my shoulder so hot and intense that I was grateful for the radiating agony of breathing through broken ribs to distract me.

Beyond the stabbing clutch of every breath, my side felt funny—heavy and sort of caved in. I tried to look toward the fighting vampires, but the movement tilted my world on its axis, and I dropped into a dizzy spiral. I clutched at my head, hypo forgotten, as a storm of howls and growling filled my ears. The noise was growing closer, almost at my feet. Unable to turn my throbbing head, I moved my fingertips along the cool blades of grass, anything to distract me from the nauseating waves of pain. I closed my eyes, losing myself in the welcoming darkness behind my eyelids.

I lost track of time. I opened my eyes to see the leaves moving gently over my head, then drifted off. There was a crunch and a screech, followed by silence. I awoke to find Cal kneeling at my side. He moved me to lean against him. I howled at the movement, clutching my injured arm to my chest. The vocal effort had me coughing, blood bubbling over my lips and into my good hand.

"Cal," I rasped. He gingerly moved me into his lap, cradling my face against his neck. I whimpered, my uninjured fingers curling around his shirt collar.

"Shh, it's bad," Cal whispered. "You're losing a lot of blood, and there is internal damage."

I carefully moved my head back to give him my best unimpressed glare, under the circumstances. "Duh."

My inappropriately timed sarcasm seemed to lift his spirits, or at least the corners of his mouth. They quirked up, then quickly dropped down. He stroked my cheek, so softly I could barely feel it. "Iris, you could—you could die. Do you want me to turn you?"

My hand dropped away from his chest. And for a moment, I wanted to say yes. I wanted the pain to be over. I wanted everything to stop. I wanted to stay with Cal forever. But there was Gigi to consider. Poor Gigi, who had already lost her parents and counted on me to be her whole family. If I was a vampire, if I "died" before she turned eighteen, they would take her away from me. I wanted to give her time to adjust to the idea. I wanted to have my last human moments with her, eating Peanut M&M's and watching John Hughes movies. I didn't want to show up on our doorstep with fangs.

And even with the crippling agony, I remembered the not-so-small problem of Cal's wanting to leave my little backwater town the minute he could make tracks. And since he seemed to have just killed Mr. Marchand, that minute had arrived. When he'd asked me whether I wanted to be turned, he never specified that he would stay with me while I adjusted to being a vampire. What if he became bored with me? What if he didn't know how to love someone after so many years? What if he turned me, only to leave me the moment I rose? I couldn't handle that. Better that he left me human and damaged than alone for a foreseeable eternity.

"No." I wheezed. "No. Get me to a hospital. Find Gigi."

Cal's expectant face fell for a second, and then he recovered and smiled down at me. He murmured something in Greek and kissed me on the forehead, just as I passed out.

17

Once your vampire guest "leaves the nest," it's doubtful that you'll hear from him again. The undead are not big on thank-you notes and hostess gifts.

—*The Care and Feeding of Stray Vampires*

I woke up. And Cal wasn't there.

Gigi was sitting by my bedside, her head slumped against the mattress, drooling. There was a car-battery-sized box of Godiva truffles on the nightstand, along with a stack of Teresa Medeiros novels and an arrangement of white and purple irises. Next to the chocolates, Gigi had placed a picture of the two of us dressed in western gear for her high school's Fall Festival. Our arms were slung around each other, and we were grinning like loons, which may have had something to do with the deep-fried Snickers bars we'd just consumed.

My eyes grew hot and prickly as I looked down at her sleeping face. I slipped my good hand over the dark, silky strands of her hair. I remembered braiding it into pigtails for the Fall Festival and the first time I'd helped her pin it up for a dance. Tears slipped down my cheeks.

She was growing up so fast. I'd almost missed it. I could have missed everything.

Ben came through the hospital-room door, trying to balance two fancy coffees and a bag stuffed with the blueberry scones that Gigi loved. I wiggled my uninjured fingers at him, and he stopped in his tracks.

Ben Overby had made a special trip across town to the Hollow's lone Starbucks to get my sister to eat. His stock had gone up in my book, exponentially.

"Hey!" he exclaimed, grinning at me. "You're awake!"

Gigi's head shot up from the mattress. Her face had wrinkles where the rough sheets had bunched under her skin. And there was a patch of dried drool on her cheek. But Ben's eyes lit up at the sight of her, even when she shrieked like a banshee and launched herself at me.

"Don't you ever, ever do that again!" she cried, hugging me with one arm and slugging my leg with the other. "All that talk about being responsible, and do what I say, and then you get into a fistfight with vampires!"

"Well, technically, being thrown into the tree did most of the damage," I said, yelping in pain when she halfheartedly slapped the side of my head. "I'm sorry!" I huffed as her weight squeezed the air out of my lungs. "Ow! Ben, get her off me!"

Ben looked pretty damned amused as he set the coffee and pastry aside and pulled my sister back into her chair. She promptly burst into tears and buried her face in Ben's shirt. "Sorry, Miss Iris. She's had three days to bounce between panic and pissed-off. You gave us quite a scare."

"Three days?" I exclaimed.

"Ophelia Lambert, that creepy vampire chick, picked us up at the Dairy Freeze after you were brought here," Ben said. "We called her as soon as we got to a main road, told her she needed to get to the Marchand house. She said the same thing you did, to get to a well-lit, populated place and stay there. She came to pick us up, said Mr. Marchand was dead and you were hurt."

"Marchand is dead?"

Ben nodded. "Cal poisoned him, gave him some of the same stuff he was given but a much bigger dose. Ophelia said you would understand that. She told us that you were brought here but not to worry about the bills, because the Council would take care of whatever the insurance didn't."

"Massive internal bleeding!" Gigi yelled with sudden authority.

"You had massive internal bleeding," Ben informed me calmly while my sister raged. "A few broken ribs, a wound on your arm that required surgery, a lot of broken bones on your left side, and a punctured lung."

"Severe concussion!" Gigi added between sobs.

Ben nodded. "And a concuss—"

"Severe!" Gigi cried.

"A severe concussion," Ben finished, patting Gigi's back. "Your legs are OK, though. That's something."

Gigi continued to cry softly. I reached out to touch her but gasped at the searing pain in my arm. "I'm sorry, Geeg, I really am. No more fistfights with vampires, I promise."

"I was all alone!" Gigi cried, untangling herself from Ben and throwing herself back on my chest. I wheezed at the impact and the radiating waves of agony in my ribs. "The doctors kept asking me questions about living wills and DNRs and insurance. I didn't know anything about that stuff. They shoved all this paperwork at me, and when I said I was only seventeen and couldn't sign it, they called Child Protective Services! They said I might have to go to foster care if you didn't wake up. I guess I never realized what would happen if—if something—if you—"

"Shhh," I said, patting her head.

"I'm so sorry if I've ever been mean to you or made you feel lame because you were trying to take care of me. I know you work hard and worry a lot and give up stuff to make sure I'm OK. And if I ever make you feel like it's not worth it, I want you to kick my ass."

"OK."

"And ground me. In fact, I'm thinking of grounding myself after that bullshit I pulled with John. I can't believe Ben put up with it. Oh, but can I be ungrounded on April 23? Because that's the prom, and Ben asked me."

"Watch your language," I said as she dabbed at the tears on my cheeks. "And sure, you can go to the prom. We'll go dress shopping as soon as I'm out of traction."

"OK." She sniffed, brightening a little when talk turned to silhouettes and color choices, whether it was tacky for Ben to match his bow tie and cummerbund to her dress.

As my sister chattered happily and Ben cautiously picked through the Godiva box, all thoughts of lying vampire Romeos and nearly dead sisters were abandoned for corsage floral schemes. I couldn't help but wonder where Cal was. I was hurt, injured while saving him, and he couldn't come to the hospital to check on me? Had he gone back to the house to check on Gigi while I was unconscious? Had he already left town?

I cleared my throat, trying to focus on something beyond the hot tears gathering at the corners of my eyes. When Gigi finally took a breath, I focused on the boy standing awkwardly at her side. He was looking everywhere but at me, which made me think that my hospital gown was a little more revealing than I'd previously believed. I plucked nervously at the robe, tightening it at my throat. "Ben, I've been meaning to ask you, but I've been unconscious. How did you find us?"

Ben blushed. "There's this new app for the iPhone called FriendRadar. If a phone that's on your contact list is within a hundred feet, it will ping until you're standing right in front of that person. It's supposed to help you find your friends at the mall or the movies or that sort of thing. But I rewrote the software to increase the range. I was supposed to be picking up Gigi at your place the night John took you guys. When I got there and saw the house tossed, I turned on the app and followed Gigi's signal."

"How much did you increase the range?" Gigi asked.

Ben cleared his throat and averted his eyes. "I probably shouldn't tell you that. It's not entirely, um, condoned by the FCC."

"You're a genius," I told him. "You have permission to

date my sister, for real this time. No curfews, no restrictions, no base limits."

"Thanks, but I'm pretty sure that's the painkillers talking," Ben assured me, squeezing Gigi's shoulder affectionately. "We can talk more about dating rules later."

Gigi's mood darkened suddenly. "I should have dated you all along. This is all my fault. If I hadn't fallen for John's crap, Iris wouldn't have gotten hurt. You know, that night at the movies, I was texting him because he wanted to know where I was. He was trying to figure out how much time he had to search our house and then jump us. Asshole."

I patted her cheek, wincing when the IV pulled at the skin of my wrist. "Geeg, you're not a bad kid. You've never made me regret taking you on. Question my sanity? Yes. But never regret. Even with the John thing. You just made a series of really bad decisions, which is something I can identify with."

"You mean with Cal?" she asked.

I wiped at my eyes. "Letting Cal into the house. Forgetting that Mr. Marchand was a vampire just because he happened to look like a cuddly old man. A series of really bad decisions."

"Never trust a man who looks like Colonel Sanders," Ben agreed sagely.

I laughed, swiping at my cheeks. Gigi frowned. "What do you mean, letting Cal into the house was a mistake?"

"Well, do you see him here?" I asked angrily. "I mean, the man turns our lives upside down. I'm attacked at his house by the same creep who messed around with your brain to pump you for information. I nearly get killed trying to save his butt. But is he anywhere to be found? No. I'll bet he lit out of the house as soon as the Council vacuumed up Mr. Marchand with their little Dirt Devils."

Gigi shrugged. "I don't know. I haven't been back at the house long enough to see if he's still there."

"Where have you been staying?" I asked, my eyes narrowed.

"Over at Miss Andrea's house," she said, adding quietly, "and at Ben's."

Ben added hastily, "Our rooms are on different floors. And my parents said she can stay as long as she wants." He laughed. "My dad didn't ever think I'd get a girlfriend. He and Mom are thrilled."

I tried to calculate which could be more dangerous to my sister's well-being, staying with her hormonal, adoring boyfriend or being exposed to what Dick Cheney considered appropriate conversation in front of a teenage girl. I pressed the little red button that released my pain meds and wondered how often I was allowed a dose.

Better yet, did they sell York Peppermint Patties in the gift shop?

"And for the record, Cal's at the Council offices. Ophelia said something about needing to debrief him," Ben said, looking at Gigi with an expression of acute male discomfort.

"I'll bet she did," I muttered.

I felt a strange, warm sensation spreading from my arm through my chest. It took me a second to recognize that it was the morphine drip. I sighed, relaxing into the stiff hospital mattress, as Gigi tried to turn the topic back to more pleasant matters: their "sucky" prom theme, "Almost Paradise"; a scandal at their rival school involving the valedictorian, the shop teacher, and Chatroulette; the stream of vampires that had been showing up at our house to leave little presents on the porch. And not lame presents, either—spa gift certificates, bottles of wine, exotic plants. Gigi said that the vampires had started visiting the night after my accident to offer tokens of appreciation, now that my address had become common knowledge on the vampire news network. Because Ben and his parents weren't comfortable with so many vampires approaching the house with Gigi there, he said that Jane and Andrea had been appointed to accept the gifts.

"I wonder if I have to write thank-you notes," I mumbled. "Do vampires do thank-you notes? Geeg?"

I looked over to see Gigi dozing off, her head tilting back uncomfortably against the hard plastic chair.

"Ben, why don't you take Gigi home to get some sleep?" I asked. "That angle can't be good for her neck."

"But you just woke up!" Gigi protested weakly as she raised her head.

"So you know I'm going to be OK." I sighed. "Go home, get some sleep. In your own room . . . on a separate floor from Ben's. Ben, would your mother be willing to sleep somewhere between your bedroom doors as a precaution?"

"Where do you think she's been camped out for the last week?" Ben muttered.

"Fine," Gigi said, yawning widely. "But I need to go home and grab some clothes."

"Be careful, OK?" I told her. "If you go by the house and anything seems off, don't even go inside, just drive to Ben's."

Gigi stepped closer, leaning over the bed rail as she kissed my forehead. "What if Cal's there? What do you want me to tell him?"

With fresh pain consuming me, I wasn't sure how to answer. I shook my head.

"Why are you crying?" Gigi asked, pushing my hair back.

"Because you're yanking on my IV."

I dozed off and on throughout the afternoon, grateful for the private room. I was sure that Ophelia had arranged it, because my insurance company certainly wasn't going to cough up for it.

I woke up to fingertips trailing gently over my cheeks. Soft lips pressed against my temple. I felt the corners of my mouth tilt up. "I love you." I sighed, opening my eyes and expecting my vampire to be sitting at my bedside.

There was a strange squelching noise a foot from my bed, shoes turning on freshly cleaned tiles. My eyes fluttered open. The deep brown eyes I expected to be hovering near were usurped by baby blue.

I recoiled, yelping when the movement pulled at my IV restraints. "Paul!" I exclaimed.

"Hey, Petal," he said softly. "I've got you."

"Hi," I whispered, squinting up at him. "What are you doing here?"

"Well, where else would I be?" he asked, pushing the hair back from my face. "My girl's hurt, I come running."

"I'm not—"

"My girl. I know," he conceded. "I let you go. I wasn't smart enough to hold on to you."

"I think there were equally 'not smart' actions on both sides," I admitted.

"Could you forgive me?" he asked. "Iris, I can't tell you how I felt, hearing that you were hurt. I didn't know what I would do if something happened to you. I don't want to be without you. I want to ask you if you could consider marrying me. I'll be a good husband to you. And I'll make more of an effort with Gigi. I didn't realize how important you two are to each other, until I saw her reacting to seeing you in this hospital room. Won't you please marry me?"

He pulled a black velvet box from his pocket and showed me the little round solitaire that would have looked very elegant on my hand. He pressed the box into my palm, but my fingers refused to close around it.

It would be so easy. I could have a normal life, with a normal, if unexciting, man. I could have the white-picket-fence fantasy, a husband, a house, kids, and a dog. No more drama. No near-death experiences. No having a backup plan that included being turned into a vampire.

But it would be a lie. I didn't love Paul. I never did.

I had affection for him. I wanted to be his friend, the kind of friend he didn't have sex with—and that was it. I wanted to see him at the Piggly Wiggly without feeling awkward.

I closed the box, squeezing his hand. "I really appreciate it, but no. I can't."

He frowned, nodding. "Can I ask why?"

"Because you're right. We could make this work. We could put our noses to the grindstone and make this a marriage. But it shouldn't be that hard, Paul. And in that whole speech, you didn't mention loving me."

He sank back into his chair, looking a little sheepish. "I didn't, did I?"

"We don't love each other like married people should."

He protested, "But we could—"

"No, Paul. That's my final answer."

"I've really lost you, haven't I?" He smiled sadly. "To that vampire?"

I nodded. "You've lost me, as much as I lost you. I'm sorry, Paul."

"Well, at least I tried." He sighed. "But if my mama asks, I made a grand sweeping gesture that you were just barely able to resist, OK?"

"I'll tell her there was groveling involved," I promised.

"Thanks. She's always liked you," he said.

"Would have been nice to know that when we were dating," I muttered.

He chuckled and leaned in to kiss me. I ducked away, making him pause.

"No?"

I shook my head. And as he was backing away, we heard a cold voice from the doorway.

"Is there a problem here?" Ophelia was standing in the doorway, wearing a tight white minidress that could be termed a nurse's uniform, in the porniest sense of the word, complete with a starched white cap.

"No," I said, yawning. "My friend was just leaving."

Paul frowned at Ophelia but squeezed my hand and left without a fuss. "Good-bye, Iris."

"Good-bye." I sighed. "I'm glad to see you, Ophelia."

"I see the pain meds are kicking in," she said, sauntering closer. She looked over her shoulder. "Close the door, would you?"

A lankier vampire followed her, shutting the door behind him.

"Oh, shit!" I yelped, springing out of my languid state. "Ophelia, that's—"

"Mr. Dodd, I know. I thought the two of you should be formally introduced, since he is about to offer you the rarest of gifts. The vampire apology."

"I'm sorry?"

"No, that's his line."

"I'm sorry," Mr. Dodd muttered.

"For?" Ophelia prompted.

"For being 'grossly inappropriate' when I met you at my house, leading you to think that I was a threat to you, when I was supposed to be observing and protecting you." He said it in a monotone so flat that he could have been reciting a telemarketer's script.

"What?"

Ophelia said, "Mr. Dodd was supposed to make contact with you, just enough that you would remember his face and not panic if you happened to see him. Instead . . ."

Awkward silence.

Ophelia kicked his ankle and hissed. "Instead . . ."

"I came on to you," he mumbled. "Usually, when I put on the charm, ladies prove quite receptive." He followed this remark with a sullen little sneer, then resumed looking down at his feet.

"He was watching you on the rare occasions when you ventured into public at night," Ophelia said. "We knew that Cal couldn't be with you, and I thought it would be helpful for you to have some protection. I didn't mean to give you something else to worry about."

"I'm sorry," he muttered again.

"That night at the movies!" I exclaimed.

"I didn't mean to scare you."

"You sent me running home into the arms of a crazy teenage vampire stalker."

"I *said* I was *sorry*."

"You know, somehow that doesn't quite cover it," I shot back.

"Oh, there will be time for groveling," Ophelia assured me. "Mr. Dodd is in charge of guarding your door here at the hospital. He'll be waiting outside every minute of every night."

"I really don't think that's necessary," I protested.

"He will fetch you magazines, chocolates, cuddly

stuffed toys. And he will taste-test every meal the staff brings you, to make sure it hasn't been tampered with."

"Won't eating human food make him sick?" I asked.

Ophelia gave Mr. Dodd a nasty grin. "Yes."

Ah, that would be the point of this exercise in humiliation.

I settled back against the pillows, resigned to having a grumpy, resentful vampire bodyguard. Again, I wondered about Cal, but pride and the desire for continued blissful ignorance kept me from asking Ophelia. I wasn't going to lose any sleep or time on him, I promised myself. If I never saw his face again, I would survive. If he showed up here, I might be willing to speak to him. But that was about as much consideration as I was willing to give him at that point.

"Wait, so if he was keeping an eye on me, what was up with Mr. Crown? Why was he at the movie theater?"

"Well, I'd just managed to find a copy of the welcome basket delivery schedule, listing Peter as the contact for Cal's house. Before I could make it to Peter's house to question him, one of his more loyal humans at the Council office contacted him to warn him that I was coming."

I scoffed. "Mr. Crown has loyal humans?"

"Some people like cranky, anal-retentive men." Ophelia shrugged. "Crown called Dodd, knowing that he was following you, and the pair of them attempted to contact you at the theater."

"I think we need to clarify the definition of 'contact,' because Mr. Dodd seems to think it means 'chase the subject and her minor sibling into a darkened parking lot.'"

Mr. Dodd's mouth opened to protest, and I cut him off with a raised hand. "If you give me another half-assed apology, I will smack you with this IV pole."

Mr. Dodd cleared his throat. "I was going to say that Mr. Crown believed that he was being framed by Mr. Marchand. He thought that if he delivered you and your sister safely to the Council for questioning, it would go a long way toward clearing his name."

"Because calling you and explaining himself was the less reasonable option?" I asked.

"Vampire logic is difficult to explain. However, Mr. Crown does send his regards and promises to come by for a visit later."

"Oh, good," I muttered.

Ophelia seemed to close the business portion of our visit with an overbright smile. "I'm told that puzzles and board games are a typical way for humans to pass their time in a hospital," Ophelia said. "Do you prefer Scrabble or chess?"

"Like I'm going to play games of strategy with you under the influence of opiates." I snorted.

"Well, it's not like you'd win without the influence of opiates," she observed dryly.

"Scrabble it is," I decided.

"Go fetch the board from my car, won't you, Mr. Dodd?" Ophelia asked sweetly. "And on your way back, be sure to stop by the cafeteria to bring Iris a nice human breakfast. I'm sure she's hungry."

The grumpy, chastened vampire loped out the door with a resentful glance over his shoulder. Part of me felt sorry for Mr. Dodd, who would be vomiting Jell-O and broth for the next few days.

I got over it.

18

I closed the front door behind me with a snick and leaned my head against it. One more day down. Until what? I had no idea, which was sort of depressing. I just knew that I'd survived another day.

I dropped my messenger bag by the table, wincing at the effort it took from my still-tender muscles. I was healing. Stairs were still difficult. Gigi had sweet-talked Ben into helping me during my first few days back at work. It stung my pride, but I couldn't lift anything heavier than ten pounds with my shattered shoulder. With tales of my "heroic efforts" to help Cal through his ordeal spreading through the undead gossip circuit, referrals had tripled. I needed Ben's help. Plus, I'd had to hire Jolene as my full-time assistant and apply for a loan on a second Dorkmobile.

Cal had been gone for nearly a month. I'd come home

from the hospital to find the house empty, his tent neatly folded in the basement. He'd left a fangwort flower pressed between the last pages of my mother's cutting journal. And that was it.

I wasn't keeping track of the thirty-two days since he'd made love to me. I hadn't marked the thirty days since I'd told him I didn't want to be a vampire like him. And I certainly wasn't aware that it had been two weeks since I'd had any sort of update from Ophelia. Despite being grateful for my assistance, she didn't seem to think it was healthy for me to continually check on Cal's progress in closing the investigation.

Time was the enemy, but it was all I had. Gigi was set to graduate from high school in a week. She'd attended the prom with Ben, wearing a gorgeous yellow strapless gown that set off her dark hair beautifully. Ben had arranged for a wrist corsage consisting of yellow gladioli. Gigi had rolled her eyes but accepted it gracefully, particularly after I pulled her aside and told her that the flowers symbolized infatuation. To receive a gladiolus implied that the recipient had pierced the giver's heart with passion. Gigi had pinked up prettily, while I prayed that Cal's "pepper spray" lecture had been effective.

Gigi had decided on the University of Kentucky, where she planned to major in nursing. Watching the staff at the hospital take care of me had had a profound impact on her. And it didn't hurt that Ben was majoring in information systems there. She had a roommate lined up. She was collecting towels and sheets and the dolphin posters required to decorate her dorm room. After

August 1, I would be an empty-nester, and I wasn't sure how to feel about it.

Somehow I didn't think that working more hours was going to be a big comfort to me. Maybe Mr. Rychek could tell me where he got Diandra's hypoallergenic cat.

Returning to a darkened, empty house was something I needed to get used to. I sighed, dropping my purse onto the hall table and trying to remember what I had in the fridge. Jolene had organized some sort of casserole brigade among her aunts to feed us while I was laid up. For days, we'd gorged on meatloaf, pot pie, chicken-and-rice casserole, and pasta salad, none of which appealed at the moment. But making dinner for just myself was a singularly depressing thought. And eating Jujubes for dinner, though appealing, couldn't be responsible. Maybe I needed to consider one of those sad, single-lady "dinners for one" cookbooks.

I didn't bother turning on the lights as I made my way to the kitchen. The house was spotlessly clean. I'd gone into a sort of dusting frenzy the previous week, as it was one of the few household chores I was allowed. Gigi mastered the heavier tasks but did mention that she was glad the dorm had a cleaning staff. I planned to let her figure out that meant that the main hallways and communal bathrooms were cleaned, not individual rooms.

I set my cell phone on the kitchen counter. My foot caught on something on the floor, and I went flailing down. "Yipe!" I shrieked as I fell on top of something rather firm and smelling of leather and oak moss.

"We have got to stop meeting like this," Cal's voice

said, all smug and cool as I struggled to pull my face out of his chest. "We are terrible at staying away from each other, Miss Scanlon."

I righted myself, pushing up on my elbows so I could see his happy, relaxed face. He was fully recovered. His face had filled out a little, and his color was even. He'd lost that tired look around the eyes. He trailed his fingers over the ridge of my cheekbone, stroking the skin reverently. "Iris, aren't you going to say anything?"

Oh, I had plenty to say.

"You prick!" I yelled, smacking out at him. "You jackass! You moron! You insufferable, arrogant ass-monkey!"

"Ass-monkey?" He chuckled, catching my wrists and holding off my blows. "I see you've gotten past your reluctance to curse. I don't think 'ass-monkey' is a word, by the way."

"It is now! I just made it up!" I brought my knee up so I could catch his balls.

Or I would have if he hadn't dodged. Stupid lightning-quick vampire reflexes.

He dodged my kick, caressing my thigh as he gently forced my leg into a less injurious position. He nuzzled my throat. "Well, as an insult, it's highly effective, so congratulations."

"What the hell do you think you're doing here, lying on my kitchen floor?" I demanded. "And by the way, did you get your sword back? I think I should have asked that before I started beating on you."

"Yes, I got it back." He drew his hands over my hair, drawing me closer. "And I'm down here because I wanted to start over. So I came back to where we started, so to speak. I couldn't figure out a way to get you to my kitchen floor without tipping you off."

"Did they medicate you heavily while you were gone? I mean, they had plenty of time to get the dosage right."

He looked sheepish. "I'm sorry. It took a while to get all of the details wrapped up."

"And obviously, you were in a remote location where phone signals could not reach."

"Until recently, I wasn't sure that you would be willing to see me," he said. "I thought you'd moved on."

"What the hell are you talking about?"

"I came to the hospital the night you woke up," he said. "I had finally managed to satisfy Ophelia's demands for basic information about Waco's killing. During her debriefing, the only thing that kept me sane was that she was receiving regular updates on your condition from Jane. I came to your room and found Paul there. He was touching you, and you were smiling. You told him you loved him."

"I thought it was you!" I exclaimed. "I was drugged out of my mind and woke up to someone stroking my face. I assumed it was you."

"I'm sorry it wasn't. I'm sorry I wasn't there for you. And when I heard you say those words to someone else, even if it was a mistake, it broke my heart. I didn't know it could break. I don't want to be away from you ever again. I don't want to be anywhere without you. Or Gigi. If she'll have me."

I sat up, leaning against the cabinets. My lips twitched, but I bit back the smile while he continued.

"I panicked. I put you in danger. I put Gigi in danger. I was so sure you were going to decide that being with me wasn't worth it that I ran at the first sign of rejection. I should have talked to you instead of running away. If Gigi hadn't tracked me down to knock some sense into me—"

"Gigi? Really?"

"Well, Gigi and her sweetheart. Did you know Ben can track cell-phone signals from up to ten miles away? Gigi came to see me at my new Council housing and told me that I was, quote, 'a total dumbass' if I didn't see how much we loved each other."

I loved my sister. I really did.

"And you didn't call me after my baby sister kicked your butt because?"

"I couldn't call," he said. "The Council can be very persuasive when they're trying to convince you not to retire. You see, I've learned a lot about my vampire brethren over the years, things that would make life uncomfortable for the vampire hierarchy if released to the general public. I had to make arrangements for certain packets of information to be left in key locations so that if I or anyone I cared about came to harm, that information would be distributed."

"How does your local Council supervisor feel about this?" I asked, thinking of the bloody revenge Ophelia could be planning at this very minute.

"Who do you think helped me set it up?" he asked. "She likes the idea of having her own freelance consultant in her backyard. And she likes you. She wants you to help plan the wedding when Jane finally gives her permission to marry Jamie. Jane says hello, by the way, and that you're still on for Girls' Night at River Oaks next week. I believe Gabriel, Dick, Jamie, and I are expected to do some sort of manly bonding activity involving gaming equipment."

That seemed awfully settled. For someone who spent so much of his time fighting attachments, Cal was practically drawing up a potluck rotation with my friends.

I crossed my arms over my chest. "You're staying nearby?"

He grinned, pulling me into his lap. "I was thinking very close by. It's a very convenient location. Beautiful gardens, spacious underground accommodations, and it's Iris-adjacent."

I snorted. "Surely you don't think I would bring a vampire into my home. Do I look particularly stupid to you?"

He chuckled, recalling our very first conversation. "No, I make a habit of only loving brilliant women. Besides, I already know where you live."

"Don't you threaten me! There are a lot of handy, breakable wooden objects in this room. As I have mentioned before, I'm not above living out one of my fonder Buffy fantasies."

He waggled his eyebrows. "Considering what Buffy did with Angel *and* Spike over the course of seven seasons, I think I'd be OK with that."

"How do I know that you're not going to walk out on me again the next time things get rough?"

"I don't do that. Not anymore."

"Considering that you just did it, I have a hard time believing that," I shot back with a little more vitriol than I'd intended. I blew out a long breath, ruffling the bangs curling into my line of vision. "You hurt me."

"I'm sorry. But you can trust me never to do it again. Open my wallet."

I sighed. "If you offer me an obscene amount of money right now, I think you should know that I am capable of hurting you. You're bigger than creepy John, so it may take me a while, but I *will* take a chunk out of you."

I flipped open the expensive-looking leather contraption, and an engagement ring slid out into my open palm. He slid the ring onto my finger. I took a moment to admire the respectable square-cut diamond, offset by little flowers engraved in the platinum band. He kissed my hand and tucked it against his chest. "I'm thinking a Halloween wedding. Gigi would appreciate it. And think of the many ways you could use trick-or-treat candies as part of the theme. Candy corn and chocolate kisses as far as the eye could see."

I laughed, pleased at how well he knew me. "I've already got two weddings booked for that night. Newly made vampires just love getting married on Halloween," I replied. "How about next spring? It would give me more time to plan."

"Winter solstice. The longest night of the year," he countered.

"I'm still saying spring."

"Which means you never quite learned how negotiating works."

Why did everybody tell me that?

I barely resisted the urge to smirk at him. "How badly do you want to marry me, Mr. Calix?"

He grumbled. "Done."

"I love you," I told him.

"I love you more than anything I have known or seen in my long, long life. Marry me, stay with me."

"Done." I laughed and kissed him. "So, did you have a plan B if I said no? Because it would be hard to bounce back from lying prostrate on the floor in the dark with any dignity."

"I have several extra-large bags of M&M's stashed in your china cabinet," he admitted.

"You think I can be bought with bulk candy?" I asked, lifting a brow. He smiled winsomely. "OK, you were close to the mark."

I wrapped his arms around my shoulder and tucked my face into this throat. "I'm sorry if I hurt your feelings when you asked if I wanted to be turned. I just wasn't ready yet. I'm still not. There are some loose ends I need to wrap up, with the business, with the human world, with Gigi. I want to have some time with her yet, to say good-bye to things like cheeseburger night and talk to her about wills and health insurance. I want to take her on a real vacation before she starts college, somewhere sunny. I can't exactly do that if I'm a vampire."

Cal nodded, pressing a kiss to my temple. "I understand. Beachcombing is considerably less fun when you're worried about bursting into flames."

"How about we wait until Gigi's sophomore or junior year of college?" I asked. "She'll have time to adjust to the idea of me being turned. She won't be around for the scary new-vampire phase. By the time she comes back for a visit, I shouldn't be a danger to her."

"Done. But what about your business?"

"Right now, it's going great. I'll have time to build it up a bit, hire some daytime people, and move into a more managerial role."

"What will you tell Gigi?"

"I will tell her that we love her. And we're her family, whether we're living or not. And with a three-thousand-year-old future brother-in-law, she will have the coolest family sitting at graduation."

"Graduation?"

"Graduation, birthdays, Christmases, and any number of events that require you to wear a silly sweater or staple twisted crepe paper to the porch. This is the price of being part of a family," I told him, toying with his shirt buttons. Cal grimaced. "Too late to back out now."

"In terms of the sweater, how silly are we talking?"

"Cal."

"On a scale of one to ten?"

"Cal!"

"Am I allowed to negotiate terms?"

I cupped his chin in my palm. "It will make Gigi happy."

"Damn it, you know my weakness."

"I love you."

He groaned. "That's my other weakness."

"And by that, you mean . . ."

"I love you, too."

"Wonderful. Now, let's get you off the floor," I said, slipping my hands into his. At my hip, my BlackBerry jangled to life with "Flight of the Bumblebee." Cal's eyes flicked toward the offending device, apparently resigned to the idea that he would be sharing me for eternity with a ridiculous novelty ringtone. Nuzzling my nose against his throat, I unclipped the phone from my belt and slid it onto the countertop. He grinned down at me, kissing me soundly. I wound my arms around his neck and sighed.

"Let it ring."

Turn the page

for a sneak peek

of the next entertaining romp by

MOLLY HARPER

Witch Hunt

Coming soon from Pocket

If you are fortunate enough to receive a message from the other side, pay attention to it.
—*A Guide to Traversing the Supernatural Realm*

My week started with spectral portents of doom floating over my bed while I was trying to have anniversary sex with my boyfriend. It was all downhill from there.

Stephen had not been pleased when I'd pushed him off of me, rolled out of bed, and yelled, "That's it! I'm going!" at the image of a crow burning against my ceiling. I mean, I guess there are limits to what men are willing to put up with, and one's girlfriend interacting with invisible omens is a bit out of a perfectly nice investment broker's scope. He seemed to think I was huffing off after taking offense to that counterclockwise tickle he'd improvised near the end.

Of course, telling him about the increasingly forceful hints I'd received from my noncorporeal grandmother for the last two weeks would have made the situation worse. Stephen tended to clam up when we discussed my family and their "nonsense." He refused to discuss my Nana Fee or the promise I'd made to her that I'd travel all the way from our tiny village to the wilds of America. So I'd tried ignoring the dreams, the omens, the way my alphabet soup spelled out "HlfMunHollw."

I tried to rationalize that a deathbed promise to a woman

who called herself a witch wasn't exactly a binding contract. But my grandma interrupting the big O to make her point was the final straw.

And so I was moving to Half-Moon Hollow, Kentucky, indefinitely, so I could locate four magical objects that would prevent a giant inter-witch-clan war and maintain peace in my little corner of northwestern Ireland.

Yes, I am aware that statement sounds absolutely ridiculous.

Sometimes it pays to have a large tech-savvy family at your disposal. When you tell them, "I have a few days to rearrange my life so I can fly halfway across the world and secure the family's magical potency for the next generation," they hop to do whatever it takes to smooth the way. Aunt Penny had not only booked my airline tickets, but also located and rented a house for me. Uncle Seamus had arranged quick shipping of the supplies and equipment I would need to my new address. And my beloved, and somewhat terrifying, teenage cousin Ralph may have broken a few international laws while online "arranging" a temporary work visa so I wouldn't starve while I was there. Not everybody in our family could work magic, but some members had their own particular brand of hocus-pocus.

Given how Stephen felt about my family, I'd decided it was more prudent to tell him I'd accepted an offer for a special six-month nursing fellowship in Boston. The spot came open when another nurse left the program unexpectedly, I told him, so I had to make a quick decision. He argued that it was too sudden, that we had too many plans hanging in the balance for me to run off to the States for half a year, no matter how much I loved my job.

I didn't want to leave Stephen. For months he had been a bright spot in a life in need of sunshine, with the loss of my Nana Fee and my struggles to keep the family buoyed. And yet, somehow, here I was, sprawled in the back of a run-down cab as it bumped down a sunlit gravel road in Half-Moon Hollow, Kentucky. The term "cab" could only be applied loosely to the faded blue Ford station wagon, the only working taxi in the entire town. We had a fleet of two working in Kilcairy, and we only had about four hundred people living inside the town limits. Clearly, living in Boston until my early teens hadn't prepared me for life in the semirural South.

Yawning loudly, I promised myself I would worry about cultural adjustments later. I was down-to-the-bone tired. My skirt and blouse were a grubby shambles. I smelled like airplane sweats and the manky Asian candy my seatmate insisted on munching for most of the thirteen-hour flight from Dublin to New York, which had been followed by a two-hour hop to Chicago and another hour on a tiny plane-let. I just wanted to go inside, take a shower, and sleep. While I was prepared to sleep on the floor if necessary, I prayed the house was indeed furnished as Aunt Penny promised.

While the McGavock clan had collectively bankrolled my flight, I needed to save the extra cash they'd provided as "buy money" for my targets. Living expenses were left to me to figure out. I would have to start looking for some acceptable part-time work as soon as my brain was functional again. I squinted against the golden light pouring through the cab windows, interrupted only by the occasional patch of shade from tree branches arching over the little lane. The sky was so clear and crystal blue that it almost hurt to look out at the odd little clusters of houses along the road. It was so tempting just to lay my head back, close my eyes, and let the warm sunshine beat hot and red through my eyelids.

"You know you're rentin' half of the old Wainwright place?" the cab driver, Dwayne-Lee, asked as he pulled a sharp turn onto yet another gravel road. I started awake just in time to keep my face from colliding with the spotty cab window. Dwayne-Lee continued on, blithe as a newborn babe, completely oblivious. "That place always creeped me out when I was a kid. We used to dare each other to run up to the front door and ring the bell."

I lifted a brow at his reflection in the rearview. "And what happened?"

"Nothin'," he said, shrugging. "No one lived there."

I blew out a breath and tried to find the patience not to snap at the man. Dwayne-Lee had, after all, been nice enough to make a special trip to the Half-Moon Hollow Municipal Airport to pick me up. Dwayne-Lee had been sent by Iris Scanlon, who handled various business dealings for my new landlord. His skinny frame puffed up with pride at being tasked with welcoming a "newcomer," he'd handed me an envelope from Iris containing a key to my new house, a copy of my lease, her phone number, and a gift certificate for a free pizza delivered by Pete's Pies.

Anyone who tried to make my life easier was aces in my book. So from that moment on, I was a little in love with Iris Scanlon. Less so with Dwayne-Lee, who was currently nattering on about the Wainwright place and its shameful conversion from a respectable Victorian home to a rental duplex after Gilbert Wainwright had moved closer to town years before. I closed my eyes against the sunlight and the next thing I knew, the cab was pulling to a stop.

Wiping furiously at the wet drool trail on my chin, I opened my door while Dwayne-Lee unloaded my luggage from the trunk. Separated from the other houses on the street by a thicket of dense trees, the rambling old Victorian was painted robin's-egg blue with snowy white trim. The house was two stories, with a turret off to the left and a small central garden separating the two front doors. Given that the opposite side of the front porch seemed occupied with lawn chairs and a disheveled garden gnome, I assumed that the "tower side" of the house was mine. I grinned, despite my bone-aching fatigue.

I'd always been fascinated by the idea of having a tower as a kid, though I'd long since cut my hair from climbing length.

The grass grew scrabbled in patches across the lawn. A section of brick had fallen loose from the foundation on the west corner. Knowing my luck, there was a colony of bats living in the attic to complete that Addams Family look.

"I'll have bats in my belfry." I giggled, scrubbing at my tired eyes.

"You feelin' all right, ma'am?" Dwayne-Lee asked.

"Hmm?" I said, blinking blearily at him. "Oh, sorry, just a little out of sorts."

I pulled a wad of cash from my pocket and handed him enough for my fare and a generous tip.

Dwayne-Lee cleared his throat. "Um, ma'am, I can't take Monopoly money."

I glanced down at the bills in my hands. They were the wrong color. I was trying to pay Dwayne Lee in euros. "Sorry."

With Dwayne-Lee compensated in locally legal tender, I took my key out of Iris's envelope, unlocked the door, and hauled my stuff inside. My half of the old Wainwright place consisted of two bedrooms and a bath upstairs, plus a parlor and a kitchen downstairs. It was a bit shocking to have this much room to myself. I was used to living in my Nana Fee's tiny cottage, where I still whacked my elbows on the corner of the kitchen counter if I wasn't careful.

At some point, the house appeared to have been decorated by a fussy old lady fond of dark floral wallpaper and feathered wall sconces. The house was old, but someone had paid some attention to its upkeep recently. The hardwood floors gleamed amber in the afternoon light. The stairs were recently refurnished and didn't creak once while I climbed them. The turret room turned out to be a little sitting area off my bedroom, lined with bookshelves. I ran my fingers along the dusty shelves. I loved a good book. If I stayed long enough, I could put a little reading chair there . . . if I had a reading chair. I'd need to do something about getting some more furniture.

Despite Aunt Penny's assurances, the rooms were furnished in only the meanest sense. There was a table and chairs in the kitchen, a beaten sofa in the parlor, plus a dresser and bare mattress in the front bedroom. Sighing deeply and promising myself I wouldn't mention this to my aunt, I drew the travel sack—a thin, portable sleeping bag for people who were phobic about touching hotel sheets—over the bare mattress. The travel sack was a Christmas gift from Stephen. I smiled at the thought of my dear, slightly anal-retentive boyfriend and resolved to call him as soon as it was a decent hour overseas.

I found blankets in the bottom drawer of the dresser. I wasn't too keen on using them as covers, given their moldy state, but I thought they would make a good shade for the window so the sun wouldn't keep me awake. I boosted myself against the dresser to hang one . . . only to observe that some sort of Greek statue had come to life in my garden.

He was built like a boxer, barrel-chested and broad-shouldered, with narrow hips encased in ripped jeans. Thick sandy hair fell forward over his face while he worked. His sculpted chest was bare, golden, and apparently quite sweaty given the way it glistened while he planted paving stones near a pristine concrete patio.

I wavered slightly, grabbing the window frame, my weakening knees coupled with jet lag causing me to collapse a little. Was this my next-door neighbor? I wasn't sure if I was comfortable living so close to a he-man who could lift giant stones as if they were dominoes. And when had it gotten so bloody hot in here? I hadn't noticed I was warm in the cab . . . Oh, wait, it was time for he-man to take a water break. He took a few long pulls off a bottle from his cooler and dumped the rest over his head.

My jaw dropped, nearly knocking against my chest. "You've got to be kidding me."

Just then, he looked up and spotted me ogling him from above. Our eyes connected . . .

And he winked at me like some lothario gardener out of a particularly dirty soap opera! I spluttered indignant nonsense before tucking the blanket over the window with a decisive shove.

I pressed my hands over dry, tired eyes. I didn't have the mental reserves for this. I needed to sleep, eat, and bathe, most likely in that order. I would deal with the man reenacting scenes from *A Streetcar Named Desire* in my garden at a later date. My shoulders tense and heavy, I crawled onto the mattress, bundled my shirt under my head, and plummeted into sweet unconsciousness.

I woke up bleary and disoriented, unable to figure out where the hell I was. Why was it so dark? Was I too late? Were *they* here already? Where was my family? Why couldn't I hear anyone talking? I lurched up from the mattress and snagged the blanket from the window, letting in the weak twilight.

As soon as I saw the paving stones, I remembered the flight, the mad taxi ride, and the Adonis in the back garden.

"Oh." I sighed, scrubbing my hand over my face. "Right."

I stumbled into the bath and splashed cool water on my face. The mirror reflected seven kinds of hell. My face was pale and drawn. My thick, coffee-colored hair was styled somewhere near "crazy cat lady," and my normally bright, deep-set brown eyes were marked with dark smudges that weren't entirely composed of mascara. I had my grandfather's features, straight lines, delicate bones, and a particularly full bottom lip. Of course, that meant I looked like my mother, too, which was not something I liked to dwell on.

I stripped out of my clothes, standing under the lukewarm spray and letting it wash away the grime. Long after the water cooled, I climbed out of the tub, only to remember that I hadn't thought to bring any towels into the bathroom with me. Aunt

Penny had stuffed a few into my suitcase because she knew the house wouldn't have them. But my suitcase was downstairs, next to the door. And I was stark naked.

"Moron," I cursed myself as I took a sprightly, shivering walk across the bedroom to retrieve my jacket. I took the stairs carefully—because I wasn't about to die in a household accident wearing only an outdated rain jacket—and carefully avoided windows as I made my way to my luggage. The towels, somehow, still smelled line-fresh, like the lavender and rosemary in Nana Fee's back garden. I pressed one to my face before wrapping it around my body toga-style.

I mentally blessed Aunt Penny for packing some ginger tea in my bag, which was good for post-flight stomachs. I retrieved the tea bags and cast a longing glance at the kitchen. Did the "furnished" bit include dishes and cups? I could function—I might even be able to dress myself properly—if I just had some decent tea in me. Even if it meant boiling the water in a microwave.

I shuddered. Blasphemy.

If I set the water to boil now, it would be ready by the time I picked out clothes. Multitasking would be the key to surviving here. There would be no loving aunties to make my afternoon tea, no uncles to pop into town if I needed something. I was alone here with my thoughts, for the first time in a long time. And considering my thoughts of late, that could be a dangerous thing.

"Staring into space isn't going to get the tea made," I chided myself. Securing my towel, I made my way to the stove, careful to avoid the windows. I didn't know if my neighbor was doing his sweaty work out in the yard, and I didn't fancy being winked at wearing this getup.

Setting the tea bags on the counter, I began rummaging through the cupboards, finding dirty, abandoned cookware, but no kettle or cups. I opened the top cupboard nearest the refrigerator and—

"ACCCK!" I shrieked at the sight of beady black eyes glaring out at me from the cupboard shelf. The furry gray creature's mouth opened, revealing rows of sharp, white fangs. It swiped its paws at me, claws spread, and hissed like a brassed-off cobra.

I let loose a bloodcurdling scream and ran stumbling out of the kitchen, through a screened door, and into the moonless purple light of early evening. With my eyes trained behind me to make sure . . . whatever it was didn't follow me, I slammed into a solid, warm object. The force of my momentum had me wrapping my arms and legs around it as I struggled away from the fanged menace.

"Oof!" the object huffed.

The object was a person. To be specific, the shirtless, sweaty person who'd been standing in my garden earlier. Dropping a couple of yard tools with a clank, he caught my weight with his hands, stumbling under the impact of struggling, panicked woman. Certainly as surprised to find me in his arms as I was to be there.

Slashing dark eyebrows shot skyward. The full lips parted to offer, "Hello?"

Oh, saints and angels, I was doomed. He was even better-looking up close. Tawny, whiskey-colored eyes. A classic Grecian nose with a clear break on the bridge. Wide, generous lips currently curved into a naughty, tilted line as he stared up at me.

Completely. Doomed.

Focus, I told myself, there's a mutant rodent in your cupboard, waiting to devour your very soul, then terrorize the townsfolk.

"In my kitchen!" I shouted in his face.

"What?" The man seemed puzzled, and not just by the fact that I seemed to be wrapped around him like some sort of cracked-up spider monkey.

"In. My. KITCHEN!" I yelled, scrabbling to keep my grip

on his shoulders while leaning back far enough to make eye contact. Despite my all-out terror, I couldn't help but notice the smooth, warm skin or the tingles traveling down my arms, straight to my heart. He smelled . . . wild. Of leather and hay and deep, green pockets of forest. As my weight shifted backward, his large, warm hands slid around my bottom, cupping my cheeks to keep me balanced against him. "Th-there's a creature!" I cried. "In my kitchen! Some demon rat sent from hell! It tried to bite my face off!"

The fact that his hands were ever so subtly squeezing my towel-clad ass managed to subdue my mind-numbing terror and replace it with indignant irritation. I didn't know this man. I certainly hadn't invited him to grope me, spider-monkey climbing or no. And I had a perfectly lovely boyfriend waiting for me at home, who would not appreciate some workman's callused hands on my ass.

"You can move your hands now," I told him, trying to dismount gracefully, but his hands remained cupped under my left cheek.

"Hey, you tackled me!" he protested in a smoky, deeply accented tenor.

I narrowed my eyes. "Move your hand or I'll mail it back to you by a very slow post."

"Fine," he sighed, gently lowering me to my feet. "Let's get a look at this creature in your kitchen."

Struggling to keep my towel in place, I led him into my kitchen and tentatively pointed toward the home of the Rodent of Unusual Size. I could hear the beast hissing and growling inside, batting at the closed door with its claws. I was surprised it hadn't managed to eat its way through yet. But somehow, my would-be rescuer seemed far more interested in looking around, noting the pile of luggage by the door.

"Haven't had much time to unpack yet, huh?" he asked. I glared at him. He shrugged. "Fine, fine, creature crisis. I'm on it."

He opened the cupboard door, let out a horrified gasp, and slammed it shut. He grabbed a grimy old spatula I'd left on the counter during my rummaging and slid it through the cupboard handles, trapping the monster inside. He turned on me, his face grave while his amber eyes twinkled. "You're right. I'm going to have to call in the big guns."

He disappeared out the door on quick, quiet feet. I stared after him, wondering if I'd just invited help from a complete lunatic, when the early evening breeze filtering in through the back door reminded me I was standing there in just a towel. I scrambled over to my suitcase and threw on a loose peasant skirt and a singlet. I wondered what he meant by "big guns." Was he calling the police? The National Guard? MI-5?

I was slipping on a pair of knickers under my skirt just as my bare-chested hero came bounding back into the kitchen with a large, lidded pot and a spoon.

"Are you going to cook it?" I gasped, ignoring the bald-faced grin he gave my lower quadrants as my floaty blue skirt fell back into place.

"Well, my uncle Ray favors a good roast possum. He says it tastes like chicken," he drawled, holding the lid over his thick forearm like a shield as he tapped the spatula out of place. "Personally, I have to wonder if he's been eating chicken that tastes like ass, but that's neither here nor there."

I darted away as he opened the cupboard door. A feral growl echoed through the empty house as he maneuvered the lid down and the pot over the front of the cupboard. He used the wooden spoon to reach over the grumpy animal and nudge the possum into the pot. He slapped the lid over it, turning and giving me a proud grin.

"Thank you." I sighed. "Really, I don't know what I would have done—"

The giant rat began thrashing around inside the pot and making the lid dance.

"I want that thing tested for steroids!" I yelped.

"It's just a baby," he said, placing one of his ham-sized hands on the lid. "These things burrow in pretty much wherever they want to, doors and walls be damned. A cousin of mine went to tuck his daughter in one night and found one cuddled with her stuffed animals."

"This is a baby?" I peered down at the dancing pot. "How big do the mothers get?"

He shrugged. "Better question: where is his mama?"

"Oh," I groaned as he opened the back door, crossed the yard, and gently shook the possum out of the pot and into the tall grass near the trees. I called after him, "Why did you have to say that? I have to sleep here!"

Climbing my back steps, he looked far more relaxed than he should have been after evicting a vicious furred fiend from my kitchen. Shirtless. "I have to sleep here, too. And if it makes you feel better, there's a good chance that the mama could be sleepin' under my side of the house," he told me. "I'm Jed, by the way."

I giggled, a hysterical edge glinting under the laughter, as he extended his hand toward me. "You're kidding."

He arched a sleek sandy eyebrow. "I'm sorry?"

I cleared my throat, barely concealing a giggle. "No, I'm sorry. I've never met a Jed before."

He chuckled. "I'd imagine not, with that accent and all."

Now it was my turn to raise the bitch-brow. He of the sultry backwoods drawl was mocking my accent? That was disappointing. Since landing in New York, I'd worked hard to control whatever lilt I'd picked up since moving in with Nana Fee. It wouldn't do for the locals to know where I was from.

"Your accent," he said, his forehead creasing. "Boston, right? 'Pahk the cah in the yahd?'"

I blushed a little and regretted the bitch-brow. I'd forgotten how muddled my manner of speaking was compared to my new neighbors' Southern twang. My accent was vaguely Boston, vaguely Irish. Nana Fee had tried to correct my lack of R's in general and attempted to teach me Gaelic, but the most I picked up were some of the more interesting expressions my aunts and uncles used. Mostly the dirty ones. So I spoke in a bizarre mishmash of dialects and colloquialisms, which led to awkward conversations over what to call chips, elevators, and bathrooms.

"Oh, right," I said, laughing lightly. "Boston-born and raised."

Technically, it wasn't a lie.

Jed looked at me expectantly. I looked down to make sure I hadn't forgotten some important article of clothing. "If you don't give me your name, I'm just going to make one up," he said, leaning against the counter. "And fair warning, you look like a Judith."

"I do not!" I exclaimed.

"Half-dressed girls who climb me like a tree are usually named Judith," he told me solemnly.

"This happens to you often?" I deadpanned.

He shrugged. "You'd be surprised."

"It's Nola," I told him. "Nola Leary."

"Jed Trudeau," he said, shaking my outstretched hand. "If you don't mind me sayin', you look beat. Must've been a long flight."

"It was," I said, nodding. "If you don't mind, I think I'll just go back to bed."

There was a spark of mischief in his eyes, but I think he picked up on the fact that I was in no mood for saucy talk. His full lips twitched, but he clamped them together. He held up one large, work-roughened hand. "Hold on."

He disappeared out the back door and I could hear his boot steps on the other side of my kitchen wall. He returned a few moments later, having donned a light cotton work shirt, still unbuttoned. He placed a large, cold, foil-wrapped package in my hands. "Chicken-and-rice casserole. One of the ladies down at the Baptist church made it for me. Well, several of the church ladies made casseroles for me, so I have more than I can eat. Just pop a plateful in the microwave for three minutes."

I stared at the dish for a long while before he took it out of my hands and placed it in my icebox. "Do local church ladies often cater your meals?"

"I don't go to Sunday services, so they're very concerned about my soul. And I can't cook to save my life. They're afraid I'm just wasting away to nothing," he said, shaking his head in shame, but there was that glint of trouble in his eyes again. He gave me a long, speculative look. "Well, I'll let you get back to sleep. Welcome to the neighborhood."

"Thanks," I said as he moved toward the door. I locked it behind him, turning and sagging against the dusty curtains covering the window in the door. "If there are any greater powers up there—stop laughing."

I massaged my temples and set about making my tea. Jed seemed nice, if unfortunately named. And it was very kind of him to give a complete stranger a meal when he knew she had nothing but angry forest creatures in her cupboards. But I couldn't afford this sort of distraction. I'd come to the Hollow for a purpose, not for friendships and flirtations with smoldering, half-dressed neighbors.

Just as I managed to locate a chipped mug in the spice drawer, a loud, angry screech sounded from somewhere left of my stove. I turned and fumbled with the locked kitchen door, yelling, "Jed!"